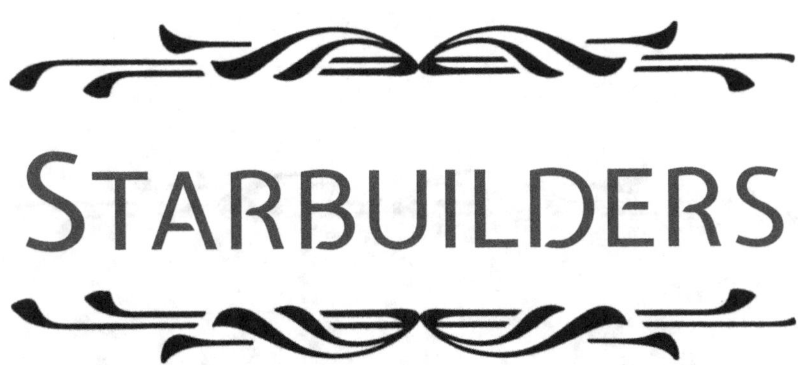

STARBUILDERS

BY J.P. PRAG

SINGULARITY

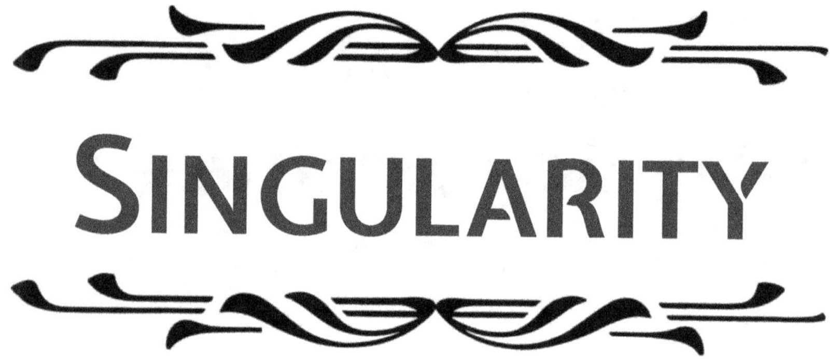

 MAP TO THE STARS

PRELUDE I

Continuing to shiver in spite of the thick pelts and waterproof skins he was wearing, Nothaar Akii considered what he could do to rectify the situation. Although the necessary protective attire had been specially harvested from creatures native to the area and treated in a way to help keep the extreme cold at bay, Nothaar was still finding it difficult to understand how the beasts could survive outside in such conditions. Deciding to put aside his own discomfort, Nothaar instead turned his head to the right and asked in the language that his host spoke, "This is it? This is as far as we can go?"

"Yes," the old man named Baubu Yoordi confirmed, "Just as you asked, I've taken you to the southernmost point in the land. This cliff juts out further than anything else, thus making it the true end of the world."

Nothaar rotated away from Baubu and looked out over the dark and choppy salt sea. Given the fairly limited amount of time the sun would have shined overhead on that day, they had to use what useful light there was to complete the trek out to this locale, take in the boundless nothingness, and then make the return journey to Baubu's village. And all this had to be accomplished before the night fell and the predators that stalked under the cover of darkness discovered their presence. *There's still so much I don't understand*, Nothaar thought to himself. Expressing his concerns aloud, Nothaar declared, "These extremely short days are so distressing to me. Nothing like this happens where I'm from."

"It's the reverse in the summer," Baubu explained before a knowing, yet good-humored look spread across his face. "If I can convince you to stay that long, you'll see days when the sun goes to sleep for just a short while."

"The summer..." Nothaar trailed off, lost in his own thoughts and pangs of homesickness. "That's another thing that doesn't fit. When it's summer here, it's winter back at my birthplace. Everything is inverted down here in the southern lands."

"From my perspective," Baubu harrumphed, "your northern homestead is the backwards one. You said your village was on the northernmost tip of the world?"

"That's right," Nothaar confirmed. "Even the stars above changed as I crossed the great desert. I mean, of course, where the new stars have appeared, not where the old stars used to be."

"I'll have to take your word on all that and what your motherland is like," Baubu conceded, "having never gone very far to the north myself. However, I can confirm that the stars you have seen here are not the ones of my youth. Before the... the... what did you call it, again?"

"The *Sky Shift*," Nothaar answered in an almost reverent whisper. After all, it had practically become his religion and calling.

"Right, right," the elder Baubu acknowledged. "My memory is not what it once was. Nonetheless, I had one of my young pages go through my observations, and she concluded that the *Sky Shift* you say happened at your village also transpired at the same time as the one here. It all seemed to occur simultaneously twenty summers past."

Nothaar displayed his melancholy acceptance before responding, "Not that I doubted it at this point in my journey, but that confirms it: the *Sky Shift* was a worldwide phenomenon that took place everywhere at once. In every village I've been to that has a *Keeper*, they've been able to validate the *Sky Shift* happened on practically the same day, give or take a little difference depending upon how far east or west they are when the sun goes to sleep and the moon awakens."

"Are you absolutely sure it was everywhere?" Baubu challenged his visitor.

"What do you mean?" Nothaar asked in confusion.

Flashing him a mischievous expression, Baubu queried, "Do you believe there is nothing beyond the endless salt sea?"

Aware that he was most likely falling for one of Baubu's riddle-filled traps again, Nothaar nevertheless responded, "It's called 'endless' for a reason, is it not? I've seen no reason to consider otherwise."

Laughing, Baubu said, "Well that, my newfound friend, is where you're wrong. I know with almost certainty that there's more out there, far beyond the horizon we can see from this particular vantage point."

Trying not to feel insulted by his geriatric guide, Nothaar instead swallowed his pride and pursued what he was really after: information. "Please, tell me about it," he implored. There was nothing Nothaar desired more than to discover the complete truth, and the only way he was going to get it was if he learned about... everything.

"How about a trade?" Baubu offered. "From one *Keeper* to another."

"You don't have to be so formal with me," Nothaar countered. "I don't really do all those rituals and things. At the risk of offending you, I don't believe the *Knowledge* should be contained only by *Keepers* like us and our small pool of assistants. Instead of withholding what we learn to a precious few, I would like to see the *Knowledge* spread to the entirety of the masses."

In response to Nothaar's declaration, Babub's visage instantly became devoid of any readable emotion. Nothaar internally snickered as he recognized that Baubu was using a technique he was quite familiar with and employed prodigiously himself: the masking of all intents and feelings. Without a trace of his genuine reaction, Baubu plainly stated, "That is borderline blasphemy."

"According to some I have met," Nothaar willingly offered without so much as an attempt at self-censorship, "my thoughts are quite heretical, already beyond any tolerable or reasonable behavior. I will tell you that I've been... removed... from several villages by other *Keepers* for uttering such a treatise."

"And yet you still hazard saying the same to me?"

Baubu tested. "Why would you do such a thing when I could just as easily cast you out and leave you to perish alone in the wild over the remainder of the long winter?"

Instead of answering, Nothaar just sighed and articulated, "Besides never getting this cold or staying dark for so long at the northern edge of the world, there are many differences I can opine on. For instance, although it can snow up there, rarely does it accumulate beyond a few fingers-width in depth. During some winters, there is no snow at all. As I traveled south from my village, things became hotter and hotter until I reached the wastelands. After crossing them and continuing to head downward across the countryside, the climate became much more like what I was accustomed to. Yet, I came to discover that the territories below the desert wastes are much larger than those of the north. At some point, I came to find winters more like these. True, this is the worst I've seen, but I'm not afraid. Despite leaving my home with no frame of reference for what winter could be, I've adapted and will continue to do so."

"Why tell me all this?" Baubu solicited.

"For two reasons," Nothaar began. "First, I want you to know that should you expel me, I'll still find a way to survive, so your threats have no bearing. Second, I wanted you to hear what freely sharing the *Knowledge* sounds like without the constraints our profession and dogma put upon us."

Baubu stared at Nothaar in complete silence for several moments more. Nothaar held his gaze, not breaking eye contact as the wind whipping around them provided the only accompaniment. Finally, Baubu blinked, started cackling, and declared, "I like you Nothaar. You're unconventional for sure, but maybe we need a little bit of that to shake things up. People can become so complacent and think they should do things as they have always been done. More so, it's quite clear that the world is changing in ways we cannot control and predict. Unfortunately, I won't survive long enough to see this through. It'll take someone like you to lead us to the other side of whatever is coming... whatever has already come."

"Thank you, Baubu," Nothaar accepted with both sincerity and humility. "That means a lot, especially coming from someone as venerated as you. Your reputation has actually extended quite far and wide from here. I've heard your name in my ears for many seasons now, and am glad to see you have lived up to the grandiose expectations others have heaped upon you, whether or not you were aware how you're regarded elsewhere in the world."

Clearly surprised and not even attempting to hide his feelings anymore, Baubu looked down at the snowpack and disclosed, "I had no idea my name was spoken outside my own village in any context..."

"You would be amazed at everything there is to see and learn!" Nothaar exclaimed.

Looking up, Baubu sadly professed, "I'm afraid I missed the opportunity to do what you're doing and tour the whole land. My youth is far behind me, and I fear I may have squandered it, after all. Nothaar, tell me about the rest of our scattered brothers and sisters, if you would. It would gladden me to be taught through what your eyes and ears have perceived."

"I will," Nothaar quickly agreed with a gesture that indicated his concurrence, "after you tell me what is beyond the apparently not-so-endless salt sea."

"You are tenacious!" Baubu remarked. "Very well. I assume you'll want to hear from the primary source directly, too, so I'll summarize. The fishermen who go out in the summer often claim they have caught sight of another land even further to the south. However, this place has been described as being made entirely of ice! According to their oral tradition, some of their ilk have even ended up landing or wrecking there, and that during the peak of the season the sun never sets."

"Astounding!" Nothaar granted. "Although, it's a bit suspect. If they wrecked their boats on this land of ice, how have these stories returned to us?"

"I don't know how it is where you come from," Baubu replied, "but fishermen here never go out alone. There are always several vessels traveling together as a safety measure. These seas are quite rough and treacherous. Even in the heat of summer, boats have run into large blocks of ice, some of which have washed up on our shores."

"And yet, despite all these detailed accounts and signs of something more to be learned," Nothaar interrogated Baubu, "you never thought to confirm the incontrovertible truth? You chose not to go out there yourself to find out for sure?"

Signaling his disapproval at such an idea, Baubu confessed, "I never much cared for being on the water. I can barely stick my feet in the ocean without becoming nervous. Besides, the fishermen have far more important work to do than drag a curious *Keeper* around on some wild adventure. They must use the precious time they have to gather vital sustenance for our people. As you can clearly see, we need a lot of provisions for the winter, so preserving the bounty of the summer harvest is critical for our survival. It's a difficult existence, but quite rewarding. I could never ask them to give up days and days of their life-sustaining profession just to satisfy my own inquisitiveness, even if they were willing."

"I understand," Nothaar granted. "It's much the same where I come from... and everywhere else I've been, for that matter. Come, let's return to your village; I'm getting quite chilled. On the way, I'll tell you all about the rest of the world."

PRELUDE II

Side-by-side, Nothaar and Baubu began walking back towards the village. En route, they idly chatted about the various locales that Nothaar had visited and the groups that were inhabiting them. Their conversation never settled on any topic in particular and instead bounced around, driven solely by the whims of the participants. As their voyage took them upon a well-worn path, Nothaar remarked on how he could practically feel the history of the trail itself. "It's quite clear that your people have been coming this way for generations," he noted.

Baubu gave him another one of his playful expressions and—with a sparkle in his eyes—confirmed, "Yes... especially the young lovers. Privacy is difficult to come by, and many people like to escape to a romantic hideaway where they can take in the breathtaking view of the end of the world. I'd be lying if I didn't admit to a few rendezvous and liaisons out there myself during my formative seasons."

Laughing, Nothaar admitted he found the idea appealing, although, he divulged, he was not as young as when he set out on his journey of discovery.

"How long has it been?" Baubu inquired. "When was the last time you saw your home?"

Suddenly pausing in his tracks and almost causing

Baubu to careen into him, Nothaar began counting on his fingers. "I set out early in the season, fifteen springs past. My spring, I mean, so your autumn. Therefore, it's been fifteen autumns and a part of this winter, now."

"And how many springs/autumns had you lived before you left?" Baubu delved further as he started walking again, forcing Nothaar to catch up.

Nothaar did not need to count as he knew that number by heart. "Twenty of my own."

"Ah, not so young, but not so old," Baubu observed. "This is my eighty-third winter."

Giving him a look of surprise, Nothaar tried to process the idea of having seen so many seasons. Based on this fact, Baubu was the oldest person Nothaar had ever met, but he never would have guessed it by how spritely the octogenarian was. Although he could easily have outpaced the far older fellow as they continued strolling, Nothaar chose to match his relatively impressive pace, becoming even more spellbound with how well Baubu continued to function.

When they reached a point where several paths intersected, Nothaar quickly chose what he instinctively felt was the correct route. "You remember the way back after only coming through here once before?" an apparently amazed and impressed Baubu asked.

"Not exactly," Nothaar admitted. "While my memory is better than average, it's just that I've developed a good sense of direction and the ability to 'read' the roads as if they were a book. It's like the footpaths have their own vernacular, and I've learned to speak it fairly fluently."

"Just as you've quickly picked up our tongue, as well," Baubu remarked. Nothaar gave Baubu a sign of appreciation at his observation, but otherwise offered no additional comment. They were quiet for a while until Baubu tried a different tact by soliciting, "So, you promised me some of the *Knowledge* you've accumulated during your long journey from one end of the world to the other over these past fifteen autumns. While we've talked about some generalities, I'd like you to give me some deeper *Keeper*-level analysis. For instance, although you've only spent a short amount of time with us, how do we compare with the other settlements? Are we very different from them?"

Nothaar gave a small chuckle before declaring, "While there are many things I would call 'unique' to your culture—just as I would say about any of the places I've been—taken altogether, I would surmise that all people are far more similar to each other than they would expect. Even things that on the surface appear to be different actually seem to have sprung from the same root."

"Please expound upon this," Baubu encouraged.

"Well," Nothaar began, "you mentioned my ability to pick up your tongue rather easily. I'll tell you, if the members of my village heard us conversing in this way, they would find the entire thing incomprehensible—and not just the esoteric topics. However, in the words you use, there are commonalities with my native language... and all the other ones I've encountered. There is no trick to being able to learn and understand these diverse ways of speaking; I have found that they all must share some type of common foundation. Long ago in the past, we most likely all expressed ourselves with the exact same terminology. Yet, over the many long seasons, as our villages have remained isolated from each other, our descriptors and pronunciations have drifted apart, thus creating numerous dialects with distinctive elements. But because the evidence points towards the existence of some progenitor language, I've been able to decipher what that might have been and use it as a basis for finding the communal facets across the majority of words spoken by all varieties of people."

"Even the *Language of Children*?" Baubu pressed.

Nothaar again halted their progress as he thought about how he wanted to explain this subject. Deciding that Baubu would understand what others seemed incapable of comprehending, Nothaar started moving again before he commenced enlightening, "No, not the *Language of Children*. It's completely different and has nothing in common with all the assorted iterations of the tongues of people. Believe me, I've been everywhere in the world—save for this possible new land of ice you've brought to my attention—and, going by how all other people speak, I do not see where it could have originated from."

"And yet, despite this lack of a 'base' from which to begin, you've been able learn it," Baubu stated as an absolute fact, not a question.

Displaying a gesticulation of disagreement, Nothaar clarified, "As best as I can, given the limited time I've spent working on it during my short stays at each of the settlements. There are things about the *Language of Children* that are so foreign and odd that it makes it almost impossible to understand. Even the rules for grammar—which are relatively the same throughout every other local dialect I've heard—are not shared by the *Language of Children*! The order for subjects, actions, and descriptors are completely different. If that were not enough, they have a myriad of words that I've been unable to translate or make any sense of. Somehow, though, they all understand each other perfectly as if these seemingly meaningless sounds are full of the most profound significance."

"Hmmm..." Baubu offered in response. "Then, this gets to the core of my inquiry. Is the *Language of Children* spoken here the same as the one used by the next generation everywhere upon the earth we tread?"

"I mean, I really can't say for sure..." Nothaar attempted to dismiss.

"There's no one more qualified than you to answer the question," Baubu interrupted. "I want your professional opinion based upon your experience as a talented linguist and traveler."

Pondering for a moment longer, Nothaar put to words what he'd been secretly harboring within him, the impetus that made him leave his long-forsaken homeland. "Yes. Despite how strange it sounds to our ears, it's an identical abnormality. Unlike the physical deformities they all have in one form or another—and despite the fact that those bodily changes vary wildly in their manifestations—the

Language of Children is a precisely replicated affliction. It's as if they have all been... possessed... by the same verbal tic, the same words, the same grammar, the same hidden meanings and mysteries."

"I find it interesting," Baubu declared, "that you use the word 'possessed' to describe their condition. Are you a believer of the power of demons and spirits and gods, all directly impacting the world of the living?"

If it were any other *Keeper*, Nothaar would have probably maintained the secrecy of his sentiments, but Baubu had proven himself to be very open and nonjudgmental. "Whether demons and spirits and gods are real or not, this is not their handiwork. What is happening is some type of natural process. Although I cannot fathom what it might be, they are still children, flesh-and-blood like any other birthed preceding the *Sky Shift*."

"True, true," Baubu quickly agreed, "but there is something I have noted as a key difference. You may have quickly become fluent in our tongue, but our youngsters have the most difficult time learning the language of their own people. Where you are eloquent, they will stutter. Tell me, what do your private contemplations sound like? Do you ruminate in the words of your native tongue, the ones I use, or something else entirely?"

Describing his inner monologue, Nothaar elucidated, "My thoughts shift to the language I am using. There's usually a period of adjustment of several cycles of the sun and moon for it to take effect, but basically, one morning, I wake up thinking in the language of the village I'm presently inhabiting."

"I've asked the young ones the same question," Baubu explicated, "and every single one has said they only hear their own *Language of Children* in their souls. In order to speak to anyone born prior to the *Sky Shift* twenty summers past, they must literally translate everything in their mind before speaking, each-and-every time."

"I hadn't thought to ask that!" Nothaar exclaimed. "What an interesting development. But what does it mean? How's it possible?"

Giving Nothaar a look of disappointment, Baubu said, "I was hoping you'd be able to tell me that. It appears that you're just as much in the dark as the rest of us. All I know for certain is that prior to the *Sky Shift*, only the deaf, dumb, or deficient could not learn our tongue. Yet, since that point, everyone born in this generation struggles, including some extreme outliers. We have, unfortunately, some kids who lack the ability to speak the language of their contemporaries; yet that does not make it any easier for them to learn the words of our village. It's almost as if the *Language of Children* is still within them, but inaccessible in some indescribable way. Sadly, due to not having a way to tap into that strange vernacular, they are outcasts even among their own peers."

Thinking back on his experiences, Nothaar took note of how the youth were not changing in a homogenous way. Some had barely any noticeable phenotype modifications while others looked completely different but could not—as Baubu had just highlighted—speak the *Language of Chil-*

dren as naturally or at all. Nevertheless, he anecdotally perceived that the rate of deviation was accelerating, and a higher proportion were being born that seemed to have many more of the wide array of transfigurations happening in concert.

"I could teach them," Nothaar suddenly offered, "and you as well, and anyone else who wants to learn, how to speak the *Language of Children*... at least, as well as I am able put the words together."

Visibly lightening up at his suggestion, Baubu avowed, "This would be a good distraction over the long winter and the nearly endless nights. Speaking of which, we should probably pick up our pace if we want to get back to the village before nightfall. That is, unless you'd like to meet the beasts that your cloak is made from. And you can trust that they will be out for bloodthirsty revenge if they catch you wearing the skin of their relatives!"

Baubu broke out in a hardy laugh at his own joke, but began to walk with a brisker step, just the same.

PRELUDE III

After arriving back at the village, Nothaar and Baubu retired to the older man's hut. There, Baubu's assistants had kept the fires burning while they were away; thus, it was actually quite comfortable inside. Nothaar was amazed at the ingenuity that went into insulating the building to keep so much heat in the interior while letting all the smoke out. Sweating from their vigorous walk, Nothaar was quick to shed his warm layers. Still, the cold felt like it had seeped as deep as his organs and was stubbornly refusing to allow his internal body temperature to return to its expected normal level.

In order to banish Nothaar's chilly core, Baubu advised a rather straightforward solution: building an inner-fire. As the two seated themselves upon stuffed cushions on the floor, one of Baubu's aides brought over bowls filled with a fish broth that had been heated in a cauldron hanging above the nearby fire. Much like in Nothaar's homestead, Baubu's people also preserved foodstuffs by smoking, pickling, and other such methods in order to make sure they had enough to eat through the winter season and into the spring before fresh options became readily available. Due to this, the contents of the dish were mostly pureed such that their previous forms were no longer obvious. Still, the scent was distinct enough that Nothaar had no doubt as to their origins.

When Nothaar took the provided wooden spoon towards his mouth, Baubu warned, "Be careful with how quickly you eat it. It's impossible to tell until afterwards, but some batches may not be digestible for you."

Nothaar gave a knowing gesture, having experienced such situations many times before himself. "Over my long journey," Nothaar elaborated, "this issue with some food becoming disagreeable seems to be happening at a higher rate. I wish I'd thought to document it at the beginning of my quest, but it took many cycles of the seasons before I even recognized the pattern. At first, I thought it was a condition unique to the southern lands, but every *Keeper* has assured me that this isn't how it was in the past."

"Therefore," Baubu interjected, "it was not just poor meals that spurred you to leave your home village?"

Laughing as he took his first spoonful, Nothaar explained, "No, no; I quite liked the cooking they did where I came from. We have some aromatic spices that I have not come across since I entered and crossed the wastelands. Sadly, my supply ran out long ago, otherwise I would offer you some to zest up your own serving of soup."

"Oh? Do you find the meal bland?" Baubu teased.

Although Nothaar actually did feel that way, in deference to his generous host, he graciously expressed that it was not a significant concern to him before declaring, "Honestly, I prefer to experience a locale as it customarily is without contaminating it with my preferences."

Baubu gave him a thoughtful look before responding, "But you're the one who just told me that you want to spread the *Knowledge* with no restrictions to all the laypeople. Is that not the definition of 'contamination'?"

"I doubt most average folk would understand the wisdom we could share, anyway," Nothaar asserted with some bitterness. "Or would care to know to begin with."

Quickly picking up on Nothaar's tone, Baubu assuaged, "I know how you feel. It can be difficult being... different... from the rest of the people around you. Feeling the drive to take up our calling of maintaining and building upon the *Knowledge* makes people like us stand out, and not always in a beneficial way. Even some of my own kin have difficulty seeing the value in what we do. Not all of them, mind you, but their opinion is shared in one way or another by the vast majority of people who reside here. 'Is it safety, shelter, or sustenance? No? Then we don't have a moment to even consider it.'"

"It's as if I've had that exact same conversation hundreds of times before!" Nothaar exclaimed. "While at my home, I quickly noticed the *Sky Shift*, as well as the slight fuzziness that now pervades the sun and the moon. I tried to convince the others in my village to just look up and confirm it for themselves with their own eyes, at least to verify that I was not the only one seeing it. After all, it's not uncommon for people in our profession to lose their wits and start to see the imaginary as real. Without corroboration, I knew that I couldn't trust my potentially biased sight and conclusions."

"And did they do as you asked?" Baubu inquired.

"Not many, no," Nothaar confirmed. "It took quite a while to get others to start to notice these things; and I could only convince a handful of them to assist me, at that. Yet even among that group, they did not think it was particularly important or worth pursuing. 'What does the position of the stars have to do with me?' they would ask. Another would say, 'Who cares if some wandering stars have left and new ones have arrived to replace them? Perhaps they've finally gone off to wherever it was they were going while the new ones appeared simultaneously?'"

"An intriguing proposition," Baubu thoughtfully pondered. "Sometimes the unschooled can be the most insightful, being so unencumbered by the *Knowledge*."

"I ruminated on that very idea for several summers," Nothaar confessed. "As you say, it certainly seemed reasonable and plausible. We don't know where the stars are going on their treks, especially the wandering ones. There was a certain logic to it with some stars exiting and new ones arriving. Still, it bothered me that all the stars left together at once, literally overnight, after their exact locations and paths had been documented over many *Keepers'* lifetimes. In my village, each successive generation of *Keeper* has been even more fastidious than the prior at recordkeeping. While it's not much by the standards of some of our ilk, there were still hundreds of drawings of the movements of the stars and other observations that I had access to that the general residents did not. The more I thought about it, the more this schism seemed to be a complete inflection point unlike any other.

"This became especially clear once the post-*Sky Shift* newborns started to appear in the world as changed beings, and later when they began speaking the *Language of Children*. I thought the two events must have been connected, but I could not confirm it until a traveling trader— Vedoori was his name, I believe—emerged and set up shop for a season. I obsessively interrogated him and he became quite annoyed with me. Vedoori didn't notice things the way people like us do; he didn't detect the *Sky Shift* at all. Still, I was grateful for the one thing he could confirm for me: he said that progenies like the ones we were birthing at my village were also being born everywhere he had been, and that they were speaking a babble nobody understood. That was all the evidence I needed to substantiate that there was something more going on than just what we could see in front of us, and I resolved to head out the following spring. I realized that I actually had a dearth of information, and I needed to leave in order to fill in the gaps so as to get real answers."

Baubu requested that Nothaar confirm that the spring he left was his twentieth one. Once he had done so, Baubu asked, "A man of your age going on a quest like this; did you not have a family already?"

Exposing his embarrassment, Nothaar explained, "As a person who stood apart as I did, I could not woo any of the women in my hometown. If I may be frank, I'm quite jealous with how *Keepers* seem to be generally more revered and taken care of here in the deep south. I cannot emphasize enough that it's not that way up north. As a consequence of this, my occupation did not provide me with any excess wealth so that I might potentially purchase a mate instead of convincing one to join me willingly."

"You poor man..." Baubu attempted.

"It's fine," Nothaar cut him off. "I didn't really feel a burning desire for the opposite sex, anyway."

"Ah, I see how it is," Baubu observed. "You are one of those men with the soul of a woman within you, then."

"It's not really that," Nothaar demurred. "An attraction to other men is not what I felt, either, though I have nothing against it and have met many such individuals on my journey. I liked these people well enough, but I wasn't sexually drawn to them. Besides, I had other things I was much more interested in. Men, women, family—none of those really hold my interest as much as learning all there is to know about this world of ours.

"For instance, as I was traveling village-to-village, I found that the percentage of irregularities of all kinds was the same anywhere I went. While some local residents believed that having traits like containing the soul of the opposite sex was an abomination that needed to be purged, others thought that these people were unique and special and needed to be cultivated and worshipped to appease the gods. But no matter how they viewed the condition, the number of such individuals as a ratio to the total population was always relatively the same. In other words, this characteristic appears to be a naturally occurring phenomenon."

"And you believe this theory is relevant to our current predicament?" Baubu queried.

"Yes," Nothaar readily agreed. "With what we've seen thus far since the *Sky Shift*, everyone must reset their expectations and attitudes so that we can deal with what's happening with the younglings. Unfortunately, history has already shown that we cannot expect the denizens of our world to react so logically. I have seen places where they eradicated all the newborns in their quest to purify themselves. Elsewhere, I came across the shells of what once were thriving settlements. From the few survivors I met, it sounded like they devolved into civil war and left nothing but destruction and dead bodies in their wake. Sadly, these types of reactions are not unexpected. Such is the way of small-minded people who fear what they do not understand... and do not want to understand."

Giving a sound signifying defeated agreement, Baubu propositioned, "As a man many seasons your senior, I believe you should reconsider your stance on forsaking a family of your own, or even just seeking out pleasures of the flesh. There is far more to life than only building upon the *Knowledge*! For instance, we have many eligible women here, several of whom would be happy to have someone for a mate who is not a fisherman. Besides, I'm not sure how many seasons I have left, and could use an official *Keeper* apprentice to take over for me permanently."

"Baubu, I am flattered, humbled, and honored by such an offer..." Nothaar initiated.

"However..." Baubu started for him.

"However," Nothaar continued without pausing, "my work is not yet complete and my journey is far from at its conclusion. I want to compile all of my findings into a collected opus, written both in my native tongue and the *Language of Children*. Picture an open book with pages on each side. The way I imagine it is that on the left will be the lexes that any *Keeper* and some learned people would be able to read and recognize, and then on the right I could use the *Script of Children*—or, at least as well as I can write it based upon my own comprehension and ability to determine the purpose behind these glyphs."

"You never cease to amaze me!" Baubu cheered. "You've even learned what their squiggles mean?"

"Sort of," Nothaar granted. "At least, I know it decently enough that I can create a phonetic translation table. This is information that's not just invaluable right now, but will be crucial in the future. As such, I see it as my duty to retrace my steps and spend time in each village translating my tome into their own distinctive tongue and script. That way, every *Keeper* will have access to the same reference document, just one that's been custom tailored for their audience."

"I see how it is," Babu commented. "You see this work of yours as some type guide to bridge communications across the generations."

"More than that," Nothaar contended. "We can't just focus on our problems in the here-and-now and how we're going to deal with them. Don't get me wrong; they're critically important to address, too. But if we project out into the far future, we might find that the *Language and Script of Children* could supplant all of our vernaculars. Given that, these books may end up being the last archive of who our people used to be."

"This is quite a task and burden you've given yourself," Baubu remarked. "How long do you believe such an undertaking will take?"

"If I were to estimate," Nothaar postulated, "I would imagine that it'd take the same amount of time: another fifteen springs."

"My word," Baubu punctuated. "By the time you return to your home village, you'll have seen at least fifty full cycles of the seasons!"

"True enough," Nothaar certified. "Although I'd like to believe I have tens of springs more beyond that like you, it would be quite unusual. Because of that, my return should give me enough time to train my own successor and maintain the unbroken line of the *Knowledge*."

"A mighty obligation indeed," Baubu acknowledged, "especially since you've mentioned that you weren't particularly appreciated up there. Although I've been a bit flippant about the naysayers I've dealt with in this village, from what you've described there is downright hostility towards *Keepers* where you're from, and the north in general. As you've plainly witnessed, here, the condition is fairly the opposite. Or to put it more bluntly: we have much to offer a person like you."

"I have noticed," Nothaar agreed, "and it is quite

tempting. But I also recognize that among all these pages and helpers that there must be someone you're already considering for your replacement. You don't strike me as someone who leaves anything to chance, so you must be shaping one of them into your planned successor."

"While your presumption has a certain amount of truth to it," Baubu confessed, "none have demonstrated to me that they have the capacity and skillset comparable to what you have shown in just a few short days: insight. As I said before, this is the primary critical skill that will be necessary to lead us during this unprecedented age and transition into whatever the future may bring."

"If I promise that I'll think about it," Nothaar beseeched, "that I will genuinely consider your offer, will you stop pestering me about it?"

When Baubu did not give any immediate response, Nothaar quickly added, "Besides, I'm not planning to go anywhere anytime soon. If possible, I would like to peaceably spend the winter here writing my composition and then translating a copy into your own language and script. I'm confident this will take the rest of the season and then some, so you can guarantee I'll have plenty of time to contemplate your proposition before I'd need to set out in the spring. Would this compromise be acceptable to you?"

With one of his roguish expressions spreading across his face, Baubu declared, "I don't mind at all... but don't be surprised if one night a granddaughter of mine crawls under your blankets and asks you to help keep her warm."

STELLIFEROUS

CHAPTER 01

Nothaar Akii had left the village near the southern edge of the world tardier in the spring than he would have preferred. Over the long, dark, and cold season, the settlement's *Keeper,* Baubu Yoordi, had finally succumbed to his advanced age in the middle of his eighty-third winter. While Nothaar had originally found the geriatric man to be spritely and full of life, spending more time with Baubu had revealed how precarious his health situation really was, and how scared he was for his people's future. *It seemed like all his actions were an intentional feint, trying to manipulate me into staying and taking over for him,* Nothaar divisively thought as he continued his lonely trek through the now fully blooming woods. *He even waited to die until he met me, using his passing to the next world as a way to get me to supersede him in this one!*

For whatever reason, it appeared to Nothaar that Baubu did not trust any of his assistants—not even from his own bloodline—to assume responsibility over his role as a *Keeper.* He refused to officially apprentice any of them, and thus it looked like the long line of the *Knowledge* would be broken with his demise. However, Nothaar did not share Baubu's opinion about his subordinates and he had elected to stay on long enough to train someone else to be Baubu's true replacement. Her name was Anlynx, and she was one of Baubu's granddaughters. Nothaar was well-versed in the methods of propaganda and knew that having someone from Baubu's lineage would make the other villagers accept the transition more easily. Given Baubu's long reign, this would be a critical component of assuring that Anlynx inherited all the fidelity and confidence that Baubu had engendered from the people of his community.

Anlynx was not as convinced as Nothaar and, like her recently departed ancestor, tried to convince Nothaar to remain in their settlement. Pressed naked against him underneath a pile of furs, she asked, "Would it be so bad if it was you instead of me? We could even continue these little sojourns of ours on a more regular and… official basis."

As Anlynx started tracing her fingers up Nothaar's inner thigh, he felt tempted by the offer. To break the spell she was casting over him, he bluntly inquired, "Tell me: the first night that you found a way to roll under the sheets with me, was that of your own volition, or was it at Baubu's directive?"

"Couldn't it be both?" Anlynx queried as she attempted to maintain her sultry tone. Nevertheless, she had pulled her hand back in a telltale sign of being upset by Nothaar's disturbing insinuation. "Did Baubu urge me to get close to you, perhaps even to seduce you? Yes, yes he did. But I wanted to do that on my own anyway, and would have done so with or without his encouragement."

"I wonder how I could possibly accept or know if that

is the unadulterated truth or not?" Nothaar pushed back. "How could you absolutely and unequivocally discern that about yourself? Even before I began coaching you, Baubu had taught you quite a bit of the *Keeper's* way. You used many of the techniques against me..."

"...and you let me because you liked it!" Anlynx finished for him, flashing an expression of satisfaction and desire that almost made Nothaar believe that it could be sincere.

Still, Nothaar contemplated at the time, *now is the moment to be resolute. I must break Anlynx of any notion that I'm going to reside here at the bottom of the world with her. This will be her final test.*

"My dear Anlynx," Nothaar began, "I have enjoyed every moment with you, especially those without any encumbrances separating us. More so, I hope we can prolong taking pleasure and solace in each other's arms for whatever time lingers for me here. But the new plants have started to push their heads through the snow, and the old ones have started to bud. It's a sign that spring is here and that I must begin the next phase of my mission."

At this, Anlynx shot up to a sitting position and let the furs fall away and expose her chest. "And what if I told you I was pregnant with your child?!" she shouted.

Closing his eyes for a moment, Nothaar knew the inflection point had come. "It would make no difference," Nothaar coldly replied. "I will abandon you and the baby. How many new parents are out there that need my *Opus on the Language of Children* so that they can raise their own offspring? You already have the benefit of my experiences; they still need me to provide the *Knowledge*."

This pronouncement had finally overwhelmed Anlynx as she started crying uncontrollably. She refused to let Nothaar console her, and, really, he did not honestly try very hard to do so. The crueler he was to her, the more likely she would be to finally realize that he was not meant to share a life with her. Eventually, she got her emotions under control, collected her clothing, and left his hut without another word.

From that day forward, they never shared a night of passion again. Things became quite tense between them, but Anlynx redoubled her efforts under Nothaar's tutelage. It was she who declared that she was ready to be officially anointed the *Keeper of the Knowledge*, and Nothaar quickly acquiesced and granted her the title. Within a few more turns of the sun and the moon, he was on his own, never having been allowed to examine Anlynx to learn if she really was impregnated with his offspring, one who would undoubtedly be yet another one of the transmogrified children.

Ruminating over these scenes in his head as he trudged along, Nothaar was suddenly shaken from his stupor by a loud, concussive blast of sound. Looking up, he caught sight of a ball of flame streaking diagonally downward through the sky, leaving a trail of fire in its wake. "A falling star!" Nothaar exclaimed aloud. If any of the plants and woodland creatures within earshot had a retort for him, they did not share it. Watching the celestial entity descend, Nothaar ascertained that it would soon hit the ground and, as such, he braced himself for the expected explosion and resulting shockwave.

However, once the massive object dropped out of sight below the treetops, nothing happened. *Strange*, Nothaar thought, *there should have been a large blast by now, visible even at this distance*. Perusing his memory, Nothaar remembered that he had seen a similar event before, in an age prior to the *Sky Shift*. Further, he had studied several accounts from other *Keepers* in the far-flung past. *Something is very different about this one*, he considered before electing to head in the direction he had last seen it plummet to the earth. Based upon his own experience and what he had read, he presumed that there would be a unique rock at the landing site. Falling stars had brought rare and highly valuable metals and gems, commodities he could use for trade. Although storytelling and doing administrative tasks could buy him lodging and some meager meals, having extremely desirable tangible goods would open up a slew of potential resources that he would need on this quest and duty of his.

Despite the fact that Nothaar tried to reach the descended heavenly gift as quickly as possible, it still took several rotations of the sun and the moon. As he approached the area where he reckoned it must be, his worst fears came true; someone else had come upon his prize first. It was evening when he finally reached the area, although he was quite perplexed and thought he must have been mistaken. The forest looked completely undisturbed.

There were no signs of scorching or destruction that should have accompanied such an occurrence, nor really any evidence at all that anything unusual had happened. Instead, things were oddly quiet, except for the distant voices of whoever had come across his desired prize before him. Cursing under his breath, he pushed his feet onward.

Using the cloak of the nighttime darkness, Nothaar slowly approached the strangers' camp. He was hopeful that maybe they would be willing to work with him and split the bounty, but wisely knew they could also be jealously guarding their valuable find. It would not be the first time Nothaar had been met with violence when trying to strike a deal, so he wanted to know what exactly he was up against.

Getting as close as he dared, Nothaar was still unsure where things stood and what was going on. Peering out from behind some bushes, Nothaar saw that the unidentified people had set up a campfire and were sitting on the other side of it. Due to this, he could not make out their faces, features, or anything else about them. He thought that he could see the outline of two individuals, but that did not mean that others were not nearby. Now that he was close enough to surreptitiously observe their camp, Nothaar could finally make out what they were so loudly and indiscreetly saying.

The words completely shocked him to his core.

Chapter 02

Deciding that he must take a calculated risk, Nothaar stepped out from his hiding place and presented himself. He positioned his hands into the universal gesture of peace, demonstrating that he was not brandishing a weapon. After making a noise with his throat to ensure that the strangers would notice him and not be taken unawares, Nothaar began in the dialect he had heard from them, "Greetings be to you, fellow travelers. Me hear you speak *Language of Children*, too. You speak *Language of Children* good; me very impressed. *Language of Children* very difficult for people not children!"

At Nothaar's words, the other two jumped up from their seats. It seemed to Nothaar that they had been completely oblivious of the fact that Nothaar was there until he had spoken. *How could they not have sensed me?* Nothaar wondered. *I did little to mask myself once I came out of my concealment. If they lack critical instincts like these, how might they possibly be surviving out here?*

Instead of responding to him, the one to Nothaar's left pulled some type of bent-shaped object from their belt, held it in their hand, and pointed it at Nothaar. It was difficult to make out any details about the item, but Nothaar was quite sure that even if the sun were shining brightly overhead, he would have no idea what its purpose and function were. However, he could recognize a threat when one was being directed at him. *Perhaps they can't see me?* Nothaar considered. *That would explain why they're not even acknowledging the goodwill sign I'm making.* Moving his contemplations to speech, Nothaar declared, "Maybe you no can see. Me make signal of goodness. No harm does me want to you do."

The one brandishing the... thing... whatever it was... finally broke their silence and demanded, "Stay where you are, or I'll shoot you dead!"

The voice sounded male to Nothaar, but was cracking under the declaration. It was quickly obvious to Nothaar that this man—perhaps boy—was not used to being intimidating and did not know how to do so effectively. Even still, Nothaar decided to take his warning seriously. Besides, he was quite confused by what this person had said and wanted some clarifications. He was familiar with much of the *Language of Children*, even expressions he had no translation for, but here was a term he had never heard before. To this he queried, "'Shoot'? No know word. What 'shoot' mean? Me know many languages. Please speak you natural tongue and then me better able talk you."

There was silence between all of them before the one to Nothaar's right moved towards their companion and put their hand on the first one's arm. "Lower your gun, Ifu," a female voice that sounded gravelly with age commanded the young man. "It's a native, and certainly not a danger to us."

At this pronouncement, the one apparently called Ifu did as requested. The woman spoke up again and announced, "Please be at ease, stranger. But also know that what we are speaking is our natural tongue. We have no other language with which to converse."

Well, this makes even less sense, Nothaar pondered. Giving voice to his opinion, Nothaar noted, "No can see you good, but you no sound like child. One say Ifu maybe child. If Ifu child, make logic that speak *Language of Children*. You, female, no sound like child. Sound like old lady, seen many seasons."

The seemingly elder woman started cackling, apparently greatly amused by Nothaar's observations. Nothaar was heartened by this, hoping it would lower the tension between all of them and lead to some type of détente. Once she was done laughing, the still unnamed woman admitted, "Your ears are quite sharp, friend. I am old, so very old. Hell, I'm so ancient that I've lost count! Last I checked, I had lived several hundred years, but even that was a long, long time ago."

This new information made Nothaar's head swim even more. He was not sure if he was translating the words correctly, but he recognized another one he had never heard before. "Please explain, what 'year' mean?"

"Damn it, Syraaq," Ifu cursed to his partner, "this thing doesn't even know what a 'year' is! What are we supposed to do with that?"

"Now, now, Ifu," Syraaq cajoled. "Don't take for granted that all of our words have direct parallels. Let's attempt a different tack with this one, try to see how things are progressing from his perspective. Mister... uh... what should we call you?"

"Me name Nothaar, clan name Akii," Nothaar offered, hoping that familiarity would breed some type of trust and understanding between them.

Syraaq attempted Nothaar's name, but it sounded jumbled on her lips. "Alright, Nothaar. As you've heard, my name is Syraaq with the... what did you call it... 'clan name' of Sec. My easily agitated young companion here is Ifuwukoogeeq, which is actually his full name as his... group... does not have clans or, what we call family names. But he just goes by 'Ifu' for short, and is personally insulted if you use his entire handle."

"Me understand," Nothaar conceded. "Many people use small name. Me call you Syraaq, him Ifu. Everyone happy now, yes?"

"Almost," Ifu menaced.

"Hush you," Syraaq gently admonished. "Let's see if we can bridge this cultural gap. Nothaar, do you measure the passage of time? Like, do you know when you are supposed to plant crops?"

"Of course!" Nothaar bellowed, insulted by such an odd recrimination. Even people without the *Knowledge* were aware of such basic concepts. "Is simple, all people understand. Count each season: spring, summer, autumn, winter, back again."

"Ah, now I grasp how you recognize the transition of a period," Syraaq declared. "Nothaar, there's no need to feel offended; a 'year' is just the entire span for all four of those seasons to have transpired. You could also think of it as how long it takes to make a full trip arou—"

"He definitely won't follow that!" Ifu interjected.

"No, me get idea, me have same concept," Nothaar argued. "Me live thirty-five springs. Little off due to me come from far north where seasons reversed, have to fix number in head. You from south?"

"Let's put that aside for now," Syraaq deflected. "Now that you fully appreciate what a 'year' means, I believe you'll have a different question entirely."

Thinking back to Syraaq's earlier statements, Nothaar made a noise of surprise. Both Syraaq and Ifu flinched with the latter yelling, "What the hell was that?!"

Are these people complete idiots? Nothaar deliber-ated. *They don't even recognize a common sound of astonishment! And yet, they seem to know so much more. It's clear they're hiding something from me, even if I can't see their faces yet in order to read their expressions. On the other hand, they seem to think that I'm the fee-bleminded one—or at least, that's Ifu's attitude. Perhaps I should stop being so diplomatic and get a little belligerent with them. That should help establish our stations. I'll start by calling them out on the obvious contradiction Syraaq previously made.*

Giving rise to these deliberations, Nothaar yelled with thinly veiled disgust, "Syraaq, you lie before. This not good way to start exchange. Why you lie about age?"

"I did no such thing," Syraaq calmly explained. "Everything I have said is true to the best of my memory."

"No is possible," Nothaar quicky retorted. "No people live eighty, ninety springs. Most die very earlier. Me just send *Keeper* Baubu Yoordi to realm of spirits. Baubu oldest person me ever know. Baubu lived eighty-three winters."

"And yet he'd be but a babe to me," Syraaq chuckled.

Nothaar was not discouraged and continued, "More proof: you sound old, you say me right to think you old, but me still no see you yet. Changed children, people speak *Language of Children* only twenty springs. You speak perfect *Language of Children*, therefore you must be child. Pretend to be old with fake voice, trick me. Why trick me? Me no understand, but me know you lie."

Satisfied that he had properly confronted Syraaq and Ifu's fabrications, Nothaar placed an expression of victory upon his countenance, even though the other two could not clearly see him either. Instead of admitting their deceits, though, Syraaq started howling in laughter. "If that is what you believe," she said as she continued to snicker, "then let me dissuade you of your own false pretenses."

Syraaq then walked around the campfire with Ifu closely behind, still nervously tapping the strange object he had put back in his belt. With the two clearly visible, Nothaar found himself once again speechless. Suddenly, he felt himself doubting everything he had learned, all he had done to maintain and add to the *Knowledge*. It would not be the last time.

CHAPTER 03

Standing before Nothaar were two people—if that word could be applied to them—that did not look like any other person Nothaar had ever seen before. Examining the duo as well as he could by the light of the campfire, Nothaar saw that they shared a skin tone coloration similar to the children, but it was somehow more pronounced and vibrant. If anything, the youngsters looked like they were a dull mixture of the complexion of people born before the *Sky Shift* with what Ifu and Syraaq had wrapped over their frames. As observed by Nothaar, the stark differences Ifu and Syraaq possessed did not end with just their pigmentation.

Among the recent generation, no two progenies were exactly alike. Each one seemed to have an unpredictable combination of physical characteristics and unusual bone structures that altered their faces and bodies far from the norm of the pre-*Sky Shift* populous. Even their internal organs were often rearranged, as Nothaar was able to learn by performing autopsies on those who unfortunately died early for any number of reasons. Conferring with other *Keepers* during his journey, Nothaar also found that the infant mortality rate had jumped up significantly. Since the mutations had come, babies were far less likely to survive their first season. A larger percentage were stillborn than from before the *Sky Shift*, also spreading a great sadness among grieving parents and villagers. *Baubu was right*, Nothaar thought, *this new era is quite difficult and will only become worse before it gets better. It will require strong guidance from all the Keepers of the Knowledge if we are to somehow get past this age of transition.*

Still, what Nothaar was mulling over only concerned the offspring he was familiar with. In Ifu and Syraaq, Nothaar recognized the amalgamation of every single phenotype he had seen in various children—plus more he had never witnessed or gathered from other *Keepers*—combined into singular beings. Both Ifu and Syraaq shared all these features. More so, Nothaar was also forced to accept that Syraaq was being honest with him. She showed obvious signs of advanced age, even if she did not align with how Baubu had appeared. Whereas she was staying still as the firelight danced off her wrinkled skin and pale, thin hair; Nothaar detected that she stood with a slight bend in her back. There was no doubt that she was in some advanced phase of life. *Even if Syraaq lied about how many winters she's seen,* Nothaar surmised, *she has been through at least several multiples of twenty of them. That means she must have been born this way before the Sky Shift, but that's impossible. I haven't witnessed, heard, or read about anything like this happening before that point. What are these... these...?*

So completely distracted by their faces alone, Nothaar barely noticed the clothing they were wearing. As he attempted to take it all in, he realized that what they had on did not appear to be made of materials harvested from animals or plants, at least none that he had ever seen. Even the patterns and colors were unattainable by his estimation. While he had certainly seen dyed fabrics among the many settlements he had visited, nothing compared to the crisp lines and exactness of the fit and cut that these two sported. Beyond these features, their outfits were also as far unalike from each other as Nothaar's was from either of them.

Beginning to feel faint, Nothaar kept himself from potentially losing consciousness by managing to squeak out, "You no people. You magic creatures! Try to wear face and skin of people, trick people, trick me. Somehow learn talk, learn *Language of Children*. Make mistake. Children no like regular people. Should look like Nothaar if want to trick, not children."

"There's no subterfuge here," Syraaq claimed. "I give you permission to touch my face, my hands, anything on me if it will help you conclude that I'm as real as you are, and that what you see is exactly how I came into this shared existence of ours... give or take a few age spots."

"Syraaq, you go too far!" Ifu scolded. "You can't let this thing touch you; you have no idea what type of pathogens he may be carrying. Do I need to remind you that we have very little functioning medical equipment available to us, especially ones that could identify and isolate some new disease and clear it out of our systems? Even leaving the ship and breathing this air has been a massive hazard that I'm not sure we should have partaken, especially considering the situation we find ourselves in now."

"First off," Syraaq countered, "this man is no mere 'thing' or some other mindless beast or plant. Standing before you is another living and thinking being with a name, a name he wants to be called: Nothaar. Show him all the proper respect that he is due and deserves. This man, this incredibly animate and breathing archetype, is exactly the profound example of what you convinced me is so important to protect.

"Second, we're going to have to leave here eventually, so it'll be best if we can build some natural immunity and use what we have on hand to keep ourselves safe before we are forced to head out."

"Slow down!" Nothaar cried. "Me no understand half words that said. No can keep up speed, no can list all new words me hear."

No one spoke for a few moments until Ifu stepped around Syraaq and declared, "Nothaar, I apologize. I have treated you unkindly. As different as I appear from you, you look the same to me, so very strange. I've never seen anything... anyone... quite like you before. It's taking me some time to wrap my head around it."

Nothaar quickly responded, "Me, regular people from before *Sky Shift*, strange one to you? Do you come from land with no regular people?"

"Just the opposite..." Ifu began.

"Even if claim be people, not spirit, not evil sprite," Nothaar interrupted, "Ifu and Syraaq still make mistake with bad fake names."

Ifu looked like he was about to argue back, but Syraaq put a hand on his shoulder to stop him. Instead, she asked, "What makes you think our names aren't real?"

"You names not like any of people," Nothaar explained. "Me travel from point most north where me village home be to point most south. Go east, west, across wasteland, everywhere. Me meet all people, learn all tongues, hear many names, understand how names and words made. You names just random combination sounds, not even like each other."

"Wait," Ifu beseeched, "what do you mean that our names are 'not even like each other'?"

Nothaar took a deep breath as he contemplated how he would explain. In his own tongue he would find it exasperating to expound on the ideas of linguistic theory, but in the *Language of Children* it was exceedingly difficult. He was well aware that he was speaking without the proper lexes and grammar, especially as he was listening to Ifu and Syraaq prattle on. Even though he could not keep up with them or grasp everything that was being said, it was clear that they were completely fluent and comfortable in a way Nothaar could only dream about.

Deciding that the method by which he approached the topic with Baubu would be best, Nothaar attempted, "Most people only speak one tongue, tongue of home village. Me visit many villages, hear and learn their tongue. After just few tongues, me start to hear pattern, same sound coming from past. Like root of plant. On top, many different leaf, look like own thing. At bottom, come from same base. In past, me think, all people speak same tongue. Many village stay apart long time, change tongue. Tongue come from one, become many, you understand?"

"I believe we do," Syraaq confirmed. "Please, go on."

"Words, names, the same," Nothaar continued. "Names also come from root. Change, yes, but share past. In other village, name 'Nothaar' be 'Nodarc'. See, same name, different speak?"

"So, what does that have to do with us and our names?" Ifu challenged, although Nothaar did not detect any bravado or malevolence behind it. Instead, it seemed like Ifu was pushing him into revealing something, something that Syraaq had already apparently intuited.

Without wasting a breath, Nothaar answered, "Ifuwukoogeeq and Syraaq Sec no share root with any tongue from before *Sky Shift*. Also same with *Language of Children*, names no come from there. But more! Is clear no share root with each other."

"Whoa there," Ifu forced Nothaar to pause. "You picked all of that up just after hearing our two names?"

"Not just names," Nothaar admitted. "Also accent. Ifu and Syraaq speak *Language of Children*, speak perfectly. Words all same, but inflection on words different. Same word, say slightly different, hit syllable different. Two look like all parts from children together, speak as children do, but small differences. Ifu and Syraaq, if real names, not from same place. Born different place, grow up different, be different."

"Holy shit!" Ifu exclaimed. "Syraaq, we've stumbled upon a fucking prodigy!"

"He is an incredibly smart one," Syraaq confirmed, but with some trepidation in her voice. "Nothaar, our names are real, but you are completely correct about everything else. Just like your name does not spring from the... *'Language of Children'*... neither do ours. Our names predate it, as well. But we don't call the words we speak what you do. For us, it's simply known as the *'Lingua'*.

"Just like all of your children, everyone who looks like us speaks the *Lingua*. It's one of the many things that bonds us together. Nevertheless, there are differences, cultural ones mostly, between our various... homes. Not only were Ifu and I born many years apart, but we also originate far, far away from each other. You are very insightful, Nothaar, and I'm curious what else you may know about us without having to be explicitly told."

"Me show," Nothaar offered.

At this, Nothaar brought his travel sack to the ground and started to pull something from the inside. As he began to do so, Ifu suddenly whipped his bent object from his belt and commanded in a sharp tone, "Slowly! Do not make any sudden movements!"

Now that he could see it better, Nothaar saw that Ifu's... weapon, he supposed... was made out of polished metal and other materials he did not recognize. However, it appeared to be several pieces fitted together. *At the very least,* Nothaar considered, *he could certainly bludgeon me with it, but that does not appear to be the intimation he is making with pointing it at me. He seems to be implying something could be launched from it, like a spear or an arrow. I don't see how that's possible, but Ifu certainly believes so. Maybe some type of tiny spear is on the inside that can be thrown out somehow? Perhaps this weapon is not meant to be used on people, but on small game?*

Deciding not to chance it, Nothaar slowly brought out his prized possession until Ifu visibly calmed down and put his armament back in his belt.

"What do you have there?" Syraaq asked.

Nothaar opened the pages and showed them to the two odd strangers. "This me *Opus on Language of Children*," Nothaar proudly proclaimed. "After *Sky Shift*, me travel world to learn all that happen, make book so all people can learn from Nothaar experience. Me make book gift to all villages of world."

"Ifu, do you see it?" Syraaq inquired with alarm. "Nothaar has learned our letters, too. And, look here! If I'm not mistaken, he's created a type of phonetic translation from the *Lingua* into his own tongue, and vice versa.

"Oh, Ifu, I'm so sorry for ever doubting you. You were right all along. We've done a terrible thing here."

Chapter 04

"What you do?" Nothaar probed with concern. "Ifu and Syraaq do something bad? How fix?"

Instead of answering him, Syraaq changed the subject—as she seemed quite apt at doing—by querying, "You've said a term a few times now, and I'm wondering what it is. This *'Sky Shift'* that you've mentioned, could you explain to me exactly what that means?"

Feeling whiplash at the sudden alteration in topic, Nothaar decided that he should answer Syraaq's inquest for now. Eventually, he figured, he would get all his questions answered, too. That resolved, he also knew that he could retake control of the conversation and pull some details out of these two. "Me be *Keeper of the Knowledge.* Syraaq and Ifu understand?"

In response, Syraaq and Ifu looked at each other in what Nothaar interpreted as confusion, though it was not how he himself would have rendered such an expression. They both made the same gesture that Nothaar also did not recognize, but reckoned that it meant that they were unsure. As such, he continued. "*Keeper* is job. Most job of people in village get food, make tool, protect, do acts that easy to see how stay alive. *Keeper* in all village. Learn all can, use what learn make life better. Tell stories, record history, observe world. Not all see *Keeper* be useful. Must train from old *Keeper*, be given title of *Keeper*. Many rules, many traditions. Hard work."

"I think I get the gist of it," Ifu offered. "You're some type of scholar, teacher, historian, philosopher, mathematician, priest, administrator, and a slew more of tasks and responsibilities. Basically, anything not related to the immediate survival of your village. Because what you do is not tangible, the other denizens often don't think you do anything valuable."

"Me no understand most word," Nothaar conceded, "but me think you get idea. Have *Keeper* in Ifu village?"

"Umm..." Ifu said as he appeared to be trying to find the right terminology, much to Nothaar's delight. Anything that knocked Ifu off kilter would be useful for Nothaar's purposes of controlling the flow of data. "Yes, sort of, but not in one person. Where I'm from, you could say that most people do the work of a *Keeper*. Even then, they would focus, specialize, in just one of those activities."

"Where I'm from, too," Syraaq acknowledged.

Nothaar gave them a quizzical look before declaring, "No possible most people be *Keeper*. Most people no want be *Keeper*, but most people need do work for food, for shelter, for safety. If all *Keeper*, how eat?"

"Let's just say food isn't really an issue back at our homesteads," Syraaq dismissed Nothaar's concerns. "Now, we get what a *Keeper* is, so how does that relate to the *Sky Shift*?"

Nothaar plastered on a relaxed mannerism to hide his

true reaction. *This one is wily,* he thought. *Syraaq saw right through my technique and threw it back at me. I guess I have no choice but to be cautious. If I keep things directed towards Ifu, I'll probably have a better chance of acquiring the information I seek.*

With this plan in mind, Nothaar turned away from Syraaq and inquired, "Ifu, you know what you want do with life when you small?"

An expression that Nothaar could only surmise was sadness came over Ifu. *Interesting,* Nothaar mused, *I wonder what that's about? I've hit on some nerve and regret.* As if in answer to these thoughts, Ifu declared, "Yeah, I thought I did, but I was wrong."

I was spot on, Nothaar internally gloated. Instead of pursuing that path, though, Nothaar expounded, "Me want be *Keeper* before me know what *Keeper* was and do. As small Nothaar, me begin track stars on own, Old *Keeper* notice, take small Nothaar on as apprentice."

"That's quite an impressive feat for a young boy to decide to undertake on his own," Syraaq announced with gusto. "Not everyone would be willing to look up and keep track of everything happening above them."

"Be no very hard," Nothaar countered. "Very few number stars, can follow all. Wandering stars most easy, make patterns all... year."

"Wandering stars?" Ifu asked in bewilderment.

"He means planets and other large local celestial bodies," Syraaq translated. "He just doesn't realize it."

It was now Nothaar's turn to show his confusion as he

delved into Syraaq's words, "What mean? What be 'plan-it'? What 'cell-est-tail'? Please explain. Me need understand so me can speak *Language of Children... Lingua...* good. Is necessary so me can help all, fix mistake Syraaq and Ifu say they make."

Once again avoiding giving him a direct response, Syraaq instead summarized, "So, when you were young, you started tracking the stars overhead. Thus, twenty years ago, you quickly noticed a sudden change. The stars you had known your entire life were gone and replaced with a whole new set. More so, most of the stars became the wandering type. Whereas before there were only a few of them, now almost all of them were wandering stars. Does that about cover all of it?"

Shocked at having it all laid out so plainly without him having to explain it, Nothaar could only make a gesture of agreement.

"I'm afraid I don't know what that particular gesticulation you are making means," Syraaq asserted. "You'll have to use your words."

"Yes," Nothaar agreed, "Syraaq understand all about stars, say everything right. But me learn something new, too, about language. Tongue not just words, tongue also movement of body, hands, face. Me believe all movement same all people, but not Syraaq and Ifu. You no understand Nothaar, me no understand you. Words not enough. Much more to do. Me no notice children doing different movements until Syraaq and Ifu start doing. Now think back, see same in story in head. Have to update opus."

The color left Syraaq's face and she suddenly appeared ill. Turning to her companion she said, "Ifu, this is terrible. We shouldn't contaminate this place any further. It goes against everything we believe in, all we're fighting for. You were the one who convinced this obstinate old fool that what she'd been doing her entire life was wrong. Wouldn't allowing this be far worse?"

Something is off, Nothaar contemplated with apprehension. *I thought that Syraaq was in charge and commanding the young Ifu, but their roles are actually reversed, just like the seasons between the north and the south. Syraaq has apparently gone through some crisis of faith and has found a new religion in whatever it is that Ifu is preaching. She's looking to him for direction and guidance; he's the real ringleader here.*

"No, Syraaq," a suddenly more confident Ifu pronounced. "Don't you see the opportunity right in front of us? Nothaar is already beyond 'contaminated', and he did it to himself, all on his own. We had nothing to do with it, which is exactly what I've been saying all along! He's the perfect specimen for everything we have talked about. If he came back with us..."

"Back with us?!" Syraaq abruptly interrupted. "Ifu, you impetuous dupe; we can't take a non-*Common* back with us. Heck, there's no way we can possibly get anywhere ourselves right now, anyway. Even if our vessel were not a complete wreck, Torch Drive Ships were only designed for traveling in interstellar space; they have no capabilities to get off planet."

"Syraaq, Ifu, please slow down!" Nothaar pleaded. "Me no can understand all words. No nice to do to me, no nice to speak of Nothaar like Nothaar no here."

Chuckling to herself, Syraaq verbalized, "Well, he's certainly got us there; we are being incredibly rude! Nothaar, on both of our behalves, we apologize. You are an obviously very bright and learned... person. That said, I fear that Ifu is right about you. You, perhaps, are too smart for your own good. Now that you've seen us and talked to us, I don't think we'll ever be able to let you go."

At this pronouncement, Syraaq pulled an object from her own belt that looked similar to the one Ifu had, but with some small noticeable differences. Nothaar did not have enough time to appreciate them, though, as he briefly saw something come flying out of the hole in the front of the item, followed shortly by a pinch in his chest. And then, there was nothing but blackness.

CHAPTER 05

Nothaar awoke with a splitting headache, worse than any prior occurrence he could remember. Even when he partook in the substances that were supposed to open his mind to mystical possibilities or lower his inhibitions, the aftereffects were nothing compared to this sensation. Then, as his wits started returning, he found it was not just his head that was in pain. First, there was a burning sensation in his chest at the point where he remembered the pinch happening before he passed out. Beyond that, his shoulders felt out of position, like they were being pulled the wrong way. As he tried to realign them from his prone position on his left side, he discovered he was unable to do so because his hands and feet had been bound and tied to each other behind his back. If that were not enough, he then felt a pressure that indicated the need to empty his bladder, but could not figure out a way to do so from his present bodily arrangement without soiling himself. He supposed it was a blessing that an accident had not happened naturally while he was comatose.

The only thing that was not causing him discomfort was the giant cushion below him. It was large, and Nothaar estimated that two or more people could easily fit atop it with room to spare. More so, it was soft, spongier than anything in Nothaar's experience. With a pang of regret, Nothaar judged that Anlynx would have loved it as she often complained about still being able to feel the earth beneath her back as they partook in each other's ecstasies. He tried rolling around and found that the massive pillow contoured to his body as he moved. This, in turn, had the effect of making it impossible for him to find a purchase in order to push himself upright.

Eventually, Nothaar was able to keep rolling over until he fell out of the colossal padding and landed with a thud upon the ground, adding another layer of radiating soreness. From his new vantage point, though, he saw that the area he had been sleeping within had been raised above the floor in its own structure, like a special container just for slumbering. It was so unusual that he almost missed his next shocking discovery.

Whereas the supportive zone was comfortable and warm, his landing spot was cold, hard, smooth, and shiny. In surprise, Nothaar thought, *It must be made out of metal, but I have never seen so much in one place! Metal that can be shaped is so rare that I have only ever seen a handful of weapons and a bit of jewelry fashioned from some of it over the duration of my entire life and travels. Yet here, they are wasting metals to just be a surface to stand upon. If they have such resources, why would Syraaq and Ifu be so determined to take control of the falling star? Certainly, they don't need the wealth contained within it if they have access to all this!*

The thought of the two strangers brought Nothaar

back to reality. He realized that Syraaq and Ifu must have done something to him to make him lose consciousness, some type of spell or potion. Either way, what Nothaar was observing around him gave some solace as it was proof that his memories of them and their unique qualities were genuine and not a figment of his imagination or a sign that he was losing his mind. At least, Nothaar hoped that was the case and that he was not somehow creating this un-fathomable realm within some deep, dark recess inside his battered brain.

Taking stock, Nothaar tried to make sense of all the oddities that were placed before his eyes. He was unaware of any record in the *Knowledge*—factual or fiction—that described a space where metal was so prodigiously avail-able that it could be used as a building material. Throughout his journey, no other person he had met had presented or proposed such a concept, either. As such, it was inconceivable to Nothaar that there could be this much metal in one location, nonetheless have it extended all the way up the walls and into the ceiling.

Looking up, Nothaar found he needed to squint. Light was coming from above, but he could not figure out its source. The roof did not appear to be open to let in the sun. And yet, illumination was emanating from that exact direc-tion. *What type of strange trap have I managed to fall into this time?* Nothaar wondered as he continued to inventory everything around him, which did not amount to much. De-spite these quandaries, Nothaar was glad to be able to make some practical improvements. Now that he was on something solid, he could wiggle his way up to a kneeling position, sitting on the back of his heels. Getting there took almost all his energy, and he panted with exhaustion from the effort.

Suddenly, the wall across from Nothaar slid away, appearing to eat itself. "What sorcery be this?!" he yelled out in the *Lingua* to no one in particular.

In answer, Syraaq and Ifu walked through the now available portal. "No magic here," Syraaq assured him as she made some type of motion with her hands and arms that Nothaar decided must have indicated the use of mystical implements. "Everything you see before you is science. Or, if I may borrow your parlance, an application of the *Knowledge* for the comfort of all people."

Growling in annoyance, Nothaar spat, "What you do me? How me here? Where here?"

"Ifu, please hold your firearm out for Nothaar to see," Syraaq requested. Without a word, Ifu pulled the bent metallic object from his belt and held it in both hands so Nothaar could look at it. Syraaq then explained, "This device is called a gun. It is a projectile weapon, meaning that it uses an explosive power to push a smaller object outward. Imagine that there is a miniature rock or a round ball of metal inside the hole you can see. Now picture it flying out with the speed of the fastest thing you've ever seen. Whatever that is, multiply it many times over. What would happen if it hit you?"

"If go that fast?" Nothaar began. "Would go straight through Nothaar, come out other side."

"Very good," Syraaq cooed as if she were praising a young pupil, a tone Nothaar had heard from his old master during his own early apprenticeship to become a *Keeper*. "When Ifu threatened to 'shoot' you last night, that is what he was saying. That ball inside, we call it a bullet. There are ways to deflect them, but you absolutely do not possess such technology. The bullet would have pierced some vital organ and you would have died instantly."

"Syraaq, you have gun," Nothaar refuted. "You 'shoot' me, yet me alive."

Syraaq returned an expression that Nothaar could not quite construe, but her eyes were saying she was being mischievous. It reminded him of Baubu, and he wondered what else the two geriatrics might have in common. "I'm surprised you can remember that," she decreed. "Yes, there are actually many different types of guns for various functions. The one I used was non-lethal, or, rather, I hoped it would be for you. It shoots out a dart, what you might think of as a tiny spear or arrow made out of metal. Inside that dart was a very strong substance that makes people sleep, what we call a sedative."

"Hope no kill me?" Nothaar delved. "No know if do that, yet do anyway? Syraaq no good person."

"No, I'm not a good person," Syraaq readily agreed. "But with Ifu's help, I'm trying to become a better one."

"I'm sorry Nothaar," Ifu apologized, now seemingly playing the role of the rational peacemaker. "Syraaq moved too quickly for me to react. She wasn't thinking about the consequences. The sedative is designed for people like us, like your changed children. There's no telling how it'd affect someone like you."

"Why sedative potion work different on me?" Nothaar inquired. "Should be same. Nothaar people like Ifu, like Syraaq, like children."

"No, you're not," Ifu countermanded. "All of the people born before this *'Sky Shift'* of yours are something different, something... alien. We perused through some sections of your *Opus on the Language of Children* last night. From that, we know you're aware that the newer generation have changes that go beyond the skin and into their insides—that their organs are moved or are different, new, or missing. It's more than that, much more than you can even see."

"What me no can see?" Nothaar demanded.

"You lack the tools and the frame of reference for us to even begin to answer that question!" Syraaq scoffed.

"For now," Ifu quietly tried, "you'll just have to take my word for it. Let's just say that even their blood has been changed in such a way that it works differently, that it's more like ours than yours."

A fright suddenly came to Nothaar as he asked, "But you blood no good for all children, yes? Babies die, more than before. Less life, many sad parents."

Ifu looked away, apparently torn. Syraaq chose to respond for him, "Yes, Nothaar. The changes, as you've so eloquently documented, are slow. Your progeny, your future generations, they are turning into something not unlike us. But for a long time, it will be a mix. Some of these combinations can survive, a large percentage of them cannot. In time, though, there will be no more of your type and only people who look like us, talk like us, act like us. They won't die with such frequency anymore. Actually, with other updates, they will expire far less often and will live longer and longer. Someday, they will even be able to stay alive as lengthy a time as me, if not more so. After all, we are always improving our skillset related to longevity, as we are in all fields."

Flashing his disapproving visage towards Syraaq and Ifu, Nothaar declared, "Me need urinate."

CHAPTER 06

After a bit of negotiation, Ifu rebound Nothaar's hands in front of him so he could use them somewhat normally. More importantly, Ifu also loosened Nothaar's restraints around and connected to his feet. With these adjustments, Nothaar was able to stand up and walk around freely, although only in a slow shuffle. Whereas Nothaar had asked to be completely untied, Ifu insisted that he couldn't do that, at least not yet. *Even though he's pretending to be my ally,* Nothaar contemptuously thought, *it's quite clear that he's a proponent of what Syraaq did, as well as continuing to hold me against my will.*

Once his bonds were relocated, Nothaar was surprised to discover that they were not actually rope like he originally suspected. Although they acted in a similar fashion, they did not resemble anything he had ever seen or felt before. Prior to this occasion, every type of cord he had come across had been made of some sort of plant fiber, but this one was constructed from a surprisingly flexible material that seemed almost impossible to rip or fray. Unexpectedly, Ifu did not tie knots to hold the line together; instead, the fabric—for lack of a more accurate word—appeared to adhere to itself. *How had Ifu so effortlessly separated them,* Nothaar wondered, *while for me they won't budge no matter how hard I struggle?*

Putting all that aside, Ifu brought Nothaar over to a wall and waved his hand at it. When he did so, the partition once again ate a piece of itself, revealing another room, albeit a much smaller one. At the sudden disappearance of the metal barrier, Nothaar jumped backwards as he let loose a frightened shout. Due to his encumbrances, he started to lose his balance and fall backwards. Whether by choice or instinct, Ifu caught Nothaar and assisted in keeping him upright, and thus helped avoid another round of bruising and pain, at a minimum.

Once Nothaar was steady again, Ifu turned to him and said, "You can go ahead, I'll wait out here."

As Ifu continued to look at Nothaar expectantly, Nothaar decided his best bet was to just head inside the smaller room. Once there, though, he was not sure what was supposed to happen next. Giving voice to his confusion, Nothaar asked, "What me do now?"

Outside, he heard Syraaq chortling and then say, "Ifu, you better go in there and show him how to use a toilet! You have to realize: he's never seen such a thing before, especially not one designed for interstellar travel. Now, I'm no expert, but there might be some difficulties depending upon what orifices he uses to exorcize waste!" Syraaq apparently found the situation intensely uproarious as she could not stop laughing at her own comment.

Ifu came inside and declared, "I'm sorry, Nothaar, this is going to be a bit embarrassing for both of us." After this, Ifu proceeded to remove some clothing and demonstrate how to use the toilet so that expelled bodily fluids and other ejecta could be caught and sent away somewhere. He then explained that they actually collected all these expulsions and reused them, which caused Nothaar to feel nauseous at such a notion. Attempting to backtrack, Ifu struggled with his words while endeavoring to clarify that they purified everything. "For instance, urine becomes potable water," Ifu insisted. "It's all very clean and safe. We do exactly what nature does, except faster!"

Nothaar was hardly convinced, but at that moment he did not have to worry about adding water to his body, only getting rid of some. Thankfully, he and Ifu were fairly similar in physiology, so he figured he could use the toilet in the same way that Ifu had shown him. After expressing so and asking for privacy, Ifu quickly acquiesced and eagerly bowed out of the room and into the larger one. On his way to exiting, Ifu further expounded that Nothaar could shut the opening by waving his hand a certain way at the portal, and to do the same in reverse to let himself out. Nothaar was too concerned about potentially being trapped inside with only the toilet for company, so he opted to leave the gateway open, forcing Ifu and Syraaq to listen as he did his personal business.

Much relieved, Nothaar shambled his way back to the main area. There, Syraaq was waiting with a cup in her hands. The chalice was unlike any Nothaar had ever seen, made of yet another material he did not recognize. It was so perfectly rounded that he wondered how any person's hand could possibly make it that way. *The artisan that forged this must be one of the most gifted people in the whole world,* Nothaar contemplated. *I've never seen such craftsmanship before. This one item alone might buy me an entire season of provisions, it's that amazing. Perhaps I should forget about the falling star and just see what I can... appropriate from here?*

Taking the container from Syraaq, Nothaar brought it up to his face and took a whiff. There was no smell at all, not even from the cup itself. "What this?" Nothaar asked.

"Just water," Syraaq tendered.

In disgust, Nothaar immediately dropped the cup, which clanked on the hard metal floor, though did not shatter. Water spilled out everywhere, but did not stick around long as the floor seemed to drink it until it was dry. "You give Nothaar urine water?!" he accused with revulsion.

"Ifu, what the heck did you tell him in there?" Syraaq chided with disappointment.

"I tried to explain the recycling and reclamation system a bit," Ifu clamored in his defense.

"Why would you do that?" Syraaq shot back. "Can't you tell that Nothaar is already scared and lost, out of his element and depth? His people live in huts and use the woods as their bathrooms. They haven't even invented the latrine yet!"

"How do they have paper and bound books, food preservation and detailed astronomy, but not have things like... that...?" Ifu complained.

"Technological development is not a straight line," Syraaq reprimanded. "Every group evolves at varying paces in differing fields depending upon their needs and the pressures they are dealing with. In a land of peace, would they develop weapons of mass destruction?"

Without waiting any longer for Ifu to reply, Syraaq bent down to pick up the cup and walked over to the wall. There, a niche appeared after she made a gesture and she fit the cup within the newly formed space. Nothaar then heard a tinkling sound. Once it ceased, Syraaq took the cup out again and said, "Watch me, it's perfectly safe." At this, she took a sip. "Now you," she pronounced while offering the cup again.

Nothaar still resisted taking the drinking goblet while saying, "Syraaq, Ifu both say things work different on them than on Nothaar. Syraaq maybe kill me because she no know for sure. How me know this safe?"

Ifu took the cup from Syraaq and swallowed a large gulp himself before asserting, "Water is universal. No matter where you're from, water is always the same, give or take an extra neutron or the spin of a... you know, never mind that. For all intents and purposes, water is just water, and everything that lives needs it exactly as it is. It's one of the things that binds all life together."

After hesitating some more, Nothaar finally took the cup from Ifu's hands and drank. He hadn't admitted it to them or even himself how parched he was, and the water was incredibly refreshing and cool. "Very good water," Nothaar agreed. "Taste clean, no mineral, like source of river."

"As I told you," Ifu avowed, "we purify it. That is water

and nothing else. You've probably never had water quite like this before, not even if you sipped directly from a rainstorm overhead."

"Are you hungry?" Syraaq suddenly asked.

In response, Nothaar's digestive system started grumbling. He had last eaten the morning before he met Ifu and Syraaq, and he had no idea how long ago that had been considering there was no way for him to tell either the length of time he had been unconscious or even what part of the day it was then. Nevertheless, based upon the indirect evidence he had been able to gather, he felt quite confident that at least one turning of the sun and moon had passed, but probably not much more than that.

"I'll take that as a yes," Syraaq decided. "Do you have any food in your pack that we can give you?"

"Yes," Nothaar affirmed. "Have provisions, been dried for winter, early spring, long travel. No matter which ones, all taste much same. Old from last autumn now."

Ifu excused himself before departing out the open hole in the wall and quickly coming back in with Nothaar's pack. Digging around inside, he pulled out some foodstuffs and handed them to Nothaar. As Nothaar began to gnaw on a piece and soften it with his saliva, he noticed that both Syraaq and Ifu were looking at him intently. Feeling that maybe he could start to turn the tide towards his side, Nothaar proffered, "You want some me food? You hungry, need eat? Me have lots, can share." It wasn't true at all, but Nothaar hoped that showing kindness would get his captors to start to change their behavior towards him.

Surprisingly, both flinched away, even more than Nothaar had done earlier with the water. "Nothaar food no good?" he asked.

Syraaq explained, "Just like the sedative affects us and you differently, so does food. Water may be universal, but food is incredibly specific. We cannot digest and absorb the nutrients from your provisions. We do have our own—limited—supply of goods to eat, so don't worry about that."

"No can eat me food?" Nothaar probed for clarification. "Children can eat me food. Children be like Syraaq, like Ifu, yes?"

"Yes, and no," Syraaq contradicted both Nothaar and herself. "Like we talked about earlier, they are in a period of transition. Someday, they won't be able to eat food like you have there, either."

"Then all die!" Nothaar concernedly yelled.

Ifu made a signal that Nothaar interpreted as telling Syraaq to let him try. After doing so he said, "Just as the children are changing, so are all other living things. In time, Nothaar, there would actually not be anything for people like you, from before the *Sky Shift*, to eat. But don't worry, no one alive today will be around to see that day; it's still a long way off, many generations from now."

Something abruptly clicked in Nothaar's understanding as he noted, "Happen now. Some food, no can eat, even same batch. One plant good, neighbor bad, no way tell. Cause many problems!"

"It's, unfortunately, what happens throughout this type of changeover period," Ifu sighed. "And it's not just people that are dealing with this. Every type of creature of the land, sea, and sky is going through their own version of the transformation you are seeing in the plants and children. Most are very subtle, but they are just as dangerous for those that try to eat them."

"Meanwhile, since we can't get new food here, we have to make our own rations last for as long as it takes, too," Syraaq added.

Nothaar turned towards Syraaq and queried, "As long as takes for what?"

Instead of answering, Syraaq shifted her gaze to Ifu and they shared some deep, apparently sad glance. Finally, Ifu broke the silence and declared, "We need him to come with us. Nothaar is the evidence we set out to find in the first place that proves that what we do... did... as Starbuilders was morally wrong and reprehensible in every way. If we're ever going to get through to the government and alter things for the betterment of all life, we have to start being honest—with them, and with ourselves."

Seeing his opening, Nothaar chimed in with, "And with Nothaar. Need trust Nothaar." As he spoke, Nothaar indicated towards the ropes that still constrained him as their reluctant prisoner.

CHAPTER 07

Ifu and Syraaq debated amongst themselves on the potential merits and detriments of releasing Nothaar from his restraints, with Nothaar providing the occasional additional argument in his own favor. "Me no attempt run away," Nothaar offered, although even he didn't truly believe that contention. "Beside, me no know where here be, no can go anywhere. Need Ifu and Syraaq show me how leave, go back to where was, where star fell. Only then maybe me able leave, if Syraaq no shoot me again and make me sleep and hurt all over."

Despite Nothaar's plea lacking his complete sincerity, this assertion appeared to finally make a breakthrough with his wardens and they agreed to fully untie him. Still, Nothaar got the impression that they were not granting him his freedom, and that it would take a lot more to make that possible. Fueling these trepidations, before they removed Nothaar's bonds, Syraaq and Ifu discussed some subject that Nothaar could not follow before Syraaq left the room and came back with yet another gun-looking device. This time, to assuage Nothaar's immediate concerns, she first put it up to her own arm and apparently made it shoot. She then did the same to Ifu before finally finishing the identical procedure with Nothaar. He felt a small pinch followed by a burning sensation that went around his entire body. For a moment, he thought she had poisoned him with another one of her miscalculations. However, as quickly as the heat came, it swiftly dissipated. Syraaq was studying him during the whole ordeal and, after the sensation passed, she verbally confirmed with him that he felt normal once again. Upon receiving a positive affirmation from Nothaar, Syraaq seemed to stare off into nothing before turning to Ifu and declaring, "It's working perfectly; it'll be safe to cut him loose now."

As Ifu began undoing Nothaar's shackles, he said to Syraaq, "I'm surprised it worked with his physiology. Are you sure his system won't just purge them or something?"

"No, I'm not" Syraaq admitted, "but I'll keep an eye on it. So long as they can leech energy from him, though, I'd imagine all should be good."

Apparently satisfied, Ifu finished his task of unleashing Nothaar and said, "There, Nothaar, feel better?"

Rubbing his wrists, Nothaar declared, "Much more, yes. But what do now?"

"I believe a tour is in order!" Ifu announced with a surprising amount of chipperness. "Follow me, if you will."

After what Nothaar surmised to be a surreal and uncharacteristically polite offer, Ifu walked through the opening in the wall with Syraaq following closely behind. Not seeing any other options, Nothaar exited next, only to find himself in a long, featureless corridor. It appeared to be made of the same metals as the room he was just in, but otherwise offered no additional clues as to its purpose or where, in general, Nothaar found himself. Syraaq came around behind him and waved at the hole they had just traversed until it closed back up, replaced by a wall. "Me pack still inside!" Nothaar shouted in alarm. Losing his rucksack would mean that he truly was lost. He stood no chance of surviving in the wild without his supplies.

"It's not going anywhere," Syraaq assured him. "If you want, you can go back in there." At this, she made a different motion and the opening reappeared again. Nothaar stuck his head inside and saw that it was the same room and his possessions still sat where Ifu had put them down. "How make hole in wall come and go? Walls somehow build and break selves."

"In your villages," Syraaq began, "you live in permanent huts, right?"

"Yes, most do," Nothaar agreed. "Some live caves, some near wasteland only grass, some stone, some wood, some mud. No agree on best way."

"Alright," Syraaq said, "and do you have doors, something to block the entrances?"

"Of course!" Nothaar roared. He was getting tired of Syraaq and Ifu assuming that people like him were some type of savages who just thoughtlessly roamed the land. "Need doors keep warm inside, cold winters. Also, keep animals out. Very basic. People no beasts."

"I apologize," Syraaq demurred. "I didn't mean to imply otherwise. We've only been in your... land... for a few days and there is much we don't know about you, your people, and your... capabilities."

"What land Syraaq from?" Nothaar probed. "Come from land of ice?" Since Nothaar had recently learned from Baubu that such a place could potentially exist, it would explain a lot about Syraaq and Ifu. *Perhaps there are many other lands beyond the great salt sea,* Nothaar considered. *I thought I knew about all of the locales in the world, but I must admit that I was mistaken. As far as I'm aware, no one has attempted to cross the endless expanse to see what may be out there. It's obvious now that it's not the end of the world as we once thought. If the Knowledge was wrong about this, what other parts of our beliefs are incorrect? I'm already aware that Syraaq and Ifu come from separate homelands. Whatever is happening here must have happened in their villages first. I wonder if it occurred with Syraaq's people at an earlier time than Ifu's? For how long and in how many areas is this transformation happening?*

Chuckling at Nothaar's question, Syraaq declared, "Far from it. Although, there is also a land of ice where I come from."

"Multiple lands of ice?!" Nothaar bade in shock. Over the past few cycles of the moon, his worldview had certainly been challenged more than he ever considered possible. *Damn that Baubu Yoordi,* Nothaar cursed inside his head. *I would have been better off not having my perspective disrupted like this.* Then, feeling remorseful, Nothaar apologized to the memory of the departed *Keeper* and for taking his frustrations out on him. More so, Nothaar admitted to himself that despite what was transpiring and the situation he found himself in, he preferred to always learn more and let the truth fall where it may, no matter the consequences and repercussions.

"We're getting off track," Ifu interrupted. "We haven't even left the doorway yet.

"Wait," Nothaar commanded as he stepped back out into the hallway. "You mean hole in wall be really door? Where door go when open?"

Sighing with a clear indication of annoyance at being further delayed, Ifu explained, "It goes into the wall. Make the same gestures as Syraaq just did and, this time, watch closely what actually happens."

Doing as instructed, Nothaar was able to make the door appear and disappear multiple times. Finally, he noticed that it was actually sliding inside the wall. "Wall really hollow, door go inside!" Nothaar declared with delight at his discovery.

"Not completely hollow," Ifu countered, "but for your purposes, that's true enough."

"How magic work?" Nothaar requested.

"What magic?" Ifu perplexedly asked.

"Me no know magic, no have magic power," Nothaar expounded. "Yet me make door move. How possible? Is me magic now?"

"It's not magic!" Ifu shouted.

"Nothaar," Syraaq tried in a quieter tone. "It may look like magic to you, but it's really just tools. We have given the door a way to see and respond to us."

"Door can see?" Nothaar queried. "Still sound magic."

"You're going to just have to trust us on this," Syraaq insisted. "It'll make sense... eventually. Imagine showing that book of yours to someone from before the *Knowledge* began. They would think it was magic, too."

"Before the *Knowledge*?" Nothaar concernedly questioned. He never considered that such an era might exist, but there was an undeniable logic to it. *The Knowledge had to start at some point,* Nothaar internalized, *so there must have been an age when it didn't exist.*

Instead of pursuing this topic further, Nothaar began to look around in the long, empty space they were in. There was not a lot new to see as each segment appeared almost exactly the same as the next as far as his eyes could gather. Finally, as a way to change the subject and satisfy his own curiosity, Nothaar observed, "Room inside door no as big as area in now."

"There are more rooms," Syraaq declared as she walked a few paces down the metal walkway, signaling Nothaar to follow her. Once he closed the gap, she instructed him to do the same motions as he had executed with the previous doorway.

Doing so, another entrance appeared. Nothaar walked inside to find a room with a layout nearly identical to the one he had just been in. He then went along the walls making the same gestures he remembered seeing Ifu use earlier until another passageway appeared. There, unsurprisingly, he found another smaller toilet room. Closing it, he returned to where Syraaq and Ifu were waiting and shut the door behind him.

"All rooms same?" Nothaar inquired. "All have toilet room make urine water?"

"There are some differences here and there," Ifu patiently answered in a much calmer tone than before, apparently coming to realize his exacerbations were not helping the situation. "But yes, you can generally expect all quarters to have an en suite lavatory."

"How many?" Nothaar delved. Without a strong understanding of his environment, Nothaar knew that he would remain at a tactical disadvantage. He hoped that if he presented the inquiries innocently enough that Ifu and Syraaq would willingly give up vital intelligence.

"How many what? Rooms?" Ifu questioned. "I... don't really... Syraaq, do you know what the capacity is here?"

"Of this class?" Syraaq asked. "I'm not sure, either. Maybe if we walk around a bit, I'll get a better sense and can make a proper estimate."

"Good idea," Ifu agreed. "Let's get more than a few paces away from where we started and take a look around. Are you finally ready, Nothaar?"

CHAPTER 08

What happened over the next indeterminable stretch of time was a complete blur for Nothaar. Ifu led the charge as their party passed through many corridors that all looked very much the same to Nothaar, took ladders up and down, and went into even larger rooms that Nothaar could not make any sense of. Although Syraaq was constantly panting as she tried to catch her breath while keeping up with her younger and faster companions, she still sometimes tried to explain to Nothaar what he was looking at and the purpose to each of these spaces. Nonetheless, Nothaar lacked anything to compare them to and, thus, could not truly understand what was happening. After a while, Syraaq finally cried out, "Ifu, I'm old; I can't keep going at this pace! Let's go to the mess hall and get some food and drinks before we continue."

Whatever this "mess hall" was, Ifu quickly acquiesced, apparently in need of a break and some refreshments himself. By that point, Nothaar was so dumbfounded and turned around that he had no choice but to continue to follow them lest he be lost forever. Eventually, their group came to another nondescript area with only one discerning feature: the largest door-hole Nothaar had seen to date. For some reason it was already open, so they walked right through without pausing. Inside, they were in an area that Nothaar estimated could fit a small hamlet—including all its buildings and people—if everything in such a hypothetical community were condensed together onto a single parcel. Instead of that, though, there were many raised square and rectangular metallic planks scattered throughout. Each of these freestanding flat slabs were surrounded by several shorter ones, usually one or two on each side. The comparatively diminutive objects also had a flush surface, but each was at about a half the height of their taller and wider associate. They further distinguished themselves by having a perpendicular attachment on a single flank against their outside edges.

"Oh, thank goodness," Syraaq exclaimed as she pushed past Nothaar and Ifu and went over to the closest of these setups. There, she pulled one of the smaller pieces away, sat upon it with the erect component to her back, and then scooted it closer to the larger slat. "My aching legs," she complained as she rubbed them with her hands. Nothaar noted that despite their seemingly fantastical abilities, Syraaq and Ifu were very much mortals and dealt with the same bodily limitations of any living being.

"Nothaar, take a seat," Syraaq offered as she indicated towards another one of the contraptions she was sitting upon next to her. "Ifu, be a dear and fetch me some buttered toast and tea."

Maintaining his position, Nothaar watched as Ifu started to rummage through some bags that were haphazardly scattered upon the ground. All of them were agape and other smaller bags were spilling out. Ifu threw several of these miniature sacks aside before apparently finding at least one of the things he was looking for.

"Why are you still standing there?" Syraaq inquired, snapping Nothaar out of his study. Imitating Syraaq's previous actions, he found himself sitting upon the hard surface. From that viewpoint, he noticed that his arms were around the same height as the taller piece.

Squirming in his position trying to get comfortable, Nothaar asked, "This how Syraaq and Ifu eat meal?"

"What do you mean?" Syraaq confusedly asked.

Nothaar clarified his thoughts, "Sit on hard block, put food on taller block?"

"Oh..." Syraaq began, "do you not have tables and chairs?"

"Me no know these words," Nothaar answered.

"I see," Syraaq said. "So, when you want to sit down in your hut, what do you do? Do you not have furniture of any kind?"

"Again, me no know that word 'furniture', either," Nothaar avowed. "However, Nothaar people sit on pillows on floor. More comfortable than hard block."

"Now I get it," Syraaq claimed. "Well, what you are sitting upon is a 'chair' and what is in front of us is a 'table'. Not all chairs are this uncomfortable; many are made so that they have cushions... I mean pillows... built into them. Unfortunately, the people who designed this mess hall thought it should be more utilitarian than comfy."

Before Nothaar could ask any follow-up questions, Ifu

came over to the table, took a seat himself, and threw two of the smaller packages in front of Syraaq, leaving another three and a pitcher of some kind in front of him. "Figured I might as well join you," Ifu stated.

"Giving yourself a feast, eh?" Syraaq probed.

"Looking at what's available, it's clear that there's no way to take it all with us," Ifu highlighted, "so I might as well binge now."

At this pronouncement, Ifu lifted the pitcher and poured a liquid—which Nothaar recognized as plain water—out of it and onto his packages. Nothaar's eyes widened as he saw the parcels start to transform as they drank the offering, becoming other shapes entirely. Eventually, he noticed steam rising from some of them, as if they had been heated over a fire. Smells began to assail Nothaar's nose, some which were delightful and others that were nauseating. He was so transfixed by what was happening, though, that he completely missed Syraaq doing the same and new items appearing in front of her on the table. When he did finally turn towards her, he at last recognized something. "Syraaq, you have bread!" he proclaimed with awe.

Syraaq paused with the slice of bread close to her mouth, placed it back down, and said, "So, your people have some type of bread, huh?"

"Bread very important," Nothaar proclaimed. "Gather grain head, use all winter make bread. Also make spirit drink starting same way, but use more water. Other ingredients necessary, too."

"Of course they invented alcohol before toilets," Ifu derisively commented. "Gotta have your priorities, right Syraaq?"

Snickering in response, Syraaq made some motion of agreement before bringing her slice of bread to her mouth and taking a bite, seemingly very satisfied with the result.

"Can me see?" Nothaar asked, indicating towards another piece in front of Syraaq.

After chewing and swallowing her first nibble, Syraaq pushed what she had called "toast" towards Nothaar and said, "Sure, but remember not to eat it. It won't agree with you."

Nothaar mimicked a sign of agreement he had seen Syraaq and Ifu give each other and went to pick it up, but immediately dropped it. "Ow, is hot!" he remarked. "How hot? No fire, just water."

"I'm going to eat and enjoy my tea," Syraaq declared. "Ifu, you explain it." She then brought a cup with steaming liquid to her lips, another surprise to Nothaar as he had not seen Ifu bring over any container like that to hold Syraaq's tea.

Showing displeasure at having to put down his own meal, Ifu left their company and picked up another one of the petite containers from the ground. He then put it in the center of the table and asked, "What do you see here?"

"Is small bag," Nothaar responded.

"Do you notice anything else about it?" Ifu pushed.

Taking a closer look, Nothaar let out a sound of annoyance at having missed it before. Ignoring Ifu and Syraaq's clear confusion and discomfort with the indiscernible-to-them noises he was releasing, Nothaar noted, "Has picture painted on top, and letters from *Language of Children*! Err... me mean, *Lingua*..."

"Can you read what it says?" Ifu urged.

"Me think so," Nothaar declared with some trepidation. Slowly, he began to read, sounding out the lexes and his overall understanding of the *Lingua*. "It say, 'fish-flavor soup, hot'. Me get right?"

In response, Ifu took the pitcher of water and poured it on the packet. Before Nothaar's eyes, it grew and transformed, becoming a bowl with a broth inside and chunks floating in it. Even a spoon grew out of it as the liquid momentarily boiled before stopping and letting the steam disperse. It breached Nothaar's sense of smell and an overwhelming feeling of nostalgia hit him as he recalled the fish soups of Baubu's village and his own long forsaken hometown. He had to stop himself from diving right in, reminding himself that he would not be able to digest what was in front of him, at best.

Giving Ifu a skeptical look, Nothaar lambasted, "And Ifu say no magic, right? Ifu make bowl, spoon, meat, and heat with only water, but still no magic."

"None whatsoever," Ifu claimed as he opened his hands wide to the side, wiggling his fingers.

"Then how?" Nothaar demanded.

Pausing a moment before speaking, Ifu explained, "In order for our food to take up as little space as possible, we remove all the water, dehydrating it."

"Nothaar people dry plenty food," Nothaar interrupted. "Make jerky, you see earlier."

"We go a lot further than that," Ifu clarified. "Our food is made into a fine powder, as are the component pieces for bowls and plates and utensils. When you make bread, do you add some type of fungus or something to the wet grains to get it to grow?"

"Yes, children use word 'leaven'," Nothaar confirmed.

"Okay, good," Ifu stated. "We have something similar, but even smaller: tiny helpers that are so miniscule that you can't even see them. Once water is added, a command is triggered and they then mix things together, rebuilding everything back to their original configurations: the containers, the utensils, even the food itself."

"Chunks of meat, too?" Nothaar countered.

"We don't harvest live animals," Ifu declared with some unbridled disgust undercutting his voice. "If we want a protein like that, we grow it."

"You grow animal like plant?" Nothaar scoffed.

Giving himself another brief hesitation, Ifu retorted, "Again, more akin to fermenting and baking it like a bread. Once you have an understanding of the concepts the way our people do, you find out the methodologies are relatively the same. True, there are some individuals who still occasionally consume the flesh of live animals, but they are few and far between nowadays. It just isn't efficient or practical enough to feed a large population."

"Then how make hot?" Nothaar dismissed.

"By the stars, how am I supposed to explain the laws

of thermodynamics and how endothermic reactions work to you?" Ifu cursed.

"To be fair," Syraaq suddenly chimed in, "how well do you really understand those principles? I'm not afraid to admit that I barely get it. Nothaar, we don't need to know how it works; we just live in a universe where we know that it does and smarter people than us built the products that take advantage of these tenets.

"And we're going to need to hope they knew what they were doing because we must carry as many of these packets as possible. In order to do that, it means each has to be incredibly light. That is why you are seeing all those bags with our foodstuff scattered across the floor, Nothaar. We're packing ourselves, for a very long journey."

"How long need food for?" Nothaar quizzed.

This brought another round of laughter from Syraaq before she answered, "If I were to guess, I'd say several years. And in all that time, all the food we'll ever be able to consume can only encompass what we can carry out of this very room."

"Why so long?" Nothaar grilled. "No go home, go land where food can have?"

"You have many 'why' questions," Syraaq chided, "but I'm afraid the answers will be gibberish to you without a lot more context. Where to begin with someone as primitive as you?"

"Syraaq!" Ifu called, aghast. "You can't use that word with him! As you reminded me of earlier, that's the type of prejudice we must expel from our minds if we expect to succeed. We must purge our own predispositions, otherwise we'll have lost before we truly get underway. Nothaar is a sapient being, and that is where we have to adjust our beliefs to align to."

Greatly distressed, Nothaar called out, "What 'primitive', what 'prejudice', what 'sapient'? All drivel in me ears. These no words hear from children."

"But they do intrinsically know them," Syraaq cryptically asserted. "They just haven't had a reason to use them yet. Sadly, the time will come, though... it always does."

Not satisfied with her response, Nothaar let his frustrations get the better of him and refused to continue conversing. Ifu apparently picked up on his pouting and decided, "I don't think just talking about all these foreign notions is getting us anywhere. We're going to need some visual aides to explain things to Nothaar."

"I didn't think I would need to remind you about how dire our situation is," Syraaq refuted, "but we are running on low-power mode here. The generator is destroyed beyond repair—or, at least beyond the skillset of the two of us to fix it—and we can barely keep the lights and basic life-support functions going. If we had any extra juice, we could have activated the elevators instead of being forced to climb those awful emergency ladders!

"More so, this situation cannot and will not last. The further along we get into the spring and summer, the more the trees overhead will start to sprout additional leaves and block out all remaining light. We're barely collecting enough radiation from Nothaar's Quantum Shifted sun using the last-resort solar collectors on the outside skin of the ship. It certainly doesn't help that we just barely have the nose of our transport poking out above the surface so that we go unnoticed. Not that that preventative measure really did us any good, though."

"Then we'll do it analog style!" Ifu pronounced as he got up from the table, leaving his now cold and forgotten food behind.

CHAPTER 09

Groaning as she stood up, Syraaq started to follow Ifu as he began heading towards the large doorway. Looking at the piles of plates, bowls, cups, utensils, and uneaten food, Nothaar asked, "Syraaq, you leave all here like this? No clean? No save scraps?"

"We do save the scraps, per se," Syraaq claimed. "Remember before when you spilled your water on the floor and it all got absorbed? Well, the table will do the same with whatever we leave on it. Nothing goes to waste; it will all be recycled into something or other down the line."

"Animal or insects no get into storage?" Nothaar probed further, concerned about what may happen should Syraaq's and Ifu's food supply be eaten or filled with eggs, feces, or other contaminants.

"There are no living animals or insects of any kind in here," Syraaq stated. "If one somehow got on board, they would be quickly exterminated. As it is, we had to convince the *Eh-aye* that you were not a foreign object that needed to be eradicated."

Not following this line of reasoning, Nothaar questioned, "What... who be *Eh-aye*? Others here?"

Before Syraaq could answer, Ifu poked his head back inside the mess hall and called, "Where are you guys?

Come on, follow me already!"

Without another word, Nothaar and Syraaq did just that. Once again, they walked through the featureless corridors and, occasionally, up ladders to levels that looked much the same. The size was astounding to Nothaar and he could not believe they could keep walking and still be inside. Thinking about his unfinished conversation with Syraaq, he queried, "House only for you two? Or others here, like *Eh-aye*? Why no see?"

This question actually brought a rare chuckle from Ifu who in turn explained, "No, this isn't some massive mansion for just the two... or three of us, from your perspective. The *Eh-aye* isn't a person, it's a... let's just say an invisible helper without a body."

"Is captured spirit?!" Nothaar asked aghast.

"Again, there is nothing mystical or divine involved in anything we do or that happens here," Ifu corrected. "The *Eh-aye* is another tool, something we mere mortals built. Just like with the little helpers I told you about that assist in reconstructing our food, the *Eh-aye* is similar."

"Ah, so Ifu and Syraaq no detain spirits," Nothaar concluded, "but build them, instead."

Sighing, Ifu declared, "Sure, Nothaar, if that helps you accept how it works."

"But I wouldn't say that we specifically built the *Eh-aye* ourselves," Syraaq interjected. "Someone else did that. We wouldn't have the first clue on how to go about making an *Eh-aye*, even a simple one! Like any tool, we know how to use it, not how to make it from scratch."

"Me understand," Nothaar declared. "Me can use metal knife, but no know how make one. Is very special skill. Can read in the *Knowledge*, but no have experience in undertaking task. Takes many years to learn."

"Exactly," Ifu agreed.

"So, *Eh-aye* no person," Nothaar pressed, "that mean Ifu and Syraaq only people in giant building. Why?"

"Well, to be honest," Ifu began, "we stole it."

"Stole?" Nothaar questioned. "Why steal home? How do? Cannot just pick hut up, take with. If could, me no need sleep outside."

"All will be answered, I promise" Ifu assured Nothaar. "But to clarify your misconception, this is not a domicile of any kind; it's a vessel for transport."

"Not sure words me know or use right, or understanding what Ifu and Syraaq been saying," Nothaar offered. "Can make more clear?"

"Do you have boats?" Syraaq quickly asked before Ifu could come up with any response.

"Yes," Nothaar acknowledged, "boats go out on salt sea, get fish. Me village in far north get lot of fish. Same with village in far south where me just was. Away from coast, some fish in pond, but people in villages there no eat much fish. Me happier near salt sea, eating fish. Feel like home. Been long time since there."

"Alright," Syraaq accepted, "then I want you to think of what you're inside of right now as a very big boat."

"Boat here feel like could hold many villages," Nothaar contended, "include all people and huts. Biggest boat me see sit eight people, that all."

Instead of responding to Nothaar's challenge, Syraaq asked in an apparent non sequitur, "Nothaar, I think I know based upon your earlier words and reactions, but I need to confirm something. Tell me, how do you count?"

When Nothaar displayed pure confusion upon his façade, Syraaq requested that he show her with his hands, saying the numbers aloud. Putting up his left hand, Nothaar began counting with his fingers starting at one and finishing at his fifth and final digit. At Syraaq's urging he continue, adding his right hand and finished at ten before returning to his first grasping appendage to continue counting the double digits. "Ten-one, ten-two, ten-three, ten-four..." he was enumerating before Syraaq cut him off and declared that was fine enough.

"Thank goodness, it's exactly as I judged it to be!" Syraaq announced with an exhalation of relief. "You are base-ten, just like us."

Feeling he was getting lost in so many unanswered questions and new terminology, Nothaar decided to follow-up anyway, "What be base-ten? Why good?"

Syraaq appeared to ponder for a moment before she elucidated, "Some people count to another number like five or eight before they go into a second numeral. So instead of ten-one, ten-two, ten-three, it would be eight-one, eight-two, eight-three."

"Very confusing, very strange," Nothaar contended.

When Syraaq agreed, Ifu suddenly broke his recent silence and noted, "Even if you were something like base-eight, it wouldn't matter. In the end, one of the future generations of the children would convert to base-ten, one way or another. That said, it'll certainly make things easier for communications between all of us in the meanwhile."

Before Nothaar could delve deeper into what Ifu meant by his enigmatic remark, Syraaq chimed in with, "Now that we recognize that you use base-ten, I need to know how big a number do you understand? If I asked you what ten tens were, what would you say?"

Annoyed by such an infantile query, Nothaar flippantly responded, "Ten tens is hundred. Ten hundreds is thousand. This simple math. Can go much higher. You want Nothaar to count all way to million?"

"Excellent," Syraaq proclaimed instead, ignoring Nothaar's outburst. "Since we've gone around the ship quite a bit, I can now more accurately answer your earlier quandary, and you'll be able to understand my response."

"Which one?" Nothaar sardonically pushed back. "Many question no been answered, only adding more to pile as walk around... big boat."

Syraaq patted Nothaar's shoulder and declared, "We're trying, too. It's not just you; we're frustrated by what's transpiring because we don't know the best way to properly communicate with you, either. This situation is new to us. Truthfully, we didn't really come up with a plan on how we might share necessary information with... someone like you. I believe it's going to be a long time before we truly understand and trust each other."

"Syraaq think be possible?" Nothaar argued.

"I do," Syraaq affirmed. "Before I met Ifu, I doubt I would have, though. Somehow, he has helped this old lady open her eyes for the first time. You should have a little faith in him, too, and in us, both."

"Must be earned," Nothaar perfunctorily stated.

"That's... fair enough," Syraaq capitulated. "Well, anyway, as a demonstration of our dedication to you, and to prove that we're not ignoring you or trying to deflect from you learning about the true nature of our sudden appearance in your midst, I will tell you what I have concluded after walking this great distance:

"There are approximately four-thousand personal cabins on this ship, with many designed for multiple occupancy. We could probably fit six thousand people in here comfortably."

"Six thousand!" Nothaar yelped. "That twice more than biggest settlement me ever see. Me once see longhouse that maybe hold fifty villagers, all standing, but not bigger. Used for special times. That place also not able to sleep in, not right for that. Big boat beyond anything me see. Why need so much space? Travel normal mean less room, somehow this place have more."

"Ha! This vessel is really nothing," Syraaq contended. "Actually, this ship was originally situated inside a much larger one—like a baby in the womb—and that parent craft housed hundreds of thousands of people. Like Ifu said, we stole it from that grander vessel to make our escape. Unfortunately, as good as the *Eh-aye* is at being able to do a multitude of activities, it cannot pilot alone. Just like with your metal knife forger, there is a certain skillset and level of experience that is required to complete these tasks. Lacking both, we couldn't control our trajectory, and we crashed right where you found us."

Nothaar gave a gesture of disagreement before declaring, "No is possible. No salt sea here, inland many days walk. How could boat get far from water?"

Syraaq gave him a look that Nothaar would later learn indicated delight. "We didn't travel by sea; we came from the sky!"

Before Nothaar could ask anything more about this incredulous revelation, Ifu announced that they had arrived and opened a portal into another realm of existence.

CHAPTER 10

Following Ifu's lead, Nothaar and Syraaq entered another large, cavernous space. It was not as big as the mess hall from which they had recently departed, but its purpose completely eluded Nothaar. Most notable to him, though, was that it was the first place aboard their supposed "boat" that he had seen where the floor was not made of a shiny metallic material. Instead, it was some type of soft, compressive substance. While nowhere near as responsive as the large pillow he had awoken atop of, it was still a relief on his feet compared to all of the hard surfaces he had traversed to get there.

"What this room?" Nothaar finally asked when neither Ifu nor Syraaq offered an immediate explanation.

"It's a gym," Syraaq replied. When Nothaar did not give her any indication of understanding the word, she expounded, "A gym is a place where people go to do physical activity in order to help keep their bodies healthy and—for some—to look sexually attractive."

"Most people me know look to do less hard work, not more," Nothaar countered.

Giving what Nothaar was beginning to consider one of her signature chuckles, Syraaq contended, "I'm sure your populace partakes in an excess of manual labor, but our denizens are—for the most part—far more sedentary. As you correctly observed and commented on when we left the mess hall, we don't even need to clean up after ourselves! We have many... helpers and tools to do what your people probably have to do by hand."

"You keep slaves?" Nothaar prodded with disgust in his voice. While it was not common, he had come across villages—especially ones near the wastelands—that did press others into involuntary servitude. Usually, they were from a neighboring settlement that had been raided. Nothaar had not tended to spend too much time at places like that lest he potentially find himself also forced to remain against his will.

"Not slaves," Syraaq corrected. "We have apparatuses, what we call machines, which look like they are doing work only a sapient being could accomplish, but they are not alive like you and me. They are, in truth, custom designed and forged to do specific tasks as we have taught and ordered them to."

"Like *Eh-aye*, like tiny food makers, like door that can see," Nothaar offered.

"Yes, exactly," Syraaq confirmed. "The door is not alive; therefore, it cannot be called a slave. It's just a thing, an object. It doesn't think or care in the way we do. All it does is exist as a door, nothing more, nothing less. Yes, it's fancier and does more specific actions than any door you may have encountered before, but in the end, it's still just something that's used to block an entryway and can be removed when needed."

"Because door open self," Nothaar probed further, "Syraaq people no have strength in arms to open doors?"

This apparently hit Syraaq as particularly amusing as she started chortling uncontrollably. Once she got herself under control she declared, "Yes, Nothaar, I think you could actually look at it that way. Since most of our time is not spent doing all the basic physical stuff necessary to sustain life, we do what we call exercise. For instance, someone may pick up those objects on the rack behind you—what are known as weights—and pump their arms up and down. Only then might they build the muscle required to open doors, even though there are only a few rare occasions when that would be a needed skill. It's all part of how we maintain our overall well-being."

"No open doors, but do exercise to pretend open doors," Nothaar summarized. "Seem pointless."

"Perhaps you're right," Syraaq conceded. "There are certain groups that think like you do, who say they want to live a more 'natural' lifestyle away from all our techno—all our helpers and tools. And that is their choice and they are allowed to follow that path, that belief, if it makes them happy. All people are free; or, at least, as free as they can be within the confines and rules of their cultures."

"You're wrong about that," Ifu suddenly chimed in from the other side of the gym, where he had been gathering various accoutrements while Nothaar and Syraaq were debating. Walking over, he continued, "Nothaar, there's a larger government overarching all our societies. Yes, Syraaq and I originate from different and distant places compared to each other, but even then, we belong to a greater collective that can make directives about everyday life. More so, that far-off body renders decisions not only for all people like us, but for ones like you."

"How?" Nothaar questioned. "People in village a day walk away no can control another. How can place that me no know exist tell me how live life?"

Instead of answering him, Ifu bade his companions follow him back to where he had piled up various pieces of equipment. Once there, Ifu asked, "Nothaar, please describe the shape of the world to us."

Although confused by the sudden shift in topic, Nothaar began to describe the contours of the land as he knew them from both the *Knowledge* and his own travels. As he was doing so, he elaborated on some of the specific places and features he had passed through, such as the tall mountain ranges and the great wasteland desert that bisected the tinier north from the behemoth south. Finally, at this, Ifu cut him off and queried, "When you walked through the desert, what was the shape of that line?"

This area of inquiry did not register with Nothaar, so he expressed, "Not sure what you mean. Walk through desert in line, so shape be straight line."

"In other words," Ifu interpreted, "you are saying it was basically flat."

Nothaar confirmed his assessment as they went through a few similar examples. After several of these, Nothaar finally understood what Ifu was getting at and asserted, "World mostly level. Have some mountains that go up, valleys go down, but yes, Ifu correct, is flat."

"I'm sorry to inform you," Ifu contradicted, "but that is completely wrong."

"How wrong?" Nothaar shot back. "Me agreeing with what Ifu say. If me wrong, Ifu wrong."

"I didn't say the world was flat," Ifu insisted. "I was trying to understand your perspective and just repeated your own conclusions back to you. But here, let me show you how it really is."

Upon this pronouncement, Ifu picked up a bright green ball—about the size of both his arms outstretched at an intermediate angle—and put it in front of Nothaar. At first, Nothaar was astounded by Ifu's ability to pick up such a massive object with ease, but once he was able to examine it, he found that it was made of a lightweight squishy material and completely hollow on the inside. The ball could not have been heavier than a bait fish.

"Nothaar," Ifu began, "this is the shape of your world. When you walked through the desert, it was not a flat, straight line. Instead, it was on a curve."

"That make no sense," Nothaar argued. "Me have eyes, can see ahead. It all flat. Would notice curve like hill. Ifu not there, cannot know."

"Yet, when absolutely nothing was in front of you," Ifu calmly retorted, "it looked like the world just ended at some point. There was a horizon."

"Of course," Nothaar acquiesced. "Me always see horizon. In desert, on cliff at edge of world, atop mountain—horizon always visible somewhere."

"Edge of the world, huh?" Ifu threw the phrase back at him. "What would make you think anywhere was the edge of the world? The horizon looks like it's cutting everything off, but you kept walking and that supposed limit continued moving further and further away from you. You have never reached the horizon, consequently you have never been to the end of the world or anywhere else. Just because you couldn't reach it, doesn't mean something is not there."

After pausing for a moment, Nothaar whispered, "Land of ice beyond great salt sea..."

"You're still thinking too linearly," Ifu interrupted. "Let's focus on just places you know are real and the horizon. The horizon is the curve of a ball. The ball is just so big that you are only seeing a little bit of it—really, the least that you possibly could see given your relative size compared to the entire globe."

Nothaar closed his eyes and tried to picture what Ifu was saying, but the proportions still did not fit. Opening them again, he told Ifu as much.

"Fine," Ifu granted, "close your eyes once more." After Nothaar had done so, Ifu resumed, "Think of the ball we have here in front of us in the gym. Now, imagine that you are a very tiny insect, the teensiest one you know, maybe some type of body parasite that lives in your hair. If you were that miniature bug and were crawling along on the surface of that ball, how would it look through its eyes?"

Doing as requested, Nothaar created the whole scene in his imagination. Losing himself in the daydream, he spoke aloud, "It look flat, like regular line, with horizon. Similar to when me walk sometimes, no feel go up, but find me high above after time. So subtle, so long period, no notice changes. Short steps flat, all steps together curve!"

"Yes, yes!" Ifu exclaimed. "I knew you'd get it! You see, the world is not flat nor does it have an end. It's a sphere, which means it goes on forever. If you had land everywhere or took a boat out on the ocean, you'd eventually end up right back where you started."

Leaving his mind's eye, Nothaar returned to reality and began tracing a finger across the exercise ball in front of him until he did exactly as Ifu described. *On a sphere, Nothaar pondered, no matter which direction one headed out in, they would return to where they began, just as Ifu stated. If I had the proper boat and supplies, I could have left from Anlynx's village and kept heading south until I reached my home in the north again. Or I could have begun this whole journey by leaving my village and going north, landing in the far south. From there, I could have walked home over fifteen... years... It would have cut this entire venture in half. What a revelation this is! There is so much our people could do with this information. I must get this into the Knowledge and let the other Keepers know as soon as possible.*

Suddenly, Ifu was kneeling next to Nothaar and placed a hand over his fingers that were still tracing pathways across the make-believe world. In delight Ifu announced, "But it doesn't end there, Nothaar, not even close!"

CHAPTER 11

Watching Ifu go through the items he had collected from around the gym, Nothaar saw him select a medium sized yellow-orange ball and cradle it in his arms. "Arg, this one's heavy," Ifu complained as he scuttled over to an open area on the floor. "Syraaq, find a ball you can take for a walk, too."

Grumbling to herself, Syraaq began looking through everything until she found a ball similar to the large green one that Nothaar was still perched in front of, except it was only as wide as her chest. "Got it," she announced. "Now what?"

Ifu put his ball down near his feet and pointed towards the edges of the room. "I'd like you to make a wide orbit around me, as far as you can go. Make sure you stay in a mildly ovular shape and keep an even pace."

"I see where you're going with this," Syraaq responded in a conspiratorial tone. At this declaration, she began to do as Ifu requested. "I suppose you're going to want me to rotate on my axis?"

"If you can," Ifu answered. "I don't want you getting too dizzy and falling down or anything. I'd appreciate it, though, if you could."

"I'll see how I feel," Syraaq offered as she started to

twirl around as she also paced in a loop around the room. After just a few turns, she gave up on the revolving and declared, "Whew! I'm not nearly coordinated enough to pull that off."

"That's fine," Ifu conceded. "However, Nothaar, it's not going to be optional for you. I'd like you to pick up your ball and start to spin while walking in a circle around me, too. Please make sure you are closer than Syraaq is, but also try to slow your pace down enough to be kind of the same as hers. It doesn't have to be perfect, though. Can you do that for me? Obviously, you'll complete your circuit faster than she will simply because it's shorter, but don't worry about that."

"Me try," Nothaar affirmed before launching into his own mimicry of Syraaq's actions.

Once everyone was following Ifu's choreographed routine, Ifu then said, "Okay, Nothaar, if you can, I want you to look out and follow Syraaq with your eyes whenever she is in your line of sight. Does that make sense?"

"Maybe should have picked smaller ball," Nothaar sarcastically responded. Still, despite the difficulties, he did as Ifu requested.

After making several passes encircling the room in this way, Ifu then posed, "Now, Nothaar, if you were looking up at the night sky, perhaps over the length of an entire year, is there something that Syraaq and her ball remind you of?"

At first, it was not clear to Nothaar what Ifu was apparently hoping that he would see. After several more times through these sequences, though, an idea began to percolate in his mind. When it crystalized, Nothaar dropped his ball, let it bounce away, and declared, "Pattern is same as wandering star across sky!"

"Exactly!" Ifu cheered. "Except it is no star at all. These are what we call planets."

"Hear Ifu and Syraaq use word before," Nothaar noted. "Still, me no sure understand what difference."

"A star," Syraaq interjected as she stopped walking around and threw her own ball to the side with a grunt, "is like your sun. It's a ball, yes, but one that is full of heat and light. A planet circles around a star, just like we were doing with Ifu as our sun."

Another consequence of this surprising announcement immediately jolted into Nothaar's consciousness. As the implications of their team activity started to sink in, Nothaar began, "World no at center of all creation..."

"Go on," Ifu excitedly encouraged. "You're on the right track, standing on the precipice."

Taking this cue, Nothaar resumed, "Sun at center. Me world... me planet... just one of many going around sun. And moon... moon... how does moon work? Switch place with sun? No, not make sense."

"Just as a planet goes around a sun," Ifu hinted, "so, too, does a moon go around a planet."

"There are other moons?!" Nothaar howled. For some reason, this idea threw him off far more than learning his world was just one of many planets and that they were all surrounding the sun. Without waiting for an answer,

Nothaar then asked, "What about regular stars, not wandering ones? They also... what word you use... orbit sun?"

"Not quite," Syraaq gently chided. "They are all suns in their own right, each with their own set of planets orbiting around them. The only reason they look so small to us is because they are very distant. That said, and more germane to our conversation, you should be made aware that there are also many different types of planets. Among them, some are very special, just like your world that we are all currently inhabiting."

"What you be implying?" Nothaar prodded, feeling intense dread at the answer he realized he must already have surmised but couldn't bring himself to believe.

Syraaq looked at Ifu, who gave some silent motion that appeared to give his permission before she stated, "Nothaar, Ifu and I come from two such places."

"Right, me know," Nothaar insisted, fighting against the truth bubbling to the surface and all that it suggested, all that it would mean for his understating of how existence functioned. He continued grasping at the impossible, trying to maintain his denial. "Come from lands far away, lands me not know about before. Ifu and Syraaq lands different from each other."

"No, Nothaar," Ifu corrected. "We don't just come from different lands; we're from other planets entirely. We were each born on our own spheres, nowhere near this one, and even distantly isolated from one another's."

Overwhelmed by the notion Ifu and Syraaq were presenting, Nothaar forced himself to act like the *Keeper* he was trained to be and start asking the right questions to add to the *Knowledge*. For clarification, he interrogated, "Ifu and Syraaq travel heavens? Boat no go by sea, but go across sky? Boat fall from sky and crash in land of Nothaar people? Have own world not same as me world? No come from lands of this... planet?"

"Right," Syraaq encouraged, seemingly oblivious to Nothaar's extreme discomfort. "And we have to leave your world as soon as possible. We don't belong here. Honestly, we can't stay here indefinitely."

"What... be you...?" Nothaar trailed off, not sure even he knew what he was asking anymore.

"We've told you before," Syraaq contended. "We're not gods nor monsters nor spirts nor magic. We are just flesh and blood people, people who are very much mortal and alive; just the same as you."

"Well, not the same exactly," Ifu disagreed. "And that, in itself, is the problem. As we've made clear, we can't eat most your food, or probably any of it, which means we're on a countdown until our own supplies run out. If we are to survive, we have no choice but to leave and go back to the—what did you call it?—the heavens."

"Unfortunately," Syraaq added, "our ship, our boat as you think of it, is broken. Even if it wasn't, it lacks the capabilities to leave a planet. However, there is a place on this globe that we can go that will give us the ability to depart and go back to our own homes."

Hearing these topics again with a renewed understanding, Nothaar pressed for additional details. "Me understand no can eat food of Nothaar planet. Planet different, too removed, too different. But Syraaq and Ifu not of same planet, right? How come can eat same food, no problem? Why people not of same planet very similar?"

"Oh boy," Syraaq reproached, "that is going to take a lot of time to explain."

"Time we don't have," Ifu interrupted. "Not if we continue to stay here. Nothaar, we can explain everything, but all of these subjects, they're not so easily answered without the proper background information. It took us half a day just to agree on the shape of the world. Do you begin to fathom the vast gap between you and us in your understanding of the universe? You have no idea what you don't know, but I've got a pretty good handle on it now. You may have the *Knowledge*, but we have millions of times more of it containing concepts and ideas you've never even dreamed were a possibility.

"The crux of our situation is this: we need to make a very long and difficult journey so that we can escape your world and get back to our own homes, and we would like you to come with us. And I want to be very clear about this—it is a necessity for you to join our mission."

Sensing a threat and seeing Ifu almost reflexively touch his gun in the holder along his waist, Nothaar asked the most pertinent question, "Why me?"

Syraaq must have noticed Nothaar looking at Ifu's gun because she walked over to Ifu and pushed his hand away from the weapon before declaring, "Finding someone like you was the whole reason we stole a Torch Ship in the first place. Nothaar, you know that things are happening here since your *Sky Shift*, uncontrollable things. With so much already in motion, we probably won't be able to stop what is transpiring on your planet and to your people. But with your help, we might be able to prevent it from happening to some other species on another planet in the future."

Although she was pleading with kindness, Nothaar could see she was just as desperate as Ifu was. At that moment, he recognized that if he did not agree to their plan that he was as good as dead. Thus, he submitted to their will and agreed to accompany them... wherever it was going to lead him.

CHAPTER 12

Stepping into a world of greenery for the first time in at least an entire cycle of the moon, Nothaar blinked in the dawn light. Happy to finally be outside Ifu and Syraaq's stolen Torch Drive Ship—a concept they still hadn't expounded upon to him yet—he inhaled a deep drag of the cool early morning spring air. Letting it go, he took a real look around at the campsite where he had originally found his captors. Amazingly, the pit they had for their large bonfire was nowhere to be seen. It did not appear as if anything was unusual compared to any other part of the forest, aside from two obvious exceptions.

Turning around, Nothaar got a good look at the nose of the Torch Ship—appropriating the mildly shortened name that Ifu and Syraaq often used while discussing the vessel—that he had just stepped out of. Almost the entire structure was buried beneath the surface, with only a comparatively small, rounded pyramid-like point visible above the ground at about the height of two people. It was just enough to create one of the sliding doors so that a single individual could pass through at a time after ascending a long ladder. Nothaar was unsure why, but Ifu and Syraaq had let him go on ahead before them. He wondered if it was some type of test to see if he would seize the opportunity to try to run away. Thinking about the prospect, Nothaar had to admit to himself that he was quite tempted by the possibility, but decided against taking the risk at that stage. If he was going to escape, he would do it at a time and place of his choosing so that they would be caught unawares. *An attempt at this juncture would be premature and most likely fruitless*, Nothaar surmised in his native tongue. *I need them to trust me so they'll drop their guard.*

While the skin of the Torch Ship obviously had a lot of metallic components comparable to the interior, something else stood out in Nothaar's eyes. Having seen some of the materials aboard the vessel and had them explained to him, Nothaar now recognized that there was a layer of glass with imbedded machinery inside it. Even the metal underneath was quite dark; not quite black, but certainly close. Seeing it in the daytime, it was no wonder why he had not noticed it during that murky night with the campfire distorting his vision. Despite being close to the color of a midnight sky, Nothaar had learned that it ate light like the plants did and used that to make the many amazing feats he had witnessed within the ship's internal confines.

Next to the cone that was peeking through the earth like a newly sprouted tree was something Nothaar could not quite identify. In some ways, it looked like a transport cart that people who harvested food often operated to move their goods around. *Actually*, Nothaar considered, *it's closer to the wagon that Vedoori—the trader who visited my village and whose inspiration set all these events in motion—had. The food gatherers' carts tended to be two-wheeled and about half the size of an adult person. Vedoori's wagon had four wheels and was so big that he could sleep inside it. I believe during one of my incessant interviews, he told me as much. But with something that big, travel is incredibly slow. That concern was part of the reason I opted to start this journey with nothing but what I could carry on my back.*

Early on in the planning sessions for Syraaq and Ifu's intended new adventure, the two off-worlders seemed to become quite distressed to discover that there were no what they called "beasts of burden" available on the planet. They elucidated that on many worlds there were large animals that could be domesticated and put to work for the purposes of helping and serving people. "It's a fairly conventional thing to see as a species grows and evolves," Syraaq had told him. "The fact that you've reached some of the milestones in your development that you have, nevertheless how far you've become dispersed across the entire continent—all without the benefit of tamed and trained creatures available to you—is quite re-markable, a real testament to your kind's fortitude. I'm sure there are plenty of xenoanthropologists out there who would love to do a study on your society."

"Me thought you say you no have slaves," Nothaar contended. "Would not forcing animal to do work be just that? Much crueler than killing and eating, which you no like that Nothaar people do."

"We don't engage in animal husbandry anymore," Syraaq insisted. "Well, at least for the most part. There are an unfathomable number of *Commons* that populate tens of thousands of worlds in our alliance; no one can account for all of them."

Apparently, Nothaar had ascertained, Syraaq and Ifu's peoples were collectively known as the *Common*. Even though they were from different planets, they insisted that they were the same, and that all other people were like them, too. The only exemptions to this rule were the few worlds like Nothaar's that had been recently discovered by the Starbuilders—the organization that Syraaq and Ifu had apparently been employed by before they absconded with the Torch Ship. Nothaar did not have a separate name for his own species; they were just "people" to him and every-one else. Since he did not even recognize until he met Syraaq and Ifu that he was on a sphere-shaped planet to begin with, his world did not have a separate name, either.

Ifu had then spoken up, offering, "Besides, animals are not sapient. Only a sapient being can truly be enslaved."

"This not first time use word," Nothaar had observed. "Still, me no understand. Please explain."

Syraaq, in her typical fashion of attempting to mediate understanding between everyone, had answered, "Think about those plants that populate your world. They are alive, yes, we can all agree on that?"

"Of course," Nothaar quickly acquiesced, wondering who would argue that a plant was not alive.

"Good," Syraaq continued. "Although they may be alive, they are not what we'd call 'sentient'; that is, they do not feel and react in the way an animal would."

"New word, too," Nothaar complained. "But grant, plant and animal different type life, respond to world in very unlike ways."

Appearing to consider her next move, Syraaq then proposed, "And what about you, Nothaar? What separates you from the animals in the same way the animals are distinct from the plants?"

Pushing down his feelings of being demeaned and underestimated yet again, Nothaar actually considered Syraaq's words as an objective, academic exercise. Finally, he answered, "Me no just react with instinct. Me, all Nothaar people, think in head, and not just about how survive. Also think about purpose of life, of place in world, of mysteries, of past and future. Not just living to be alive, living to find meaning."

"Exactly!" Ifu suddenly interjected. "And that is the difference between sentience and sapience. You, Nothaar, are sapient, just like us. And as rare as life is, sapient life is a miniscule fraction of that."

Due to the lack of draft animals to assist in their journey, Ifu and Syraaq had debated the best way to transport their party and all of the goods they intended to take with them. Aside from all the food and equipment that Ifu said was necessary to "clean and purify" water—among other concerns—Nothaar had convinced them to bring items that might be valuable for trade like raw ores and precious gems. His mind was forever attached to the riches the falling star was going to bestow upon him, and he was still getting over his disappointment that nothing like that was to be had. "Going need help of people," Nothaar had argued. "Me also need more food. Can hunt, gather, fish, but will need more. Must go by villages. Syraaq and Ifu will need stuff, too, right?"

Syraaq and Ifu were quite concerned with getting anywhere near the other villages and their inhabitants, and wanted to eschew contact as much as possible in order to avoid what they termed "cultural contamination". It was the same with the materials they would use for exchange; Ifu spent significant time with the *Eh-aye* to figure out ways to take existing resources available on the Torch Ship and modify them to look like they were completely unformed and natural, taking extreme efforts to ensure that they did not appear fabricated in any way.

Because of Ifu and Syraaq's concerns, they also worked with Nothaar on creating an accurate map of the world based on Nothaar's memories and records, notably the locations of all those settlements. They obviously had some plan and destination in mind, but thus far had refused to share that information with Nothaar. Whatever their scheme was, Nothaar had come to realize that they were plotting a course that would keep them as far away from other people as possible. However, until that moment, Nothaar had no idea why they were having such an issue figuring out which way to go.

Standing before Nothaar was what Ifu and Syraaq must have agreed upon to act as their conveyance mechanism. It was another glass and metal monstrosity with an exterior that almost exactly matched what Nothaar had seen of the Torch Ship. He supposed, then, that it would also consume sunshine in order to function, which meant that Ifu and Syraaq's envisioned path must have been outside the deep woods. Looking at the sheer size of the gargantuan apparatus, Nothaar had no doubt that it would do poorly in such an environment, anyway. Along its massive length, eight rubberized—a material that Nothaar had also recently become acquainted with, especially in the gym—wheels were affixed on each side. Examining the façade closely, Nothaar discovered that there were seams along its length between the wheels, indicating that the machine could bend like a segmented insect.

"She's a beauty, isn't she?" spoke a voice coming from behind Nothaar, catching him unawares. Nothaar realized he must have been completely engrossed in his inspection as he was surprised to discover Ifu had climbed out of the Torch Ship and walked over to where he was standing without him hearing or noticing.

"She? What she?" Nothaar confusedly asked as he looked around for Syraaq, the only female among their crew that he was aware of.

"Oh, sorry," Ifu submitted. "It's a habit among my culture to impart genders on inanimate objects, especially automata like these, what we call a vehicle. I don't want to confuse you; it's still just another one of our verbal contrivances. It doesn't have the soul of some poor, hapless woman trapped within."

Chapter 13

Hearing Ifu belittle him once again, Nothaar took a deep breath to calm his nerves and still his reaction. He supposed, though, that Ifu had some reason to warrant his particular choice of explanation. Over the past cycle of the moon, Nothaar had made many, apparent, faux pas while trying to understand how Ifu and Syraaq's technology worked. Holding that thought at bay, Nothaar instead asked, "How get vehicle outside? Too big go up ladder, out door of Torch Ship."

"It wasn't moved outside in that way," Ifu explained. "We printed the components inside the ship and then had the robots drag them outside and assemble the whole thing out here."

Robots… Nothaar ruminated, turning the word over in his mind. *My first encounter with them was another one of those situations in which I was wholly unprepared for.*

While earlier Ifu and Syraaq had described various things as "helpers", Nothaar had learned about the many different forms these assistants had taken. For instance, there was the disembodied *Eh-aye* that existed in an ether of pure thought and energy. However, Syraaq had revealed that *Eh-aye* required a receptacle of some kind to contain it, what she had called a "storage medium". Further, she had said that their own version of the *Knowledge*—what they called the *"Archive"*—required something similar, and that it was critically important that they be able to bring this device with them.

"We also have a very personal version of the *Archive* that we cannot abandon," Syraaq had insisted. "If we lost the regular *Archive*, it's no big deal; there are millions of copies of it. The one we have is only a partial version, anyway. But our personal *Archives* are always being added to and we can only do a backup at select intervals."

"What backup mean in this case?" Nothaar inquired. During their conversations, he had come to realize that many words had multiple definitions, some of which he did not have any context to draw meaning from.

"In this usage," Syraaq clarified, "it implies making a copy. Like you told me you intended to do with your *Opus on the Language of Children*. Unlike what you would have to do manually by hand, though, we have the ability to create a reproduction rapidly and automatically."

"More your invisible helpers, like *Eh-aye*," Nothaar observed.

"Yes," Syraaq readily agreed. "The last time we did a backup was before we stole the Torch Ship, so everything we have and will do could be lost if we... misplace... it before we can leave your planet."

"No understand," Nothaar interjected. "Why no just write down, keep track?"

"We don't write on paper," Syraaq attempted. "You cannot see it, but we have, oh, I guess I'll call it invisible books. They are only observable to people like us who have had a machine, what we call a computer, installed in their eyes. The computer endows us with many special functions and abilities, of which writing is only one minor feature. Right now, you probably wouldn't really understand the rest of them, though. That said, what I want you to appreciate for the time being is that nothing is stored on the computer in our eyes, it's just a way for us to access our data and information. For that, we need a storage medium, too. The Torch Ship has a large capacity for stowing all this, more than enough for the entire complement of people it could possibly carry. We'll need to take ours with us, along with some other critical stuff."

"Still no clear," Nothaar insisted. "Just no use eye computer, use other way for writing."

"As I said," Syraaq began with an unmistakable undertone of irritation, "there is more to it than writing. I didn't want to get into this just yet, but it appears I have no choice. We have what we call programs, what you might think of as more things like the *Eh-aye*, except with specific purposes. We need them in order to do particular operations. Without getting into what those might be, let's just say they are like appendages to us. If we lost them, it would be the same as you losing a hand or a foot. That is how essential they are to us and our survival."

Deciding not to pursue the topic any further, Nothaar let the conversation end with Syraaq's pronouncement. He wondered if he would ever completely understand what she had been alluding to.

Aside from the computer programs that existed in some hidden realm, there were what he learned were called "nanobots", which were machines so small that no one could see them. These nanobots were responsible for things like rebuilding the food, plates, and utensils from the contents of Ifu and Syraaq's sustenance packs. During one incident when Syraaq had accidently cut herself with a knife to the point of bleeding and ripped her sleeve, Nothaar had watched with astonishment as both her skin and the clothing healed themselves. Syraaq had explained that there were similar nanobots that specialized in restoration, and that even the outside of the Torch Ship used them. At that moment, Nothaar assumed that the new vehicle before him must also have had nanobots that would instantly repair any damage the exterior or wheels might suffer along the way.

The next level up on these mechanical servants consisted of a wide range of tools known as the "automata". Among the automata were items like the doors that responded reflexively to certain inputs. As far as Nothaar could tell, the automata were always fashioned for a specific role and then were given a usually singular task to accomplish. Since Ifu had called the vehicle an automata, too, Nothaar expected that it would respond to similar interactive methods, whether those be touch, voice, or something else entirely.

But then there were the robots. When Nothaar initially stumbled upon one, he was completely shocked. Before him stood something that vaguely looked like another member of the *Common* race, except that it had metal skin, was naked, and appeared rather androgenous due to its lack of genitals. "Who you?!" he shouted with alarm. After all, Ifu and Syraaq had been very clear that they were the only two people aboard.

"I am Unit Gee-Bee-Ex-Eight-One-Seven," the strange creature had responded.

"Hello," Nothaar tentatively tried. "Me name Nothaar Akii, from this planet. You from other planet, like Ifu and Syraaq?"

"I was constructed on this vessel," it responded, "based upon a design originating from..."

The story continued for quite some time, but Nothaar could not follow along. Once it stopped talking and just looked at him expectantly, Nothaar asked the next obvious question. "You... you no like me, no like Syraaq and Ifu. What be you?"

At this query, it started to tell the same tale again, completely verbatim. Although he did not want to be rude, Nothaar finally decided to interrupt its diatribe and tried to clarify that he was looking for a much higher-level answer. It took several more attempts before it finally declared, "I am a robot."

Since this was a new term, Nothaar followed up with, "What robot?"

"Robots are mechanized automations that are assigned specific tasks by *Commons*," Unit Gee-Bee-Ex-Eight-One-Seven began. "All robots have the ability to perform both individually or as a group using interconnected artificial intelligence algorithms. Typically, robots are given assignments that are hazardous to *Commons* or require a superior level of strength and dexterity. Unlike other automata, robots are not specialized and can be adjusted for both routine and unexpected activities."

As Nothaar started to open his mouth to ask a follow-up question, the robot disrupted his intentions by requesting, "Sir, with due respect, if you have further questions, you should consult the *Archives*. I am falling behind in the expected schedule of my assignment. It is against my programming to not complete my duty in a timely manner."

Before letting it go, Nothaar did manage to ask, "What be you assignment?"

Without hesitation, the robot declared, "My mission, as it has been since coming online, is to continue to hide the impact of the Torch Ship's landing zone by moving and filling in dirt and plants from around the general surrounding vicinity while avoiding all other lifeforms. This undertaking will be considered complete when any evidence of the Torch Ship having been here is completely removed or disguised to such a degree that no sapient being would be able to notice. If that is all, sir, I would prefer to return to this labor."

"Of course..." Nothaar conceded as the robot ran off without so much as saying farewell.

A short while later, Nothaar confronted Syraaq. "You want build trust, but you make terrible lie!"

"What are you espousing this time?" Syraaq sardonically replied. Nothaar had come to her similarly charged a few times and she was beginning not to react at all. This was unlike Ifu who still took everything as an afront.

"Me meet slave," Nothaar highlighted. "Is robot named Unit Gee-Bee-Ex-Eight-One-Seven. It tell me what you make it do."

Barely looking up, Syraaq just displayed the *Common's* expression for trivializing amusement and avowed, "Robots aren't alive, Nothaar."

"Very alive!" Nothaar countered back. "Is sapient, like you say. Talks, thinks about life, looks at past and future, offers advice."

"No, Nothaar," Syraaq calmly professed. "They are just very sophisticated machines that give the appearance of being sapient; it's all part of a trick. It makes them easier for us to interact with, but they lack any free will whatsoever. You may even be judging that if they are not sapient then they must be sentient, but that would be a false assumption, too. They are much closer to a plant than anything else on the web of life, but even that is a stretch."

"How you mean?" Nothaar probed.

"Well, think of it this way," Syraaq pronounced. "What is the one thing that all life wants to do, whether it is a plant, a beast, or a person?"

Nothaar considered for a while before announcing, "Want have offspring, make more life, life like itself."

"Exactly!" Syraaq clapped. "And, if all goes well, that offspring grows and reproduces on its own, too. But robots don't do that. They are built exactly as they are. They don't have a desire to procreate, or any desires at all. In reality, they do as they are told without thought, without reaction, and even without instinct. Inside, they are empty shells devoid of anything that living beings like us have to offer. There is an ancient word that is rarely used even among *Commons* nowadays that would fit here: they are golems."

Still unsure, Nothaar again chose to put the conversation aside for another time. That came during a meeting in the mess hall in which they were all discussing the logistics of their journey. In truth, Ifu and Syraaq were conferring as Nothaar did not have much input or influence on the decisions that were being made. This time, though, he asked, "What about robots?"

"What about them?" Ifu retorted.

"No can leave behind!" Nothaar insisted.

"We don't really have a choice on the matter," Ifu claimed. "We can only make our transport so large for efficiency and safety's sake. And even if that wasn't a consideration, robots take a massive amount of energy to keep functioning. All of that power is going to be required just to keep our conveyance moving, operating the *Eh-aye*, running our machinery, and making sure our copy of the *Archive* continues to be accessible."

"Will kill robots just for comfort things?" Nothaar accused, completely aghast.

"Oh geez..." Syraaq cursed.

"What's going on here?" Ifu asked Syraaq.

"He still thinks the robots are alive and that they'll die if they're left behind," Ifu clarified.

A debate then ensued on the definition of life, sapience, and consciousness that went late into the night. Nothaar walked away unsatisfied about the lines in the sand that Ifu and Syraaq drew, but he also realized that he barely comprehended what was happening around him at that point. He had no choice but to admit defeat again, especially as he learned that many of the robots had already succumbed because they could not acquire the fuel they needed due to the current condition of the Torch Ship.

CHAPTER 14

Syraaq exited from the bit of the Torch Ship poking above the surface and asked, "Why is the vehicle parked so close? That's going to be an issue."

"Hold on, I'll fix it," Ifu declared. However, he made no movement and instead seemed to look off into nothingness. Suddenly, the wheeled automata started to silently creep forward as if by its own volition until it was what Ifu must have deemed a safe-enough distance away.

It's like Ifu can control the vehicle with his mind, Nothaar reflected. *I know that's not exactly how it works, though. There's some type of connection between their brains, the computers in their eyes, and the rest of their tools, but I'm unsure what it is. Either way, I'm beginning to recognize the signs of when they are using it, like that blank stare Ifu was just giving.*

At one point, Nothaar had heard Ifu refer to his technological enhancements as "ocular implants", but one set of new terminology was enough for Nothaar. It was not clear to him why the *Lingua* was so inefficient that it used multiple words to describe the same thing, but he had long since lost his desire to pursue the topic further. Instead, as the vehicle was evidently then placed at a safer location, Nothaar asked, "Why need move?"

Syraaq expounded for him, "When our Torch Ship entered your planet, we were coming in very fast. Certainly not at the speeds a Torch Ship is capable of since we had engaged the breaking sequence, otherwise we wouldn't have survived the impact, nor would much else. However, if we had done things correctly, we would have ended up in your world's orbit instead of on its surface. The only way to save ourselves was to basically blast a giant hole ahead of us on our trajectory and try to slow down enough for a softish landing. It mostly worked, but ended up destroying the energy production system. After that happened, we decided to bury the ship and try to put things somewhat back to the way they were. Thus, the first thing we did was send the robots out to complete that task."

"In only few days," Nothaar noted, "noble robots do much work. When me reach you, no see any indication of hole or fire or damage any kind."

"We had a lot more robots when we landed," Syraaq informed him. "Over time, they either broke down entirely from the work, could not charge back up fast enough to continue, or just plain malfunctioned. Either way, they're almost all dead now, and the last few that remain will join them shortly."

Before he could stop himself, Nothaar reflexively cringed at this description. Ifu must have noticed as he quickly retorted, "She doesn't mean 'dead' for real. It's a figure of speech and a way of anthropomorphizing non-living things that we do for ease of dealing with them, like how I referred to the vehicle as a woman."

"You did?!" Syraaq inquired. "What type of woman is our land-based transport?"

"Ifu say is beautiful," Nothaar tattled.

"Well, I didn't know you swung that way, Ifu," Syraaq joked. "I mean, no judgement, but if I knew that was your thing, I would've worked harder to save one of the robots from ending up in the scrapheap."

Even though Syraaq was cracking herself up and Ifu was taking the berating with false indignation, Nothaar did not find the sentiment amusing in any way. Nevertheless, Nothaar not showing any reaction in general was something Syraaq and Ifu said they were quite used to as they recognized that Nothaar did not always follow along with what they were saying. Nothaar let them continue to hold on to that belief even as he learned more of the *Lingua* and its nuances. He surmised that it would be best if the *Commons* continued to misjudge him and remained ignorant of his full capabilities.

"Anyway," Ifu spoke above the din in an attempt to regain order, "We should also get ourselves further away from the ship since we appear to be all set and ready to go. Last chance: does anyone have anything else they want to retrieve from the Torch Ship before it's too late?"

Syraaq made a movement that Nothaar now knew indicated a negative response, and he mimicked it as well. All he had was his own rucksack with all its accoutrements, and that was currently slung over his back. He was starting to run low on food, though, and would need to do some hunting and/or gathering in the near future in order to replenish his supplies. Although he had expected to arrive at the next nearest settlement well before then, it was not like anyone knew he was coming and would realize he was absent. No one would ever look for Nothaar; if he never appeared anywhere again, his disappearance would easily be dismissed the same as any person who went missing within the vast wilderness between villages.

Once all three of them had moved out of the way, Ifu took on a faraway look as he appeared to once again slip into his private realm. All Nothaar could tell was that Ifu held up his hand and made some gestures. At the end of the sequence, it looked like Ifu used his pointing finger to press something, but Nothaar could not imagine what that might be. A few short moments later, though, the ground started shaking beneath their feet. Peering downward, Nothaar watched as loose grains of dirt started to move towards where the part of the Torch Ship was peaking above the surface. Then, the earth that was closest to the craft started to swirl inward, like a sinkhole was forming. In short order, the dark metal and glass began to melt before his eyes, its structure collapsing underground. As it slipped below the surface, more topsoil and plants fell towards it and whole trees toppled. Yet, as quickly as it commenced, the earthquake ended and all was quiet. Aside from the obvious disturbance at ground level, there was no sign that anything had ever been there.

"What happen?" Nothaar yelped. "What Ifu do to Torch Ship? Was Ifu and Syraaq home, yes?"

"The Torch Ship was never our home," Ifu proclaimed

by way of an explanation. "It was just a ferry, a boat for the heavens, as you would say. But it can't go there anymore and we have to move on. However, we can't leave it behind. You already stumbled upon it; what would happen if someone else discovered it?"

"They be contaminated," Nothaar summarized, using the descriptor he often heard during Ifu's orations.

"Exactly," Ifu approved. "Because of that, I made the only logical choice: I destroyed it using rapid molecular decomposition."

Before Nothaar could even ask the question, Syraaq noted, "Basically, there are microscopic bonds that hold everything together. For instance, water is not actually a monolithic substance; rather, it is a combination of two things, what we call elements. Two atoms of elemental hydrogen and one atom of elemental oxygen combine together to make one molecule of water. What Ifu did was sever that bond between the hydrogen and oxygen, thus setting them free and turning them back into what they once were. Except, of course, it was on a much more massive scale with a lot of different molecules."

"Why would two... elements... change property when join together and become... what you say?... molecule?" Nothaar pushed back.

Syraaq gave a gesticulation that implied that she was unsure. "Who knows?" she rhetorically asked. "Despite the incredible span of time the *Common* have been trying to unlock that mystery and many more like it, we still don't know for sure, or even really have a good line of inquiry to follow. We understand almost all of the rules of the universe and how to manipulate them into doing our bidding, but we have no idea why most of them work. It just is what it is."

"Sound like you have faith, believe in magic spirit," Nothaar accused.

"Maybe..." Syraaq trailed off without further argument.

"Even so," Ifu interposed, "the job is not done. The remains are radioactive. That is... what I mean... hmmm... they are a type of poison. Everything living in this immediate area might get sick and die, especially if someone tries to dig a hole here later. We have to call someone in to clean up our mess. It's not just protocol for situations like this, but the morally right thing to do. No *Common*—at the very least no current or former Starbuilder like us—would ever want any harm to befall any living thing on this globe. Life is just too precious and too rare to let something bad and destructive like that happen."

"Call?" Nothaar delved. "What this word mean?"

Ifu glanced towards Syraaq, who in turn queried, "Do you have a way to relay messages over a long distance, like with smoke from a lookout or with fire torches?" Once Nothaar had confirmed that he had seen such things, she continued, "We do something fairly similar, except over the vast expanses between planets and other spac—other ships in the heavens."

"Smoke and fire no can travel so far," Nothaar prodded. "How call work?"

Cutting Syraaq off from making any reply, Ifu ordered, "Let's hop in the vehicle and get underway. We'll try to explain en route."

CHAPTER 15

Using another one of his silent commands, Ifu apparently requested for the vehicle to expose individual entryways for each of them. This time, the doors opened by curving along the surface of the transport and ending up on the roof. "Pick a bunk," Ifu suggested as he strode towards the portal closest to the front. Syraaq quickly followed behind and went with the one in the middle, leaving Nothaar no choice but to select the last option available.

Pulling himself upward off the ground, through the egress, and towards the interior of the vehicle, Nothaar found that there was a long bench available for him on the inside. Testing it out by placing a hand on it, he discovered it was made of the same soft material as the giant pillow—the bed—that he had first awoken upon after he was apprehended. Syraaq turned around from her own seat and declared, "See, I told you there were chairs and such that were much more comfortable. We're going to be trapped in here for almost the entire day, every day, so we might as well do it in luxury."

"I designed it to function like a futon," Ifu added from two rows away. "That way, it can lay completely flat like a real bed for when we sleep. There are also personal dividers that can be put up. Nothaar, you'll have to manually ask the *Eh-aye* to lift yours since you do not have the necessary implants and modifications to directly interact with the operating system. Now, please sit down and buckle up; I don't want you to smack your head as we get underway."

Not understanding half of what Ifu said—especially the request to "buckle up"—Nothaar took his seat and asked, "But where going? Still no tell."

Before answering, Ifu seemingly had requested the doors to close back down and for the vehicle to slowly begin to get underway. At the pace it was going, Nothaar was quite sure he could have walked faster. Nevertheless, he was amazed that he was not feeling most of the bumps and divots that he knew littered the forest floor.

Finally, Ifu responded, "Generally, we're going to be heading in a north-west direction. Our destination is where the ocean meets the land at the equator."

"And equator is where?" Nothaar delved. Now that he knew which direction they were heading, he could make some suppositions about what to expect along the way. In particular, Nothaar had a strong suspicion about what villages and peoples Ifu and Syraaq would be trying to avoid, as well as the potential fresh water sources they would need to stop at to bathe and replenish their stores. More so, it also gave him the opportunity to begin to fabricate his own escape plan. As he was calculating whether it would be worthwhile to try to enlist the help of others to capture Ifu and Syraaq, along with their technology, Nothaar realized that trying to detain the pair would be a death-sentence for them due to the lack of a readily available supply of the sustenance they required. *For every-one's sake, Nothaar considered, it would be best to just let them go on their way and leave our planet for good. After all, they have declared themselves to be criminals and ad-mitted that even being here is against the will of their government overseers. I imagine that should they actually get away from here, no one else would be coming. It doesn't appear like they have a lot of support among these Starbuilders they've mentioned, nor from the general pop-ulous of the Commons.*

"Ifu, this is awkward," Syraaq suddenly complained. "Is there some type of conference room mode here?"

"Yeah, yeah," Ifu confirmed, "hold on."

Following those words, the benches started to bend and shift, sliding around each other until they formed a circle. During the process, Nothaar was thrown from his place and landed hard on the floor with a thud. He picked himself back up and splayed onto his bench just in time before a table grew from the area on the ground where he had just been lying.

Once everything stopped repositioning itself, Syraaq scolded, "Nothaar, why weren't you wearing your seat belt like Ifu told you to do?"

"Me no know what that be," Nothaar complained as he rubbed the bridge of his nose from where he hit it.

"Look at me," Syraaq demanded. "You see these re-straints that are attached to me and the bench? Now watch this." With this pronouncement, she then demonstrated for Nothaar how to secure himself so that he would no longer go flying while they were in motion.

After he had done so, Syraaq declared, "Ah, this is much better. Always good to be able to see some friendly faces when talking with them."

"Oh, I'm sure we're going to get really sick of each other's faces after a while," Ifu sardonically remarked.

"Before then," Nothaar reproached as he reinserted himself into the conversation, "still need to explain equator... and how going do call."

"Right, right," Ifu agreed, brushing off Nothaar's legitimate concerns. However, Ifu had yet to begin to fill in any of the details.

In his stead, Syraaq elaborated, "So, a while back, you told us about how the stars above your head changed as you walked southward. You wrote quite a bit about it, too, in your *Opus on the Language of Children*."

"You finish reading me book?" Nothaar interrupted. "Is very long."

"Yes, we both did," Syraaq attested.

"Although, to be honest," Ifu interjected, "it was rather challenging considering your limited vocabulary and what we might call your... poetic style describing things you didn't have words for. Thankfully, I'm a fast reader."

"Anyway," Syraaq attempted again, "you chronicled that confluence in the middle of the desert, in the great wasteland, where you really began to notice how the stars were shifting and being replaced. There was no way for you know it, but that was also the same spot where the seasons flipped around, too. You just couldn't notice the change due to the extreme daytime temperature in the center of that vast, barren region always being relatively the same."

"How you know?" Nothaar probed.

"Think back to your exercise-ball globe," Syraaq continued. "There are certain features on all planets that can harbor life, and one of them is the halfway point when going from top to bottom where everything I have just described naturally occurs. This is the equator that we are talking about."

"Equator no further down?" Nothaar contended. "Me... continent... very big. Halfway through be farther south."

"No, you're thinking about it wrong," Ifu disputed. "This large landmass that you live upon and contains everything you've ever seen is not evenly split. Believe in your own observations that you wrote about: the southlands are much larger and therefore reach further downward, almost to the bottom of the sphere. By the way, we call that a 'pole'. The northern lands, on the other hand, only extend barely half that distance towards the top pole. If it was even, then the far north and far south would have very similar winter colds and summer heats, but they are pretty far off compared to each other, right?"

"Yes," Nothaar consented. "Me village in far north no like in far south. Told old *Keeper* Baubu from far south village about this. He no sure why, but now me think me see."

"Great, then what I want you to do," Ifu directed, "is consider the sun from our earlier simulation striking towards the midpoint of your world. The angle that light hits the planet at various locations is therefore consequently different. You must have noticed longer and shorter days as you traveled southbound. There are even places where the sun never sets or never rises for stretches of time, depending upon the season."

"Like in land of ice me hear about from Baubu," Nothaar offered. "Tell about before, thought you be from there. Now know not."

Making a gesture of agreement, Syraaq highlighted, "You've got the concept right. If it exists, it's probably a whole other continent down there."

Ruminating on the idea of potential other continents, Nothaar followed up with, "Be there another land of ice, in far north, at pole?"

"Honestly," Ifu commenced, "we don't know. It's why we worked with you on developing a map of your world. On our way in, our Torch Ship was so overwhelmed with other activity—especially landing safely—that it didn't scan or even take a picture of your planet from above. Both of us were on the command bridge, deep in the interior and far removed from any windows, so we couldn't have seen anything with our own eyes, anyway. Our copy of the *Archive* also lacked the pertinent details. I guess we probably should've checked what was in the local *Archive* before we stole the craft, so I'll just chalk it up to a mistake on my part!"

This was the first time Nothaar had heard Ifu actually admit to making any type of error. He was usually so full of bravado and moral indignation that it surprised Nothaar to hear him concede any fault. In many ways it was refreshing, but he doubted it would last. Instead of commenting on it, Nothaar chose to ask, "If no know planet, why go to equator? What there?"

Ifu looked towards Syraaq and they appeared to be communicating without exchanging words aloud. *Do they have the ability to send thoughts to each other?* Nothaar wondered. *If so, why do they talk out loud at all? The Common are so confusing in their actions. They don't seem to behave with any form of consistency or logic, at least as far as the examples I've seen from these two.*

After a few moments more, Syraaq spoke for the pair, "We told you that we used to work for an organization called the Starbuilders, who we stole the Torch Ship from. But we haven't explained about what, exactly, that employment entailed."

"Agree," Nothaar maintained. "Be very frustrating. Still no idea what Starbuilders do, what mean. Maybe take guess, but as Syraaq often say, 'lack context'."

"And you still do," Syraaq insisted, "thus we won't be getting too deep into that yet. But what I can tell you for certain is that there is at least one other landmass out there, and that is where we're heading."

CHAPTER 16

"You make no sense, always contradictions," Nothaar spat back at Syraaq and Ifu. "Say no see me planet, no know other continent, yet now say there be one. Give me big pain in head try keep straight you story."

"Calm down, calm down," Ifu implored. "There's a reason we're aware of this one specific place. You see, we weren't the first *Commons* to visit your world."

This was a shocking revelation and caused Nothaar to immediately halt his verbal assault. *I thought Syraaq and Ifu were an aberration,* Nothaar pondered, *and that when they left it would be the end of the Commons interfering in our lives. It appears that something more is amiss here, something much bigger than what I've been privy to.* "What other *Commons* do on me planet?" Nothaar voiced his concerns.

"Quite a bit," Ifu cryptically admitted.

"Me thought Ifu say he and Syraaq be alone, do bad on planet," Nothaar summarized from their earlier conversations. "Now say more *Commons* visit, do stuff that no talk about before."

"We'll get to all those other details later," Ifu deflected. "For now, there is one thing that's important in relation to our immediate needs. Whenever Starbuilders come across a world like yours, Nothaar, they add a certain piece of equipment. Because of that, we were able to pick up a message. It was quite faint and we almost missed it, but the conditions must have been just right for the signal to reach us. From it, we only ascertained a few data points, but it was enough to get our bearings and point us in the right direction, literally speaking, that is."

"And message tell you go to middle of planet, go to equator?" Nothaar probed.

"Not exactly," Syraaq answered, stepping back in as an intermediary. "There are certain standards that Starbuilders must follow, and one of them is that this piece of equipment Ifu told you about should be as close to the equator as possible. Further, it will be on top of the tallest mountain that is near the equator. As such, we already knew—even without any prompting—that we would have to head towards the center of your world, but that wasn't enough information. As you can tell from your own journey, the equator is a large place, and we couldn't just wander about the desert wasteland aimlessly."

"That said," Ifu interrupted, "we were also cognizant that—unless there was no other choice—it wouldn't have been installed there anyway."

"Why no there?" Nothaar pressed.

Quickly responding, Ifu explained, "By those same protocols, it should be placed as far away from native sapient beings as could be reasonably accomplished."

"Wait," Nothaar interjected, putting the pieces together, "that mean that we mu—"

"Exactly!" Ifu exclaimed without letting Nothaar finish. "We are going to have to cross the ocean!"

"You realize and no tell me before leave?" Nothaar quarreled. "What else know and no tell me?"

Ifu had an expression on his face that Nothaar had come to recognize as amused superiority. For all of Ifu's considerable pontificating on the subject of equality, it was quite clear to Nothaar that he still looked down on him. Syraaq seemingly sensed that a larger argument was brewing between the two, so she spoke up saying, "When we first met you, we actually weren't aware we would need to traverse the ocean. It was not until we picked up on the signal that we learned where, exactly, to set our heading... as well as what to expect when we got there. Now, though, we've confirmed that we must go almost exactly due west at the equator to reach our destination."

"You need go far over great salt sea?" Nothaar asked as he tried to calm himself down and speak in an even tone.

"Yes," Syraaq admitted, "very far, almost to the entire other side of the globe."

Still not convinced, Nothaar delved deeper, "And mountain there? On other continent?"

"I wouldn't call it a 'continent', per se," Syraaq confessed. "From the data we received from the... message... it's just a relatively small island. Pretty much, it looks like the mountain itself is almost the entire land area."

Confused by how this dispatch could have arrived and how it contained such information, Nothaar chose to take Syraaq's word for it and ask the next logical question,

"How we go so far? No have boat. No boat ever go far from land, always keep land so can see and go back."

"Oh, it's a problem for sure," Ifu conceded, although with an undertone of a hidden agenda he was not yet ready to share with Nothaar. "We'll have to deal with it when the time comes; we can't dwell on all our problems and things currently outside of our control."

Finally, Nothaar schemed, *I've got my opening. Ifu is lying; he's not sure how they're going to pull off getting the boat they need. He probably has some vague idea, but if he was really secure in his strategy he would make some grandiose declaration, like he always does. Good, that means I can more easily execute a turnabout on these two, and I know exactly where to make that happen.* Hiding his true intentions, aloud Nothaar began, "Okay, go to salt sea... ocean... and equator, but no have boat. Ifu and Syraaq need help get boat. No can do self, no have sla—robots anymore, need people of Nothaar planet. Me can direct to people village before wasteland. Can trade for boat. Me go in, negotiate terms, make happen for you."

Ifu opened his mouth—perhaps to object—but Syraaq beat him to the punch by declaring, "Ifu, we should take Nothaar up on his offer. Your other ideas are... fine... but this is a much better option by my estimation. Even if the boat were constructed by primi... natives... and has some structural flaws and inexact assembly choices, it doesn't have to be perfect. After all, this is going to be a one-way trip for all of us."

"Nothaar already told us his people only build small

skippers that can maybe hold eight villagers, on the high end," Ifu countered. "They don't have a large yacht to offer us that could make it around the world and meet all the other requirements and specifications. I mean, one of the major sticking points is that it would have to be able to carry the weight of this vehicle, even before we talk about the rest of our needs!"

"We already have the plans for the intercontinental sailboat that we want to use from the *Archives*," Syraaq refuted. "If we show it to Nothaar, he can transfer it to paper and translate the instructions into their tongue."

"You want to contaminate them even more?!" Ifu shouted, his outrage laid bare. "That type of technology is probably millennia away for these people!"

"But Nothaar is right," Syraaq defended her position. "The chances of us being able to build this alone without robots—even with the advanced tools we've brought along with us—are slim. In case you've forgotten, we're on a ticking clock here until our supplies run out. I wager it would be faster to let Nothaar's people do this task with their inferior materials and methodologies than for us to attempt this undertaking alone. I'm sorry, but if we are to succeed in our much larger mission and higher purpose—the whole reason we decided to come here in the first place—then compromises must be made."

Ifu grumbled under his breath for a while, but otherwise did not argue further. Nothaar took that as an indication that he had finally submitted, giving Nothaar the secret win he had been desperately hoping to secure.

CHAPTER 17

Eager to find a way to break the tension, Nothaar solicited, "Okay, me help get boat, that settled. Then we take boat to mountain on small island. But why? Still no answer me basic question of why that place need go."

Barely audible, Ifu sarcastically mumbled through clenched teeth, "Congratulations, Syraaq, you get to explain what a *Space Elevator* is to Nothaar."

Roaring with laughter, Syraaq quickly diffused the situation by seemingly just dismissing Ifu's evident tone. Maintaining her mirth, Syraaq complied with his request by saying, "Sure, I'd love to try!"

Nothaar did not see what was so funny about his question or Ifu's invitation to have Syraaq enlighten him, but he stayed silent as she collected herself.

Finally getting herself under control and wiping the tears from her eyes, Syraaq began, "Nothaar, picture our exercise-ball planets again. If you had wanted to leave your orbit and visit the world my ball represented, how would you go about doing it?"

After thoughtfully considering her words for a few moments, Nothaar answered, "Fly up very high, go over, put feet on other sphere."

"Yes, yes, very good," Syraaq encouraged. "That is,

per se, one of the potential ways to approach the problem. What you just described—in your own unique way—is what we call rockets."

Judging by the look Nothaar caught in Syraaq's eyes, she outwardly appeared to dive into her computer-vision immediately after making this pronouncement. After being gone from reality for a brief moment, Syraaq unbolted herself from her seat, turned around, and grabbed a cylinder from a niche that had appeared in the vehicle wall. Holding onto whatever she had requested, Syraaq reset her safety belt. Nothaar could tell from his position that the hollow object was semi-transparent and held a liquid inside. Syraaq clarified that it was what she called a "bottle" and that it did, indeed, contain water, though it could have been filled with any other liquid that she might have desired. Going through his own rucksack, Nothaar pulled out his empty water pouch made from an impermeable animal bladder and held it up for comparison. "Get idea, be much the same," he asserted.

"Right, right," Syraaq stuttered as she showed obvious discomfort at seeing an object made from the organ of a living being. "But all of that is beside the point. I just wanted you to see the shape of this water bottle as a visual aid, not to compare liquid transportation methods. The rockets I was talking about before, they would be in a shape like this, except with a point on top. Then, we make a fire come out the bottom. This fire is so hot, so strong, and so focused that it pushes the tube upwards. Eventually, it reaches a critical velocity such that it starts to lift off from the earth, head up into the sky, and then fully escape from the downward pull exerted by the planet."

"Escape?" Nothaar inquired. "Why need all hot fire and speed to leave?"

"Watch this," Syraaq bade. With Nothaar peering at her closely, Syraaq gently threw her cylindrical container aloft before it arced at the peak of its journey and started to return to the ground. As she caught the flying object in her hands, Syraaq elucidated, "Everything that goes up, must come down. We call this phenomena gravity. Basically, it's one of those 'we don't know why, it just is' fundamental laws of the universe. Everything in existence has a natural feature that compels them to be pulled towards each other. Actually, gravity isn't exactly real by itself; it's more like a measurable impact of the bending of space-time when talking about the fabr—"

"Syraaq, that would be off-track even for me!" Ifu interrupted. "Nothaar, forget most of what you just heard for the moment. What Syraaq is trying to say is that we're all always being pulled towards each other, physically. It's just such a very weak tug that we can overcome it by just about any movement, like walking away. But the bigger something is, the more densely things are packed into smaller spaces, the harder it is to overcome its gravity. You can't just jump up or throw a rock high enough to surmount this planet's gravity."

This description of how gravity functioned made Nothaar's mind race at the possibilities and implications. Aloud he asked, "Other planets have gravity be different?"

"Yes, you're spot on," Ifu insisted. "Gravity varies across planets and celestial objects of all shapes and sizes. However, in order for life to form naturally and survive, it must be in a very narrow range. In the middle of that particular span, we have what we call 'one gravity', or more colloquially: *one-gee*. People, animals, plants, and the rest—we can all survive in a fair amount less and little bit more, but we won't thrive. That's why it's not worth even bothering ourselves with those worlds. Nowadays, every single planet that has life embedded upon its surface has somewhere around *one-gee* of gravity."

"Before, you say life form naturally?" Nothaar probed. "Life not already there?"

"Damn it, Syraaq," Ifu cursed. "I'm digging myself a deeper hole than the one you started. Weren't we talking about interstellar travel? Geez, never mind, I'm going to give this back to you and shut my big fat mouth."

"It's alright," Syraaq entreated. "Nothaar, let me try to make this as plain as I can. Planets don't just appear fully formed with all the land and water, plants and animals and whatnot already on them. They're borne through a long process of the coming together of many other smaller constituent parts. Basically, all planets start out as just balls of nothing. Yet even among them, only a certain percentage begin their existences as rocky worlds that have a surface you could put your foot down on. Still, those rocks will—most likely—be barren with no life whatsoever. Nonetheless, if the conditions are just right, if the planet is in the right location to be perfectly warm, but not too hot or cool; if it has certain protections from the dangerous ravages of the cosmos at large; if it took shape in a very specific way... well, anyway, it doesn't matter. What is important is that if millions of little things go exactly right, then there is a remote, but non-zero, chance that life will take root and arise on that world."

There was a lot to process in that testimonial, but Nothaar did not want to pause long enough to reflect on what he had just heard. Instead, with reckless abandon, he prodded further, "There be lot of life? Many planets?"

Syraaq laughed, but it was a much more forlorn chortle than Nothaar had ever heard from her before. The sound of it made him quite uncomfortable. "Define 'a lot' and 'many'," Syraaq flatly decreed. "To you, thousands would seem like a massively huge number. However, in the unfathomable vastness that is the true universe, that would not even be a rounding error. From that perspective, no, there are very few worlds like the three of ours. Life is very, very rare. For the entire history of the universe, it has always been so. In the past, though, it used to be a little less rare, a bit more plentiful, if you will."

Plowing ahead without taking a single moment to sift through any of this new information that was being revealed at a lightning clip, Nothaar asked, "More life long ago? Why past different?"

While Nothaar refused to pause to think for a moment, Syraaq evidently decided she needed to do so before answering with her own inquiry, "Before the *Sky Shift*, as you call it, how many stars of the non-wandering variety could you count?"

Although he didn't have access to his written records from the *Knowledge*, Nothaar was quite sure he could easily answer that fairly basic query. "About eighty."

Making one of her gestures of acceptance, Syraaq highlighted, "Pretty easy for someone like you to keep track of so few, huh? Well, a long time ago, there would have been thousands of them, and that is just what you would have been able to see with your naked eyes. There were more, millions upon millions upon millions more. And those were just the ones close to you. But the cosmos, it has never stopped growing since the beginning of time. As a matter of fact, it not only continues expanding, but does so at an alarmingly faster and faster rate with each passing age. In the beginning, all of existence was close by, with everything huddled together in the smallest possible area. But now, all that is, was, and will be are extremely dispersed, and it's only getting worse. At this moment, you can still see some stars, but a day will inevitably come when the few suns that remain in a mostly cold, empty, and uncaring universe are so far apart that their light will never be visible from another one.

"That is what it means for us to be alive at this specific instant in the long history of the universe. We are here, in the *Late Stelliferous Era*, and rapidly plunging our way towards the oncoming *Degenerate* one."

CHAPTER 18

Nothaar stared at Syraaq in confusion, not sure what to make of her description of the greater cosmos and what she had just called the epoch they were inhabiting. Still, there was only one line of inquiry he could ask about. "How long been since age with many stars, now so little? And why light no able reach between suns?"

Ifu scoffed at Nothaar's inquest and answered, "It's been so long that these numbers don't even have meaning anymore. If you want to put a figure on it, it's been nearly a hundred trillion years since the universe exploded into existence and set all of this in motion."

"Trillion?" Nothaar probed. "No know number."

"It means a million millions," Syraaq offered more gently than Ifu. "Not even well-learned *Commons* can completely fathom what that quantity truly entails."

As Nothaar opened his mouth to request more information, Syraaq signaled that she was not done speaking. "To answer your other question, you don't realize this, but light is not instantaneous. Although it appears that way, it is only an illusion because it's moving so fast compared to us and how quickly our brains can even process what's going on. In reality, though, light has a finite speed and can only travel a certain distance over any unit of time."

"Even more specifically," Ifu interjected, "light is the fastest thing in the universe and nothing, nothing can go any faster... using normal physics, that is. More so, unlike everything else, it only has one possible velocity, at least in a vacuum, but don't worry about that for now. What's important is that while any of us, this vehicle, or even a rocket may go faster or slower, light can only fly ahead at full throttle. Because of this feature, we use light as our measuring stick. More specifically, we can actually calculate how far light goes in a single year.

"Now, I want to clarify something. Syraaq mentioned that millions of little things have to go right in order for life to arise on a planet. Well, one of those conditions is that the length of a year needs to be relatively the same, give or take. Honestly, it's not exact, but it's close enough. Basically, a viable planet has to orbit a sun at a distance that is within a very tight range in order for living things to be able to spring up upon its surface. Due to that, it results in the length of a year intrinsically being roughly the same. In any case, there's one standard that all *Commons* use no matter their planet of origin and whatever small discrepancies exist locally. You don't have to ask; we'll teach it to you, I promise."

"Yes, we certainly will," Syraaq agreed. "For now, though, let's keep it a bit more general. As I was saying, light treks a specific extent over a year. This length is what we call a light-year. Yes, it's a bit of a circular reference, but you get the idea, right?"

Although readily conferring the *Common*'s gesture of

agreement, Nothaar wasn't really sure that he did. Still, since Syraaq and Ifu were being unusually forthcoming, he was not going to dissuade them from revealing more from their advanced pool of expertise. He was happy to be able to acquire such snippets from their *Archive* and, hopefully, at some future point, would have the opportunity to add it to his people's *Knowledge*.

Taking his acceptance at face value, Syraaq continued, "Well, in that earlier age of the universe when there were more suns, they were also nearer to each other. Most stars—with their planets encircling them—were about ten or twenty light-years away from their next adjacent neighbor. They could get closer, perhaps as little as two or three light-years, but any chummier than that would most likely annihilate any chance for a life-bearing planet being able to form."

"That's why no life has ever taken root around any binary or trinary systems, either," Ifu added.

"Wha—" Nothaar started to ask before Syraaq again requested they put that aside for the time being. Instead, she wanted to continue her lecture on the movement of light across the heavens.

"In other words," she was in the middle of explaining, "the light you would see from those stars during your nighttime observations before the *Sky Shift* were not real-time and happening at that exact moment, but were a window into the past and how it looked ten or twenty years prior. Of course, I am being extremely generous. The massive superstructure your sun was in, what we call a galaxy, was most likely hundreds of thousands of light-years across. That means that the non-wandering stars you were watching could also have been hundreds of thousands of light-years away from your location. Therefore, that is exactly how old the light you were looking at was."

"And who knows," Ifu interrupted again, "some of those stars may have had already died before the light reached your world."

"Stars... can die?" Nothaar suddenly found his voice in the query. He was finding it exceedingly difficult to get a word in between Syraaq and Ifu's fast exchanges, especially as he was trying to decipher the true meaning behind everything they were presenting.

"If there were once billions of stars in your galaxy," Ifu harangued, "and yet there were only eighty or so by your own accounting, then what does that say to you?"

Ifu didn't even pause to give Nothaar a chance to respond. Instead, he answered his own question by highlighting, "It says that the stars must have petered out. More so, they did so at a rate faster than they could be born. Now, having read your *Opus on the Language of Children*, I know you are well aware of what happens mathematically when fatalities outpace births. The sad truth is, Nothaar, that the stars are going extinct!"

"But that would mean..." Nothaar started before Ifu quickly cut him off again.

"That's right!" Ifu declared, though it was unclear if he was actually responding to anything Nothaar had or was about to say, or was just intent on expounding upon his own rant. "The entire cosmos is in a slow demise and one day will succumb to what we call the 'heat death of the universe'. As things get further and further away from each other and more stretched out, there will come a day when a planet forms and there will be no stars to see at all. But they might be the last new life because even their star will eventually expire. And without stars, there is no warmth for planets nor people, hence the end of every-thing as we know it."

"Geez, we've gotten way off track here!" Syraaq com-plained. "Ifu, you need to shut your mouth for a few beats and let me finish getting out what I have to say here."

Although he first projected an angry countenance af-ter Syraaq's outburst, Ifu eventually relented to let her do it her way without his interference.

Once satisfied that Ifu was no longer going to subject them to any additional superfluous details, Syraaq summa-rized her main thesis. However, it excluded all the extraneous particulars about what the future had in store for all of them as they careened towards the end of time. "The essential thing that I wanted you to take from this is that some planets are relatively close to each other, and others are unbelievably far away. Those wandering stars you see in the sky now, they are all other planets. But things have... changed... for you and your planet. Within a single natural system, the furthest a planet could possibly be found would be about a light-year out, but most likely only a tiny fraction of that. Not anymore, though."

"Why?" was the single interrogative Nothaar managed

to squeak out.

With her uncertainty on how to proceed clear in her facial expression, Syraaq deflected, "We'll get to that, I swear, but you're going to have to put that aside for now. Here and now, all I want you to take away from this conversation is that there would be a long expanse to travel between any of those planets, even in the best of circumstances."

"What all this have do with rockets from bottle?" Nothaar quicky retorted.

"Wait, what?" Syraaq asked bewilderedly.

Ifu broke his promised silence by exploding with laughter. "Oh, fuck," he spoke through his never-ending chuckles, "this was supposed to be a discussion about why we need to get to that one particular island and what, exactly, the *Space Elevator* situated there even is. How the heck did we get all the way to the other end of existence with these topics?"

Harrumphing, Syraaq contended, "I just wanted Nothaar to wrap his brain around the idea that you could take a rocket up through a planet's atmosphere to reach into the great beyond, but that there is a better way. You know what? Ifu, stop the vehicle."

"What, why?" Ifu protested. "We've just barely gotten underway. I doubt we've made it very far at all."

"Too bad," Syraaq countermanded. "I need to show Nothaar something, and there is no way to do so from inside here. Let us out!"

CHAPTER 19

Instead of immediately stopping their vehicle, Ifu first instructed the interior to return to its original configuration so they were no longer sitting in a conference-style setup. From his seat in the last row, it appeared to Nothaar that Ifu was looking out the window in front of him, scanning their surroundings. After a while, he finally appeared to find an area that satisfied whatever personal checklist he was making and parked their transport there. Shortly thereafter, their doors opened and the three of them unbuckled and slid out into a small open field with grasses around the height of their knees.

"Watch out here," Nothaar advised. "Tall grass known have bloodsucking insect. Not fun get off, have strong pinchers."

Syraaq's face betrayed what Nothaar considered to be the *Common*'s typical expression for disgust before she declared, "I'll alert our nanobots so they can be prepared and be on the lookout for any invaders." After this, Nothaar watched her eyes as she seemingly entered her own personal visual space for a moment before returning with a note of satisfaction. "Done."

"Wonderful," Ifu dryly intoned. "Alright, Syraaq, we're in the great outdoors like you wanted. What now?"

Instead of answering Ifu, Syraaq went to the back of their conveyance and opened yet another door in the rear. After she crawled inside, Nothaar could hear a lot of loud rummaging, followed by several items coming flying out before she rejoined them. Since the grass was so high, she then had to go searching through it to reclaim what she had just retrieved from the storage holds.

Returning back to where Nothaar and Ifu were standing, Syraaq handed Ifu a food pouch with a bright yellow picture plastered on it and announced, "Ifu, you're once more cast in the role of a sun."

Without a word, Ifu took the offered package and held it up to his chest. Syraaq then gave Nothaar a small blue sheet apparently made out of a rubberized material, only lighter and thinner feeling. Straightaway escaping into her private invisible realm, Syraaq must have made some request because the sheet filled with air and turned into a medium-sized ball, about half the width of Nothaar's chest. With Nothaar using both hands to hold it in place, Syraaq pronounced, "Congratulations, Nothaar; you're a planet again! Now face towards your sun."

Doing as requested, Nothaar looked at Ifu, who actually wilted a little bit under Nothaar's intense gaze. Before either could make any movement or say anything else, Syraaq requested, "Nothaar, if you would, why don't you tell us how your sun moves across the sky."

Immediately, Nothaar realized that Syraaq's quiz was a trick. Every time Syraaq or Ifu asked him a question like this, it was because they were trying to challenge his preconceptions and understandings from the *Knowledge*. This time, though, he decided he was not going to take the bait. There was obviously something related to the movement of the sun that he had never considered before.

Closing his eyes, Nothaar thought back to their time in the gym, with Syraaq and him orbiting around Ifu. *There was one other element to that, though,* Nothaar recalled. *Ifu specifically wanted me spinning around. It was because of that rotation that I was able to recognize the pattern of the wandering stars. If our sun is also just a star like any other as Ifu and Syraaq contest, then it would also run on the same or a similar design.*

Nothaar opened his eyes and made a noise of surprise, one that made Ifu and Syraaq jump. Adding a mental note to moderate his own reactions and to mimic theirs, Nothaar spoke about his revelation, "As planet spin, makes illusion that sun rises and falls. In reality, one part of world face sun, is daytime. Other side must be nighttime. Revolve around and be opposite. Me notice before, too, when going far east and west. Sun have different time to wake and trade with moon. Just no know why before. Now see, see very clearly."

Turning from Ifu to look at Syraaq, Nothaar was sure he had caught a glimpse of disappointment emanating from her before it quickly disappeared. That one small slip was enough to make Nothaar realize that Syraaq was looking forward to explaining the truth to him, and was saddened to have been thwarted in her attempt.

Ifu must have picked up on the same thing that

Nothaar did because he yelled over, "Syraaq, we've got to be careful around this guy. He's picking things up quite quickly. Before you know it, he'll be outwitting both of us!"

Although Nothaar was well aware that Ifu was being sarcastic, he also took satisfaction in the fact that he was able to get one over on them. He chose to look at even this modicum of a victory as a significant achievement and a positive sign of what was still to come. In his delight, Nothaar reflected, *At some point in the not-so-distant future, I'll be able to outmaneuver them and all their advanced technology, shifting the balance of power in my favor for good.*

Hiding her displeasure, Syraaq plastered on what Nothaar considered to be a mimicry of a happy representation of acceptance as she said, "No, I'm glad you understand that. It will make this next part much easier. Why don't you find me a mildly thick and heavy stick, about the length of your forearm, if you could?"

Returning his ball to Syraaq, Nothaar searched around the perimeter of the field until he found something suitable. Once back in Syraaq's presence, Nothaar found that she was holding a length of the rope-like material that they had used to bind him before. As he darted his eyes in all directions looking for his best escape route, Syraaq assuaged, "Don't worry, this isn't to imprison you. We are long beyond the need for that. Here, why don't you give me that branch you have in your hands?"

Turning over his find to Syraaq, Nothaar watched as she somehow ordered the cord to wrap around and attach itself to the stick. *My condolences,* Nothaar confidentially expressed his regret to the constricted tree fragment, *I know exactly how you feel.*

With the stick evidently secured, Syraaq somehow made the rope split into two segments, letting the stand-alone part fall by the wayside. Meanwhile, the section that remained fastened to the fallen branch had been shortened to about half of Nothaar's height. Apparently satisfied with her work, Syraaq handed the entire contraption to Nothaar and explained, "What I want you to do is to hold onto the end of the line where nothing is attached and then spin around in a circle, like you are a rotating planet. You'll probably have to pick up your speed and get going pretty fast, so hold on tightly. Ifu and I will step back a bit to make sure we don't get hit."

True to those words, Syraaq and Ifu moved away so that Nothaar could begin the designated exercise. At first, nothing seemed to be happening, but slowly the stick started to lift off the ground. After a short while, it was high in the air and stayed there with the cord between it and Nothaar staying completely taut. "Me very dizzy!" Nothaar complained with growing nausea.

From her safe location, Syraaq called out that Nothaar was free to stop. Taking advantage of the offer, Nothaar did so and kneeled in the grass, covering his eyes with his hands in order to regain his equilibrium. Syraaq came over, took the rope from him, disentangled the branch, and returned it—along with everything else she had taken out earlier—to the back of the vehicle.

Once Nothaar was able to stand again and confirm the contents of his stomach were going to stay put, Syraaq elucidated, "What you have just witnessed is what we call centrifugal force. The upward thrust of that momentum running towards the stick and the downward pressure of gravity from where you stood allowed the connection between those two points to basically cancel out and stay straight. This is what a *Space Elevator* does, except on a much more massive scale. The tenets and principles involved are exactly the same, though, with the planet spinning very quickly and a large counterweight on the other side keeping everything relatively rigid."

"Does rope go far off ground?" Nothaar probed.

"Yes, quite so," Syraaq responded, although she did not offer any additional specifics. "It's a fair distance from a planet's surface and in the area between celestial objects, a place we call 'outer space', or the 'interstellar medium'."

Typical Commons, Nothaar derisively thought, *they never have a single way to describe something. This is already a difficult subject, yet they continually add impediments to making it simple to understand.*

Walking over, Ifu put a hand on Syraaq's shoulder, indicating he would take it from there. Aloud he clarified, "On the island with the high mountain on the equator, there is a cable like this; there is a *Space Elevator*."

"How you know for sure?" Nothaar challenged.

Not taking a moment to think about it, Ifu illuminated, "As Starbuilders, one of the things our former employers would have people like us do is install *Space Elevators* that matched these precise specifications. As I said before, it works best at a high elevation point on the equator, thus building in a zone like that is also standard practice. Ergo, one must have been placed somewhere that aligned to those criteria. The fact that we received a signal from that far-off island, and that it contained data that explained where it was located, leads us to believe there must be a *Space Elevator* in the vicinity and not some other random piece of Starbuilder equipment.

"Further, Starbuilder directives are quite clear that we must—and pardon me for using this term—do everything possible to avoid locales where so-called primitive sapient people are situated. They would want your kind to live, grow, and mature for as long as possible without discovering it. Even if someone built a boat that could cross the ocean and found the island with the tall mountain, and even if they learned how to fly, they would still probably not notice the cable. It is extremely thin and made out of a clear, nearly invisible material. Honestly, the first time any of your people will know it is there will be when they accidently run into it."

"They might discover the platform in space, first," Syraaq contended.

"Even with a telescope," Ifu refuted, "the platform—the counterweight, Nothaar—is mirrored so that it reflects the sky back during the day and the darkness overnight. That usually makes it completely unnoticeable until a species is capable of launching rockets of their own."

"What be telescope?" Nothaar interjected.

Ifu and Syraaq went back and forth, trying to expound upon the concepts of magnification and how they could be applied to looking outwards towards the heavens, making everything appear closer. Nothaar was fascinated by the potential of such an instrument and asked if they had one. Unfortunately, it did not appear that Ifu or Syraaq had thought to pack such a device and instead had destroyed any inventory they might have had or parts that could have been used to make one aboard the Torch Ship.

CHAPTER 20

Opting to attempt remaining outside the claustrophobic vehicle for as long as possible, Nothaar boomeranged the focus of their conversation back to their apparent destination. "Alright, get to island, then what happen? Climb rope to sky, reach where you say be place beyond world called outer space?"

Laughing, Syraaq decreed, "I'm afraid not. You said you scaled some mountains before, right?"

"Yes, that correct," Nothaar confirmed. "Mountains mostly towards far east of continent. Several long ranges many days walk from ocean. Me had to climb few to visit villages. Some villages on top of mountain. Easier go towards western land. Only some small hills in direction we be travel to."

"Sounds like a continental shelf is plowing in from the east, creating some uplift and helping to give shape to this supercontinent," Ifu proposed.

Completely ignoring Ifu's non-sequitur, Syraaq turned back to Nothaar and asked, "Did you notice that it was a bit more difficult to breathe at the top of the mountains, or that you could not catch your breath as well as you normally could, or that activities you found fairly stress-free below the mountain were exceedingly difficult, or even just that while walking your heart started to beat faster than normal?"

"Yes, yes, yes!" Nothaar emphatically affirmed. "Notice all list things."

"Good!" Syraaq exclaimed. "Now I can explain to you why that happens. As you might recall from this morning before we started driving away from the Torch Ship's former location, I was telling you about how even water is not one thing, but made up of several different elements."

For Nothaar, that conversation already felt like a lifetime ago, even though it had only been part of a day. He used the *Common*'s motion for agreement, thus Syraaq resumed, "Well, air is the same. That is, at least the air on a planet that can harbor life. Here on your planet—as well as my and Ifu's homeworlds—almost the entirety of the air is made up of just two elements, both of which are invisible gases to us. The most abundant is called nitrogen. While we need nitrogen for various functions in our bodies, atmospheric nitrogen is rather useless to us as is. In the air, it's more important to balance out other gasses from taking over. Also, fun fact, it helps make the sky blue!"

"How invisible substance make sky have color?" Nothaar inquired.

"Nothaar," Ifu interjected, "you're going to have to add that to your book of unanswered interrogatives for now. I don't think Syraaq wants to teach you about refraction and light scattering at this particular juncture."

"Quite so," Syraaq agreed. "What I was about to say is that the other dominant element is oxygen."

"That same name of one say earlier, in water," Nothaar remarked.

"You have a good memory for new words," Syraaq noted in return.

"Me tell you many time," Nothaar retorted, "me can learn tongues fast, even the *Lingua*."

As soon as the words were out of his mouth, Nothaar instantly regretted them. *Stupid, stupid, stupid,* he admonished himself. *I let my pride get in the way and just gave away a critical piece of intelligence, literally spilling it from my own lips. I have to turn this around so they don't notice, and do it fast. Think, Nothaar, think: how can you make them believe you're an idiot again?*

"Wait," Nothaar requested as he figured out how he could throw Ifu and Syraaq off the scent, "how come air and water be different?"

"Do you see what you started, Syraaq?" Ifu chided. "Now he wants to learn inorganic chemistry in a single morning. Nothaar, listen, just let Syraaq get through whatever it is she has to tell you and hold your questions until the end. What you are asking about are subjects even our children spend years studying to comprehend, and some go on to make whole careers out of learning more, doing research, and studying it. To say that Syraaq and I are ill-equipped to be your personal tutors on these topics would be an understatement, but I believe I may know something you could use instead."

"What are you thinking?" Syraaq suspiciously queried Ifu. It was the first time that Nothaar actually saw Syraaq direct distrust towards Ifu, so he filed that interesting development away in his brain for a potential future personal benefit.

Giving one of the *Common*'s many looks of annoyance at having to explain themselves, Ifu announced, "We'll take one of the tablets, set it up with a learning application under the tutelage of the *Eh-aye*, and instruct Nothaar on how to use it so that he can self-direct his own education. After all, we're all going to have a lot of free time until we can escape from this backwards rock."

"I'm not sure that's a good idea," Syraaq contended.

"Maybe not," Ifu granted, "but it's probably the best thing we can do in this situation."

Neither said anything for a while and seemed to just be staring each other down. Nothaar was unsure if they were communicating with one another in their heads as they appeared to be doing earlier, or if they were engaged in some type of ritual showdown. Whatever happened, Ifu apparently triumphed as Syraaq finally spoke aloud, "Fine, you win. However, you're also responsible for all the consequences that may befall us because of it."

"Of course, of course," Ifu dismissed. "Now then, can you finally get back to your story about oxygen?"

Sighing, Syraaq once again turned to Nothaar and picked up as if she had never stopped. "Oxygen is what we actually breathe, what our body uses to break down food and turn it into the energy we truly need. And before you interrupt me with your interrogations, you'll have the ability to learn all about that in your future organic chemistry and biology courses. The most important thing to note for the purpose of this conversation is that we need it, and without it we would die in just a few short... ugh, you don't have this word, do you? Let's just say very small units of time that make up part of a day.

"Now, the higher you go, the less oxygen is freely available. That is why you had all those issues at the top of mountains, due to the lower amount of it and the inefficiencies in how our bodies even intake and process the element. If you could have climbed higher, eventually there would have been so little oxygen that you'd simply pass out and suffocate. In outer space, beyond the edge of a planet's sky, there is none of it whatsoever, or so close to none that it makes no difference.

"The other thing to consider is that the further you get from the ground, the colder it becomes. By comparison, the temperature in outer space is so low that it would make your so-called land of ice feel like the desert wastelands during the peak of summer. Suffice to say that without something to convey and protect us, we cannot reach the top of the *Space Elevator* alive."

Once Syraaq finished her soliloquy, neither Ifu nor Nothaar offered any comment. They were all silent for almost another small unit of time that made up part of a day. That is, they were until Syraaq bade, "Well?"

"Oh, me be allowed speak, ask questions now?" Nothaar sarcastically cast back at her.

"Yes, Nothaar," Syraaq quipped, letting her own relatively controlled—compared to Ifu's—level of annoyance and impatience be known, "you are free to ask away. What's on your mind? I mean, related to getting off your planet, not the fundamental properties of the universe at large."

"If no can climb *Space Elevator*," Nothaar began, "then how we go to outer space?"

Syraaq was about to speak when Ifu chimed in, "That's enough, Syraaq; I've got this. Nothaar, when we arrive at the base of the *Space Elevator*, we'll have a way to send a signal outward. It won't be done with fire and smoke or whatever ways you do it, but with our advanced methodologies that you cannot even begin to fathom, much less understand. Just know for now that we are going to send a message at or near the speed of light and that someone will receive it and come pick us up.

"Specifically, when our rescuers arrive, they will drop a trolley down the line. You can think of it as a large enclosed basket that—on the outside—looks a lot like the same material the exterior of the Torch Ship had and that our current vehicle now possesses. It will slowly crawl the length of the cable until it comes to a rest at the top of the mountain. There, we'll step aboard and be taken back upwards at the same excruciatingly slow rate. The thing is, we have no idea who is going to hear our call for help. The only thing we can do is hope that it is a friendly face. In either case, we'll just have to figure out our next move once we're there."

"If me can summarize," Nothaar offered, "plan be this: Travel in sluggish, circuitous route to avoid Nothaar people. Get to village near equator on outskirts of wasteland and build boat never seen on planet before. Drive vehicle onto boat and sail to other side of world. Find single, tiny, specific island with mountain on it. Climb mountain, visit bottom of Space Elevator, and send signal to outer space. Message move at finite speed of light to distances maybe very far. Random *Common* hear dispatch, come to Nothaar planet, deliver basket down rope. Maybe good person, maybe not, make up rest of strategy later. Miss anything?"

"Nope, sounds about right," Ifu concurred.

"Then only one question left," Nothaar stated. "How long all plan take?"

Syraaq and Ifu both looked particularly depressed by this inquiry before the latter declared, "Too long, Nothaar, too long..."

CHAPTER 21

It had been about five cycles of the moon since Nothaar, Ifu, and Syraaq had departed from the Torch Ship's landing site and set out on their journey. Although the expedition had started slowly as their vehicle delicately crept its way through and out of the dense wilderness, they were able to make up for lost time once they had reached more open areas closer to the shoreline. Of course, they could not always maintain that expedient pace as many of the villages were also situated along such a beneficial corridor. On those occasions—and since Ifu and Syraaq were intent on avoiding any other sapient lifeform—their self-driving conveyance would veer back into the forest and returned them to their sluggish march.

Nevertheless, evading others was not the only reason they had to stop. Each evening as the sun went down, their transport morphed into what Ifu called "low power mode". In that configuration, Nothaar learned that all the energy it had gathered during the day was directed towards maintaining a comfortable interior environment and preserving the ability of the computer systems to keep running at full capacity. Ifu and Syraaq would not even entertain the idea of disconnecting anything they considered "essential". Even as Nothaar began to understand from his lessons with the tablet what exactly those components potentially were, he still did not agree that they were a requirement for survival or necessary for reaching their destination. Most of them simply seemed completely superfluous to him.

One day, Nothaar tried to point out to Ifu that there were capacities that could be shut down or at least have their functionality reduced in order to lower their energy needs. With the help of the *Eh-aye*, Nothaar had even calculated additional power gains that could benefit them all by changing their path from their current straight-forward route to a different one that necessitated slowing down at various waypoints. This detailed analysis had concluded that there were net fuel allotments that could be found by engaging the regenerative braking structure more often. Per usual, though, Ifu did not take Nothaar seriously. It seemed to Nothaar that Ifu considered his own suppositions to be inherently superior to anything Nothaar could come up with. Though Ifu never said such words aloud, Nothaar was certain about his impression of the situation.

As such, they plodded along on Ifu's desired trail, no matter how inefficient Nothaar found it or what the evidence showed was a better prospect. There were times they were barely making any headway, and Nothaar often took those opportunities to exit the vehicle to gather and hunt for his personal sustenance. From the late spring and throughout the summer, Nothaar's options for fresh food were quite plentiful. Syraaq had also helped him "deconstruct" his excess food into similarly sealed pouches as the

Common's nourishment so that the nanobots could reconstitute them later with the minor addition of water. "Just properly label them and don't mix them in with our supplies," Syraaq had jokingly warned. "I certainly wouldn't want to start vomiting all over my bed for mistaking your grub for my own."

Traveling northward while the seasonal temperatures rose not only naturally, but due to their specific trajectory, had proven somewhat troublesome. After being out of the vehicle for a few days, re-entering its much colder climate-controlled interior always sent a shock through Nothaar's natural physiology. Despite small issues and other similar problems, the timing had eventually worked out so that they entered the more tropical zone as the autumn would have been taking hold in the far south. Although Nothaar had often described the concept of the four seasons he was used to from where he grew up, he was well aware that the lines were not so clearly delineated in other areas around the continent. Aside from the never-ending summer heat in the desert wasteland, above and below it were strips of terrain that basically always stayed hot, too, and usually just got rainier or drier at different points during the year. To the people who lived in villages in and around those steamy ecosystems, the arrival or departure of rain marked the seasons.

Near those zones, Nothaar needed to visit villages more frequently to replenish his supplies rather than trying to find enough provisions on his own. Much earlier in their voyage, however, he had the regrettable fortune of discovering just why Ifu and Syraaq had no reason to be concerned about him potentially eloping or planning some type of rebellion against them.

On the first such occasion of Nothaar visiting a settlement populated with his own people, Ifu had parked their vehicle about a half-day's walk away and let Nothaar out. "We'll wait here until your return," he announced.

"You no come with me?" Nothaar had inquired.

"No, we won't," Ifu explained. "We need to limit our exposure to your people. If we visited as is, it would certainly raise too many questions that we should not be answering. We need to minimize the contamination of your people. Even if we wore face-coverings or something like that, we might still unwittingly let some fact or piece of information slip out. On the other hand, if we refused to speak or you said we were mute, it would only result in others interrogating you for more details."

"There... some logic to what you say," Nothaar conceded. "Children would be especially bad. If heard you speak, would glom to you. You no understand what words they should know and not know."

"Exactly," Ifu agreed. "We've done a great job thus far of avoiding your people, so I don't want to see that come to a premature end."

While Nothaar was grateful for the chance to get away from the *Commons* and be among his own kind, he was incredibly suspicious of how nonchalant Ifu was being about it. Deciding to risk exposing his own machinations, Nothaar asked, "How you know me... I... no run away and no come back? What about if I tell other people about you two, talk about *Commons*, and give to them everything I learn from *Archive*."

"Syraaq, I think it's time to show Nothaar," Ifu cryptically proposed.

"Show me what?" Nothaar concernedly queried.

"Here, let me see your tablet," Syraaq requested. Once Nothaar handed it over, she installed a new application and returned the device to Nothaar. "See this here on the homepage? Open it up."

Doing as commanded, Nothaar found he was looking at what he now recognized as the *Common*'s method for making topographical maps. Pointing to the screen, Syraaq expounded, "You've certainly noticed those marks there." Atop the diagram, there were three red dots. Two were close together and one was slightly away from the other two. Continuing her demonstration, Syraaq requested, "Ifu, would you please take a walk away from us? Nothaar, watch what happens." As Nothaar kept his eyes locked on the image, the crimson symbol that was separated from the other two slowly began to move further off. "Touch that indicator," Syraaq bade.

Lightly pressing his finger on it, a popup appeared that said it was Ifuwukoogeeq and provided some health information such as his heart rate and various figures that Nothaar was unsure the meaning of. Fearing he already knew what to expect, Nothaar pressed the other two spots, revealing containers for Syraaq Sec and a very interesting phonetic transliteration of Nothaar Akii in the letters of the

Lingua. "How this possible?" Nothaar implored.

"Nanobots," Syraaq simply answered.

"I no have nanobots in me!" Nothaar insisted.

"Quite the contrary," Syraaq refuted. "You remember back on the Torch Ship when I gave all of us a shot? I was dousing everyone with nanobots that had a very specific assignment. Unlike the ones Ifu and I also have in our bloodstreams that repair damage, these nanobots are basically tracking and charting. It takes three points to accurately find anything—what we call triangulation—and when you came along, you became our third post, so to speak. In our ocular implants, we can always see where you are; and with your tablet, you can do the same to us. This way, we should never be able to lose each other!"

Shocked to his core, Nothaar did not know how to react. He had not realized that the *Commons* had such a faculty. During his personal education sessions with the tablet, he had been trying to learn about their security protocols and what they might do. Yet, this seemed to be some ingenious, unintended use of an unrelated technology he had not even considered might exist and, consequently, had not thought to ask about. Besides, his studies had been going excruciatingly slow overall. Everything was definitely written with the assumption that readers would innately understand the meaning of the words. He would come across new terms every few beats in a sentence, forcing him to stop and try to find definitions. Those exegeses, in turn, also contained unknown terminologies, thus sending him further down into a pit of lost meaning.

Sometimes, though, it became painfully obvious just how limited Ifu and Syraaq's local copy of the *Archive* really was. They had not been exaggerating when they said they only had an extremely partial subset of what could be contained within that database. A fair amount of the *Archive* had apparently been destroyed when they left it behind on the Torch Ship before activating rapid molecular decomposition, removing any evidence of the existence of the *Commons* and their potentially perilous technology. While Nothaar would try to engage Syraaq or Ifu—mostly the former—to get answers, even Syraaq was oftentimes reluctant or unable to provide what Nothaar was looking for.

Stirring Nothaar from his thoughts, Syraaq declared, "As the advertisements say, though, 'But wait, there's more!'" She then giggled at her own joke that went straight over Nothaar's head.

"What word 'advertisement' mean?" Nothaar pressed, even though he didn't really care at that moment.

"It's a way to try to persuade other *Commons* to buy things," Ifu interposed, "usually useless stuff that we don't need. You've told us about that trader who came to your village that ended up inspiring you to set out on your prior course. Well, basically, if he put up a sign that said, 'Come get this stuff from me!', that would be akin to a type of advertisement."

"I think I get idea," Nothaar allowed just to end what he viewed as a pointless aside and get back to what he really wanted to talk about. "Anyway, what are other functions you mention, Syraaq?"

"Glad you asked," Syraaq intimated. "Made special just for you, we have the ability to monitor and listen in to your words and… let's just call it chemical reactions in your body that give away your mood. Most relevant, though, we parsed your *Opus on the Language of Children* so that the *Eh-aye* could begin to learn your peoples' native tongues. Now, every time you speak in any dialect from this world, the *Eh-aye* learns that particular vernacular a little bit more. And just as you did, it's also developing an understanding for the proto-lingo that existed as a precursor to all the modern tongues on your planet so that it can project the meanings and pronunciations of various derivations.

"But anyway, having a handy translator is not the main function and purpose we are interested in. Importantly, with this capability in place, anything you say to any other being will be reported back to us. That is, if it is of any concern. However, I doubt that will happen. The *Eh-aye* also has instructions to stop you from revealing anything untoward to your own people."

"Stop me by what means?" Nothaar solicited with horror at the possibilities.

"I'd rather you not have to find out," Syraaq deflected.

In that moment, Nothaar decided he was going to test his bonds by rushing at Syraaq with violent intentions and screaming, "Show me!"

As soon as he started yelling and turning towards her, he was overwhelmed and wracked with pain everywhere in his body. He immediately hit the ground, convulsing as he was unable to maintain his bearings.

"That's enough, Ifu!" Nothaar barely made out Syraaq shouting over his own torment.

Then, as quickly as it began, it was over. Nothaar panted on the ground for several more moments, tears flowing from his eyes. Once he felt safe enough, he started to check his own skin for lacerations, but could find none. If anything, he looked as healthy as ever.

Ifu walked over and held out his hand to help Nothaar up. Despite his rage, Nothaar took it. Once upright, Ifu entreated, "Please, don't make me ever do that again."

CHAPTER 22

Recalling his first encounter with the pain-inflicting nanobots filled Nothaar with a renewed fury. As time went on, he could not find any way in the *Archive* to purge the miniaturized machines from his bloodstream and free himself from their microscopic subjugation. If the answer existed, he either did not have access or their local copy simply lacked a record of it. On several more occasions while visiting his own people, Nothaar had unwittingly set off the automatic defenses. Yet, after each incident, he found himself unable to explain to the stunned villagers who witnessed his writhing what was happening to him. Attempting to expound upon it apparently activated the same alarm and sent him face down in the dirt. Later, when he returned to camp, Nothaar always vehemently protested to Ifu and Syraaq. With Syraaq's urging, Ifu did make some adjustments to the nanobot's tolerance parameters, especially in consideration of when Nothaar was interacting with the children who also spoke the *Lingua*.

"It shouldn't be able to kill you," Ifu calmly explained as if he was once more describing how the toilet functioned, "but I don't want you to take any unnecessary risks, either. If something were to happen to you, we'd have to somehow find a new representative to help bring the plight of your people—and all those without a voice—to the attention of our government. Maybe another *Keeper* would work out, but most likely it would have to be one of the children since we'd be able to properly communicate with them. From your own recollections and writings, it seems like you may be the only pre-*Sky Shift* person who has a solid grasp on the *Lingua* in any capacity."

Recognizing the threat to any and all inhabitants of his planet, Nothaar realized at that moment that he truly was trapped and could no longer escape Ifu and Syraaq's imprisonment. Whatever plans he may have had were completely waylaid; he had no way to overpower them. More so, he did not want anyone else to have to go through what he was dealing with. As such, Nothaar decided that in order to protect all the other people on his planet, he would sacrifice himself and willingly accompany the *Commons*, wherever it ultimately led.

As another condition of his internment, Ifu disallowed Nothaar from carrying his *Opus on the Language of Children* into the villages. Nothaar was shattered as the book was his life's work and what he had spent the past fifteen years putting together. His whole raison d'etre was to deliver his report to all the populated settlements in the world and give them a way to communicate with their own offspring, as well as deal with the transition that was obviously underway. When he argued these points, Ifu did not show any signs of being persuaded. "We just can't risk it," he had steadfastly declared.

After that pronouncement, Nothaar had decided to

memorize his opus and completely rewrite it once they arrived at the village near the equator. Although the nanobots could certainly listen to what he spoke aloud, Nothaar was unsure how much they were able to see. While they could apparently tell when he made sudden violent movements towards Ifu or Syraaq, they did not seem to truly observe what Nothaar took in with his own eyes. By Nothaar's estimation, his lack of technological augmentations like Ifu and Syraaq's ocular implants were limiting the nanobots' perception abilities.

Despite that presumption, Nothaar did not want to chance that the *Eh-aye* could figure out what he was writing down. Instead, when he stayed overnight in the villages, he composed messages in a code that only other *Keepers* would recognize and be able to decipher. There simply was not enough time for him to transcribe an entire copy of his oeuvre—Ifu and Syraaq had limited his excursions to just a few days each—so, instead, he left notes asking the local *Keeper* to either come or send someone to the village near the equator that he knew their entourage was heading towards. Once there, they would find a present that Nothaar intended to leave behind.

Thankfully, along the way, Ifu and Syraaq had proved amiable to the idea of Nothaar trading for paper and writing instruments. Since these things were quite difficult to produce, Nothaar successfully fought in favor of purchasing the items instead of trying to make them from scratch and causing their group to have excessive layovers. Furthering the groundwork around making sure that writing itself would not alert the nanobots, during his study sessions with the tablet, Nothaar had taken great efforts to demonstrate his prodigious use of such materials. Whenever the occasion presented itself, Nothaar also expounded on the idea of how he learned best by writing things down and could not easily be forced to give up a habit he had developed over his entire life, one that he had used professionally as a *Keeper*. As he hoped, Ifu and Syraaq quickly stopped questioning or paying attention to what Nothaar did with his compositions, although they continued to disallow bound blank books out of fear that he may have tried to make a copy of his seminal work.

Nothaar was forced to concede that Ifu and Syraaq's fears were well founded, so he instead attempted to demonstrate more benign circumstances when an empty tome could be put to use. At the top of that list was transferring the plans for the yacht that Ifu and Syraaq wanted to physical paper so that Nothaar could deliver the instructions and diagrams to the builders. Since this act would eventually allow their entourage to circumnavigate the globe, Nothaar had also begun to estimate how long the boat was going to take to be constructed. Knowing his own people's competencies, he estimated that the entire end-to-end endeavor would extend for almost an entire year. Due to this, in his letter to the *Keepers*, he requested that they not attempt to retrieve their gifts until a later date, perhaps not until two summers had passed. He wanted to make sure that there would be a massive time buffer in case his approximations were off or if something simply went wrong during the production process. That interval, Nothaar hoped, might allow the local *Keeper* and their assistants to make supplementary copies, and perhaps disperse them to other nearby villages themselves.

In either case, Nothaar recognized that there would be a long period of downtime once they reached their anticipated destination. He had already planted the seeds with Ifu and Syraaq that he should remain in the village during almost the entire manufacturing phase of their overwater conveyance in order to supervise and manage the whole undertaking. Furthermore, he argued, he would be able to surreptitiously make recordings on his tablet and bring them back to Ifu and Syraaq during regular status reports. That way, they, too, could also review the progress and send back additional instructions with him.

In reality, while Nothaar would indeed execute those tasks exactly as he proposed, he would also use the opportunity to create new editions of his *Opus on the Language of Children* in as many vernaculars as possible during their long stopover. Because of his planned extended stay, Nothaar had requested an even higher threshold for the punishment dealt out by the nanobots, especially including specific criteria around inscribing. He presented it as a need to survey the children and find out how much they understood, but without revealing controlled information in return. At that moment, Ifu still had not agreed to Nothaar's tender, thus he was not yet ready to test the potential refined limits of his bondage.

"We're here," Ifu announced, suddenly breaking

Nothaar out of his memories. The doors to their vehicle opened and the three of them stepped out into the dry, listless desert air.

After looking around for a bit, Syraaq proclaimed, "I don't like it. We're way too exposed here."

As with every other stop during their expedition, Ifu had chosen to park their transport a half-day's walk away from the nearest settlement. They were beyond the edge of the jungle and positioned against a sandy cliffside. Along the way, they had generally used the cover of the green forest canopy itself as a method to mask their encampment, but there was no such option at this location.

"You can no stay where trees are," Nothaar reminded them. "Harvesters from village will be come down there to get trees for your boat. Safer here, deep in desert. No one would come this way. Besides, drone can keep lookout in case anyone does. Will know long beforehand should people approach, unlikely as is."

The drone was another automata that Ifu and Syraaq had not bothered to inform him about. However, much to Ifu's chagrin, the *Eh-aye* had accidently revealed its existence. Ifu reprimanded the *Eh-aye*, but since it lacked a body to torture like the one Nothaar possessed, it did not seem to take his intimidations too seriously. Once the truth was revealed, though, Syraaq had shown Nothaar how to make the drone fly about the sky and look through its eyes via his tablet. "Of course," Syraaq had explained, "I can set my own vision to be the same as the drone's. In other words, I can see exactly as it does."

This revelation was the first time Nothaar actually felt jealousy regarding the modifications Syraaq and Ifu had made to their physiques. The way Syraaq described it, she actually felt like she was flying, too. It sounded so amazing that Nothaar wondered if he would consider mutilating his own natural being like the *Commons* did just to have the same experience. While he had not made any decisions either way, he contented himself with learning about the physics of flight and how it was even possible to do what the drone and other airborne automata were capable of.

As he did so, a question began to gnaw at the back of Nothaar's mind. Finally, he confronted Ifu with the enquiry of why they could not have built a flying contraption of some kind to transport them to their final destination instead of undertaking a relatively sluggish progression using their ground-based vehicle, followed by the need to build a completely novel seacraft. Per usual, Ifu did not offer a satisfactory answer and only contended that such a possibility would not have been viable for reasons Nothaar simply could not understand. And once again, Nothaar had no choice but to accept these words and put his own ideas and considerations aside.

"And what are we going to do about water in the middle of a vast desert?" Syraaq complained at their current desolate location.

"Seismic readings already indicate a sizeable underground reservoir," Ifu contended. "We should be able to drill down and tap into it. After all, we brought along a bunch of tools that we've barely utilized, and others we haven't even taken out once. We might as well put them to use. Anyway, we'll have to do something for the many long days ahead, or else we'll go insane from boredom!"

"Ifu, I've taken naps longer than you've been alive," Syraaq snapped. "Don't worry about me; I know how to fill up purposeless idle time."

Nothaar did not intervene as the two squabbled. Though he may have reluctantly accepted to tie his fate to theirs, it did not mean that he was interested in maintaining the peace. After letting them go back and forth for a bit, he interrupted with, "I leave in early morning, before daybreak. Travel by heat of mid and late day bad idea."

"Makes sense," Ifu agreed. "So... I guess that means this is our last night together for quite a while. What should we do to mark the occasion?"

CHAPTER 23

As promised, after a full cycle of the moon, Nothaar returned to where Ifu and Syraaq had set up their campsite in order to deliver a status report. Overall, negotiations had gone fairly well. Despite the fact that the people in the village doubted the seaworthiness of the design Nothaar had presented, they were happy to work on it in exchange for all the precious metals that Nothaar had offered. He had only disbursed a small sample as a down payment since the ores were far too heavy to carry by himself, but he had arrived back at the vehicle with a gatherer's cart so as to transport a large amount of the rare resources in a single round trip.

"Are you sure it's a good idea to give them so much at once?" Ifu challenged as they sat around a sparking blaze in the firepit. "Perhaps a payment plan would be better with deliveries at certain milestones. That's fairly standard among many *Common's* cultures."

"Nothaar people no be *Commons*," Nothaar argued. "We do barter differently. Trust important. Those who break trust often find themselves dead. Here at desert wasteland, is much worse. Although not at this village, in others nearby, believe in making slaves of betrayers, enemies, and captors."

"Ifu, Nothaar knows what's best in this case," Syraaq assuaged. "Besides, we have no real use for those minerals. All we care about is getting our boat, so just allow Nothaar to do what he thinks is necessary and let them get whatever they've asked for. If this goes sideways, then we'd need to come up with another plan, anyway. And I don't know about you, but I don't want to get bogged down in some silly contract dispute."

Ifu finally grumbled his consent and Nothaar caught them up on various other particulars. More so, he spent a great deal of time trying to set reasonable expectations. Neither of the two off-worlders were particularly happy with the tentative timeline for delivery, but they could not offer any practical way to speed up the process. Finally, with those subjects and details exhausted, Nothaar brought up what he really wanted to discuss. "Been talking to children, testing them on words and phrases Nothaar people no have parallels for. Somehow, when I use vocabulary they no should know, they intuitively understand meaning and concepts, even though lack context and frame of reference. These all things I had to learn from the *Archive*. How this be possible? They no have lessons about the cosmos like I have from the tablet. *Eh-aye* has been no help on explaining to me why youngsters understand. It have no data on what be happening to people on this planet."

Both Ifu and Syraaq were silent for several moments, looking at each other. Once more, Nothaar was unsure if they were actually communicating to each other through their minds, or just staring one another down until some-one broke. Eventually Ifu sighed and said, "I guess it's about time we let you in on all of this. Syraaq, you want to take the lead?"

Clearing her throat, Syraaq began, "Nothaar, you now understand that there are things so small that you cannot see them with your naked eye."

"Yes," Nothaar agreed, "like the nanobots."

"Right," Syraaq continued, "but those are machines. In nature, there are such entities, too, that are far, far tinier than even nanobots. The size differential in percentage from them to nanobots would be the same or more as nanobots to you. In other words, thousands, perhaps millions, of these creatures could actually fit inside a single nanobot."

"Grab your tablet," Ifu requested, "and have the *Ehaye* bring up a picture of a eukaryote cell."

Doing as bidden, Nothaar saw an oddly shaped structure with many smaller blobs inside. "A cell, in general," Ifu expounded, "is the basic structural component of life like us. While some creatures are only a single cell, you and I are made up of trillions and trillions of them. Very different kinds, to be sure, but the mechanisms are relatively the same. Most importantly, inside a cell like this one are what we call organelles. Just like your heart is an organ that pumps blood around your body, so, too, do cells have their own moving parts. Of those, the main ones we need to concern ourselves with are the part that provides energy and others that impart genetic instructions."

Nothaar questioned the meaning of "genetic instructions" and Ifu contended that it was the essence of living beings; that there were these sugars that came in certain patterns and combinations which determined how a creature looked, functioned, and reproduced. Ifu started to talk about how the instructions were only part of the equation, and that there were other things that determined the "expression" of those directives, but Syraaq let him know he was drifting far away from the core of their conversation. Realigning himself, Ifu returned his focus on what he apparently had originally intended to discuss.

"We're well aware of how to put them into any configuration to get what we want," Ifu was in the midst of saying. "But before you ask, no, we once again do not understand why. It's just another one of those mysterious universal rules that appears to be hardcoded into the cosmos. In trillions of years, we're no closer to having a true understanding of the mechanism behind these results. There are plenty of theories, but nothing that can be definitively proven."

"What's more," Syraaq added, "when life forms, it does so in its own unique way. Although we all have similar types of directions written into our bodies, they are not compatible. That is why we cannot eat your food and vice versa. And just as you could not mate with an animal and produce a genuine offspring, neither could we—you and I—breed with each other."

"Although I'd like to see you try," Ifu jokingly interrupted, "especially at your age!"

"Shut your infantile mouth!" an unamused Syraaq cussed back. "Anway, Nothaar, what I was saying is that just because we're both sapient, it doesn't have some type of universal significance that says we should be compatible or anything in all the ways that count towards producing progenies. We have this word 'evolution' that is about how species become dramatically different varieties over time, to the point of being completely new species who are nothing like their ancestors. How they get there all comes through changes found in their genetic code. But evolution is not a set path or some type of destination, with the objective of creating certain types of life that meet specific criteria. When evolution occurs naturally, it can best be described simply as when a particular feature—a trait— is beneficial enough to increase the probability of staying alive and producing viable children, the next generation will, in turn, inherit that characteristic. More to the point, the universe isn't a conscious being, thus it cannot push an agenda of any kind, nonetheless making sapient species. It just happens on a few rare occasions. Since life arises inside its own little bubbles, it's not as if different people share any specific attributes that would somehow make them able to swap genetic material."

"You say when occur naturally," Nothaar summarized, "but earlier say can put together and build code how you want it to work."

"Correct," Syraaq acknowledged. "The way we do that is we wrap what I'm going to call an 'update to the code' in a very tiny package, about a hundredth of the size of that cell in front of you. That package 'infects' the cell like a disease would and inserts the new information to be integrated and executed."

"Wait, be you saying…" Nothaar attempted, but could not quite find the right words and ideas for what he wanted to articulate.

"Yes, Nothaar," Ifu interjected. "Your children are turning into *Commons*."

"No!" Nothaar rejected, even though he had already come to a similar conclusion during their long journey. The parallels he saw in Syraaq and Ifu led him to reject any other option. *What Ifu is disclosing is the only logical deduction,* Nothaar resigned. *Still, I had no idea how it could have been accomplished, and thus have been holding on to some unwarranted hope of changing course before it's too late.*

"What's more," Ifu persisted, seemingly oblivious to Nothaar's suffering and concerns, "your entire planet is slowly turning into one compatible for *Commons* and *Common*-like life. We've already told you about how, over time, there would be no food left that you would find digestible. This is what we were talking about. The process doesn't and can't happen right away; it would be way too dangerous to suddenly shift all life to be like us. Still, gradually, it will come to pass."

"How? Why?" was all that Nothaar could manage.

"As Starbuilders," Syraaq expounded, "it was part of our job. When we found a world like yours, we would be assigned to seed the planet with these instructions so that, in the end, we can all become... homogeneous. And it's not just about food. Despite Ifu's crass comments earlier, it is about sex and procreation. Even though we could technically grow *Commons* in a vat or some other surrogate womb if we wanted, natural pregnancy and birth has a much higher success rate and statistically produces younglings who can thrive better in our universe. As much as some people believe machinery can resolve all our problems, more often than not, just exploiting natural processes is the path of least resistance.

"When the transformation process has been completed, in however many generations it will take, everyone here will be completely sexually compatible with any *Common* anywhere. At that point, the inhabitants of your world would be indistinguishable from any other *Common*. People like us could freely walk upon your earth, eat the food grown here, and produce babies with you. No one here would be any the wiser. In a forever ago age, the government determined that this was the methodology by which we were going to preserve life in a dying universe. Instead of having many different species that might wink out of existence, we'd all become one species to increase the chances that we will go on forever, together."

Nothaar was completely dumbstruck by the horror of all that had been revealed. Ifu apparently finally picked up on Nothaar's troubled expression and declared, "And trust me: we feel the same way you do, Nothaar. All of this, everything we have done, our rebellion against our own kind, is to stop this travesty from happening again. We don't believe what the government and Starbuilders have done—what we have done—to people like you is right. I know you have your reservations, but I want you to be on our side, because we are on yours."

"This is bad thing that you say you did, that Starbuilders did, before you arrived," Nothaar summarized in recollection of their earliest encounter.

"Yes, yes it is," Ifu confessed. "And there's no way for us to stop and reverse the process. Once initiated on your planet, the progression immediately became irreversible. Like I told you when we first met: it's too late to save the world you knew prior to the *Sky Shift*. Despite that, I believe, and Syraaq believes, that you can play a pivotal role in ensuring this repulsive act never happens again."

Chapter 24

"So that be it," Nothaar whimpered, ignoring Ifu's offer of cooperation. "This is end of Nothaar's people. We go, as you say, extinct."

"Not exactly," Syraaq contended. "Yes, your physical and internal structures will change. There is no doubt that your future generations will be similar to us *Commons* in all those phenotypes like size and skin tone, but not all of us are completely the same. You picked up on it when you decoded our names: your culture will survive. It's why we take such painstaking efforts to avoid contaminating your communities and to let you become whatever it is you will be without our influence. Even when your people are able to travel to outer space on their own and join the greater interstellar community of *Commons*, your unique society will live on, just as it has for our homeworlds."

"Will really be us?" Nothaar wondered aloud. "I observe that *Commons* think differently. Using brain that way will change who we be."

"You have been exposed to an extremely minimal sample size of two," Ifu reprimanded. "That's hardly enough to draw any conclusions from. You're way too bright to believe otherwise. Besides, even Syraaq and I are outliers. While there is a certain... set of instructions in our genetics that makes us risk adverse and more compliant in order to better assure the potential of sustaining life, it's not expressed the same in everyone. Heck, some *Commons* are downright lacking it, even within entire planets. Despite the seeding of this world, there is still natural genetic drift."

"There what?" Nothaar questioned.

"What Ifu is saying," Syraaq explained, "is that the genetic code and replication of it is not a seamless process. Specifically, it is not copied from parents to their children perfectly; things tend to go a little awry."

"Yes," Ifu concurred, "and the government and Starbuilders constantly try to reset everything back to baseline. Still, there are always differences that cannot be fully controlled or accounted for, especially when you are talking about trillions of individual beings. That is why you see that even Syraaq and I can have different viewpoints but still both be insurrectionists against our own kind. No, while you couldn't call it true adaptation and evolution, it's still variance."

There was silence then, except for the crackling of the fire. After a while, Nothaar chimed in by asking, "What about the *Lingua*? Still no explain how that works."

"It's really much the same," Syraaq claimed. "There's a lot you can do with genetic encoding—if you know how. Since our people have long ago mastered it, we were able to actually program the entirety of the *Lingua* into our very essences. We come out of the womb already knowing the *Lingua*, even when we cannot express it."

"What about new words?" Nothaar challenged. "Find unknown thing, make new tool, going to need new term to describe it."

"I will admit," Syraaq began, "that stuff like that is quite difficult for us. We don't really have a good mechanism to teach language since there is generally no need to do so in a formal setting."

"Really, though," Ifu added, "we would just seed the word through a genetic update to all *Commons*. As you might imagine, it will take hundreds of years to roll something like that out, but in cosmic terms, that is barely any time at all."

"It never ends, then," Nothaar lamented. "Over time, Starbuilders always be manipulating people, changing them into what they want."

Syraaq looked away before divulging, "You're not wrong, and I, sadly, have been a part of that machine for a long, long while. Somehow Ifu opened my eyes to the horrors and terrors of what we do... did. I'm not sure why I was never able to see it before. Maybe it was my own wiring that simply broke down with age and normal degradation? *Commons* have barely changed at all in countless millennia simply because we are incapable of it."

"Our genetic alterations have hamstrung us from ever transforming, progressing, and growing," Ifu added, "and, most importantly, finding new solutions to our much larger problem: the heat death of the universe. Without diversity, there is no chance that we will be able to overcome basic universal physics."

"It takes a lot to push us out of our comfort zone," Syraaq continued. "We need to be shaken up. You, Nothaar, can be that impetus. You are the proof that we should not be converting life into us, but should allow it to flourish and come into its own. An array of potentialities is the most likely key to our collective survival."

"You always talk about yourselves and your needs," Nothaar spat. "But you people almost forever been *Commons*. Cannot help with transition. How my kind be able to exist in such a different... universe?"

"Actually," Syraaq corrected, "it is not a cut and run operation. Yes, the Starbuilders do try to leave you alone to develop as a unique society, but they return at regular intervals to check in on you and make adjustments. For instance, your planet's rotation cycle time is slightly off of the *Common*'s standard, and it has been messing with Ifu's and my sleeping patterns, what we call circadian rhythm. These figures need to be exact for *Common* physiology, so the Starbuilders will return to speed up or slow down your axial revolution as needed."

"How can do that?" Nothaar solicited. "Cannot just have giant automata use hands to spin world. Now I know likely size that planet must be and that no ship can be so big that it be larger than planet. Things get that big, collapse under own gravity, turn into balls."

"There are a number of ways," Syraaq expounded, "depending upon what's right for the situation. Asteroids could be thrown towards the planet at an oblique angle, giant engines could be installed, whatever works. That is part of the job and there are people who specialize in figuring out and implementing the best and least destructive solutions. They could even use a Quantu—"

"That's not the only thing Starbuilders have to consider," Ifu suddenly interrupted. "Remember before when we talked about the length of a year? Well, Starbuilders will also adjust your orbit to get it closer to standard. And as Syraaq was alluding to earlier, they are going to be back to check the progress of their genetic updates and drop further seedings to help things along. They won't let your species die out during the conversion process; they'll make sure that your people are prepared for what's to come."

"If Starbuilders make genetic update," Nothaar attempted, "cannot we do same, annul what done?"

"What would that accomplish?" Ifu refuted. "Even if we had the means—which we do not—they could just as easily come back and override what we had done. No, the only way this ends is if they agree to it themselves, if our government decides to set out on a whole new path."

"And you see no way to stop them?" Nothaar pleaded as a last resort. "Even using force, weapons? Cannot change Nothaar people if no can be here."

"Against that much power?" Ifu contended. "No, none of us would stand the slightest chance. Are you thinking that you could unite everyone in your world and mount some sort of counteroffensive? Or that we could recruit other *Commons* to this noble cause? Well, we have some ancient fiction stories like that, too, ones that tell tales of little backwater planets like yours being able to topple galactic empires. Unfortunately, that's not how this society and government works. Besides, if your people were really a problem, Starbuilders could easily erase your entire world from existence without needing to come anywhere remotely nearby themselves. It's been done before, to my understanding."

"Stop scaring Nothaar!" Syraaq demanded. "Nothaar, life is far too precious to do anything like that nowadays. In all my long existence, I've never seen anything close to that happening. Starbuilders believe in a deliberate and hands-off methodology. If they found a species showing aggressive or antiestablishment tendencies, they would probably just introduce a genetic update to make the people more docile and open-minded. I mean, on the whole, that is; individual aberration will always exist. Still, a subtle change in mindset would propagate through the populous over thousands of years until it became a dominant trait. No, there is no realistic way of impeding the Starbuilders with violence or rebellion of any kind. As Ifu just stated, the only way to make a difference is to do so from the inside.

"Nothaar, we want to get you in front of the government so that they can hear what you have to say. Like we've been telling you: it's far too late to stop or change the course and fate of your world. But with your assistance, we can ensure that it will be the last one that has to go through this."

"I wonder," Nothaar probed, "how much you still agree with Starbuilders? Syraaq, you say you work for them for almost entire lifetime, Ifu much the same for shorter span. Had to have impact on beliefs, even if do not like some specific actions."

"Fair enough," Syraaq allowed. "There are certain things that we are proponents of. We believe in the overall mission of trying to save and preserve life, and to bring all sapient peoples together. The universe is vast and mostly empty, and only becoming more so. There is no way we can abandon a species like yours to struggle alone in some dark corner of the cosmos, to live out your existence without the benefit of ever knowing there are others like yourselves out there. Our *Archive* is full of examples of what ensues when a spacefaring culture reaches a certain milestone in their technological development but cannot find any signs of other life."

"What happens?" Nothaar probed.

"They all die," Syraaq forlornly noted.

Chapter 25

Feeling a hand on his shoulder, Nothaar turned around and found Syraaq standing slightly behind him with her arm outstretched. "Still feeling seasick?" she asked with a twinge of concern in her voice.

"No, not anymore," Nothaar assured her. "I have gotten somewhat used to it. Being far out at sea is certainly considerably different than fishing within sight of the shoreline, though."

Syraaq used the *Common*'s gesture for appreciative understanding and joined Nothaar at the yacht's upper-deck portside railing. "It's been a long, long time since I've been able to enjoy the sweet salt air of the open ocean," she confessed. "Most of my life has been spent between worlds, living and working on a spaceship of one kind or another. This... what has it been... a year and a half or more now that I've been on your planet? I can honestly say that I'm not looking forward to it coming to an end."

"Do not worry," Nothaar assuaged her. "*Eh-aye* thinks it will be another seven or eight cycles of the moon until we reach our destination."

With a bemused expression, Syraaq nonchalantly dismissed Nothaar's comment and instead responded, "Let's teach you a new word in the *Lingua*. Instead of constantly saying 'cycles of the moon', you can call each one a 'month'. Technically speaking, a month is a couple of days longer than the entire timeframe from one full moon to another. Nevertheless, for all practical purposes, and my sanity, they're the same thing."

"Noted," Nothaar acquiesced. It was hardly the first new terminology Nothaar had picked up over the ensuing interval between delivering the plans for their ocean transport and casting off from the shores of the only land he had ever known. He now felt much more comfortable and confident when speaking the *Lingua*, and had even begun to shift his internal voice into the language of the *Commons*. "Then it will be seven or eight... months... until we make landfall at this island of the *Space Elevator*."

"You know what, Nothaar?" Syraaq proposed. "You will be the first of your kind to ever set foot on that particular piece of real estate. You should give it a proper name, one based on your own native tongue."

"What would be the point?" Nothaar bemoaned. "I will be the only one of my people to ever hear the name. They will never know that I was there, nor would they be able to speak the words. Whoever 'discovers' this island in the future will surely only speak the *Lingua* and, as such, will give it a name more soothing to your own ears."

Something sparkled in Syraaq's eyes as she claimed, "That's not completely true. On my homeworld, many cities and ancient structures still bear their original nomenclature, or at least something pretty close to it. As you observed when we first met, Ifu and I have monickers that are not based on the *Lingua*, either. Despite the fact that your people haven't even figured out how to implement proper sanitation yet, they will still leave behind an unusually large document trove. Given that, I'm absolutely positive that some future archeologist will eventually come along to rediscover and reconstruct your historical tongue. And assuming that is going to happen, then we should leave that person a little... gift."

"A gift?" Nothaar inquired. "What is going on in that batty old mind of yours?

Syraaq darted her eyeballs left and right and then turned around. After seeming to confirm that they were indeed alone, she whispered in a conspiratorial tone, "This has to stay between us, you got it?"

Nothaar paused for a moment before stating the unsaid obvious implications, "Ah, so Ifu would not approve, huh? In that case, I am quite interested to hear your idea."

Laughing, Syraaq continued, "Among many cultures, including my own, we have a tradition called a 'time capsule'. What we do is make a box that is impermeable to water or anything else that might be detrimental to its contents. Once we place whatever items we choose inside of it, we bury it to be found by some yet-to-come generation. It's almost like a type of immortality; a way to say hello to those who we would otherwise never meet and tell them who we were, what we did, and why they should care. Some think of it as a way to say to them that, for a brief moment, we mattered."

"You just entomb this 'time capsule' in a random spot

and hope someone accidentally comes across it someday?" Nothaar asked, completely flabbergasted.

"Not exactly," Syraaq admitted. "Usually, they are placed somewhere important and/or obvious, such as in the cornerstone of a new building or underneath a statue. A statue, by the way, is a work of art tha—"

"I have learned about statues," Nothaar interrupted. "No need to go into detail."

"Look how far you've come!" Syraaq clapped with joy. "Not just in your fluency of the *Lingua*, of course, but with how much you've absorbed from the *Archive*. Well, in that case, let's get back to time capsules. As I was saying, in a lot of cases, there are explicit instructions on when they should be opened."

"We would not have the luxury of directing anyone to a specific location or proposing a date for them to retrieve the package," Nothaar lamented. "How would someone even know to look for it?"

"My thought is this," Syraaq explained. "There are certain areas that someone trying to understand the past would be more likely to explore and want to excavate. Since we can take an educated guess on where that would be, we can put the time capsule right in their conjectural path! And can you imagine their face when they find this box made of obviously futuristic technology and filled with ancient writing? You could even leave a translation matrix from your tongue into the *Lingua*. It would be the discovery of a lifetime for some poor sap who would have to come up with some theory for how any of this was possible and be forced to prove that it was not just a hoax!" Syraaq couldn't continue as she started cackling at the hilarity of her own proposal.

"Oh, a practical joke then," Nothaar summarized. "It is... what was that term Ifu used? Ah yes, very 'on brand' for you."

Wiping her eyes, Syraaq declared, "The best humor also comes wrapped in truth and deeper meaning. Yes, it would be completely hilarious, but it's also a chance for you to say your goodbyes. Nothaar, you'll never be able to return to your own homeworld."

"I know that already!" Nothaar snapped. Immediately regretting raising his voice, Nothaar contritely added, "Sorry, my tone was uncalled for. I suppose I have been thinking about that fact quite a bit recently myself."

"Do you want to talk about it?" Syraaq queried.

There was no way for Nothaar to know if Syraaq sincerely cared and wanted to help unburden him or not, but it did not matter to him, anyway. Instead, he replied, "No, thank you. What I would rather know is this: how will we ensure that this box of yours is able to survive the ravages of time?"

Examining Syraaq's face, Nothaar recognized the look of incredulousness in the manner of the *Commons*. "You doubt that we have such capabilities?" she challenged.

Reviewing what he'd learned about the *Commons* in general—and Syraaq and Ifu specifically—over the last nine or so months that had gone into building their yacht, Nothaar was quite sure that if they thought it was possible, then he had no reason to doubt that it was so. Although Nothaar had been convinced that it would take at least a year to build their sea vessel, Ifu and Syraaq had labored tirelessly to come up with creative ways to speed up the process. Among the heretical acts they partook in was using their advanced tools to actually fell and prepare trees while the harvesters were away. Additionally, they drilled a hole to access fresh water—what they called a 'well'—near the reaping site, thus making it possible for the people from the village near the equator to not need to carry as much liquid with them. With less encumbrances, their hired hands could stay in the area longer and do more of the necessary groundwork.

Regrettably, Nothaar had some difficulty explaining how these amazing happenings were being undertaken without anyone noticing. He made ridiculous claims about having other teams of people out there doing specific tasks; that they were all working together, but separately. The harvesters wondered how it was possible that they never once came across these mysterious helpers, but Nothaar made excuses and invoked his status as a *Keeper of the Knowledge* and all its secret wisdom. That excuse did not work with the local *Keeper*, though, and their relationship became extremely strained.

While it did not matter to Ifu and Syraaq, the situation with his fellow *Keeper* was quite concerning for Nothaar. Because Ifu and Syraaq—most likely more so the latter—were willing to bend their own rules and risk some cultural contamination, the project took much less time than

Nothaar had hoped to have to spend on his own goals. In turn, he had been unable to make as many copies of his *Opus on the Language of Children* as he had originally planned. More importantly, his chilly relationship with the village's *Keeper* made him concerned about the fully completed editions ever getting into the hands of those who needed them. Nothaar's entire scheme was dependent upon everyone playing their role, and he was no longer confident that his own desires would still be executed by those he had entrusted his life's work to. He felt that everything he had sacrificed, nonetheless everyone he had abandoned, might all have been in vain. Dejected, Nothaar recognized the unfortunate truth that he most likely would never know the outcome.

Since he couldn't express any of his trepidations to Syraaq, Nothaar instead verbalized, "I suppose you must have some decent notion, otherwise you would not have offered. Very well, we shall make this time capsule that you recommend. I can see the value in it... and the humor."

"Well, when you put it that way," Syraaq mocked, "it doesn't sound very funny at all!"

Plastering on a false expression of amusement that Syraaq had sincerely used on him many times in the past, Nothaar attempted to project a jovial mood as the two companions continued to chit-chat and toss around potential names for their island destination. Eventually, though, his old worries bubbled to the surface and Nothaar admitted that he had been feeling quite perturbed.

"What are you so annoyed about?" Syraaq delved.

"Like you said," Nothaar expounded, "we have been together for a year and a half or more, and yet I am still barely any closer to the truth."

"You've got to give me more than that," Syraaq prodded. "Tell me what it is that you need to know so badly."

Taking the opportunity presented to him, Nothaar announced, "You promised me that once we were out at sea, you would finally explain the reason behind what Starbuilders do. I am tired of waiting, and I am completely done with all the subterfuge. What has been done to my world, my people, my children?"

"You already know that," Syraaq curtly countered.

"And you know what I mean!" Nothaar immediately retorted. "I am not talking about the hows and whys of genetic manipulation. What I need to understand is: what is the secret behind the *Sky Shift*? What has happened, and how was it done?"

"Oh," Syraaq managed. "I see. Well, I guess our nice day in the sun together, just enjoying this sea breeze, has come to an abrupt end. Let's go below deck and find Ifu; this is going to take a lot of... well, everything... for you to understand, and I don't have enough energy at my age to do it on my own."

Chapter 26

"Oh, geez!" Ifu complained. "We have to explain how the entirety of the *Commons* society, infrastructure, and methodologies work? Right now?"

"Yes!" Syraaq pushed back. "Why, do you have something better to do? As far as I can tell, we're all just basically doing nothing while we wait for this floating bucket to get us somewhere new."

After several more moments spent grumbling, Ifu finally conceded with, "Fine, fine. Gather around, everyone, and I'll try to make quantum physics as crystal clear as possible to a being whose people haven't even invented the wheel yet!"

"You know very well that my people have had wheels for thousands of years," Nothaar corrected Ifu.

"It's called 'hyperbole', Nothaar," Ifu rejoined. "You can ask the *Eh-aye* about it later. For now, just stop taking everything I say so literally and personally!"

"Enough you two!" Syraaq intervened in an apparent attempt to stop the brewing argument between her companions. "I can't handle all of your male hormones constantly getting in the way of us having an agreeable, harmonious time aboard this ship."

Nothaar caught Ifu using his righteous glare towards

Syraaq, and then Syraaq completely disarming him by brushing it off. *Syraaq is obviously not intimidated by Ifu,* Nothaar thought, *and, as such, there is no way for him to bully her like he can do to me. I wonder if it has always been that way, or if things have changed between them over time? From what I have been able to glean, I do not think this is how Syraaq imagined her later years going.*

Once they were all seated around a table in the galley, Ifu began tapping the surface in front of him with his fingers and rhetorically asked, "Where to begin?"

"I believe gravity is a good starting point," Syraaq accommodatingly offered despite Nothaar estimating that Ifu hadn't really asked her.

"We have already discussed gravity in some detail," Nothaar countered. "Plus, the *Eh-aye* has also helped me learn a great deal about it. For instance, I am aware of the analogy of the fabric of space-time, and how gravity is really the bending of that sheet."

"That's actually rather useful," Ifu cheered. "It gives us a reasonable place to begin. Syraaq is right; gravity will be the best way to broach this topic."

"If you say so..." Nothaar trailed off, not interested in receiving a lecture on something he felt he had a pretty decent handle on.

Seemingly picking up on Nothaar's dismissal, Ifu contended, "Okay, smart guy, tell us what would happen if someone shoved another sun in the exact same location where your central star sits?"

Harumphing at the easy question, Nothaar answered,

"Gravity dictates that they would orbit each other in closer and closer spirals until they merged, bringing their masses together in the same area. Sometimes this amalgamation might just make a bigger sun, other times it may result in just a denser and hotter one."

"Alright," Ifu conceded, "but what would happen if we kept sending more solar bodies toward it? How big and/or dense could a single sun get?"

"There... there would be no limit..." Nothaar unassuredly responded. He realized that he had not considered that there could be an upper threshold.

"Just to check," Ifu interposed, "you do know that the more gravity pulls on you, the slower you will move and the more energy you will need to escape its grasp, right?"

"Of course," Nothaar assuaged, much more confident in this line of reasoning. "It is like rocketry. One would need more power to escape a planet with more gravity."

"But what about light?" Ifu challenged.

"Pardon?" Nothaar asked, looking for clarification.

Syraaq decided to enter the fray by explaining, "Nothaar, as you're well aware, light has a finite speed, and therefore the same can be said about its energy."

"Wait," Nothaar tried to gain a moment to think. "Be... are you implying that there is a point when gravity is so strong, that light would be stuck inside, like a bottomless pit of some kind?"

"A black hole," Syraaq responded. "That's what we call it. Not only are they real, but they're also one of the most populous celestial objects left in the entire universe.

Someday, when all the other remaining stars are gone and we are deep in the *Degenerate Age*, they will still be there. No, they won't be shining brightly because they can't. Instead, they will continue to suck up anything that happens to cross their paths, including each other. This will go on for trillions multiplied by trillions of years, if that term would truly have the same meaning by that point."

"And this... era of black holes..." Nothaar attempted, "it will go on and on forever, until everything becomes just one big black hole?"

"Not exactly," Ifu corrected, "But you have stumbled upon an important aspect. Eventually, even black holes can evaporate back out to the greater universe. At least, that is what we think based upon the mathematics. It's all very complicated and so far out into the future that it almost makes no difference. However, more pertinent to our conversation, yes, black holes can get extremely large, what we have termed supermassive."

"Okay," Nothaar acquiesced, "You obviously know about these things better than I do, so I will defer to your experience on this. That said, I am still not sure why it is relevant to the purpose of Starbuilders."

"Patience," Ifu recommended. "We are working our way there."

"Fine, fine," Nothaar flippantly discharged.

Ifu stared at Nothaar for a moment longer. Nothaar thought he could almost see Ifu calculating in his head whether it was worth his time to continue, but eventually he elected to do so. "The math tells us something else, too.

A supermassive black hole could, theoretically, host in its orbit tens—if not hundreds—of thousands of worlds that are the correct size and mass to host life. By these estimations, the planets could also circle around it at a distance of up to ten light-years out. That way, spherical bodies could be spread out so that some would be relatively close to each other while most would be light-years away."

"Can you imagine it?" Syraaq added. "Having two planets that are orbiting ten light-years from the center of a supermassive black hole, but on opposite sides. Even if you could travel near the speed of light, you cannot go through a celestial object with that much of a gravity well; you have to go around. Thus, it's not twenty light-years in a straight line, but more like thirty to fifty light-years to get there, depending upon the path you'd be forced to take to avoid running into any of the other globes."

Quite confused by this hypothetical situation, Nothaar probed, "But what would be the point? Life needs light to survive and thrive. I could have told you that even before I met you and learned about the *Commons*. Simply, if there was no light because it cannot escape the black hole, then the planets would just die."

Contorting his face in what Nothaar had come to recognize as happy superiority, Ifu announced, "It's almost like you would need to... Build... A... Star..."

"Build a star?" Nothaar repeated. "Why would someone need to..."

Nothaar abandoned the rest of his sentence as his mind took off in every direction. He couldn't make sense of any of it; there was just too much that he did not understand about how the universe functioned. Despite his intensive studies, he was still coming to the subject from far behind. The *Commons* had access to this data and information from their earliest formative years. In contrast, Nothaar felt that he might as well have been living in a cave for the thirty-five years he had lived on the planet before meeting them. Comparatively, he realized, in many ways he had been doing just that. Suddenly, the gap between the extraterrestrials and himself began to feel humbling, and he recognized that Ifu had every reason to feel the way he seemed to. The truth Nothaar had not been wanting to admit to himself because of his own personality clashes with the off-worlders became clear: they really were superior, at least in their knowhow.

Bowing his head in defeat, Nothaar whispered, "Starbuilders, that is what you said you were. I have not paid enough attention or thought about it plainly. You do more than just live and survive in this universe; you are actively involved in its construction. Though *thou art mortal*, you still take on the job of the gods to rewrite the heavens.

"Please, I would be grateful if you would tell me how."

Chapter 27

"There's no need for that," Syraaq assuaged. "Raise your head up high! True wisdom is recognizing what you don't know. Hubris is trying to compensate for a lack of knowledge by claiming there is no more to be had. Perhaps, now, you are ready to listen and not fight?"

"I am," Nothaar kowtowed. "You are correct: I was not predisposed towards hearing your and Ifu's words before. Today, though, I am beginning to appreciate just what a drop in the ocean my understanding has been. I promise you, I am finally prepared to just take heed."

"Good," Syraaq allowed. "In that case, Ifu, how would you like to proceed?"

After a thoughtful moment, Ifu answered, "I believe we need to go back to propulsion, first."

"I agree," Syraaq acquiesced while Nothaar said nothing, letting the *Commons* come at the problem—one that was encapsulated by him—in their own way.

"There are two ways to move in the universe," Ifu began. "The first is with propulsion. This ship we are on, we are using the wind energy to move us across the surface of the ocean. Before, in our vehicle, we used power from the sun to turn the wheels and push us forward. You are aware of rockets and how much force is necessary for them to overcome gravity and get off a planet. These are all examples of propulsion.

"In the same vein, even Torch Ships use propulsion. What we have not been clear with you in the past is just what these vessels do. In outer space, in the interstellar medium between large celestial bodies, the effects of gravity are so small that you and everything else would appear to be floating; rather uncontrollably, I might add. If you took one of those rockets beyond the edge of your sky—something the descendants of the people populating your world will most likely do in the future—once it's just a little bit beyond the confines of the planet, everyone would look like they were swimming through the air. In reality, they would actually be falling back towards the ground, but the rate would be so slow that it would make no difference whatsoever and could be easily overcome. Remember, gravity is weaker the further you get from the center of an object. As such, we call this state 'being in microgravity'. Some call it *zero-gee*, but that's not accurate, and I want to be precise for you. I've been made aware that unintentional inaccuracy in the name of expedience has been a disrupting issue in our conversations."

"I appreciate it," Nothaar claimed. "Please, go on."

"Very well," Ifu accepted Nothaar's entreaties. "The way a Torch Drive Ship works is by constantly increasing its speed to simulate *one-gee* on board. The methodologies to make this happen are far outside my purview, but from what I do understand, the ship needs an exact course because halfway through it has to flip around and start breaking in reverse, thus creating the same feeling of downward pressure for its occupants. That's not exactly what is happening technically, it's more like the floor coming up to meet a person, but that is how our sensory organs interpret the sensation.

"Those velocities, though, cause something else to change. What happens is that the perception and reality of time elapsing extends in a way that is not obvious to the occupants of the ship. The strange truth is that the faster you go, the slower time moves. Even if someone were to travel fifty light-years on a Torch Ship, those aboard would only experience..." Ifu suddenly paused as his eyes and face betrayed that he had slipped into the virtual realm that Nothaar could not see or access—or, frankly, could comprehend. Nothaar guessed that Ifu wanted to consult with the *Eh-aye* on something, most likely to solve some equation.

After a brief interlude, Ifu continued as if he had never stopped, "... less than eight years themselves. So even though more than fifty years would have passed outside the ship, only eight happened inside the vessel. In as basic of a way as I can explain this concept, time depends upon where you are looking from. This is what we call the 'observer effect'. Where the so-called observer happens to be and how fast they are moving determines how many years they experience between events.

"That is also part of the reason why years have far less meaning to people like Syraaq and myself. We've spent considerable portions of our lives being propelled by Torch

Drive technology. Due to this, the number of years we have been alive do not correlated with the total number of years that have passed on our homeworlds, at least not as far as an observer who has never left there would reckon. This is what is known as 'time dilation'."

"I will admit," Nothaar disclosed, "that this is a lot to take in, and I am having trouble wrapping by brain around all of it. These are concepts that are so far outside my experience that I am not sure I will ever be able to fully grasp the basics of what you are telling me."

"Do not beat yourself up too harshly," Syraaq intervened. "Most *Commons* never leave their own planets, and therefore have not had to go through and deal with all the consequences of traveling across the universe. Almost none of them make the necessary effort to absorb this information and contemplate the ramifications. We'll happily go over the finer details with you again and again. Be proud of what you have understood to this point, and we'll build upon it later."

"Okay, I will try," Nothaar conceded, although he was no longer sure if he could. He was feeling completely overwhelmed, but did not want to stop Ifu since he was being so open and amiable with him.

Right on cue, Ifu spoke again with no preamble, "So that is one way to go about getting places. The universe, though, is unbelievably large. Honestly, we cannot really tell how big it is, but estimates range from hundreds of billions to trillions of light-years across. The physics start to break down if you want to traverse that distance the traditional way."

"Traditional?" Nothaar prodded. "Propulsion, I suppose, is really the 'old' method of doing things, then?"

"I wouldn't put it that way, exactly," Ifu disagreed. "It has its purposes, and I'll get to that shortly. First, though, I want to tell you about how we Starbuilders have been able to cross these vast, unfathomable distances and discover worlds like yours."

Remaining silent, Nothaar anxiously awaited the answer as Ifu appeared to be gathering his thoughts. Finally, Ifu attempted, "Nothaar, this is going to be the most difficult concept yet, so I'm going to try to keep it as simple and high-level as possible for now. One thing you need to understand is that there are two things we could call reality. One is the universe at the level we experience it, with all its rules and what we could boil down to one idea: causality. You do an action and there is a reaction to it. As strange and sometimes crazy as the results may be, there are solid and dependable laws that we can write guidebooks about to explain these deterministic results. However, there is a realm far below our own that we can barely see with even the most advanced tools."

"You mean like the microscopic domain, with the nanobots and the generic packages?" Nothaar quizzed.

"No," Ifu corrected, "far tinier than that. Do you remember what we talked about with the elements, how water is made up of hydrogen and oxygen?"

"Yes," Nothaar recollected. "I also recall that oxygen is the element that we all need to breathe."

"That's correct," Ifu conciliated, "but even elements are made out of different sub-components. And some of those parts consist of other even smaller pieces. Eventually, though, you will get down far enough that you will be at a layer known as the quantum."

"That is definitely a new word for me," Nothaar admitted. "It has not come up during my lessons with the *Eh-aye* at all."

"I'm not surprised," Ifu noted. "This type of science is the part where most people just give up on trying to follow it fully. You see, within the quantum realm—for lack of a better descriptor—everything that works up here completely breaks down. For this discussion, the only thing that's important is to highlight that you could not definitively say a quantum particle is in a particular place. These quantum particles exist on a probability spectrum, and this range extends throughout the entire universe. It's only when we witness the particles that they pick an extant position. When we look away, they go back to being potentially everywhere at once."

"I am... not sure I understand," Nothaar confessed.

"Don't worry about it for now," Syraaq counseled. "Let Ifu take you the rest of the way, then we'll come back here later. I promise, this is not the last you'll hear about this."

Once Nothaar gave the *Common*'s gesture for agreement, Ifu did just as Syraaq suggested. "Here's the thing: the arithmetic says that any quantum particle will most likely be exactly where we expect it. In other words, you are precisely where you are because the quantum particles that you are ultimately made out of are collapsing their probabilities to say that this location is where they belong. That all said, there is a non-zero chance of making any single one of them appear anywhere else in the universe. We call this phenomenon a Quantum Shift. The plainest way to put this is that we have a technology that allows us to perform Quantum Shifts at will."

"By that logic," Nothaar summarized, "then you could appear anywhere in the universe instantly. Why, then, would you bother with *Space Elevators* and Torch Ships? Why are we on this journey at all? Could you not just perform a Quantum Shift to your homeworld?"

"That's not how it works," Ifu contested. "Very specialized equipment is necessary—technology that is highly controlled. Even among our own kind, access to information on how a Quantum Shift functions is extremely contained. I mean that up to and including at the genetic level. We have coding that prevents us from being able to properly learn how to use and implement it. The only way around this is to have a deliberate modification made to your genetic programming. Even trying to hack your own genes can result in death if not done properly. At the same time, the nanobots we all carry in our bloodstream are on the lookout for such attempts, and will attack if they detect such an event.

"To be very clear, that is how serious our government takes this potential threat: that they are willing to kill another *Common* without so much as a trial or a review of the facts first. Uncontrolled familiarity and access to

Quantum Shift technology would be incredibly dangerous. Someone with nefarious intentions could easily destroy a planet, a star, even a supermassive black hole. Due to these possibilities, there are also laws, even for those who have the proper approvals. One of those is that we do not perform a Quantum Shift within one light-year of any celestial body... except under specific circumstances that I'll get to later. For now, though, just be aware that the grand vessel we were on before we left in the stolen Torch Ship, that was what is known as a Quantum Ship. But a Quantum Ship is still just a Torch Ship, only with the additional capability of performing a Quantum Shift.

"But that's just the beginning! There's so much more we can do with Quantum Shift technology, and therein lies the real reason we are known as Starbuilders."

CHAPTER 28

Although Nothaar was feeling queasy at just the idea of potentially destroying whole worlds full of life with a mere execution of some incomprehensible, abstract technology, he did not interrupt Ifu's train of thought. Instead, he remained silent so that Ifu would continue to reveal the details behind the secrets of the Starbuilders. He could almost sense that they were about to hit the crescendo of that enigma.

Whether he noticed Nothaar's internal struggle or not, Ifu barreled ahead with his explanation around Quantum Shifts and how they were implemented. "On our Quantum Ships, what we do is jump a large distance and start mapping anything our sensors can see for hundreds of thousands of light-years in all directions. Of course, we have to keep moving to simulate gravity, so hopefully we have somewhere noteworthy to head towards. Nowadays, though, these waypoints are fewer and further between. Even within Syraaq's lifetime, she's noted a decline in useful discoveries."

"That's anecdotal," Syraaq corrected. "The Starbuilders' fleet is massive, so I can only speak from my own experiences. Besides, putting it that way makes me sound even more ancient than I feel."

Ifu giggled a bit at Syraaq's quip before continuing, "The mapping process is usually done just to give us an idea of where to head towards next. If we detect a sign that there is possibly something of interest out in the ether, then we jump towards it and start the mapping process all over again. Rinse and repeat this same set of instructions ad nauseum until we come upon something worthwhile."

"What would be considered 'worthwhile'?" Nothaar interrupted, wanting to make sure he understood.

"Well," Ifu responded, "you know that we are looking for planets that contain life, especially sapient life. To be fair, the way we do it, it's like looking for a single grain of sand across an entire solar system, but it really is the best method we have. We are fanning out in every direction possible—at least, given the limits of the resources available to us. Even though there are an extremely large number of *Commons* compared to your own kind, we can only build and staff so many Quantum Ships. There are logistical limits to what we're capable of.

"That all said, Nothaar, we don't just care about worlds like yours. Sometimes there are planets that already host life, but do not have anything even remotely approaching sapient. Other times, there are globes that seem to have almost every indicator necessary to sprout living beings, but for some reason do not. In either case, we can reappropriate those worlds for our own purposes. A planet lacking sapient life can be reprogrammed the same as yours has been, making it suitable for *Commons*. Should it be a baren place, we can undertake a process called 'terraforming' in which we make subsisting possible. Let it be known that this is not the ideal solution. On these empty rocks that we terraform, it's a constant struggle for life to maintain its tenuous hold; it's much better if life arises naturally on its own without interference. Still, the *Common's* population is constantly expanding. As such, we must have other planets at the ready where we can export our excess populace. A single ball can only hold so many people comfortably without causing the complete wrecking of its environment."

"It's fair to note," Syraaq interposed, "that we're not always looking for planets that can harbor life and serve our purposes that way. Oftentimes, we just need metals, molecules, and other such resources. We will harvest these useful celestial objects to get what we need to continue to support our society and the efforts of the Starbuilders and groups like them. Acquiring reserves from wherever we can find them is a big part of the job!"

"Quite so," Ifu agreed. "Another thing we do is drop off and pick up communication buoys and probes. Nothaar, I can see your confusion already. You can think of them as automata that are created to send messages across the vast distances of outer space. After all, while out on missions, we do need to be able to send and receive reports and orders from home. If we put these out using traditional means, it would take billions of years at the fairly limited speed of light. But with a Quantum Ship, we can cut that down to just a few years, or at least decades."

"Thank you for clarifying," Nothaar offered.

"My pleasure," Ifu beamed. When combining Ifu's elated response to this show of appreciation with his earlier reaction to Nothaar's prostrating, Nothaar sensed a pattern was emerging. He quickly recognized that stroking Ifu's ego with compliments and groveling made the *Common* much more accommodating and palatable to be around. While Nothaar was coming to accept his own shortcomings compared to Ifu, Syraaq, and the rest of their ilk that were out there in the greater universe, it did not mean he was willing to relinquish his personal struggle for freedom. However, knowing that day would not come any time soon, Nothaar resolved to use techniques like these ones more often in order to make his protracted captivity be as comfortable as possible. At the same time, Nothaar admonished himself for letting his own temperament get in the way of doing so sooner. He was determined not to let his emotions get the better of him any longer.

"But this is where we can return to the question of Quantum Shift application," Ifu proffered. "We don't just find these things, Nothaar; we take them with us. We relocate whole planets with their single moons—one of the requirements for a life-bearing world—out of their native solar systems and into the orbit of a supermassive black hole, one that all *Commons* live around and call home. We have made our last stand against a dying universe by gathering all sapient life there. Long ago, the earliest *Commons* decided that it would be best if all remaining sapient beings were close together, otherwise we'd never be able to interact with each other on a regular basis; certainly not in a universe this big, dispersed, and empty."

"Wait right there!" Nothaar franticly insisted. "Are you saying we are in orbit of the *Common's* supermassive black hole right now? That we left my home solar system and are now within yours?"

"That's correct," Syraaq gently answered. "That was the *Sky Shift* you observed more than twenty years ago. The stars above your head appeared to change because they actually did. You and your planet are deeply embedded in the realm of the *Commons* now."

"That does not make any sense, though," Nothaar argued. "It is like I highlighted before: if a black hole truly traps all light within itself as you previously detailed, then how can life continue to exist? Why do I see the sun overhead even now? How come, since the *Sky Shift*, it has continued to rise and set each and every day?"

"Great set of questions, and ones I was just about to get to," Ifu claimed. "You see, although we permanently moved your planet to be within the *Common's* system, we wouldn't actually transfer your sun here—or anywhere, for that matter. Stars like yours, Nothaar, are the real prize, the greatest treasure, and we are very wary of doing anything that might upset them. You have no idea how few of your class of stellar object still exist, and how infrequently they form innately nowadays."

"In case you're wondering," Syraaq interjected, "we've tried, unsuccessfully, to forcibly produce stars that match our criteria. I mean, not us personally; those attempts were last made long, long ago. The point is, things did not go well. I'll get into the reasons some other day, though. I'm sure we'll have the opportunity to go into depth about it, but it would be better if we could connect to a more complete edition of the *Archive* so I could show you the videos and data."

"Then we will set it aside for some future date," Nothaar agreed.

After signaling his concurrence by performing the *Common's* motion for accord, Ifu recommenced, "For life to flourish, it needs a very specific output of energy from a star at a highly specific distance. Unfortunately, stars that align to these conditions have a relatively short life, usually around ten billion years or so. Yet even that is not quite right because later in their existences they are no longer life-giving entities, but instead become destroyers. In reality, the useful window is only about seven or eight billion years."

"The suns of our homeworlds," Syraaq added, "expired long ago, many billions if not trillions of years before your star was even born. In order for our worlds to maintain their presence, we must have the light and energy of suns like yours to regularly replace the ones that are lost."

"How is that possible?" Nothaar probed.

"In the orbit around where your planet once was," Syraaq expounded, "there are now a large number of round, hollow-looking collectors. What they really are, though, are Quantum Shift machines. You could almost think of them as real-time portals. Sunlight hits the edges and powers the devices. They, in turn, preform a Quantum Shift so that the light and energy that reaches the center is instantly transported towards a planet. A ring is placed at a relatively stationary juncture near said planet, simulating the effects of having a sun really being there. From an observer on the planet, things would appear pretty much as they always had."

"Except, to a keen watcher like myself," Nothaar hypothesized, "the sun would look slightly fuzzy."

"That's right!" Syraaq confirmed. "This is because—since the Quantum Shift is constantly happening—there's something akin to drag happening. It's not exceptionally perceptible to the average person; and, if you've never seen a non-Quantum Shifted sun, you'd never know the difference, anyway. Nevertheless, it's a well-documented phenomena in the Starbuilders' training manual, thus I immediately knew what you were getting at when I read about it in your *Opus on the Language of Children*."

"Wouldn't a constant Quantum Shift inside a solar system go directly against the protocols you just told me about?" Nothaar challenged.

"True enough," Syraaq admitted, "but these devices, along with the movement of planets to our system, are the only exceptions to the rule of how far away a Quantum Shift must happen from a celestial object—the one light-year distance law—just due to the nature of where it is necessary to place them."

"In truth," Ifu clarified, "we somewhat lied to you a bit before. Back in the gym when we first met, I set up the orbits to look like how they were before we preformed the

Quantum Shift of your planet to our system. Now, you orbit around a supermassive black hole like all the other worlds, and your sun—at least a facsimile of it—does actually circumnavigate your planet. We do everything we can to make it appear like you are orbiting around it, but eventually your people's understanding and technology will reach a level where they will recognize that's not the case and something is amiss."

"Why would you ever do such a thing?" Nothaar protested as he realized that it no longer mattered if he saved himself; his world was forever tied to the *Commons* and there was no hope of escaping their clutches.

"Amazingly, our predecessors were inspired by a book," Ifu elucidated. "It was one of those stories about a species that self-destructed, but it contained some novel ideas of just what Quantum Shift technology was capable of. It's called... uh... Syraaq, do you know?"

"Oh," Syraaq exclaimed as she was seemingly caught off guard. "I think it was 'Compendium of' something or other... some species' 'End', perhaps? I forget, and I doubt I ever read it; probably only heard about it during my school days forever ago. If you're really interested, when we reconnect to the main *Archive*s, I'm sure we can find it or introduce you to some professional historian who could help out."

"As for your inquiry about why, Nothaar," Ifu rejoined, "this is where Syraaq and I diverge from the Starbuilders of yore. There is a contention among them and throughout the government as a whole that—although they are knowingly abducting people and planets en masse from their home systems and transforming them into *Commons*—that these actions serve a higher purpose, some greater and more precious good. They believe that despite everything they do to individuals like you, you'll be able to develop normally without interference before you are ready to join the greater galactic community."

"And that is what you disagree with?" Nothaar prodded. "That is where you draw your moral line?"

"Yes," Ifu contested. "And you are the proof that what we are doing as Starbuilders is wrong."

"You have made that declaration before," Nothaar stressed. "How do I prove such a grandiose contention?"

With a satisfied expression, Ifu explained, "Just the act of moving your planet and causing a so-called *Sky Shift* affected your development because you noticed! Put aside the speed of genetic changes that were delivered to your planet; there is no doubt now that your natural path diverged due to that very singular component of our involvement. You recognized that something was awry, and set about to learn what it was and to do something about it. That means that we did change your destiny, for lack of a better word, as a species. You corroborate that the entire Starbuilder's creed is based on a falsehood. That is why you and you alone can be the impetus to stop this travesty from happening to anyone else.

"I want to be clear: what Starbuilders do is very important. We need to find other life-bearing worlds and the suns that power them. These things are critical for our collective survival. But instead of forcing you to become one of us and join our system, we should allow you to come into your own in your home system and only approach you when you are ready. Keeping tabs on your development would not be particularly difficult and we could easily visit at regular intervals. I mean, what is even a few million extra years to our society? That's basically nothing, and we could easily afford to wait. When the time is right and if your people approved, we could turn you into *Commons* and have you join us. Nevertheless, it should not be done against your will and, more so, without your consent."

Syraaq quickly added, "This is why we rebelled, Nothaar: for you, and people like you yet to come. As a long-time Starbuilder, I committed every sin that Ifu has described. Along the way, misgivings were always creeping around in the back of my mind, at least subconsciously. Honestly, I wasn't really sure what I was feeling, and I tried to push all of it aside and suppress those heretical thoughts. For a long time, it worked.

"Yet, somehow, in an immeasurably large universe and despite the extensive fleet of Quantum Ships, Ifu and I found each other. We became close and Ifu put words to the doubts I'd been suffering my entire life, but could not find a way to express. Once we realized that there were two of us, that we were not alone, we knew that we could not stay and continue performing our heinous duties. On a crew and supply rotation jump back to the *Common*'s system, we took advantage of the situation to steal a Torch Ship and make our escape. Before we did so, we heard about your world, the latest discovery and delivery from just twenty years ago. After deciding that your planet was our destination, we immediately set out. Sadly, we weren't prepared to be insurgents. That is how we ended up in the mess we are in now. However, since it led us to you, I wouldn't have it any other way. I must thank you, Nothaar, for making our dream of achieving a better life for others—especially non-*Commons* who don't have a say in the matter—one step closer to becoming a reality."

CHAPTER 29

Staying perfectly still while his eyes patiently swept through the crystal-clear water, Nothaar at last caught sight of his prey. Slowly, he lifted his spear above his head and waited for the exact right moment. When it came, he quickly thrust his weapon under the briny depths and through the fish. It was a direct hit into its torso. As it writhed under his sharpened point, he swiftly pulled his prize out of the sea and held it above his head. Nothaar carefully began to make his way from the nearly knee-deep liquid to the shoreline. Meanwhile, at the edge of his spike, the fish continued to flop around, making a futile last attempt at escape—a useless effort considering its fatal wounds. Amazed at the creature's tenacity, Nothaar took a moment to wordlessly thank and honor the fish for its sacrifice, making a promise to himself that he, too, would never stop fighting should he be ensnared in a similar trap.

Strutting his way further up the beach and far from the water's edge, Nothaar came upon his slick metal table that had been repurposed from a piece of their former land vehicle. Pulling the fish off his spear, he put it down on the surface, retrieved his axe, and rapidly severed the beast's head in order to end its suffering. With that done, he began his ritual of gutting and priming the meat, thinking ahead to how we would prepare it for consumption—deeply missing the aromatic herbs of his old home in the northlands. Soon enough, the scavengers that also made this miniscule island their home started to let themselves be known. Some had even become brazen enough to approach Nothaar. He threw the scraps towards those daring few, attempting to reward their docile behavior. Silently, he once more wished they would come closer and help alleviate his loneliness.

This had all been part of Nothaar's daily routine since he, Ifu, and Syraaq had landed at what he had christened 'Portal to the Stars Island'. At least that was what he told Ifu and Syraaq it meant in a transmuted version of the *Lingua*. In his own native tongue, it had a much more lyrical sound and was a bit of a pun that did not translate between their vernaculars. Syraaq had quite a good laugh when Nothaar revealed the name and its meaning, greatly confusing Ifu. Since Ifu was not privy to Nothaar and Syraaq's secret scheme to leave behind a time capsule, he did not realize how this would be a rebellious act that would give a cryptic clue to some future generation.

Otherwise, Nothaar spent his days gathering foodstuffs from around the tiny speck of land. Despite its diminutive size, it had a large amount of resources that met Nothaar's immediate needs and then some. If there were more people, that would not have been the case, but for one being it was far more than enough. Ifu and Syraaq had advised Nothaar to take significantly more excess goods than he needed and to continue to deconstruct his meals into packages that could be reconstituted later. "At some point," Syraaq explained, "we'll be able to get our hands on a grow-tank and reprogram it to make something edible for you. But until then, you'll need a steady supply of staples and calories to keep you going. Then, it'll be your turn to go through the careful rationing that we've had to endure this entire time!"

Unfortunately, Nothaar found, the supposed prorating system that Syraaq and Ifu had been executing had not been anywhere near enough. The two *Commons* were presently doing everything they could to minimize their energy output so they would need less food. Due to this, they had become lethargic and spent most of their days just lying around in their cabins. Their personal homesteads had all been built out of pieces of the intentionally deconstructed ship, leaving Nothaar alone most of the time. Nothing out of the ordinary happened most days, so there was equally little to talk about. It was getting to the juncture where he could go days without seeing or talking to either of the two off-worlders, and they did not seem bothered by this.

When they first arrived, there had been a flurry of activity. Their first goal was to scale the steep mountain and reach its snowy peak. It took nearly an entire month just to find a route that would meet their purposes, and equally as long to make it happen, especially after many false starts and retreats. "We should have thought of a way to bring an automata with us that could cut out and pave a road," Ifu had complained.

"I didn't think," Syraaq interposed, "that I would be the one to remind you that we cannot leave a trace of our existence nor any obviously discoverable evidence that we were ever here."

"Yeah, yeah," Ifu dismissed through his huffing endeavors at catching his breath. *Apparently*, Nothaar had silently observed, *Ifu is far less adept at handling higher altitudes compared to Syraaq and me. His struggles are actually slowing us all down.*

Once finally atop the formidable mound, Ifu revealed the anchor point for the *Space Elevator* and proceeded to tap into its communications system. "I've set up a wireless network," he announced. "We should now be able to able to directly interact with the broadcasting array from anywhere on the island. That way, we don't have to stay up here and can set up camp at the base of the mountain."

"But will we not have to ascend the mountain again to meet our saviors?" Nothaar had disputed.

"Of course," Ifu agreed. "However, we'll have plenty of time. It'll be nearly a year, at best, between when we receive a response to our request and someone actually shows up. We'll have plenty of warning and time to prepare for that eventuality."

True to these words, once Ifu had confirmed that their distress signal was being sent out at repeating regular intervals to the wider universe at the slow speed of light, they made their way back down to the much warmer sandy shoreline. It was then that they opted to dismantle the yacht and use it to build shelters, tables, chairs, and other useful implements. They did the same with much of the vehicle, leaving part of it to act as a power station and central server, then disassembled the rest and fashioned the various pieces into tools and workspaces. Ifu assured Nothaar that, in the end, they would destroy all of it using the same rapid molecular decomposition technique he had performed on the Torch Ship by which he and Syraaq had arrived on Nothaar's world.

"Will that not contaminate this tiny island with radiation?" Nothaar concernedly asked. "There are many flora and fauna that call this region home, and they should not be subjected to a death sentence due to your navigational mistakes and negligence."

"You don't need to fret that much," Ifu assured him. "What's left of the vehicle and our other accoutrements is barely a speck compared to the volume of the Torch Ship. We'll bury everything we brought with us as deeply as possible and hopefully prevent any potential leakage that could be dangerous to the life around here. Some future explorer may find a small hot spot, but their rather minimal exposure should not be a major worry. Besides, with any luck and well before then, we'll be able to get a clean-up crew to come down the space elevator and remove any remnants of our contaminants."

Having no further arguments, Nothaar let the issue and proposed solution stand as Ifu had laid it out. Otherwise, aside from small matters like these, every day was focused on the challenges of ensuring their collective survival. It had become clear to Nothaar that Syraaq and Ifu were starting to waste away. When he spent time contemplating what would happen to him should they die, Nothaar realized that he would be completely trapped on this fleck of sand in the middle of an endless ocean for the remainder of his life. As far as he was concerned, there was no guarantee that anyone would ever respond to Ifu and Syraaq's plea for help. Even if some other *Commons* eventually made an appearance, Nothaar did not believe it would be in his best interest to be discovered by them as they might view him as just another "contaminant" that needed to be cleaned up.

Similarly, Nothaar was painfully aware that no one was ever coming from the mainland to rescue him. Although the designs for the massive water vessel were now a part of the *Knowledge*, building another ship and piloting it were entirely different skillsets. No one knew nor cared where he went after he departed the supercontinent, so there was no hope of anyone arriving from that direction. The only option that remained to Nothaar, he believed, was if he could somehow reconstruct the yacht or some other suitable craft. Lacking proper transport, there would be no way for him to escape; thus, he would live out the rest of his days being completely removed from his own kind. Thinking about it again only made him feel more isolated and forlorn.

Syraaq and Ifu were always making grand plans for Nothaar, whether he agreed to them or not. One day, Syraaq had said, "When we get picked up, we'll have to hide your... unique features... under a mask, gloves, and long clothing. Don't worry, we thought about this before we left the Torch Ship and created outfits that should fit you. They are all made out of the same fabric we *Commons* use. I wish we had decided to make a few more changes of clothing for us, though, just for some variety."

"Will it not be odd for me to have my face and other body parts covered all the time?" Nothaar challenged.

"Nonsense!" Syraaq claimed. "As you're well aware by now, the unique, original base cultures and societies of most worlds are preserved and live on long after the transformation into being *Commons* takes hold. Among these, many cover their features, so it wouldn't be out of place at all. No one would notice or mind."

"Otherwise," Ifu had added, "if you were as plainly exposed as you are right now, all anyone would be able to see would be some freaky alien. I cannot stress enough how we *Commons* only ever see others that look exactly like our own kind. Catching a glimpse of anything else would be unsettling, to say the least. Just because we have a wide range of tolerated and accepted ethnicities and beliefs, it does not mean we don't have xenophobic tendencies in other areas. Given that, can you imagine what would happen if someone got one peek at you? Everyone—including the authorities—would freak out and accuse us of abduction and interference!"

They would think that, Nothaar derisively had ruminated, *because that is exactly what you are doing. Of course, I cannot say that out loud out of fear of what your painful reprisal may be.*

On another occasion when he was feeling particularly morose and Syraaq and Ifu were looking abnormally ill, Nothaar had asked what he should do if they did not survive until other *Commons* arrived.

"Even if we die," Syraaq declared, "you should go on with the mission without us. Pretend to be a mute or that your vocal cords are injured. You can use the tablet and have the *Eh-aye* speak for you."

"I agree," Ifu said as he rolled over in his sickbed. "Although you've come a long way, it's still very obvious when you speak that the *Lingua* is not your native tongue. It will make you stand out as a non-*Common*, and that is not something you should reveal until the time is right or you can find other trustworthy allies."

"You'll have to keep pushing forward, somehow," Syraaq rejoined. "You absolutely must find a way to get yourself in front of the government and show them that what they've been single-mindedly pursing for all this time is just plainly callous. It's the only way we can stop this madness, for the good of all those yet to come."

Despite their entreaties, Nothaar was unsure if he could or wanted to fulfill Syraaq and Ifu's wishes.

CHAPTER 30

The door slid into the wall and Nothaar stepped into the room he had been told was called the "sickbay". Removing his full face covering—which he had come to find rather restrictive and annoying—Nothaar asked with as much positive energy as he could muster, "How are my two patients doing today?"

Ifu attempted to shift in his bed into a sitting-up position, but failed beneath his own weight. "Still apparently malnourished and weak," he whispered.

Coming over to his side, Nothaar worked the controls on the bed to lift Ifu into an upright configuration. At the same time, Nothaar carefully moved the various lines attached to Ifu's veins that were directly pumping nutrients, medicine, and nanobots into his bloodstream. The fact that Ifu could talk in a coherent sentence at all was an improvement, Nothaar noted. Looking over at Syraaq, Nothaar observed that she remained comatose. A mask had been placed over her mouth in what Nothaar supposed was an effort to increase the amount of oxygen she was receiving, but otherwise nothing had changed over the past several days. A medical robot had explained to Nothaar that despite the advanced technology and deep understanding of physiology the *Commons* had access to, it was still up to

Syraaq's body to finish the repair job itself and bring her back from the brink.

Since no other *Commons* were around and the only other witnesses were the robots, Nothaar took advantage of the opportunity and removed his gloves and other remaining concealing garments.

"What are you doing?" Ifu admonished—although with only a minüte amount of force—as he finally got a good look at Nothaar and apparently realized that the non-*Common* had publicly revealed himself. "You shouldn't take a risk like that. What if someone here were to discover your secret? Could you imagine what might happen?"

Nothaar rearranged his face into an unhappy expression in the style of the *Commons* before answering, "I am afraid I have some bad news for you. Captain Bipauc figured it out almost immediately."

"What?!" Ifu sort-of yelled as he attempted to jump out of his healing chamber.

"Easy there!" Nothaar admonished as he gently pushed Ifu back down and realigned all the lifesaving equipment. "You should know that the captain is of a similar opinion to you and Syraaq. They have commanded me to continue to wear my disguise and not communicate with anyone else on the ship. However, it was necessary from the onset to reveal myself. Without you and Syraaq in any condition to assist me, the Torch Ship immediately recognized me as an outside contagion. At the beginning, it was easy enough to believe we were all covered in so much flotsam that the sensors could not tell the difference, but after the decontamination procedures, it was quite clear that I did not belong. Captain Bipauc pulled me aside and interrogated me, before making the proper adjustments to the internal systems. As such, I am quite safe to be myself in here, as well as in my quarters and the captain's private office."

Pausing for a moment, Ifu surmised, "You've... you've already told me this before, haven't you?"

"I have," Nothaar confirmed. "You do not appear to be fully cognizant yet and are having difficulties maintaining your memory. Nevertheless, we have not been able to converse this easily before now, so I am hopeful that you are showing signs of progress. Syraaq, on the other hand..."

Once more, Nothaar looked over at Syraaq. This time, Ifu turned his head to follow Nothaar's gaze. "What happened to her?" Ifu queried. "What happened to me, to all of us? How did we even get here? Where... is here?"

"What is the last thing you remember?" Nothaar inquired in return.

Closing his eyes, Ifu was silent for several moments before beginning, "The response to our emergency beacon came relatively quickly, much sooner than we ever could have hoped. It didn't make any sense. The speed of light is finite. We shouldn't have heard anything for a long time, maybe even two years! Nothaar, how could this be—"

Nothaar cut Ifu off, stopping a rambling perseveration he had heard before in an earlier fever-induced rant. "Captain Bipauc's Torch Ship was already en route to my world. They received your distress call and responded to it so quickly because they intended to visit my planet for their own reasons and purposes."

Ifu looked at Nothaar with concern and suspicion. "Captain Bipauc?" was all he managed to solicit before seemingly losing his train of thought.

"Yes," Nothaar confirmed. "Captain Qeraat Elii Bipauc of the private-industry Torch Ship named 'Reimagine', or so they introduced themselves to me as. The captain is... I am sorry, I do not have the right words in the *Lingua*... a person with the souls of a man and woman entwined so they are both and neither gender at the same time. There is not exactly a word for it in any language from my home-world, either."

"It's fine," Ifu assuaged, "I get what you mean, any-way. So, this is a non-governmental vessel?"

"I fail to recognize how I would know or define the dif-ference," Nothaar retorted.

"Never mind that then," Ifu dismissed. "Okay, so we received the response we had been waiting for and exe-cuted all our planned preparations before beginning to ascend the mountain to the *Space Elevator*. When the time came, we started the difficult journey to the peak. And then... and then..."

"And then you and Syraaq lost consciousness," Nothaar finished. "I had to pick you up and drag you one-by-one to the top."

Of course, Nothaar had considered just leaving them and letting them die right there, thus freeing himself from their custody. However, he could not bring himself to actually end their lives, even through inaction. Also, he had some selfish reasons for his choices as he had no idea what the repercussions on his own nanobots would be if the two extraterrestrials were no longer around. Due to this uncertainty, Nothaar felt he could not take the chance of endangering his own life by risking theirs. It seemed to him that all their fates may had been notionally tied together, whether he had wanted to admit it before that moment or not.

Keeping these deliberations to himself, Nothaar instead stated, "Your lack of activity over the preceding months left you woefully unprepared for the necessary physical exertion. More so, you could not ingest calories fast enough to make up for your lack of eating prior to the ascent. This, accompanied with the change in altitude and ensuing oxygen deprivation—hypoxia, it is called—caused your bodies to shut down."

Staring at Nothaar with shock and awe, Ifu probed, "And you determined all that on your own?"

"Of course not!" Nothaar beamed with delight at having impressed Ifu with his summary. "The medical robots worked with me to figure out what happened. I am merely repeating their prognoses."

Relief came over Ifu's face as he declared, "Oh, good, I was concerned for a bit there."

"Why?" Nothaar quizzed. "Is there something wrong with me learning these facts and concepts?"

"No, no, it's not that," Ifu attempted. "It's just that, well, it would be surprising... what I mean... that is..."

Deciding to save Ifu from his own spiral into offensive and demeaning prejudices, Nothaar continued his story, "Well, anyway, after getting you and Syraaq to the base station, I did not really know what to do. However, I undertook whatever action I could in order to keep you and Syraaq alive by maintaining your bodily warmth and forcing food and water down your throats. Still, I had no way to know what actions would be necessary and appropriate to respond to our would-be saviors, but eventually I did see something slowly descending from the sky. When it landed, there were thankfully other *Commons* inside who helped bring you and what remained of our supplies—including your precious and extremely heavy data storage medium and my comparatively lighter personal supply of food—into the interior of the transport. Per your prior instructions, I used the *Eh-aye* on the tablet to speak. Nonetheless, as I already revealed, Captain Bipauc saw right through my subterfuge."

"How long ago was that?" Ifu grilled.

"It has been about a month, perhaps a few days shy of that, since we came aboard," Nothaar replied.

"And during the succeeding interval since then," Ifu reacted, "you've spent significant time with this Captain Bipauc character... alone?"

"That is correct," Nothaar confessed. "The captain is quite a gregarious individual. Syraaq would get along with them quite famously, but I do not believe you would share the same opinion."

At the mention of her name, Syraaq let out a groan.

Nothaar walked over and signaled one of the medical robots to join him. "This is a good sign," the unit assured him. "Any type of non-autonomic response demonstrates that she is on the mend. You should also talk with her, not just the other patient who is conscious. Studies have shown that certain areas of the brain light up when people in comas are spoken to."

"Will it really help?" Nothaar bade.

"That is debatable," the unit admitted. "However, it would not hurt. Here, I will put a real-time scan of Syraaq's brainwaves on the screen behind her so that you can watch as it changes with the input you provide. Music is oftentimes beneficial, but I lack any records to know about the patient's preferences. As her friend, you would be better equipped to decide what she would find stimulating."

Looking back toward Ifu, Nothaar requested, "Ifu, you have known Syraaq much longer than I have. What do you think she would like?"

Suddenly, Ifu looked miserable, and tears started to stream down his face. "I... I... don't know," he blubbered. "I just... don't know. In all our time together, did I ever really get to know Syraaq personally? Oh, Nothaar, I'm such a failure, such a terrible friend. How could I have done this to her? How could I have imperiled her life like this? How could I not even know what her favorite song is?"

CHAPTER 31

After leaving Captain Bipauc's office, Nothaar, Ifu, and Syraaq—the latter of whom was still temporarily confined to a medical-transport chair until she could gain enough strength to safely ambulate on her own—retired to Nothaar's quarters. Nothaar did not want to go back to either Ifu's or Syraaq's rooms since it would result in him needing to don his coveralls for yet another trip through the hallways of the Torch Ship *Reimagine*. Thus, Nothaar offered his own private place for a debrief simply so he could put his disguise away for the rest of the day. Once they were inside, he quickly shed his concealments and took a deep breath of the unobstructed air. That first hit of crisp ventilation never ceased to please Nothaar.

Although Ifu had basically recovered from his injuries, Syraaq was progressing at a far slower pace. However, even Ifu eventually accepted the medical robots' identical prognoses that Syraaq's advanced age was a detrimental factor in her recuperation, and it was a minor miracle that she was alive at all. Syraaq, at first, did not appear to be too happy to have survived, but had slowly been changing back to her old, cantankerous self. Just that morning, she had teased Nothaar that she intentionally lost all her body weight in order to make it easier for "a strapping specimen of masculinity like you" to carry her the rest of the way up to the mountain top.

"Well," Nothaar began as a way to kickstart the conversation, "I believe that went quite decently. Captain Bipauc actually sounds like the exact kind of ally you said you were looking for, who I was to seek out in the event of your demise. We were very lucky, in that regard. And, since my world was Quantum Shifted into your system, they had already been monitoring it and planning on making regular visits as they, too, do not believe that indigenous planets should be taken out of their home environment. What more could we have hoped for?"

Instead of rapid agreement, Nothaar was surprised to discover that Syraaq and Ifu were staring at each other in that knowing way, exchanging their secret language. *Something is obviously wrong with what I said*, Nothaar thought, *but I cannot for the life of me fathom what it might be. I thought Syraaq and Ifu would finally be happy that we found more Commons like them, but for some reason this seems to have made them unmistakably despondent and concerned.*

"No, Nothaar," Syraaq gently corrected, "Captain Bipauc is not like us at all. I can see how you would be confused and think so, but I'm sorry to report that they are actually a danger to us and our mission."

"How so?" Nothaar probed, completely confused. He felt like he had been participating in an entirely different meeting than them. *Perhaps it is just that I have spent more time with Captain Bipauc than they have?* Nothaar considered. *After all, I have had months of one-on-one time with the captain while this is the first time my companions have had the opportunity to really sit down with them. Maybe it is just a trust thing at this point.*

"Ifu and I," Syraaq attempted, "we are, what we'll call, *Reformists*. As we discussed long ago, we believe that it is morally wrong to Quantum Shift a planet with sapient life on its surface into the orbit of our supermassive black hole without the consent or knowledge of that world's inhabitants. But in the end, we do approve of the idea of the overall *Common*'s society and Starbuilders' mission, especially in relation to the harvesting of solar radiation from sun-like stars in order to sustain all the other populated spheres that are here. These people... they don't exactly share those beliefs. They are *Decentralists*. Did you not hear how what Captain Bipauc is proposing is different than what we want to accomplish?"

"Frankly, I did not," Nothaar avowed.

Looking perturbed, Syraaq continued, "Nothaar, this group, they're extreme radicals. They don't believe in having a central system to home all the *Commons*, but would rather take their planets and move them into the systems and orbits of stars like yours."

"I can see the logic in what was propositioned," Nothaar interjected. "There is a danger with having all sapient people in one place. Mayhap it would be beneficial and safer to spread life out into many smaller colonial groupings. With Quantum Shift technology, no one would be more than a couple of years away. If anything, that would make these globes closer from a travel perspective compared to using a Torch Ship to make a thirty to fifty light-year journey within the current setup."

"And I don't think you picked up on some very concerning subtleties and key differentiators," Syraaq persisted in her argument. "It's not just about having planets sharing a singular orbit around some far-strewn sun, but also changing the *Common* themselves. Instead of making all life align to the *Common*'s standard, they would rather change their genetic makeup to match the natural life in the system they move to."

"What would be so bad about that?" Nothaar spat. "What was wrong with my species before you seeded my world with your genetic manipulations? Becoming more like the natives the Starbuilders discover might actually teach you lessons and give you the diversity you need to avoid the heat death of the universe."

"It's one thing for your species to choose to maintain your base genetic profile," Syraaq countered, "but another thing entirely to create a splinter pool away from the *Common*. This creates isolation and strife, separate nations that may want to go to battle with each other. If we have many genetic bases, then which one is the 'real' *Common*, eh? Can you imagine the type of race war that would ensue on a universal scale, especially considering the capabilities we have? Have you not read more about how destructive quantum technology can be in the hands of unhinged individuals with no central superseding controls?"

Nothaar had to pause and made a *Common*-style gesture that indicated he was deeply considering Syraaq's words so that neither she nor Ifu would interrupt his train of thought. *I have to admit*, Nothaar pondered, *that Syraaq has a point. It appears that I have not properly considered the disparities and inherent dangers in these two seemingly similar philosophies. If I had made my way here alone, I most likely would have blindly cast my lot with these so-called 'Decentralists'. Truthfully, I still barely understand the greater cosmos I am now a part of, and could easily be led astray.*

Giving voice to these thoughts, Nothaar conceded, "I am sorry, Syraaq, I see what you mean now. I had not fully meditated on the implications of what Captain Bipauc and their crew want to do. It also brings some of my prior conversations with the captain into a new light."

"What do you mean?" Syraaq inquired. "What happened between you and Bipauc?"

Gathering his words, Nothaar explained, "Captain Bipauc has been trying to learn about me, my people, and our culture. They have, in particular, focused on how others from my world might react to new celestial objects or a mass of visitors from another world. More so, given this new information, they appeared to have been testing the limits of what the denizens of my planet would accept before violence erupted. I do not believe the captain was particularly enthralled with my answers."

"Yes," Syraaq agreed, "they were testing you, trying to gain intelligence and see where you would fall within their grand plans. Nothaar, they just want to use you for their own ends, but you may have barely dissuaded them by helping them realize that you wouldn't be a very good spokesperson for their cause."

Someone wants to use me for their own purposes and personal crusades, huh? Nothaar derisively sneered to himself. Aloud he asked, "Were they hoping to put me in front of the government, as you are?"

"That can't be it," Syraaq retorted. "Like I said, what they were discussing, what they are proposing, it's fanatical and... and... and..."

"And illegal," Ifu finished, finally breaking his long silence. "I would even go as far as to say it's heretical. We cannot become more intertwined with this crew and their viewpoints. Picture going before the government with a bunch of zealots that are against the basic tenets of our entire society. If our important message were lost and we got laughed out of the room, that would be the best possible result. The more likely outcome, given the obvious blasphemy, would be excommunication."

"To where?" Nothaar audibly wondered.

"It's a euphemism," Syraaq clarified. "There is nowhere to go; it would basically be a death sentence."

"I thought the *Common's* government believed in preserving life at all costs?" Nothaar countered.

"Life in general, as a concept, on the grand scale," Syraaq corrected. "On the individual level, with trillions of us, what is one small flame? Sometimes, in order to save the collective, you have to kill the singular."

"Seems hypocritical," Nothaar asserted.

"Maybe so," Ifu allowed, "but that's a fight for another day. For now, we have to start working on a plan to get away from these fanatics."

"Ifu, I hate to be the bearer of bad news," Syraaq interjected, "but we are in the middle of interstellar space and there's no smaller Torch Ship to steal this time. Getting in an escape pod—even if we could somehow accomplish it on this unfamiliar craft—would be of no help since those types of dinghies only have very basic propulsion. The gist of it is that we're stuck with our erstwhile hosts, at least for the time being."

"Do you know where we're going?" Ifu suddenly queried. "We must be heading somewhere, otherwise we would not be under the effect of false gravity. You can't just fly a Torch Ship around without a destination or in circles or something; it would mess up the equations and fuel requirements and whatnot."

"I have no idea," Syraaq admitted. "You've heard all the same information I have. Bipauc hasn't exactly been forthcoming in their intentions and plans."

"I know," Nothaar pronounced. "The people on this vessel mistakenly believe that because I cannot speak, I therefore cannot hear. They freely let gossip slip from their lips in my presence."

"Well, don't leave us hanging," Ifu beseeched. "What's our destination?"

Thinking back to what he had heard, Nothaar said, "We are heading to a planet where something called a 'conclave' will be happening. There are apparently many disparate groups that will be attending to discuss potential ways to fix the problems with the Starbuilders' methodology and avoid the end of the universe. A great number of the crew are nervous and concerned about being there, and not just because of what the government might do if it learns of this venture. They do not trust these other factions and their plans, whatever those may be. I would say the overall feeling is suspicion, and they think it is a mistake to go. Of course, they would not express these trepidations to Captain Bipauc out of fear of reprisal."

"This is brilliant!" Ifu declared. "All we have to do is convince Bipauc that we also deserve our own platform at this gathering so that we can present our arguments to the participants on equal footing. Once we do that, we'll finally be able to get off this ship. When we are landbound and everyone is distracted at this ridiculous conference, we'll have our chance to make our escape!"

CHAPTER 32

Completely exhausted, Nothaar fell into the bed pushed up against one of the walls in his lodging—what Ifu had called a "hotel". *Who knew that talking for that long could be so tiring?* Nothaar internally complained. *All I want to do is sleep, but I suppose I should have a bowl of my slop before I pass out for the rest of the evening. I presume I am also free to explore this alien city and all its sights and sounds, but to what purpose? In the end, I will still have to crawl back here for my basic nourishment.*

Forcing himself up with a groan, Nothaar walked over to the portable food vat that Captain Bipauc had fashioned for him. His own deconstructed packaged meals had long since been consumed and, not for the first time, Nothaar chided himself for failing to save some of them in order to occasionally mix them in between servings from his "basic nutrients broth", as the captain had described it. On the whole, Nothaar believed he preferred Syraaq's nickname that she could never quite say aloud without bursting into laughter: Nothaar-chow.

Sighing, Nothaar reckoned that having any sustenance was better than the alternative. Under Captain Bipauc's direct guidance, the robots surreptitiously analyzed his genetic profile and used it to develop a basic provision that would give him everything he needed—everything, that is, except the psychologically necessary components of flavor, variety, and an appetizing appearance and scent. Putting his troubles aside, Nothaar ladled out a portion and dipped his utensil in. Grimacing at his first spoonful, Nothaar was amazed that he still could not get used to its... unique properties. Still, he stuck with his supper until he could eat no more.

Letting the nanobots and other automata take care of the cleanup, Nothaar brought up the word processing program on his tablet and opened his journal file. He always felt giddy while looking at the document's name: "The Expanded Knowledge". Of course, it was written in the *Lingua*, not in his own native language. Ifu had said that they could probably get the *Eh-aye* to create an input methodology that used the nominal characters from Nothaar's aboriginal tongue, but Nothaar had decided it would be best to leave his old vernacular behind permanently. It had been years since he first encountered the *Commons*, traveled to an unknown land, ascended the *Space Elevator*, and left his homeworld. As further time slipped by, the more he had come to accept that he was never going to have the opportunity to go home again. Nevertheless, there was still something in the back of his mind that made him think it might be possible.

Putting those dangerous notions aside, Nothaar began to write:

Today was a particularly difficult one at the Conclave of Dreamers. Due to having to spend the entire conference in full regalia in order to remain hidden, as well as not being allowed to speak, these days have passed particularly slowly for me. Instead of being able to contribute my own thoughts, I am forced to just continue listening as everyone else shares... no, shouts their opinions over one another. As expected, no one has moved from their steadfast positions in any way, and thus we are no closer to producing a final document that would be able to gain the consensus of all the disparate groups here. I had no idea there were such wildly different beliefs among the Commons, but in retrospect, I suppose Syraaq and Ifu did try to warn me about it. As Syraaq said, "Give me two Commons, and I will give you two separate camps."

That was particularly amusing coming from Syraaq, considering that she and Ifu were just a duo before they met me. While it is obvious how distinctive they are from each other, it is even more interesting to see how they have closed ranks since we came to this gathering. Not once have they contradicted each other. Instead, it seems that being among differing persuasions has allowed their collective viewpoints to harden. Take today, for instance.

The breakout session began with the Heliocentralists. In their usual trite arguments, they once again rationalized that we should be going around the universe collecting whatever free hydrogen and helium remained out there and bring them to a central location to collapse into a new sun. "We would be real Starbuilders, then," they would contend, "not just some bogus terminology used for marketing purposes."

Syraaq has become the assembly's resident expert on all things related to the Starbuilders, so she was quick to counter. "As I have explained countless times," she reprimanded, "that very thing was attempted in the past and it is actually where the name 'Starbuilders' comes from. The effort was abandoned because it took more energy to collect and deliver all those elements than we ever could get out of it. In other words, it was a net loss. But even if it was not, the solution would be a temporary one, at best. It does not resolve what to do when there is no more hydrogen and helium that can be amassed or it is so dispersed so as to be, for all practical purposes, extinct."

"You cannot think of it in terms of energy," one of Heliocentralists retorted. "Is not a natural home around a real sun worth any price?"

This speech brought the Decayist party into the fray. They had been arguing much the same as Syraaq about the diffusion of core elements, but they came at the problem from what they claimed was a "reasonable economic perspective". Instead of collecting the necessary components to build new suns, they have expressed a desire to apply existing technology like the rapid molecular decomposition that Ifu used on our old Torch Ship, except they want to take it to the next level. According to one of their members, they felt it was practical to decompose other elements using "nuclear fission". Apparently, this is a process by which the protons in the nucleus of an atom are split apart, creating two separate atoms. As an example, since hydrogen has one proton and helium has two, if you force the helium protons apart, they would make two hydrogen atoms. Naturally, though, the Decayists intend to do this with much bigger and heavier elements, splitting them again and again until they reach an apparently more desirable form.

"Talk about wasted energy!" someone from the Collapsers faction bellowed. "How could that plan possibly work out?" This back-and-forth continued for some time with no headway made between the two troupes. Since the start, the Collapsers have been arguing that people like the Heliocentralists and the Decayists have been approaching the question itself all wrong. "We are all ensnared by the same conundrum," one tried to explain. "The universe is expanding and continues to inflate at an exponentially faster-and-faster rate. The only way to resolve this untenable situation is to slow down and eventually reverse the enlargement of the entire cosmos; force things to come back together until we can bring the fabric of space-time down to a more manageable size."

Per usual, this supposition brought on a round of derisive chittering and jeers. Over the din, someone yelled out, "Oh yeah? And how will you stop the 'big crunch' once you commence the process?"

A Collapser representative attempted to say it was a solvable matter they could return to later, that they had to deal with the immediate issues in front of them first, but it was to no avail. Unfortunately, the Collapsers did not help their contention since they could not even produce any hypotheses about how they might go about producing the desired retraction of the entire universe. The lack of executable details being offered gave the Rebanger Clan the opening they appeared to have been waiting for. "No, no, no," one of their band disputed. "There is no way to reverse what has happened since the Big Bang that brought our entire shared universe into being, the unique event that made all of us possible. However, what we could actually do is intentionally cause a new Big Bang and restart the cosmos all over again!"

After this declaration, the Collapsers and Rebanger Clan began to quarrel amongst themselves, basically ignoring the rest of the participants. Finally, they were vehemently roared down by the leader of the Relocateites. "Whether you want to reverse the expansion of the universe, restart it from a singularity, or adopt any of these other ridiculous plans," she scoffed, "it all comes down to one thing: energy. And frankly, there isn't enough of that readily available that we could easily harvest to pull off any of these preposterous schemes. I would implore everyone here to accept this simple truth: this universe is done for and there is no going back. The only way we Commons can survive is if we gather every bit of matter and energy that we can and use it to pierce the fabric of space-time. Then, and only then, can we leave this dying universe and migrate to a newer, younger one. In the long term, leaving our progenitor universe is our only chance for survival!"

And that motion ended any last sense of cordiality that remained between all the various blocs. After that, there was nothing but long periods of barking and recriminations, grinding the entire theoretical purpose of these meetings to a halt. Not that I had much to add to the conversation, but it was frustrating to just be there and unable to contribute anything.

Leaning over to me, Ifu whispered in my ear, "Do you see, Nothaar, what I have been talking about? These people, even Captain Bipauc and the rest of their Decentralist ilk, are all just extremists. Each of them is solely concentrating on grand astrophysical solutions, while only those like Syraaq and I are thinking about actual living organisms and how decisions like these impact their lives. There is nothing to be gained by remaining here or continuing to deal with any of them."

"Then when do we make our promised escape?" I asked in return, equally anxious to get away from the rest of the rabble. My motivations may be different, but I do share Ifu and Syraaq's distaste for these folks that are trying to play at being gods without concern for the other species that have yet to be found.

"Soon enough," Ifu assuaged. "Syraaq and I have a consultation tonight on a potential lead to get us out of here. Just be ready to go at any time. I have a feeling our getaway is not going to be as clean as I had hoped."

CHAPTER 33

With the door firmly slammed shut and locked behind him, Nothaar finally slipped to the ground, panting to try to regain his breath. Then, in a moment of panic, he swung his backpack around and made sure his most important possession in the universe was still intact. To his great relief, his portable food vat appeared to be completely undamaged and functional. He let the feeling of relief roll over him and used it to try to calm his wracked nerves. However, he knew his escape was not yet complete and there was no chance to rest yet.

As if in response to these rising concerns, he heard a sudden loud smashing sound coming from the entryway that he had propped himself up against. Jumping to his feet and stepping away, he recognized the booming voice of Captain Bipauc on the other side shouting, "I know you're in there! You can't hide from me! You have my property!"

"They don't just mean your nourishment maker," a voice whispered into Nothaar's ear. Nothaar turned to discover that Ifu had also returned to a standing position and had somehow snuck over to Nothaar's side without him noticing. "They mean you."

"I know that," Nothaar sneered in a low volume. "You do not need to keep reminding me that Bipauc basically views me as belonging to them and that I must stay with the *Decentralists* until they accomplish their goals. Believe me, I completely understand the situation."

When Ifu did not respond, Nothaar took it to mean the *Common* had nothing worthwhile to add to the conversation. Putting it aside and looking around for a brief instant, Nothaar spied Syraaq still sitting upon the ground. Kneeling down next to her, he asked, "Syraaq, are you alright?"

Lifting her head, Syraaq displayed a surprising amount of joy on her face as she declared through quick gasps of her own, "That... was... fun!"

"Syraaq!" Ifu scolded. "How can you say that? Besides, we're not out of trouble yet. All we've managed to do is reach the safe house, but now the *Decentralists* know where it is. If help doesn't arrive soon, they're going to get in and capture us."

"How did they even figure out our plans?" Nothaar asked as he began scanning around the windowless, featureless box they now found themselves inside of.

"Who knows?" Ifu attested. "They've probably had trackers of various kinds on us at all times. Maybe they just happened to see us heading somewhere they felt was suspicious and decided to follow. It's not like they trusted us in the first place, so now their misgivings have been proven correct."

"To be fair," Syraaq offered, "they had every reason to be suspicious. We actually were using them for our own purposes and plotting a way to ditch them, including conspiring with lowlife criminals."

"Hey now!" Ifu disputed. "Goqanx Guzyc and her crew are not necessarily outlaws. They just operate in a grey area that some may find objectionable."

"You mean like people who might steal a Torch Ship to accomplish a mission of greater good?" Syraaq teased in return as she pushed herself into an upright position.

"Well," Ifu hesitated, "I don't think their intentions are quite so noble. Still, they're the best chance we've got."

"Speaking of Goqanx," Nothaar interrupted, "where is she? We are going to need some assistance, and fast!"

"I've messaged her," Ifu claimed, "and let her know what's going on. I'm sure a rescue will be added to the insurmountable debt we already owe her."

Although Nothaar did not have a good grasp on how economics, barter, or wealth worked within the *Common's* arrangement, he was well aware that Ifu and Syraaq had very little of whatever was necessary in order to make a trade. Sometime in the past, Ifu had tried to explain the idea of some type of dispersed methodology that kept track both locally and universally of an imaginary token that could be exchanged for goods and services, but since nothing like it existed on Nothaar's homeworld, he was still wrestling with understanding all of it.

In an attempt to clarify the subject, Syraaq interposed herself into that earlier conversation to explain the difference between classical and quantum computing. Apparently, as far as Nothaar could comprehend, classical computing was used for almost everything average people cared about. It functioned on a mostly linear basis that could best be described as "if this, then that". Quantum computing, on the other hand, was very good at doing mathematical functions simultaneously, giving it speeds that would be impossible with the classical variety. On the other hand, due to how the quantum component functioned, it would struggle to do even the simplest tasks the classical ones did with ease. Deciding which one was the appropriate tool for a particular job, Nothaar had been told, was not as straightforward of a process as it would seem at first glance.

Most importantly, Nothaar had learned, was that the quantum computing solution was what made the Quantum Shift possible by using another feature of the so-called Quantum Realm. Syraaq had further elucidated the notion of "quantum entanglement", where an action on one quantum particle would be instantaneously repeated on another one somewhere and anywhere else in the universe. Since the worlds of the *Commons* were so distant from each other and commerce and travel happened between planets, they could not depend upon the slow speed of light to initiate transactions. Combining the properties of entanglement with capabilities inherent in quantum computing, Syraaq had clarified that it allowed them to engage in markets anywhere there was a connection. Summarizing all of that, she had said it amounted to what she called their "digital wallets".

With Nothaar still trying to wrap his head around all of these wild concepts, Ifu apparently decided it was the opportune moment to point out that Nothaar did not have such a pecuniary account and could not obtain one since it would require revealing himself. After much haranguing, Syraaq and Ifu had elected to basically sell all three of them into voluntary servitude in order to pay for their trip off planet and away from Captain Bipauc and their crew.

Thinking about all of that at the moment they found themselves in, Nothaar asked aloud, "Remind me again how willingly giving ourselves over to Goqanx Guzyc instead of sticking with Captain Bipauc is an upgrade and is going to keep us out of mortal danger?"

"I have to say," Syraaq interjected, "I'm having my own doubts now, too, Ifu. Maybe we should back out of the deal and see if we can find something else. Is there anything so special about what Goqanx is offering that makes all of this worth it?"

Before Ifu could answer, the sound of the door unlocking shook their entire party from the momentary peaceful sojourn they had been enjoying. Nothaar, Syraaq, and Ifu braced themselves up against the back wall, but there was nowhere to hide and they had nothing to protect themselves with. As the door slid open, a voice called out, "You know, I'd like to hear the answer to that, too."

Walking into the room was a *Common* woman brandishing a gun, although Nothaar could not discern what type. While he did not recognize the woman, he saw Ifu visibly relax and start to walk forward. "Oh, Goqanx, thank goodness it's yo—" he began.

"Stay where you are, Ifu," Goqanx commanded. "You haven't answered the question yet."

Going back to where he previously stood, Ifu instead responded, "What's going on here, Goqanx? I thought we agreed not to delve into each other's backgrounds, motivations, and intentions."

"Yeah, that was the plan," Goqanx concurred, "until I got an emergency beacon to come bail you out of the jam you got yourselves into. Then, I had to put myself and my crew at risk to save your little entourage. Consequently, you could say, it got me a bit curious to find out what it is, exactly, that makes the three of you so special."

"And if you can profit off it," Ifu finished Goqanx's unspoken thought.

"Now, now, that sounds like you don't approve," Goqanx mocked. Pointing her gun directly at him, she continued, "I'd recommend a change in your attitude. It would be quite beneficial to your long-term health."

When Ifu appeared at a loss for words, much less quips, Syraaq chimed in with, "What did you do to Bipauc and the rest of them?"

"Why would you care?" Goqanx retorted as she swung her gun towards Syraaq. "Aren't you trying to get away from them for reasons you still haven't articulated? Reasons I am anxiously awaiting you to give me."

Without pause, Syraaq submitted, "We have something we want to present to the government."

"The government?!" Goqanx scoffed.

"Yes," Syraaq confirmed. "And Bipauc and their people have a somewhat contradictory standing. It's a political disagreement. Bipauc is just a little more... zealous than we'd prefer and believes we are an impediment to what they want to do. As such, they desire to keep us nearby. We, on the other hand, would still very much like to leave—if you're amiable to having us, that is."

"Oh, so suddenly you don't have any 'doubts' about going with me anymore, Syraaq?" Goqanx quickly countermanded. "I don't buy it nor this 'holier-than-thou' act you and Ifu have been shoving in my face since we met. Nevertheless, if it will loosen your tongues a bit, you'll be happy to know that no one was hurt. We just surrounded them and scared them off. I might add, if you're thinking about running, my boys are still out there with their guns trained on this door, so I wouldn't suggest it."

"Why would we run?" Syraaq assuaged. "Did I not just say we wanted to go with you, willingly? Sure, I expressed a little concern in the heat of the moment, but I've come to my senses now that the danger has passed. Haven't you ever dealt with finicky and rash senior citizens before?"

Nothaar watched as Goqanx's face morphed into the *Common*'s expression of consideration and disbelief. Finally, she pointed her gun at Nothaar and said, "What about you? Nothaar, is it? I haven't heard from you yet."

Before Nothaar could utter a word, Ifu cut him off by saying, "Nothaar can't speak; he has to use the *Eh-aye* installed on his tablet as his voice. It's in his backpack. If you let him get it out, I'm sure he could respond to you."

"I don't think so," Goqanx dismissed, "and I truly doubt he can't speak. Besides, I'm certain I heard another voice that wasn't either of yours before entering; I just couldn't make out the words. There's something weird going on, and it seems to keep coming back to Nothaar. You two requested a lot of strange modifications to my ship's internal systems, which is yet more proof you're hiding something. Perhaps the answer to what you're keeping from me is under that mask. Nothaar, dear, take it off."

"NO!" Syraaq and Ifu both screamed in unison.

Goqanx pointed her gun in the air and fired once, releasing a crackling sound. A beam of light then appeared through the smoking hole where Goqanx had discharged her weapon. By Nothaar's estimation, that meant the device was some type of plasma firearm, which in turn denoted there was nothing that could stop it. One hit and he would surely be dead. "Syraaq, Ifu, please stand down," Nothaar announced. "I will do as requested. Based upon our history, I assume the truth would have had to come out sooner or later, anyway."

As Nothaar was speaking these words, Goqanx stared at him in confusion. With it still prevalent on her face and the gun pointed at the ground, she noted, "The way you speak, it's so strange. I've never heard anything like it. It's not quite an accent, it's something else entirely. Nothaar, tell me, where are you from?"

Removing his mask and exposing himself to their tenacious captor, Nothaar simply declared, "Nowhere you have ever heard of before."

For a moment, Goqanx was apparently in complete shock and made no movement whatsoever. Then, just as abruptly, she started laughing so hard that she doubled over. Her disconcerting mirth did not stop for what felt like forever to Nothaar. Every once in a while, she tried to cease her cackling, but she would look up, see Nothaar, and start all over again. At last, she managed to get control of herself long enough to probe, "Let me get this straight: you two invaded an alien world, abducted a non-*Common*, and then taught it how to talk?"

"I already knew how to talk," an indignant Nothaar responded. "And then I taught myself the *Lingua*. Syraaq and Ifu have just helped fill in some of the finer points of the language, along with general material from the *Archive* that you *Commons* take for granted."

Goqanx attempted to keep a straight face, but it was to no avail. In the end, she succumbed to another round of merriment. When she regained enough composure, Goqanx avowed, "Oh fuck, the way you speak, it's so hilarious! I don't know if it's how formal and stilted it is, or the uncanny way you pronounce words and hit certain sounds and syllables, but it's the best!"

After taking a few deep breaths to seemingly stop herself from giggling anymore, Goqanx holstered her gun and proclaimed, "Alright, alright, Nothaar, go ahead and put your hood back on. I'm going to get you guys out of here and then smuggle you off planet, just as we agreed to."

"Wait," Ifu interrupted, "so, we're good now?"

Giving him the most bewildered expression possible, Goqanx replied, "Oh, we are far from good. There is much more we need to discuss that I absolutely must have an unabridged and complete understanding around... on top of unraveling the unfathomable number of lies you've told me. Plus, there's the small matter of your ballooning restitution, one that is growing by the moment. Nonetheless, I believe those conversations will best be saved for another day when we are far, far away from this world and anyone else who might be looking for you. Therefore, my new-found 'friends', it's nigh-time for all of us to make a judicious and strategic exit. Wouldn't you agree?"

Chapter 34

"Come on lazybones," the soft, lilting voice playfully jabbed, "you've slept in long enough!"

Groaning at the light streaming in as he attempted to open his eyes, Nothaar looked up at the still gorgeous visage of his mate Anlynx. She was trying to give him an annoyed expression, but it looked more like she was being flirtatious, at least to him. Inspired by that notion, he pulled her down into their piles of pillows that adorned the floor of their shared hut and began to smother her with kisses as he groped under her clothes.

"Ach!" Anlynx yelped as she giggled and started to hit Nothaar with any cushion she could grab. "We don't have time for that right now! Maybe if you had gotten up when you were supposed to, but you have important work to do today. I can't do all of your duties; you have to actually fulfill your one agreed upon responsibility!"

Letting Anlynx go, Nothaar relented, "Alright, alright, I suppose that's true enough. I mean, how could I have accomplished all this without you? How could I have done anything without you, my love?"

"Oh, you're all sweet talk now," Anlynx swatted back, "but you were pretty mean to me when we first got together. Yet, it's clear to me now that you were all just false bravado and stupidity. Without me, you probably would have wandered the lands until you got pressed into slavery or killed or something, never amounting to anything."

Although Anlynx was clearly joking, Nothaar felt somewhere in the back of his mind that there was some veracity to what she was saying, some other lifetime he had gratefully chosen not to live. Praying silently to himself, he gave thanks that he had not let his ego get in the way of the better options that were right in front of him, ones which allowed him to have all the happiness and tenderness in his existence that he could take for granted on a daily basis. Twelve winters prior, he was determined to leave Anlynx's home village and set out on his own—guided by his erroneous belief that only he could save the world and teach everyone the secrets contained in what he then considered his seminal composition: *Opus on the Language of Children.*

I was completely blind to everything else, Nothaar lamented, *except my self-imposed so-called duty. What arrogance to believe that I was the only individual who could possibly be a savior to our people! And worse still, that it required my personal touch and intervention in every conceivable situation to be successful.*

Despite Nothaar's foolish efforts to push Anlynx away and quit the place he now considered home, Anlynx stubbornly and wisely decided not to give up on him. One day, after he had been particularly cruel in some feeble attempt to get her to reject and despise him—so as to stop her from feeling deeply connected to him—Anlynx had come to him with a proposal. It was so simple, logical, and obvious that he admonished himself for not ever considering it before. This proposition, more than anything else, made Nothaar fall in love with Anlynx and, over time, decide to spend the rest of his life with her.

"Do you remember how we came to our unanimity?" Nothaar wistfully asked.

Looking at Nothaar curiously, Anlynx walked over to him and laid her hand on his cheek. "Of course I do, my love," she replied. "After all, it was my idea. I said to you, 'Instead of trying to take this burden on yourself and force a separate onus on me, we can share our troubles and face this world together, as a team, as one. Stay here, with me, and we can act as co-*Keepers*. I will do all the administrative, spiritual, and traditional work; you can continue doing all of the research and adding to the *Knowledge*. More so, you can make all the necessary copies of your opus, take as many years as you need, and then we'll send couriers out with those editions to all corners of the world at once.' Or something like that, right?"

Responding with nothing but a sign of gratefulness upon his face, Nothaar reflected that he never ceased to be amazed by Anlynx's recall abilities. He needed to write everything down to remember it, but it seemed like Anlynx could evoke every word exactly as it had been spoken. Hearing her repeat the same speech from so long ago made his heart flutter in that stitch in time the same as it did all the way back then. "And today is that day, isn't it?" Nothaar rhetorically contended.

"That it is," Anlynx agreed without any additional comment or fanfare. Suddenly, Anlynx looked quite sad, so Nothaar asked her what was the matter. Taken by surprise, Nothaar watched as tears started streaming down her face and she declared, "After today, your mission will be complete. We struck that accord so you would be willing to linger here with me, at least for a short while. Now, now you'll have no reason, no reason to..."

Jumping to his feet, Nothaar enveloped Anlynx in his arms and started stroking the back of her head. "No, no, hush now, dry those tears," he tried. "I'm not going anywhere, not anymore. I was a different person then, a very stupid one who couldn't see the most important thing in the world was sitting directly in front of him. I've learned, darling, I really have. I have no desire nor reason to ever abandon you, or our children."

Anlynx cried into Nothaar's shoulder for a while longer before pushing herself up and finding a cloth to dry her eyes and nose. "I'm sorry," she announced, "I don't know what came over me. It was like, just for a moment, I got a glimpse into some other... some other... I don't know what, but it was like I watched you forsake all of this and, instead, some alternative, terrible life happened to the two of us, our children, and our people."

Pondering to himself, Nothaar didn't find her description to be that odd at all. Aloud to these thoughts he stated, "Strange, now that you mention it, I had a similar... I'm not sure what to call it... premonition, perhaps? It happened just a short while ago."

With her countenance quite serious, Anlynx queried, "Do you think it could be another lingering effect of the *Sky Shift*? Some new phenomena that we haven't catalogued before? It certainly wouldn't be the first new discovery since that fateful day."

Pausing for a short moment before speaking, Nothaar offered, "It could be. I'll have to investigate, check if anyone else is experiencing anything similar." Then, with a disarming expression on his face, he proclaimed, "You see, I already have a new project to explore; no need to worry about me wandering off!"

Anlynx gave him a grateful look in return and then ran over and planted a deep kiss on her mate's lips. "I've changed my mind," she professed.

"About what?" a clueless Nothaar responded.

Giving Nothaar a sultry expression and starting to pull at his night clothes she expressed, "I think we do have enough time. Since it is our ceremony, it's not like they can start without us. We'll just tell them we had important *Keeper* things to do. It's not like anyone would know any better. There's mystery and ambiguousness surrounding our profession for a reason!"

"My, how devious you are," Nothaar teasingly accused as he started to untie Anlynx's ceremonial outfit she undoubtedly had spent a large span of time setting up perfectly, only to have Nothaar ruin it with his greedy hands. "I like it," he whispered into her ear.

Before they could get any further, a smashing sound reverberated through their hut, originating from the door and piercing their sanctum. This was soon followed with the high-pitched wail of "Mooooooommmmmmyyyyy!" At first, Nothaar considered that the outburst was spoken in the *Language of Children* before he realigned his brain. As Baubu was apt to remind him, they called their own tongue the *Lingua*, which was one of the many updates he had been compelled to make to his dissertation over the years. Even calling it "of Children" had been a misnomer, especially as several more winters had passed. Now, many of those ostensible juveniles had grown up and started having babies of their own. Nothaar and everyone born before the *Sky Shift* were in danger of being replaced and forgotten. His work had changed from a way to bridge the generations to a tome more about preserving the memory of a people who would soon fall by the wayside.

"Oh, no," Anlynx whispered. "I'm so sorry. Dii must have seen me come in here and followed. She's probably been sitting outside the entryway this entire time, waiting for me to come out."

Given their state of partial undress and arousal, Nothaar could only laugh. "Please, Dii, Mommy and Daddy are not ready to come out yet," Nothaar shouted in the *Lingua*. "Can you go play and we will come find you soon?"

"No!" Dii emphatically insisted. "And you stay! I need Mommy, and I need her now!"

"Me, too," Nothaar muttered into Anlynx's ear.

Separating herself, Anlynx began to fix her ensemble while yelling in her own attempt at the *Lingua*, "Okay, baby, me come out. Need few moment more, okay?"

"Hurry!" Dii whimpered in reply.

Returning to her own native tongue, Anlynx gave Nothaar an understandably disappointed mien and said, "Apologies, my love, but the mood has been ruined. I'll make it up to you later, promise!" With that, she planted another kiss on his mouth.

"I'll just add it to your compounding debt," Nothaar joked before swatting her on the behind. "Now get out of here before you lose your opening to escaping my boundless passion!"

CHAPTER 35

Once Anlynx and Dii had departed, Nothaar began to get himself ready, as well. Dii was the younger of their two children, with Baubu being the much older one, having gone through eleven winters compared to Dii's four. Baubu had been named after Anlynx's grandfather, the former long-serving *Keeper* who had overseen the village at the end of the world in the south for several generations. For some reason, the elder Baubu had thought that Nothaar should replace him, and once again Nothaar was glad to have had Anlynx to manage the load.

The younger Baubu was nothing like his namesake, nor either of his studious parents. He didn't care about the secrets and amazements of the *Knowledge* in the least and lived only to head out to sea with the fishermen or play rough games with the other kids. Although Nothaar had done everything possible to impress upon Baubu the importance of what he was doing, Baubu did not care. On the rare occasions when Nothaar had been able to coerce Baubu into helping him understand the *Lingua*, Baubu usually made a movement with his eyes, which Nothaar had come to recognize as annoyance.

All of the children made similar and other enigmatic expressions and gestures. Each of these movements appeared to be innate, not something they were learning from one another. Nothaar had come to realize how important non-verbal cues were to communication between people, not just spoken words and written language. It was one of the many insights he had been able to uncover by not only staying in one place for a significant period of time, but by having offspring of his own that he could watch and observe growing up.

And grow up they did! Just the other day, Baubu had demanded that he be allowed to have a hut of his own, or that Dii be moved away to a separate one, preferably his parents' domicile. The homes in this village were only ever big enough for a few people in order to assist in trapping and maintaining heat over the long, cold winters. As such, it was quite normal for young children to live together in their own separate unit next door or nearby. Although Baubu had been merely precocious during his earlier seasons, this winter he had turned downright capricious.

"Me no think so," Nothaar had responded to the request in the *Lingua*. He always found it easier to speak in his son's native tongue when he was rebuking him than to try to force Baubu to speak anything else, even though he had a talent for it that he chose to ignore.

"Say 'I', Dad, not 'me'," Baubu chided. "You always make that same mistake."

"Me... I be... am sorry," Nothaar corrected his speech as he went, "but no matter the tongue, the answer is no. Your sister is too young to be on her own, and your mother and I need space of our own for reasons you will appreciate when you are older. You need to watch out for her. Your mother and I depend upon you."

"I liked it better before Dii, when it was just me," Baubu pouted.

That assessment cut Nothaar to his core. While Anlynx's first pregnancy with Baubu had been relatively easy, every attempt since had been one painful failure after another. Between Baubu and Dii, Anlynx and he had two other stillborn children, plus a host of other incomplete pregnancies and miscarriages. After Dii was born, it had been much the same. According to Nothaar's calculations, only having replacement offspring would not be enough to keep up their population. Everyone needed to have more children, but it was proving quite difficult. Whatever had changed because of the *Sky Shift* had made healthy pregnancies that resulted in full-term births an incredibly difficult task. Although he and Anlynx had been able to maintain their amorousness despite their constant heartbreaks, other couples could not and simply stopped trying or went their separate ways. Through his research and outreach, Nothaar had also seen an alarming rise in voluntary celibacy worldwide.

Now, though, Nothaar was quite certain that the issue was not isolated to people who were around before the *Sky Shift*. Individuals born after that point were having all the same difficulties and then some, no matter how old or young their partners were or whether they looked like the old generation or the new one. Nothaar feared not only the potential upcoming population crash in general, but what it would mean for the continuation of the *Knowledge* and how that would, in turn, impact the future of his children and all their descendants, if there were any to be had.

"That not nice," Nothaar had scolded. "You know how hard your mother and I worked to have another baby. You have seen our sadness at losing so many. You know how hard all parents work to have you and all your friends. You take being alive for granted. You have no idea how fragile life is, how quickly it can all be gone."

Suddenly, Baubu shifted from trying to pretend to be an adult into being the immature little boy he really was. He began to break down and cry, saying he was sorry, taking Nothaar's harsh words to heart. In response, Nothaar had attempted to console him, but he could feel the gap between them continuing to widen. At that moment, Nothaar knew with absolute certainty that Baubu would leave them behind and move to another village at the first opportunity, and they would probably never see him again. As such, he vowed to spend as much of the limited time he had left with him, no matter how painful Baubu made it.

Remembering these events from such a short while ago, Nothaar began to feel guilty. *My long-term mate apparently thinks I'm capable of abandoning all of them,* Nothaar tortured himself, *so why wouldn't my own son feel the same way? Meanwhile, my young daughter has also seemingly learned that she doesn't need me and can simply go to Mommy. And who am I to argue? Did I not perceive the same thing Anlynx did? Did I not, too, sense some other reality where I did exactly that?*

Trying to break himself from his morose meditations, Nothaar finished preparing himself for the day ahead. He could not quite shake his foreboding sensation, but attempted to put it aside for the sake of all the others. The plan for today was to lend his strength to the volunteers who were about to go out into the wider world and deliver his gift. Since he was dependent upon them, he needed to project the confidence that he wanted them to feel.

Exiting his hut, Nothaar first turned towards the forest in order to relieve himself before anyone could notice him and grab his attention. That accomplished, he snuck around the back of the village to reach the feast that had been laid out and slip some much-needed food into his system. Everyone else had probably been awake since the sun rose, but Nothaar had stayed up late the night before preparing for this pivotal notch in their history.

At the moment he had a baked roll stuffed into his mouth, Nothaar heard the voice of a small child yell out in the *Lingua*, "He's here! He's here! Everyone, come quickly, the *Keeper* is here! It's finally time to start the ceremony! Come on, come on, come on!"

Slowly, the other villagers made their way over and Nothaar lost his chance to eat anything else until after the formalities. Anlynx found her way to his side with Dii in hand. In a fruitless attempt to make her escape, Dii was relentlessly squirming against her mother's solid grip. "Where's Baubu?" Nothaar inquired.

Anlynx gave him a look that spoke words she didn't need to: Baubu was off causing trouble with his friends and not listening to her anymore. *At least*, Nothaar thought, *we share that burden, too.*

The idea of sweet treats must have enticed some of Baubu's friends because they appeared with a reluctant Baubu in tow. Spotting him, Anlynx signaled for him to join them up front, but he pretended he did not notice and cast his eyes downward to kick some rocks. "Let him be," Nothaar requested, "we'll catch up with him afterwards. I'd rather not fight with him today of all days, anyway."

"Fine," Anlynx agreed perfunctorily, "but you're going to be the one who has to talk some sense into him."

"Understood," Nothaar conceded.

Just as he was about to begin, Nothaar spotted a woman in the back that he did not recognize. *No, that's not completely right*, Nothaar contemplated. *There's something oddly familiar about her, but I'm sure I don't know her. More so, I don't recall any strangers having arrived recently, unless she just got here.*

The woman seemed to notice Nothaar staring at her and contorted her face into one of the peculiar expressions he had noted in the children. *I might read it as something akin to joy*, Nothaar considered, *but I don't think that's how she's using it. For some reason, it's making me uncomfortable.* His intent evaluation was apparently noticed, and the woman's frontal response only expand further.

Embarrassed at having been caught looking at her, Nothaar attempted to place his gaze elsewhere, but something drew him back. Even from this distance, he realized that things were not adding up. The woman had the look of someone from the post-*Star Shift* generation, but she was far too old for that. Not that she was particularly elderly—perhaps she'd lived forty-five-or-so winters, he estimated—but that was far more than were possible. Nothaar considered that maybe she just looked old for her age, but there was something else that was bothering him. With a shock, he realized what it was: she was an amalgamation of all the various features he had ever seen among the younger cohort, anywhere he had ever traveled or lived. It was disturbing to see all the various phenotypes mashed up together in one singular being.

Inexplicably feeling compelled to investigate further, Nothaar bade Anlynx wait a moment longer to start the proceedings as he walked over to the newcomer. Anlynx gave him a perplexed look, then one that he thought might be jealousy, but she made no attempt to restrain him. As he got closer to the newcomer, Nothaar found that the enigmatic woman was also dressed in a peculiar manner; her outfit made from materials he had never seen before. What he considered to be impossible colors and cuts were seamlessly woven throughout her attire, almost assaulting his eyes with their unnatural perfection. Not a single thread or whisp of lint could be seen anywhere, and Nothaar began to believe that the garments might actually be completely smooth. Peering closer, the clothing left little question as to the shape of woman's curves as it perfectly contoured around her body. In totality, the whole effect was somehow both beautiful and garish at the same time, just as Nothaar sensed the woman herself seemed to be.

Although he was still quite confused, Nothaar spoke to the peculiar woman in the *Lingua*, "My apologies if we have met before, but—as impossible as it might be to believe given your... distinct appearance and dress—I do not seem to recall such an event. I have traveled the length of the land and met a considerable amount of people, so I might have somehow forgotten. In either case, my name is Nothaar, originally of the clan Akii, and I am one of the *Keepers* of this village, along with my mate Anlynx, here at southern edge of the world. May I inquire as to what you call yourself and where you originate from?"

For a brief instant, the woman looked like she was trying to hold something from escaping the inside of her mouth. Then, she let loose a loud round of laughter that was so gregarious and disturbing at the same time that everyone turned to see what was happening. Doubling over from her own personal and inscrutable mirth, the woman could not seem to get a word out. Nothaar looked around uncomfortably as all eyes were on him, including Anlynx's, who looked disappointed in him. Turning his attention back to the cackling woman, he attempted again, "Madam, please, you are causing a scene and we are about to partake in a sacred ritual. I must ask you to get ahold of yourself or, if you cannot, to please leave the village for the time being until you are able to contain yourself."

With a few snorts, the woman finally completed her fit and wiped tears from her eyes. Putting a hand on his shoulder, she declared, "Damn, Nothaar, you never fail to make me crack up with the way you speak!"

CHAPTER 36

Removing the odd woman's hand from his shoulder, Nothaar retorted, "I am sure I have no idea what you are talking about. Now please, for the last time, identify yourself and explain how it is that you seem to know me."

At Nothaar's demand, the woman's expression immediately and unmistakably screamed incredulity. "Wait, you're serious?" she queried. "I thought this was some weird performance you were putting on. Or, hold on: is my avatar looking messed up or something and you actually don't recognize me?" At this, she turned her head side-to-side, as if she was trying to see herself. After a few spins in a circle and apparently being unsuccessful in finding a way to examine her overall visage, she clarified, "It's me: Goqanx Guzyc! You know, the greatest pirate to sail the stars? No, nothing? How about: your lord and master? Still not an inkling? Fuck, Nothaar, what in the absolute shit did you do to yourself this time?"

Nothaar could only stare at this Goqanx Guzyc character with complete confusion. She was using some words from the *Lingua* that Nothaar was not familiar with, but somehow seemed just as familiar as her. "Who... what are you?" was all that he could manage.

"I'm a *Common*, of course, silly!" Goqanx announced

with glee. "Or at least I'm the projection of one. This is quite a little scenario you've cooked up, Nothaar, very impressive. I'm guessing the *Eh-aye* had a hand in this and is helping to suppress your real memories."

"My... real memories?" Nothaar inquired, still unsure what was happening.

"Hold on," Goqanx commanded with a wicked look upon her visage. "This is going to hurt... a lot."

Goqanx quickly put her hands together in front of her and then opened them widely. When she did so, the world suddenly tore in half. On one side, Nothaar saw his home, family, and friends all looking on with concern. In his other eye was a room covered in metal with little else to see. The only thing bridging the two images was a sadistic-looking Goqanx, split vertically in the middle between the two distinct environments. Nothaar felt his mind afire, ripping apart at the competing views of reality. He hit the ground screaming in agony but managed to screech, "What have you done to me, witch?!"

"I've been called far, far, worse," Goqanx jeered, "but I have to admit, it stings a little bit coming from you, lover boy. Can't you hear my gentle heart cleaving asunder? For being so mean to me, you're going to owe me a lot more than an apology. I demand a penance, and it's going to be one that I enjoy taking!"

At those words, Goqanx slammed her hands back together and all of reality coalesced and collapsed into one space. In as painful a fashion as possible, the part of his memory that had been segmented so he could live his virtual life in peace came flooding back. Nothaar realized that Goqanx was being intentionally unsafe out of spite. The correct procedure was to slowly lower the guards so as not to potentially cause brain damage. Nevertheless, Goqanx was apparently feeling scorned by Nothaar's decision to deliberately forget her, and would most likely be okay with renting him out to yet another unscrupulous doctor who would take delight in testing their skills at repairing the damage to a sapient alien's psyche.

It was the reason he had ocular implants that connected directly into his brain to begin with. Shady characters wanted to take their turn with a non-*Common* lifeform and perform all sorts of experiments on him. Compared to the average *Common*, Nothaar actually had more machinery now shoved inside him than was customary or even healthy.

As Nothaar began to regain sensation to anything other than absolute aching fire, his eyes were at last able to set their focus on his cabin aboard Goqanx's Torch Ship. "How long were you gone for this time?" Goqanx gently asked, seemingly deciding that she had punished Nothaar for long enough, at least for the time being.

Panting to catch his breath, Nothaar responded, "Over... twelve... years..."

One of the benefits of all his new accoutrements, Nothaar discovered, was the ability to slow down his perception of time. Months could be experienced in hours—a sub-unit of time within a day that he had learned about from the *Commons* sometime along the way. Nothaar combined that ability with one for creating artificial circumstances that were projected through his ocular implants so that he experienced them as if they were happening in real-time. Meanwhile, in the actual universe, he was hooked up to medical equipment that moved him around and fed him nourishment and water.

As Goqanx had insinuated, this was not the first time Nothaar had undertaken such an endeavor, although this was by far his most ambitious attempt. He worked with his onboard *Eh-aye* to create responsive programs, a chance for Nothaar to ask, "what if?" He had tested out several other lives, experimenting with them and seeing how things might have turned out. By his estimation, engrossing himself in these alternate existences had certainly been better than partaking in his actual one. However, before this occasion, he had never attempted to restrict the majority of his own truly lived history so thoroughly behind an unreadable partition. To say that it was a risky technique would be an understatement.

"Wow," Goqanx intoned, "I think that's the longest you've ever gone. Guess I should have checked in on you a bit sooner. Anyway, sorry to wake you, but we're just a few days away from reaching our next destination, so you need to prepare for *zero-gee*."

"Where are we this time?" Nothaar cursed, letting his distaste for Goqanx drip on every word.

"Does it matter to you?" Goqanx questioned. "Or do you have some secret escape plan I need to be made aware of, hmm?"

"You know I cannot hide anything like that from you," Nothaar spat. "The nanobots report every detail of my entire life, both real and imaginary, directly to you."

Examining him like he was a piece of furniture, Goqanx pouted, "Yeah, that's true. Still, you do find ways to surprise me from time-to-time. I don't think I knew about this Anlynx woman from your homeworld before. Very pretty. But to be fair, she's either quite old or dead by now, given time dilation and all."

Holding back his desire to throttle Goqanx, Nothaar knew she was correct. Among the other things the *Commons* had done to him was find ways to apply their life-extending longevity treatments. Nothaar had no idea how old he was anymore nor how many years had passed since he'd last seen his own planet. Instead, he had just become a toy for Goqanx, something to show off on the many worlds they had visited since he unwillingly came aboard her vessel. Among Goqanx's many semi-legitimate businesses was a traveling oddity show, what she had called a "circus". Most the other exhibits were plants, animals, and artifacts, but Nothaar was the star attraction. The people came from far-and-wide to see the extraterrestrial lifeform that eloquently spoke the *Lingua* and could talk about quantum theory.

Sure enough, Goqanx had allowed Nothaar to study whatever he wanted from the *Archive*. Anything he learned seemed to make him even more valuable and interesting to those who came to see him. Many paid an extra fee to be given time alone with him, but only Goqanx was allowed to use him for her pleasure. Everything he had suffered through only made him want to escape his own existence, and he did find a reprieve in his faux diversions into alternate timelines. Nothaar did not spend all his days living in substitute realities, though he seemed to be doing so more frequently in recent years in order to keep the malaise at bay. He was free to basically do whatever he wanted, within the confines of never being too far from Goqanx and her desires, whatever they might be.

As if reading his mind, Goqanx requested, "After you get yourself together and cleaned up, why don't you come visit me in my cabin later? I'm feeling rather generous, so I'll even let you put a digital skin of Anlynx over me, if that's something you'd like to try. Actually, it might be kind of kinky to pretend to be one of your kind for a change! Oh, you know what I'll do? I'll have the *Eh-aye* put together and print out a replica outfit, just like the one she was wearing, and you can pick up untying it right where you left off."

Although Nothaar didn't say anything—nor did he believe he reacted in any noticeable way—Goqanx still seemed to easily pick up on his mystification about the fact that she was describing details she shouldn't have been privy to. "Oh, sorry," Goqanx spoke in a mockingly singsong tone as she made a gesture that Nothaar recognized as pretending to be cute, "did I not mention this before? I was spying on you through the... oh, I don't know what you'd call it... a window, a high smoke hole, I guess? Whatever that small opening in the back of your hut is called, I was checking out you and your mate going at it for a while. Whew, it got me a bit hot and bothered! Okay, okay, okay, I admit it, I was a tinge jealous!"

Nothaar suppressed a shudder lest he upset Goqanx. It wasn't like he had not fulfilled such carnal desires for her in the past. Truthfully, he didn't have much of a choice in the matter and they both knew it. Goqanx had quickly hijacked the basic nanobots that Syraaq had installed to manage his behavior and took the microscopic machines to a whole other level. If she wanted, Goqanx could completely control Nothaar's entire body. On several occasions, she had craved such a thing and done what she wanted with him. After initially trying to resist, Nothaar found his best bet was to submit to her whims.

Although Goqanx was not unattractive for a *Common*—far from it, actually—Nothaar did not want to be taken against his will. More so, Nothaar yearned for nothing more than to have time to grieve the lover and family he had just lost. With his memory fully restored, he was well aware that they were never real; but that did little to assuage his feelings related to their virtual demise and his own ensuing loneliness as a result. Nonetheless, he saw no other option but to acquiesce to Goqanx's wishes and continue to endure this violation of his very being, this never-ending rape of his body and soul. Looking directly into Goqanx's eyes, Nothaar declared, "I will be there."

CHAPTER 37

Feeling quite self-conscious with Goqanx staring directly at him, Nothaar tried to turn his face away and hide his shame. Although both of them were naked under the thick comforter that covered Goqanx's bed in her quarters, somehow having her looking intently at him made Nothaar consider himself to be particularly exposed in a way that having his own unbridled flesh exposed did not. Apparently, Goqanx wanted to continue examining him as she put her hands against his cheeks and turned Nothaar's head back towards her. Peering deeply into his eyes, Goqanx declared, "You're looking more morose than usual, my pet. Tell me, what's going on with you?"

During these post-coitus sessions, Goqanx often demonstrated something akin to sensitivity and concern in relation to Nothaar's needs. However, Nothaar was never quite sure if she was serious or was just toying with him, so he usually refused to give her anything to work with. *What benefit would it serve, anyway?* he often wondered. *It is not like she would do anything to alleviate the situation or let me go free, so what would be the point?* For some inexplicable reason, though, he felt compelled to speak on this occasion. *Perhaps I am just weak, and Goqanx is my only hope of reprieve?* he considered. *After all, I have no one else but her.* With that sad realization at the top of his mind, aloud he noted, "My recently ended virtual experience rekindled memories of all the people I have been obliged to leave behind over the years. And for what purpose did I have to lose everyone? What have I done with my life in all these years that is worthy of that sacrifice? Here I am, just another freakshow, with no friends, no family, and no future of my own."

"Ah, I see," Goqanx spoke with sympathy in her voice, but once again Nothaar was unsure if it was genuine or not. Instantly, Nothaar regretted bringing anything up at all. Nevertheless, Goqanx seemed resolved to continuing the conversation, thus he was trapped in an uncomfortable discussion about the meaning—or lack thereof—of his life with his jailer and source of his woes.

"Perhaps it would've been better if I'd allowed Syraaq and Ifu to remain aboard," Goqanx began, "at least for your sake. Honestly, I felt they were more trouble than they were worth. Not only were they always plotting and scheming, but they were terrible and inefficient workers to begin with!"

Goqanx laughed at her own evaluation, but quickly stopped when Nothaar did not join in. "Come on, Nothaar," she added, "I released them with their lives intact when I didn't have to. Wasn't that magnanimous enough for you? Haven't I shown you enough of my... softer side?"

When their party had first been taken up to Goqanx's vessel in orbit, Nothaar, Syraaq, and Ifu had been placed in a holding cell. It was only once they were underway and gravity had been restored that Goqanx came to visit and interrogate them. At first, Syraaq and Ifu had attempted to be aloof in their responses to Goqanx's inquiries, but the pirate captain had not taken too kindly to them trying to maintain their perpetual ambiguousness. Nothaar, candidly, still knew precious little of their actual plans, and, due to this, did not have much to offer. Eventually, though, Goqanx came to realize that threating and torturing Syraaq and Ifu would get her nowhere with them, but putting Nothaar in harm's way was enough to loosen their lips. One demonstration of how she had hijacked Nothaar's punishment nanobots was enough to start the tête-à-tête.

From what Nothaar had pieced together from Ifu and Syraaq's revelations to Goqanx and other earlier snippets he picked up from exchanges between the two of them, the *Common*'s central government seemed to consist entirely of just three elected representatives from each of the planets that made up the *Common*'s entire collective. This, in turn, meant that there must have been tens—if not hundreds—of thousands of delegates, an incredibly unwieldy number. Among their own massively large group, though, they assigned themselves into several divisions that focused on either legislative matters to decide the law; executive tasks to enforce the laws and perform operating responsibilities; or judicial activities to interpret the law and test its boundaries. In the end, it was a small subset of those chosen officials who actually decided the rules for trillions of people spread over their light-years-wide system circumnavigating a supermassive black hole.

The entire federal organization was housed on a single Torch Ship that was constantly traveling between worlds, but not in any type of linear fashion. It was not like their craft went to a planet and its next destination was a neighboring globe. Instead, they voyaged in a random, indeterminate pattern as designed and designated by an incontrovertible *Eh-aye*. While this was reportedly the situation, every *Common* Nothaar had ever met professed an innate distrust in allowing an *Ey-aye* to have any type of decision-making capabilities. Despite this nearly unanimous outlook, for some unknown reason this specific *Eh-aye* was allegedly part of a very special routine that was given extreme leeway. Nothaar had heard that it even had its own infamous moniker, something like *"The Sage and Her Father"*, whatever that was supposed to mean. Despite collecting these various rumors and hearsay, Nothaar couldn't really find any significant details in the local copy of the *Archive* that was available to him, and none of his companions could provide any greater detail beyond these rather superficial descriptors.

Whenever the government's Torch Ship arrived at a particular world, they would set up a temporary headquarters on the surface and stay there for several months or years, depending on the timeframe that was necessary to compete their intended duties while landbound. One of the core happenings was the election of new representatives to replace the ones who would finish their terms upon return to their homeworld. Due to the arbitrary nature of the government's flightpath, a representative may have served for as little as five years or as long as multiple millennia, from the perspective of their progenitor sphere. All that was certain was that nothing was.

When Nothaar had asked the reasonings for what he saw as a haphazard system, he was told it was due to security considerations. "Having a single location or a specific planet for the government," Ifu had claimed, "would always put it and the people who are a part of it or work for it in danger. We live in a distributed society, so the government reflects the only safe, logical, and realistic way for that to function."

Scoffing at this declaration, Goqanx had said, "That's one opinion, but some of us have very little use for the central government at all, or any government, for that matter. But that's beside the point. What I want to know is this: there is no published schedule for the government's Torch Ship. It just shows up at a planet without warning and then all proceedings get underway. How were you planning to figure out where it was going to be next so that you could possibly, maybe, get in front of the legislature and make your case?"

"Well, technically, we could just wait around on some indiscriminate planet," Syraaq jested. "I mean, it might take decades or centuries, but they'll eventually show up!"

Goqanx's expression made it clear she was not amused by Syraaq's attitude and Nothaar thought she was about to "reprimand" Syraaq, in a very painful way. As a distraction to protect Syraaq, he questioned, "But what about newly Quantum Shifted planets like my own? We do not have any representatives on the council, so how can our desires be accounted for and met?"

Quickly turning her attention towards Nothaar, Goqanx started cackling and projecting an appearance of enjoyment. "I like you, Nothaar," she announced. "These two, I could do without; but you, you're special, in all the wrong ways. Let me tell you, my dear, the central government barely cares or pays attention to the trillions of citizens it already has. It's an ineffective, useless, bloated bureaucracy that sometimes tries to get in the way of free-spirited entrepreneurs like myself. If you aren't a *Common*, they sure as hell are not going to give a fuck. As far as they're concerned, you are the Starbuilders' property and responsibility, so they'll stay hands-off until you're further along in your development and can join their pointless little club."

"No, the government is important," Ifu refuted, "and we're going to use them to help save all the potential non-*Commons* and their worlds that are yet to be discovered. Nothaar is our secret weapon to make that happen. Yes, I admit, we don't have a plan yet to figure out how to get ahead of the government and set up a meeting, but we'll be able to, eventually, somehow. Our cause is too important, therefore we will succeed in the end, no matter how many setbacks and challenges we must face and endure. I have complete faith in the merit and virtue of what we've set out to do for the universe."

All the joviality drained from Goqanx's countenance and she returned to a more serious, formal tone. "Well, until that day, you still work for me. So, unless you plan on leaving out the airlock, you have a lot to do between now and then to even begin paying down the debt you owe me. As such, I, by my own benevolence, have decided that I've heard enough about your shenanigans and ridiculous aspirations. Syraaq, Ifu, you'll each be granted your own quarters, far from each other, and be given assignments in the regular crew rotation tasks."

"What about Nothaar?" Ifu attempted.

Casually dismissing Ifu, Goqanx continued, "I have some other plans for him; don't you worry about it."

After that exchange, the three of them rarely saw each other. Syraaq and Ifu were apparently on opposite shifts and had to go out of their way to spend any time together. If they were seen heading towards each other's quarters, a security officer tended to intercept them and send them back the way they had come. They had to find ways to "accidently run into each other" in random locales. At least, that is what Syraaq had told Nothaar during one of their own infrequent encounters.

Upon reaching another planet, Nothaar finally got a taste of what Goqanx had planned for him. Crowds gawked at his very existence, ostensibly paying an ever-increasing fee to see the strange alien in their midst. As Ifu and Syraaq had explained to him in the past, the vast majority of *Commons* never left their own worlds, and certainly had not seen—much less interacted with—a different sapient lifeform. Only Starbuilders usually had that opportunity, which was one of the draws for certain people to be recruited into their organization. Meanwhile, Ifu and Syraaq were required to stay behind and only heard about what had happened planet-side upon Nothaar and Goqanx's return to the ship.

Syraaq had told Nothaar that she and Ifu had both vehemently complained to Goqanx about putting Nothaar on display out in the open and how it was dangerous for all of them as it could put them on the authority's radar. It was still highly illegal for a non-*Common* to be taken from their homeworld, but Goqanx did not appear to be dissuaded by these arguments. Goqanx herself had actually brought up Syraaq and Ifu's complaints to Nothaar on several occasions, and he recognized that she was growing more and more impatient with them. When able to find a rare opportunity to speak with one or both of them, Nothaar begged Ifu and Syraaq to discontinue their discourse. Nonetheless, they could not be deterred.

Finally, after several of these cycles of visiting planets, presenting Nothaar to paying audiences, and listening to Ifu and Syraaq protesting about all of it, Goqanx seemingly had enough. She forced Ifu and Syraaq to go down the *Space Elevator* to the surface of the world they happened to be parked at, saying that their debt was now repaid, but only under one condition: that she got to keep Nothaar in the bargain. That was the last time Nothaar had seen or heard anything about or from Syraaq and Ifu, all those years ago.

CHAPTER 38

Sitting in his clear glass cage, Nothaar waited for his first "private client" of the day. The enclosure was wholly unnecessary since Nothaar was geofenced into a specific area lest his punishment nanobots activate, but Goqanx insisted that the setup added to the ambiance and enigma surrounding him. "It makes you seem dangerous and untamed," Goqanx had told him once, "and our customers get a visceral thrill out of feeling like they've overcome some significant hazard. They like to pretend that they're great explorers doing something unique and amazing... and, most of all, scary!"

The design was based on the decontamination chambers aboard spaceships, except those all used electronic communication systems to avoid potentially sharing any germs. According to Goqanx, though, that type of technological disconnect between people would result in the paying audience deeming the experience to appear "artificial", and she wanted to make sure their encounter was as "real" as possible. Therefore, as part of setting the scene, the transparent paddock had fist-sized holes cut through it to allow sound and objects to pass unobstructed. Consequently, Goqanx's marks would perceive both false security from their protective separation barrier and deep interactivity due to Nothaar's physical availability to them.

The most recent public show had taken place earlier in the day. Per usual, Nothaar told stories from his homeworld, his people, and their various cultures, but never offered too many specific details. Goqanx wanted him to whet the crowd's appetite so that some of the patrons—in order to fully satiate their curiosity—would request additional alone-time with Nothaar. "For a significant fee, of course," Goqanx had noted with unabashed satisfaction. Since Nothaar didn't appreciate being put on display in the first place, it was not too difficult for him to hold back on discussing anything too deeply. Further, Goqanx had long ago given up the need to personally supervise his performances, thus he had a lot of leeway in deciding what he did or did not want to share. One of her bored subordinates could often be seen with the unmistakable look of someone escaping into a virtual environment while Nothaar rambled on for the locals, ostensibly trying to convert them into high-paying clients.

After these communal sessions, Nothaar was moved to his "personal receiving chambers" and the uninterested crewmember set themselves up outside to await the rubes looking for a more in-depth and personal foray. As expected, on this occasion, Nothaar did not have to linger long until some *Common* came inside. The person this time was dressed all in black with no skin showing, including a mask of some kind that covered their entire face. Just as Ifu and Syraaq had told him in the distant past, there were many cultures whose dress was very much like what he saw in front of him, thus this was not the first time such an individual in similar garb came to visit him. However, he was not completely prepared for what came out of the mouth hidden beneath the plasticized countenance.

"Hello, Nothaar," a mechanized voice saluted him. *This is new*, Nothaar thought. *Every Common in a face covering that I have ever met has always used their natural voice. I wonder why this person is choosing to disguise their speech? I suppose that among tens of thousands of worlds and trillions of Commons that some of them might have some doctrine against allowing their natural tenor to be heard. It certainly would not even be the weirdest thing I have ever seen amongst these people.*

"Greetings to you," Nothaar responded in return in the *Lingua*. "What may I call you?" *Commons* with implants frequently had freely available metadata broadcast from them, with information like their names and preferred pronouns being fairly conventional. Despite this person before him clearly using automata of some kind to interact with the world, Nothaar could see in his own visual range that they were intentionally suppressing anything about themselves from leaking out. While it was quite an unusual convention, it really did not concern or interest Nothaar that much beyond idle curiosity.

"Let's put that aside for now," the stranger replied.

"Very well," Nothaar conceded. "It is your money, and I will not interfere with how you wish to spend it. So, tell me then, what is it you want to know about me?"

Nothaar's visitor was silent for several moments before asking, "Tell me this: if you could, would you go back to the situation you were in before... all of this...?" With these words, the being in black pointed at Nothaar's restrictive compartment.

Becoming immediately suspicious, Nothaar queried, "What is it you are asking about, exactly? Are you wondering if I could leave my current employ and revert to what I was doing immediately beforehand, would I? And what would you know about me and my life at that point?"

"I've learned a lot about you, Nothaar Akii, over the past several years," the robotic-sounding proxy quickly answered, "and that's all I'll say about that subject for now. But despite what I've been able to glean, I still don't know how you'd react to an offer like this. Thus, as I said, I want to know if you'd be happier exchanging your current situation with how things were beforehand?"

"Happier?!" Nothaar scoffed. "I cannot imagine how you came across any intelligence on me, but let me be very clear: I am not happy now, and I certainly was not happy then. My choice is neither."

"But if you had to pick one," the guest insisted, "if these were your only two options, what would you do? If I presented you with an opportunity to leave your forced servitude, but the price was as I've laid out, would you be willing to pay it?"

Staying quiet, Nothaar tried to avoid answering. Everything his caller was saying felt like a trap, and one that Goqanx would be apt to set up. *If I say I preferred to stay,* Nothaar considered, *Goqanx would take delight in those words and hold them over me for the rest of my life. On the other hand, if I say I want to go back to a prior existence—even one I found profoundly intolerable—then she would use that as an excuse to painfully reprimand me and restrict what little freedoms I do have. What should I do? I cannot remain uncommunicative forever.*

While Nothaar silently pondered, his alleged customer patiently stood there without insisting he make his contemplations be known. After some time, Nothaar decided that he would throw caution aside and be honest, no matter the consequences. Part of him realized that it was because he no longer cared to continue being alive, that he actually yearned for the possibility that he could anger Goqanx enough to finally kill him and release him from his misery. With these deliberations only half formed in his consciousness, Nothaar declared, "I hate what my master, Goqanx Guzyc, has done to me and what she has ripped away from me. More so, she has made me despise myself. Do not be fooled; whatever you have heard, my life before I met her was no paradise, either. Nevertheless, at the very least, I could still hold on to a miniscule amount of hope that things could change for the better. There was a chance, as small as it was, that I could be free again to do what I saw as necessary. I do not even have that luxury anymore."

As Nothaar spoke, his supposed patron made some motions that likely related agreement, although Nothaar had to judge completely based on body language since he could not see their face. Once Nothaar was done with his riposte, the other person situated outside his prison simply stated, "Very well." And then, they walked away.

Nothaar was alone once again, completely baffled by what had just happened. Then he heard a thunk from outside, although he could not quite place what it was. His unspoken question as to its origin was quickly answered as the client in black came back inside, except they were dragging the guard from outside. A trail of blood followed behind what Nothaar then realized was a corpse.

"What have you done?" Nothaar shouted.

Instead of answering, the apparently violent stranger raised their hand to their neck and pulled off their face covering. As they beamed at Nothaar with amusement, the non-*Common* yelped with surprise, "Bipauc?!"

Continuing to display merriment despite the circumstances, they responded, "That's Captain Qeraat Elii Bipauc of the private-industry Torch Ship *Reimagine*, to you! You should use my full title, Nothaar, and show me the proper respect." They then laughed at whatever they found so comical in that statement.

"I... I... do not understand," Nothaar stammered. "What are you doing here? How are you here? What is happening right now?"

"All in due time," Captain Bipauc insisted. "First, we both have to get out of this place—completely intact, that is." As this, Bipauc put their finger to their ear and spoke aloud, "Commence operation."

Before Nothaar could even begin to inquire what Bipauc was doing, explosions and screams started pouring in from all directions. Then, Bipauc pulled a device from up their sleeve and adhered it to Nothaar's cage. "Stand back," they ordered, "and try to cover your ears, eyes, and head, if you can."

Doing as requested, Nothaar started to feel a rumble and shaking. Suddenly, the glass shattered into many small pieces and Nothaar was no longer restricted by any enclosure. "Sonic resonance," Bipauc clarified without prompting. "Everything has a frequency, and if you match it, you can make it fall apart. It's a very old technology, but it's still as effective as ever."

"It does not matter," Nothaar claimed. "I cannot leave the immediate vicinity, and, most definitely, cannot be taken too far from Goqanx. My nanobots are keyed to her and will attack me if I do not follow her explicit directives. She is probably on her way over here right now. I do not know what you are planning here, but you should run while you have the chance. Goqanx and her crew are exception-ally dangerous. Despite our history, I would not want to see you became yet another one of their casualties."

"Don't worry about that," Bipauc contended as they made their way closer to Nothaar. "Our people are keeping Goqanx and the rest of her crew plenty busy. It might even be possible that someone has managed to permanently take her out of the equation already. Still, you're right, we can't risk anything. Please hold out your arm."

Upon this request, Bipauc pulled a gun out of his op-posite sleeve. Nothaar scootched back, looking for some way to avoid the weapon. "Nothaar, stop!" Bipauc bade.

"I'm not here to kill you. This is a shot to neutralize your pain-inducing and bodily control nanobots. We're going to get them out of you, once and for all."

Acceding to the logic in Bipauc's argument, Nothaar stopped attempting to flee and did as originally instructed. "I'm not going to lie," Bipauc admitted, "this is going to burn a whole hell of a lot. I'm sorry, but it's the only way."

Placing the gun to Nothaar's arm, Bipauc triggered the device. A sensation akin to being on fire quickly began to spread through Nothaar's entire body. The internal flames grew in heat, intensity, and agony until Nothaar could not take it anymore. He faded blissfully into a dreamless blackness, one as dark as Bipauc's outfit.

CHAPTER 39

Slipping in and of consciousness as Bipauc dragged him through the chaos of the battle going on in his name, Nothaar thought he caught glimpses of people he recognized. A lot of it felt like a fever dream, so he could not be sure that what he was seeing was actually happening, but Nothaar was almost certain he spied several faces he recognized from the *Conclave of Dreamers*. It had been so long that he did not remember any of their names, but they looked much the same as he recalled. At last, Bipauc appeared to get them both clear of immediate danger and settled inside a small building. "I'm at rendezvous site sixteen," Nothaar heard Bipauc speak into the air, obviously in remote communication with someone else. "I have the package, but it appears to be damaged. Need an immediate MEDVAC at my location. Everyone else planet-side should pull out and make their way to the *Space Elevator*."

As Nothaar tried to speak, he found his voice was inaccessible. He thought he was mouthing words, but at the same time he could not feel his muscles moving. Bipauc appeared to notice and looked down at Nothaar saying, "Save your energy; we still have a long way to go."

There was a rapping at the door and Bipauc went into a private visual session, or at least that was what it looked like to Nothaar—who could not trust his own senses. Bipauc was seemingly content with whatever action they took because they got up, opened the door, signaled someone to come in, and straightaway barred the opening behind them. The woman who entered immediately began to stick things into Nothaar, making a lot of dissatisfied noises while doing so. "This isn't good," she declared. "We have to get back to the ship at once so I can have access to real medical equipment. We should also take off as quickly as possible because being under *zero-gee* will not help his condition in any way."

"All of that will take days," Bipauc complained. "What should we do in the meantime?"

Without hesitating, the apparent healer decided, "I'll put him in a medically induced coma and try to slow down his metabolism, get him into a therapeutic hypothermia state. The best thing we can possibly do right now is just try to stop a cascading shutdown of his organs, especially his brain. Who knows if we have the capabilities to reverse brain damage in an organism like him?"

"Wow," Bipauc intoned, "such an old method, it sounds downright barbaric. Do you even think that same type of solution applies to his physiology?"

Giving a gesture declaring she did not have a clear opinion, the woman highlighted, "We don't have a grasp on anything, but what choice do we have?"

Glancing one last time at Nothaar writhing on the floor, Bipauc conceded, "Okay, do it."

With no preamble, the still unnamed woman came

over to Nothaar, pressed some things against him, and then he felt and saw nothing.

After an indeterminant amount of time, Nothaar awoke. Looking around, he recognized that he was in the sickbay of a Torch Ship. More so, he knew the exact one. *This is Bipauc's personal craft, the Reimagine*, Nothaar internally remarked. *I spent so much time in here looking after Syraaq and Ifu, I could never forget it.*

As he attempted to sit up and move, a robot came over and gently pushed him back down. "Now, now, sir," it admonished. "You are still recovering from a terrible ordeal and are in no shape to go anywhere. However, I have alerted the doctor and your guardians that you are conscious, so they should arrive shortly."

Nothaar felt as weak as a newborn, thus he could not argue with the much stronger machine. Instead, he tested his own aching throat by asking, "Guardians?"

Seemingly on cue, the door to the sickbay swished open and Syraaq and Ifu came running inside. "Nothaar!" Syraaq squealed. "I'm so sorry we weren't here when you woke up. The doctor, Mouza Ori, she wouldn't let anyone be in here with you during your treatment. I just can't believe..." She trailed off in tears as she shuffled over and smothered Nothaar in a hug.

Ifu walked to Nothaar's opposite side and placed a hand on his shoulder. He looked contrite in a way Nothaar had never seen in him before. "I'm so happy to see you again, Nothaar, and I can't apologize enough for what befell you, especially because of our actions. Although I can never truly understand what you've gone through, I want you to know that I'm here for you, and I'll do anything I can to make things right for you."

Before Nothaar could even begin to ask the thousands of questions he had, another person came running in. It was the same woman Nothaar recalled from the planet, the one Syraaq must have been referring to as Mouza Ori. Looking quite upset, Mouza quickly dressed down Syraaq and Ifu for coming in before her and ejected them from the room. She then began to examine Nothaar, but would not answer any of the few queries he managed to squawk out. Finally, she just asserted, "Your only priority right now is getting better. I'll allow the captain to visit you in a few days if I'm satisfied with your progress, then you can interrogate them all you want. Until then, you are still in a delicate condition and I won't risk anything happening to you, not after what I had to do to save your life."

Seeing no other option but to agree to these terms, Nothaar slipped back into a restless sleep, although a more natural one filled with his regular nightmares. Thus, the pattern continued for several days, with Nothaar occasionally coming to and Mouza visiting to do tests. Eventually, Nothaar burst awake from one of the horrors going through his unconscious mind to notice that Mouza and Bipauc were both there, apparently in the midst of discussing him. He caught the latter part of Mouza's story as she was saying, "... physical issues are treatable and I am making great progress, but you've heard now how he screams in his sleep. That's the least of the symptoms."

"What's happening?" Bipauc inquired.

"I haven't been able to talk with him enough to make a full diagnosis," Mouza began, "but if I were to guess, I'd say it's post-traumatic stress disorder."

"Is he treatable?" Bipauc pushed.

Mouza gave Bipauc a look of contempt as she summarized, "We're barely able to do anything beneficial for *Commons*; I wouldn't even know where to begin with an alien like this. What would giving Nothaar a standard mood stabilizer even do to him? Despite all the data we were able to extricate from Goqanx's vessel before our extraction team blew it up, I'm not sure there's enough useful information to begin with. This might come as a surprise to you, but pirates and unscrupulous, so-called 'medical professionals' that were willing to put aside their oaths in order to experiment on a non-*Common* sapient being—these people were not exactly the most prodigious at proper documentation."

"Was there anything helpful in all those files?" Bipauc continued to press with what Nothaar thought was a mix of annoyance and desperation. "As you are well-aware, we have plans for this man. I want... no, require... to know if he'll be ready to go. We only have limited time until we reach our destination."

"This is an independent, intelligent, living person!" Mouza argued. "You cannot just repair him like one of these stupid robots. I won't promise anything."

Displaying his own expression of disgust, Bipauc remarked, "You know how important our mission is, right?

And how this is our one and only shot at actually doing something good in the universe? We also owe it to all the members of our very precarious alliance, several of whom died so that Nothaar could take on the essential role we've imagined for him. Nonetheless, as despicable as they were, it's not like all of Goqanx's people that went down with the ship or were taken out on the ground deserved that fate. Most of them were petty criminals, at best. To do what we did, our people had to sacrifice their blood, sweat, tears, and souls. So, it's not hyperbole when I say that we need Nothaar, or this will all be for naught."

Sighing, Mouza at last relented, "I know, I know, and just to make it clear to you: I'm a loyal soldier in our important work, too. Alright, well, there is one thing I found in Nothaar's personal *Archive*. From what I can tell—and I'm hardly an expert—Nothaar brought on much of his own cerebral and psychological injury by slowing down his perception of time and living inside virtual programs for what he perceived as years at a time. Therefore, it's not just the entire period he's been away from us, but decades more of additional time he perceives he spent in fake scenarios that always ended poorly for him."

"That sounds like an even worse prognosis," Bipauc interrupted. "I fail to see how this could help his recovery."

"I wasn't finished," Mouza rebuked. "The last one he ran was the most interesting. Somehow, Nothaar and the *Eh-aye* developed a novel method to completely partition his memories. I might be able to apply that concept to a radical form a therapy that could help him."

"You want to suppress his recollections?" Bipauc asked for clarification. "And you think that will help him get past or at least be able to deal with his mental and emotional problems?"

Her forlorn self-doubt evident on her face, Mouza rejoined, "I'm... unsure. It might be something we do here in the real world, or it might be something useful to do to him in the virtual one, despite the additional damage it may cause. In the time we have left, he could go through decades of intense psychotherapy and rehabilitation."

Having heard enough, Nothaar yelled out, "No!"

Both Bipauc and Mouza jumped, confirming that they had been unaware that Nothaar had been conscious and listening to the two of them drone on about him. Before they could attempt to talk to him, Nothaar cut them off. "My memories, real or imagined, are mine and mine alone. You do not get to decide for me what I get to remember. Yes, Bipauc, I am a broken, miserable creature who may be of no use to you whatsoever. You may have used all your resources and goodwill on a pointless quest to save me. If—and that is a big if—but if I decide to help you, it will be on my own terms. Accept it, or throw me out the airlock. I do not fear pain or death anymore."

For a moment, Bipauc looked like they were going to take Nothaar up on that offer, but instead they turned to Mouza and proclaimed, "He's your patient, doctor. You do what you and he think is best."

With that simple statement, Bipauc walked out the door without so much as a word directed at Nothaar.

CHAPTER 40

After nearly a month of further treatment, Mouza decided that it was safe for Nothaar to take his leave from the sickbay and to continue his convalescence based out of the same quarters he previously occupied during his last stay aboard the *Reimagine*. Nevertheless, she let Nothaar know that she still intended to meet with him on a daily basis to continue to work with him on his physical, psychological, and social ailments. "That said," she had explained, "I don't feel that you need to be under constant clinical observation. More so, based upon your time in captivity, I have every reason to believe it would actually be detrimental to your progress towards recovery. Listen, I know you haven't dealt with the best examples of *Common*-kind purporting to be from my vocation. Still, as a doctor, it's my duty—as it should have been the duty of those people Goqanx brought to see you—to ensure that my patients become well with no other considerations. As far as I'm concerned, Nothaar, my first priority is you and no one and nothing else. Do you understand?"

Nothaar gave the *Common*'s expression of disbelief. "How quickly you seem to have forgotten what I overheard you discussing with Captain Bipauc," Nothaar spat back. "While I thank you for your assistance in getting me away from Goqanx's clutches, exorcising my control-mechanism nanobots, and ministering my recuperation, I see no pretext for trusting that there are any altruistic motivations in all of this. You have an agenda, a reason for being here in the first place, and I must conclude that it will always come before anything else, even my own health."

Looking dejected, Mouza responded, "I'm sorry you feel that way, Nothaar. And I'm sorrier that we've given you every cause for harboring that opinion. My only solace is that I'll endeavor to show you that the *Common* race, for the most part, is not exclusively made up of what you've unfortunately had to endure. Among trillions of people, you, regrettably, have had many bad run-ins with the tiniest percentage of the worst of them."

"We will see," Nothaar conceded, although not with any deeply held consideration. He really just wanted to end this conversation and have Mouza leave him to his lonesome so that he could get used to his new/old accommodations again.

After a long stretch of silence, Mouza seemed to realize that Nothaar was not going to say anything else, so she broke the awkwardness by stating, "Well, anyway, you have free rein of the ship. I'm assuming you remember your way around. Nothing much has changed since you were last here, so things should be fairly normal and familiar to you."

"Normal?" Nothaar queried. "Familiar? No, things are quite different for me. Last time I was aboard, I had to hide who I was underneath a mask and cloak. I ate alone in my room because there was no point in being anywhere else. I know this was before your time, but I could only show my face around Bipauc, Ifu, Syraaq, and the medical robots."

"In that case," Mouza contended, "then your situation has changed for the better, overall. There's a great diversity of people and groups on board now, too, including many you met at the first *Conclave of Dreamers*. By the way, I was there, too, as a spectator, so you probably didn't notice me. That's where I decided to join Captain Bipauc and the cause. Their message of not only taking a non-interference approach, but also creating a symbiotic dispersion—it really resonated with me, both as a person and as a medical professional. As such, I asked the captain right then and there if I could join them, and they were more than happy to have me. When Ifu and Syraaq hunted us down years later, I vaguely remembered them, but more so recalled the mysterious, silent stranger that had been with them. Boy, was I surprised when they confessed who and what you were and what they had done!"

This was new information. Although Nothaar had been slowly returning to an acceptable level of physical health, Mouza had still not let anyone else visit him, especially after the incident with Bipauc. Although he was aware that Syraaq and Ifu were on the vessel with him, he had no idea why or how they got there, nor how this entire state of affairs had come together. As he attempted to process these thoughts and make sense of Mouza's unexpected revelation, Nothaar asked, "Wait, it was Ifu and Syraaq who sought you out?"

"Oh, yeah," Mouza nonchalantly confessed. "Actually, this little alliance we're all a part of—it was all their idea. You know what, it'd be better if you asked them about it. I'll message them and let them know they can come visit you now. That is, if you want guests?"

Despite desiring to be alone, Nothaar's curiosity got the better of him. "Yes, I think I would like that," he said, unsure if he actually would.

Mouza beamed with delight, apparently pleased at seeing some positivity and progress from Nothaar. "Great!" she exclaimed. "I'll get out of here and let them know. See you tomorrow, Nothaar."

At that, Mouza got up and left Nothaar by himself in his cabin. There really was not much to do as he didn't have any possessions nor anything to put away or set up, so he just laid down on the bed and stared blankly at the ceiling. He must have fallen asleep because he found himself being brought back to reality by a ringing noise. Using his ocular implants to switch his perspective to the feed from the camera outside his door, he saw that Syraaq and Ifu were waiting just beyond his entryway. Taking a deep breath, Nothaar exited the door-view and returned his eyesight to the default scene of what was in front of him. That done, he stood up, walked over to the closed portal, and let his long-estranged companions in.

After a round of hugs, apologies, assurances, and other formalities that Syraaq and Ifu seemed to feel they owed Nothaar, he bade them to be quiet for a moment so that he could ask his own questions. "Mouza told me that it was you two who actually instigated the joining of forces that eventually resulted in my liberation," Nothaar began. "Please, start at the commencement. Explain to me how this situation has come to be."

"Where do we even begin?" Ifu pondered aloud. "Well, I suppose it makes sense to start when we... parted ways. Goqanx was true to her word as she did drop us off planet-side without harming us. However, she didn't exactly help, either, as our digital wallets were completely drained and we had no resources. For a while, we lived off the charity of people who looked out for unhoused individuals. With their assistance, we were eventually able to secure employment so we could begin to refill our stores. Still, we didn't exactly have a plan for what might have come next. All we knew was that we wanted to figure out a way to find and rescue you. No matter how farfetched it seemed during our lowest moments, our only inspiration for the longest time was somehow discovering and getting to wherever you happened to be. You were never far from our thoughts, Nothaar."

"While we weren't able to figure out where you and Goqanx were," Syraaq seamlessly picked up the thread, "We did get a lead on Bipauc. It appeared they were trying to set up a new, second *Conclave of Dreamers*, especially since the last one ended after the disaster that led to our disappearance. Bipauc told us at a later point that some of the groups like the *Decayists*, *Rebangers*, *Relocateites*, and others refused to continue without our input, let alone agree to a final document. Apparently, even though we weren't of the same mindset, they still felt it was important to have equal representation in any concluding work product. Eventually, everyone simply decided to go their separate ways without any deliverable."

"Yet that is where we saw an opportunity," Ifu interceded. "We knew that Bipauc still intended to monitor your homeworld for their own purposes, so we begged, borrowed, and stole until we had enough funding to convince some other shady characters to drop us off on your old planet. We went back down the *Space Elevator*—except this time with a proper supply of food packets and accoutrements—and sent out a signal directed at Bipauc's Torch Ship. After many years, our call was answered, although with plenty of skepticism. At first, it didn't seem like Bipauc was inclined to pick us up, but their better nature overwhelmed their desire for revenge against us."

Syraaq again picked up the story, as if she and Ifu had rehearsed who would be telling which piece. "I know it's hard to believe, Nothaar, but Bipauc is actually a nice person. Under that gruff and aloof exterior, they really do care, even about you—especially about you. I've heard you already had a bit of a run-in with them, but you have to recognize the tremendous amount of pressure Bipauc is under. Keeping all these disparate and, oftentimes, headstrong people under one roof, running a ship, and financing all the necessities of sustaining everyone's existences—they have a lot going on and can come across rather curt and uncaring. I assure you, that is not really the case; it's just the stress talking."

When Nothaar didn't respond in any way or give away clues to how he was feeling, Syraaq sighed and picked up the thread where she had left off. "Anyway, when we learned about what happened at the last conclave and how Bipauc was having difficulty getting the others to agree to a new one, we offered our assistance. Having us back in the fold actually smoothed over a lot of the concerns and issues, and things finally began to get underway. Once we had everyone together, though, we surprised them all by confessing everything about you and our involvement. And that is when we presented a new plan, one that involved rescuing you. Swallowing our doubts, fears, concerns, pride, inflexibility, and recriminations against all those gathered together with differing stances, we told them that being divided was allowing the government to continue what they had been doing for time immemorial."

"Now, let's be point-blank straightforward with you," Ifu announced, "in a way—after much reflection—that I realize I haven't been in the past. You deserve better, so I don't want to manipulate you into doing our bidding. Nonetheless, in order to get all the ensembles to come together into a singular confederation, we had to make deals. Chief among those concerns you. Although you have been with us since the very beginning, we basically had to pledge your voice to all their causes. Of course, we still have the same ulterior motive: we want you to go before the government so they will be forced to listen. Coming from a sapient, articulate, non-*Common* like yourself will make any message that much more powerful, and all the parties agreed to this fact. Once they unified behind the idea of you as our chief representative—the one who will start the conversation that our experts will finish—it was only then that they could coalesce around the more important and immediate task of rescuing you."

Chapter 41

Overwhelmed by so much new information at once, Nothaar tuned out Syraaq and Ifu as they went back-and-forth around the tale of how Nothaar's rescue came together and what was next. In the middle of some detail or the other, Nothaar finally interrupted to inquire, "Wait, wait, wait; I am very confused about one fact."

"What's that?" Ifu asked.

Taking a moment to put together the right words, Nothaar queried, "Now that we are all here, all of these incongruent groups under one banner, how do we intend to intercept the government? Unless something has changed in the ensuing years during my time with Goqanx that I am not aware of, there is no way for us to know where the government is going to be next."

Neither Syraaq nor Ifu spoke. Instead, just as Nothaar remembered it always happening in his presence, they replicated their ages-old habit of staring at each other and communicating in some secret, unknowable way. Finally, with whatever transpired between them apparently completed, Syraaq simply stated, "Complete honesty, that is what we promised."

Exhaling, Ifu gave her the *Common*'s signal for agreement before clarifying, "Nothaar, this is going to be tough

"

for you to understand, but, again, it's only fair that you know exactly what has occurred while you've been away. A long while ago, we came across the government when they were set up on some world. I can't even remember the name of the place anymore. We attempted to gain an audience, but—as expected—there simply was no way to break through the first level of baseline interaction with them. Due to this insurmountable barrier, it was decided that since we had found them, we could never let the government out of our sight again. If we ever wanted to present our cases, we'd need to know where to be.

"Basically, in order to accomplish this, we began to follow the government around, stalking them from planet-to-planet as they moved around the system. Meanwhile, another Torch Ship was employed to find Goqanx's vessel and hopefully figure out where you were. Previously, we actually developed a rather novel method of sending encoded transmissions using financial transactions. Since monetary systems use entanglement and quantum computing, we could send and receive veiled messages almost in real-time, acquiring the ability to coordinate our plans. Thus, when Goqanx and her various enterprises were rediscovered, we got word pretty much immediately."

"Hold on," Nothaar interrupted. "Are you saying that you have had eyes on me for quite some time now?!"

Palpably projecting the *Common*'s expression of shame while doing his best to avoid looking at Nothaar, Ifu admitted, "Yes, Nothaar, yes we did. Although Syraaq and I were on the *Reimagine* following the government, along the way we became aware that you and Goqanx had been found and were being watched."

"Why did you not save me then?" Nothaar accused, feeling his rage begin to overflow at the realization that, worse than being alone in his suffering, his companions had allowed it to continue unabated. A powerful fury was rising from deep within his gut, and Nothaar was unsure what he was going to do with it if it reached the surface.

Ifu looked back up at Syraaq, apparently begging her to explain. She must have acquiesced because she spoke for the pair saying, "I'm so sorry, Nothaar, but there was a strategic choice that had to be made to keep every member of our coalition working in concert. Many people were quite wary about the potential of word getting out that an alien was on the loose. Frankly, we were both among those concerned voices. What we needed to do was bide our time until everything perfectly aligned. We wanted to extricate you at the exact same moment the government was approaching a nearby planet, which meant we had to wait years for the right opportunity to present itself. When it did, we pounced."

"Things are still quite tight," Ifu added. "There's a very limited window for us to make it into orbit around the world the government is about to reach and then execute the plan to get our various teams aboard their ship."

Staring at them both with complete disbelief, Nothaar could not decide where he wanted to begin. He was completely incredulous that Ifu and Syraaq has just confessed to allowing him to suffer for untold years just to keep some type of schedule. *On the other hand*, Nothaar thought, *it fits their characters and temperaments perfectly. Why should I have expected them to change? How can I be angry at them for so obviously being themselves? There is no point in being upset; it changes nothing for me or my current circumstances. Instead, I will just have to figure out what comes next.*

Giving rise to these considerations, Nothaar focused his question on the government instead of himself. "Tell me the real strategy of how you intend to get us all before the government—should we somehow make it to where they are docked in time to pull any of this off. As you have already said, they have expressed no interest in hearing from you and have already rejected your request."

With relief plain upon his face—apparently at not having to defend or explain his moralistic relativity with Nothaar's life—Ifu responded, "So, the first thing you have to know is that the government's Torch Ship is run by hired hands, just regular civilians. They sign a contract for a tour of duty, just like with any other commercial vessel. Plenty of them are true believers, usually former military types who see it as their duty to continue to serve. Others wish to become future representatives and believe that their service helps position them as the only candidates with experience and relationships with the government. Really, though, most are just folks looking to make some money and retire back to their own homeworlds. And take it from me, these wages far surpass even the very generous packages we made as Starbuilders."

"Alright," Nothaar allowed, "I can see where you are going with this around the motivations of particular governmental employees. Over the years, I have seen Goqanx and other members of her crew pay off many individuals. You think it was easy to get a non-*Common* like me down and up *Space Elevators* and have local officials look the other way as she continued to engage in an obviously illegal exhibition of an alien? People like Mouza may not want to admit it, but corruption runs deep in the *Common*'s system. Reading through the *Archives*, I have learned about many former empires and whatnot that simply grew old, bloated, and unwieldy, and see no reason to believe yours is any different."

"I want to disagree with you," Ifu contended, "but you're probably right in many ways. Listen, I'm hardly as pessimistic as you are about the current and future condition of the *Common*'s race and society, but I'm also well aware we need to change if we intend to survive. Alas, despite my desire for the higher moral ground, we have no choice but to take advantage of the cracks in the foundation where they happen to exist."

Giving Ifu a sympathetic gesture, Nothaar declared, "I understand. Go on."

"Okay," Ifu accepted. "Well, due to these unfortunate faults, we have been able to build up a relationship with many of the laborers over the years, meeting them on the ground and in space. We've learned who is not going to be helpful, and who can be exploited. As such, we have already arranged for our trustworthy—though paid-off—

allies to grant us access to the government's Torch Ship. They've agreed to smuggle us aboard and then hide us in some nook or cranny or the other, adjusting sensors in that area so that we cannot be detected. For all intents, the onboard *Eh-aye* will perceive us as if we were just another piece of innocuous cargo. Once we are embedded on their Torch Ship, we'll have years to figure out a way to set up an official meeting. After all, there's nowhere to go when on a Torch Ship; we're all equally captive!"

"And it won't just be the three of us, not anymore," Syraaq appended. "Several members from each of the groups in our alliance will be joining us. This is going to be a big operation. More importantly, we will be applying the most critical lessons we have learned since our parting: to open up and put our faith in others, and to approach our issues together as a united front. We've all mutually come to appreciate that we must work collectively. On top of that, everyone knows that only you, Nothaar, stand a chance of opening the government's eyes to how their actions are harming not just us, but the whole universe!"

"As you have said before," Nothaar summarized. "I am unsure I agree with your assessment, however, I do not have any alternative to offer. It appears that we are already well underway on this scheme of yours, so I might as well see it through to the end. Where else could I possibly go? It is not like the world I left so long ago even exists as I remember it anymore."

"No," Syraaq conceded, "I suppose not. Far too much time has passed. If you returned to the surface, I doubt you would recognize anything or anyone. You would certainly look like an oddity to them, too, some type of throwback."

"Did you see my people while you were on the surface?" Nothaar pressed. "How do they fare?"

"I'm sorry," Syraaq disclosed, "there really wasn't an opportunity for us to explore. I can tell you that the Star-builders did arrive at some point to clean up all that radiation we left behind, so that danger was mitigated. However, we never left *Portal to the Stars Island*."

"Wait, what?" Ifu interceded. "Oh, never mind, I almost forgot that Nothaar gave the island with the *Space Elevator* a name! Why's it called that, anyway?"

Chuckling, Syraaq divulged, "It's just a little inside joke between me and Nothaar."

For a moment, Nothaar actually felt that same old mirth, remembering a much simpler time, as crazy as it was. He allowed cheerfulness to grow upon his face for the first time since his emancipation, and then took umbrage with himself for momentarily feeling anything resembling joy, even for the briefest of an instant. With the cloud of darkness starting to overcome him, Nothaar bluntly requested, "Can you two please leave now. I want... no, need to be alone."

"Absolutely not," Syraaq retorted. "We cannot, and we will not. You're obviously in pain, and the worst thing in the universe we could do is abandon you once again. Not today, not ever again."

"Agreed," Ifu concurred. "We weren't able to do anything for you before, Nothaar, but we're here for you now and forever, from this point forward. Your road to recovery is going to be a long one, and I promise you that we are not going anywhere, that we are here for all the lows and highs, whatever is to come. Even if you don't hear this today, I'll repeat it at every opportunity: you are not on your own. You have us and many more people who are here for you, too. You can and should lean on us. After everything we've all been through, we're the only family we all have left."

Chapter 42

For months, Nothaar, Syraaq, Ifu, and the rest of their ragtag band had been holed up in an old maintenance corridor aboard the government's Torch Ship. Nothaar, of course, had taken his personal portable food vat with him, but the others had chosen to steal food packets from the cargo hold whenever there was an opportunity. Frankly, Nothaar observed them plundering anything and everything, not just what they needed for basic survival. Whatever line the members of their alliance drew between themselves and outlaws like Coqanx and her crew, Nothaar failed to see the difference. In either case, he had decided it was not his concern. His focus was on the core part of the mission in figuring out a way to present their cases directly to the representatives who were flying through space with them, completely unaware they were sharing the same oxygen.

By this time, their group was well aware of where and in which rooms inside the vessel the various government agencies and committees met, but they also knew they could not just walk in and reveal that they had surreptitiously been aboard all the while. At best they would all be placed in the brig; at worst, they would be defenestrated through the airlock and into an uncaring universe. Having made it this far with all their long-term dreams and aspirations, their motley collective found themselves completely stymied and paralyzed by not being able to get themselves in front of the lawmakers without endangering their combined existences.

Eventually, one day, Nothaar grew impatient and announced to the group, "We cannot go on like this. If we do not make a move of some kind, this ship will reach a planet and we will have missed our opportunity."

"I think we're all well aware of that," Ifu retorted, "but complaining about it isn't going to solve our fundamental issue. If you have a proposal for how, exactly, we can proceed, then, believe me, I'm all ears!"

"Actually," Nothaar responded, "I have been percolating on one particular prospect. Candidly, it was directly inspired by you and what everyone else here has been able to accomplish."

"Oh?" Ifu questioned, obviously enamored with the flattery. "Well, you certainly have my attention. Let's hear what you're thinking."

"My argument's main point is this," Nothaar began without fanfare. "What we need is an ally from within the government. Just as you, Ifu, and you, Syraaq, were brave enough to decide that you must be completely honest and admit the truth about me to everyone in this room and then some, so, too, must we be with a member of the legislative body. What I am saying is that we should intentionally expose ourselves to a single individual, convince them of our veracity, and incorporate them into our plot. Only once they have agreed to support us can we decide on what the next steps should be. Considering such an approach worked before to create our own pact, then certainly a similar tactic will be successful once again."

Immediately, the room descended into chaos as everyone started arguing on the merits and drawbacks around Nothaar's scheme. Ifu and Syraaq quickly lent their support to Nothaar and forcefully countered every argument that came their way. However, Nothaar noted, their influence was mostly effective because no one else had any other viable option to offer. The only useful question came when someone yelled out, "But how would we even know who to disclose our presence to?"

This was the opening Nothaar had been waiting for, and he laughed with the disturbing gregariousness he had heard Goqanx use countless times. His loud boisterousness quieted the entire room until every other member of their party was looking at him—some with concern, some with curiosity, but many with fear and trepidation. It was the exact impact he was going for. Once Nothaar was sure all eyes were on him, he explained, "Oh, you silly *Commons*. You are so wrapped up in the minutia of your lives that you never look at the big picture of what is available to you. Whereas I have had to learn about your technology and society from scratch, you take your amazing advancements for granted so much that you do not even know how to use any of your astounding tools and resources effectively. We have a treasure trove of data available to us; not only from the larger *Archive*, but all the local systems and personal editions of everyone on the ship, in the very heart of the government. Instead of wasting your time pilfering trinkets, you need to put your sticky fingers to better use.

"None of us are experts at espionage, but we do not need to be. Billions—maybe trillions—of years of experiential data are available for the *Eh-aye* to tap into in order to assist us. All it needs from us is to feed it the appropriate information and give it coherent instructions. If we... appropriate... copies of every representative's personal *Archive* and mix it with all public records available to us, we can ask the *Eh-aye* to find us the person who would be most sympathetic to our cause; or, at least, the one most likely to hear us out. This is how we discover who should be our partner in this endeavor."

There was a lot of mumbling and Nothaar could feel a certain level of discomfort rising in the room. Turning to Syraaq, Nothaar asked, "What is it? Have I said something particularly uncouth?"

"Nothaar," Syraaq tried with a sympathetic tone, "what you are describing is... well, it's not exactly forbidden, aside from the misappropriation of personal data, though we are far beyond worrying about illegal acts like that. As you've undoubtedly noticed, there's just a certain... stigma among all *Commons* against turning over decision making to computers or software. I would say it goes as far as an ingrained phobia of the potential of inorganic things becoming sapient and replacing natural life."

"So, it is a part of your genetic programming, then?" Nothaar inquired, deeply concerned with the implications.

"I would think so," Syraaq confirmed, "though I'm no expert in genetic coding and all that is or could be a part of it. Nevertheless, I would wager that if you asked any of us to do this, we would become sort-of dazed and stupefied and not be able to complete the task."

"Think about the things you were able to do with the *Eh-aye*, especially with your virtual scenarios," interceded Mouza. She had joined their company not only as one of the *Decentralist* agents, but also as a doctor, principally to continue to treat Nothaar during his recovery. While his physical wounds had seemed to have mended as well as they ever would, his psychological scars often stubbornly refused to scab over. Highlighting her concerns to Captain Bipauc, Mouza insisted that she accompany Nothaar wherever he went, ostensibly to keep up with his therapy. Meanwhile, Bipauc elected to stay behind on their craft, a shock to all considering their critical role and involvement in getting all of the disparate organizations to this point. In deference to Bipauc's absence, this technically made Mouza the most senior member of the *Decentralist* faction. Nothaar was well aware of the political jockeying that had gone along with deciding who would be a part of this operation, so there were a lot of hurt feeling even among those who made the cut.

Mouza gently expanded on her original notion by clarifying, "Things like letting a computer create a simulated existence, partitioning your memory, and having autonomous life-support units keep your body functioning were all technologies that already existed. You didn't invent anything; you just took what was already available and applied them. However, there is a reason why none of them—and notably, especially not in conjunction with each other—are very popular. Yes, there will always be the occasional genetic aberration far from the norm that will come along and create instruments like these or desire to use ones that came before, but they have not and will never catch on with the masses because, as *Commons*, we inherently despise them. On the whole, that is, of course."

"So, what you are saying," Nothaar summarized, "is you are actually incapable of doing what is necessary. You are hindered by your very engineered nature."

"I would say that is a fair assessment," Mouza agreed.

Dumbstruck, Nothaar was unsure how to proceed with this sudden problem. In all this time, it had not occurred to him how much the *Common*'s genetic programming was holding them back. The extensive years spent with radicals made him forget they were already extreme outliers, and pushing them further from the trillions of standard people would be difficult. Not being of their stock, it was impossible for him to know how their minds worked. At last, the only remaining option became clear to Nothaar.

Speaking his considerations aloud, Nothaar pronounced, "Then I have to do it alone."

"What do you mean?" Syraaq delved.

Without hesitation, Nothaar laid out his proposition, "I still need all of you to work on procuring the necessary data. I assume there is no prohibition against that?"

"Aside from violating yet another decree of the government," Ifu assuaged, "no, I don't think anything might stop us."

"I disagree," Mouza detracted. "I know I'm hardly alone in this viewpoint, but I have a real moral quandary with taking innocent people's highly personal and intimate memories for our own purposes. And, speaking specifically for myself, it would be a violation of the oath I took as a medical professional."

Ifu quickly countered, "But would you or anyone else who shares these qualms and hangups stop the rest of us from going ahead with Nothaar's idea?"

With a look of defeat clearly visible on her face, Mouza lowered her head as she said, "No, I wouldn't stop you."

Once no one else spoke up on any side of the argument, Ifu bade Nothaar continue with his intentions. Taking the reins, Nothaar expounded, "Then it is all very simple. Just as Mouza and her compatriots will blind themselves to the actions of your thievery, so, too, will the rest of you while I do what is required with the *Eh-aye*, as detestable as you may believe it is. You will not ask, and I will not tell you. The next thing you will hear from me on the subject will be the name of the government representative that we will secure with the intention of... educating... on the justness of our cause. Revealing ourselves in this way and exposing the truth will irrevocably free us from our own self-imposed imprisonment, one way or another."

CHAPTER 43

"Lauzo Wevvok," Ifu was saying to the elderly man kneeling on the unupholstered, cold floor, "I'm going to take off your gag, blindfold, and restraints now. You will not attempt to yell, attack, run away, or any other such nonsense. Motion if you understand and agree to these terms, and then I'll begin."

Nothaar watched from underneath his own loathed mask as Lauzo made the requisite gesture. Once done, Ifu did exactly as he said he would, allowing Lauzo free movement. Blinking, Lauzo flexed his wrists as his eyes circled around at all the people surrounding him inside the rebels' hideout, apparently assessing his current situation and seeking a way out. Aside from Nothaar, no one else's face was covered, and Lauzo gave the impression that he was studying each-and-every-one intently. During the preparations and planning meetings for abducting Lauzo, the group voted to keep Nothaar's identity hidden at first in order to produce a more dramatic reveal. In many ways, it was a test run for what they intended to do before the entire legislative body should this gambit with Lauzo meet their expectations and pay off.

Displaying obvious confusion, Lauzo asked, "Who are you people? I know there are hundreds of thousands of individuals aboard, but I've been here for a long time and have a pretty good memory for faces. I haven't caught sight of any one of you before. What's going on here, and, really, what is the meaning of all this? Do you have any idea who I am and what my position is?"

"We know everything about you, Delegate Wevvok," Syraaq spoke as she separated herself from the crowd, walked over to Lauzo, and slowly bent down by his side. For the first time, Nothaar realized just how much Syraaq had aged since he first beheld her. When they initially met, she had been merely ancient looking. By this point, she had become downright decrepit, at least by his estimation. Truthfully, Nothaar still had great difficulty figuring out what stage in life any *Common* may have been in considering all the various techniques they used to extend their existence. Nevertheless, even though Lauzo was also a similarly older gentleman, in comparison to Syraaq he gave the observer the impression of being downright youthful and full of vigor.

Peering over at Ifu, Nothaar realized the same analysis could be applied to him. Back on Nothaar's homeworld, Ifu had been practically boyish. The ensuing years—however many had potentially passed either from the perspective of their planets or themselves—had obviously compiled upon his visage. At the same time, Nothaar wondered how much he himself had matured, too. Before meeting the *Commons*, he had never seen a mirror before. While he had been aware of some innately reflective materials and surfaces, it was not like appraising one's self was an experience his people partook in every day. In the greater universe he found himself a part of, he could do exactly that if he so desired. Generally speaking, though, Nothaar still did not bother to evaluate his own appearance. Oftentimes, when he did so, he was shocked by his own alien-looking features. He had spent less than forty years living among beings that looked like himself. As such, he had grown accustomed to thinking that the typical *Common* was what a "normal" person should look like.

Aside from his virtual experiences, Nothaar had not seen any member of his own species since he left his progenitor sphere. Mouza had been quite contrite with him, insisting that he not partake in such fantasies anymore for his overall mental health and recovery. She specifically cautioned that Nothaar had become addicted, both emotionally and physically. Apparently, the receptors in his brain had actually been damaged by the speed at which certain hormones were being produced and absorbed. Even though he had slowed down his perception of the passage of time, events still happened inside his own body in the real universe at an accelerated rate, resulting in a significant and detrimental impact. Due to this, Mouza had been attempting to adapt medication to Nothaar's physiology, each to varying degrees of success. Although he would not admit it to Mouza, Nothaar found that the unprincipled doctors that Goqanx let experiment on him were, unfortunately, far more skilled than she was. While Nothaar knew that she meant well, Mouza's sense of morality seemed to prevent her from even considering, nonetheless attempting, the potentially hazardous treatments that might fully help him.

Turning his attention back to the scene in front of him, Nothaar heard Syraaq introduce herself and many of the other nearby coalition partners. Then, she confessed, "Despite how things have begun with us detaining you in this way, we actually hope that you'll be willing to become our ally and a voice of reason within the government, a sponsor of sorts for the greater good pertaining to the future of us as a people and the universe as a whole."

"Given the current state of affairs," Lauzo retorted, "I fail to see how that would be possible."

Syraaq returned a disarming expression as she expounded, "Many people in this room started out as enemies. There has even been violence between some of us. Yet, here we are, a united front, perhaps even friends. I'm sure you are no outsider to the idea of strange bedfellows and unbelievable alliances being made out of necessity. And from those seeds, respect and admiration can grow."

The only response from Lauzo was a harrumph, so Syraaq continued, "Well, one of the things we have learned over the years is to be candidly honest with each other, no matter the pain it may cause. As a politician, you might even find our approach to be refreshing for a change."

Lauzo actually laughed at this statement, but apparently not for the reason Syraaq intended. Instead, he intoned, "Oh yeah? Then how come you've been talking in circles? From where I sit, you are the ones being vague, speaking in ambiguous terms, and playing silly little games with me."

"Fair enough," Syraaq conceded. "Then please, allow me to lay some truth down for you. The reason we believe you will, in the end, become our compatriot is because we hacked into your personal *Archive*—and really, every single member of the government's personal *Archive*—and scrutinized them for signs of what we are looking for in a new comrade. All indicators pointed at you."

In complete shock at this revelation, Lauzo exclaimed, "Who would do such a despicable thing? Who would perpetrate such an invasion of privacy? It goes against the very tenets of our society!"

"I would!" Nothaar declared as he stepped forward. "Although others helped me gain access to the data, only I—with the assistance of my *Eh-aye*—actually reviewed any of the information and made the decision to bring you here and meet all of us."

There was a pause in the conversation as Lauzo stared at Nothaar's hidden façade with curiosity. "Your accent, your cadence, your intonation," Lauzo observed, "I've never heard anything like it. Tell me, son, who are you? Where are you from?"

Ripping off his mask to reveal his most distinguishing qualities, he announced, "I am Nothaar Akii, and I am no 'son' of yours nor any *Common*!"

"Oh... my... word..." Lauzo stuttered. He then turned back towards Syraaq and asked, "What the fuck is this? What in the holy hell have you done?"

"Hey!" Nothaar roared. Once Lauzo returned his attention back to Nothaar, he continued, "You are talking to me right now! I am a sapient being, not some lowly creature you can ignore. Syraaq is not my master; no one here is, not anymore. I am my own person. Look me in the eyes, talk to me, and treat me with dignity and respect. It is the very least I deserve after all I have been through. I demand to be regarded as an equal to any other *Common*."

Dumbfounded, Lauzo mumbled some apologies before asking, "Nothaar, was it?"

"Close enough," Nothaar agreed as he recalled that all *Commons* seemed to share the same incapability pronouncing his name correctly. He had long ago given up trying to correct them as he felt that their tongues did not seem to waggle in the necessary way.

Picking up where he left off, Lauzo queried, "Nothaar, I and many of the other members of the government have heard a rumor about some traveling circus or something like that displaying a non-*Common* that could speak the *Lingua*. Would I be making a wild assumption here if I guessed that the alleged situation was about you?"

"You would not," Nothaar confirmed. "For many years, I was under the absolute control of an outlaw named Goqanx Guzyc and her crew."

"And this Goqanx Guzyc character," Lauzo attempted, "she's the one who originally absconded with you and taught you how to speak?"

Displaying a wistful look upon his features, Nothaar began to correct Lauzo's understanding of events.

Throughout the night, Nothaar revisited his origins and encounters with the *Commons*, as well as his own journey of self-discovery. On many occasions, he glimpsed over at Syraaq and Ifu and watched them squirm uncomfortably. To their credit, though, they never interrupted Nothaar nor defended themselves from his more bitter revelations. The story then turned towards their own alliance and how it had grown out of the *Conclave of Dreamers*, and what their group was looking for from Lauzo.

As the morning came based upon the schedule that was maintained aboard the government's Torch Ship, Lauzo was practically in tears after hearing Nothaar's tale. Taking a deep breath to seemingly regain his composure, he professed, "This is a lot. There is so much I need to process, even more I need to consider. And I can't do any of that while I'm here, as your prisoner. If you want me to trust you, you are going to have to take the same risk with me. Let me go, right here, right now, with no conditions."

"How do we know you just won't turn us in to the authorities?" Ifu interrogated.

"You don't," Lauzo underlined. "That's how this is going to have to work. I can tell you that I have no intentions of reporting you, but all you have is my word. I may even believe that myself right now, but there is no telling how I'll feel once I'm outside your area of influence and have a few moments to think. Besides, you won't be able to coerce me any other way, and certainly not with controlling nano-bots or anything like that. We're the government; I have many specialized protective layers installed in me that are not available to the general populous. You think there haven't been terrorists or so-called revolutionaries in the past who have tried to take control of us or initiate a coup? What you have been able to accomplish and how it all came about are certainly novel and interesting, but hardly unique when looked at through the deep lens of history in its entirety."

Ifu attempted to argue, but Nothaar immediately cut him off. "No," Nothaar commanded, "I concur with Lauzo. This is what we all subscribed to beforehand. We have to let him go and place our faith in him. That was the whole purpose of everything we did to reach this point; it is why we specifically selected him. Lauzo, you are free to go. I hope to see you, and only you, again real soon."

Examining Nothaar with an expression of skepticism, Lauzo decreed, "Once I've had a chance to unpack all this, I'll be back. You'll see me again in a few days, one way or another. We'll then find out if your assessment of me has any credence in reality."

CHAPTER 44

A palpable measure of agitation and dread grew inside the old maintenance corridor that Nothaar and his companions had been forced to call home. Each day—really, each hour—that passed without Lauzo's imminent return only added to the growing pile of consternation. There was little any of them could do to take their minds off the matter, so all they did was debate and perseverate on how terribly things might end up for all of them in the end. Their own insecurities fueled the rumor mill, even though there were no new verifiable facts to be had.

"So what?" Syraaq loudly admonished everyone within earshot after yet another one of those lamenting sessions. "We all volunteered for this mission knowing full well that not only might it not succeed, but that we may die in the process. Are your convictions to your causes so trifling that you're not willing to become a martyr?"

There were grumbles of agreement and arguments from others about how they were true believers, and that Syraaq did not have the right to question their convictions. "Very well," she responded to no one in particular, "then just take solace in the fact that we are still here. Sure, Lauzo hasn't returned yet, but members of the security apparatus have not appeared, either. That means he hasn't turned us in yet. More so, it demonstrates that he's taking our request seriously. That is a major leap forward."

Things continued much the same as the days passed. Scouts were sent out to do reconnaissance and see if anything appeared amiss or if there were any other unusual activities within the government's Torch Ship. Though the troops were able to return with an additional supply of food packets, they otherwise had nothing to report, only noting that everything appeared as it always did. Some of the more brazen ones even tried to access data in the defense systems to see if anything was planned or upcoming, but nothing could be found.

Finally, after almost half a month, Lauzo returned to their holding area. The first thing he said was, "Rest assured, your secret remains safe. However, I want to be clear with you where my mindset currently stands: that is only true for the time being. I'm still not convinced of the veracity nor necessity of what we've spoken about. Nonetheless, for the foreseeable future, I'm willing to listen, without reservations nor presumptuous conclusions. At the same time, I have a lot of questions that I need all of you to answer unconditionally, with brutal honesty, and without qualifications. If you can agree to my terms, then we can continue to meet like this on a regular basis until I am satisfied one way or the other. Do you accept?"

While Ifu attempted to acquiesce on the group's behalf, Lauzo insisted that every individual speak and make a pledge for themselves. Once that was accomplished, he said that was enough for one day, and left them alone once again to wallow in their never-ending anxieties.

After that, though, the gap in time between visits from Lauzo was never more than a few days. He actually came back the next morning after his initial voluntary reappearance to begin his interviews. Apparently, he wanted to interrogate each person and understand their personal opinions and motivations. When discussing it among themselves, the members of the *Conclave of Dreamers* found the most frequent topic was comprehending how all of them came together, and how they intended to support each other despite their disparate viewpoints and approaches.

Most notably, Lauzo was interested in Nothaar, and spent time with him on almost every one of his appearances. Syraaq even joked that the representative was downright enamored with him. In many ways, Nothaar felt uncomfortable from all the attention that Lauzo was lavishing him with. During one of his private therapy sessions with Mouza, he told her as much, saying it reminded him of how the paying clientele used to come to see him and treated him like a performing animal.

"You should consider telling Lauzo what is going through your head," Mouza advised.

Nothaar displayed his disagreement on his face as he asked, "Would that not be detrimental to the mission? We are trying to build comradery with him and gain his sympathy. I do not want to scare him away if I am the person he is most bonding to."

Mouza could not disguise the worrisome look on her

face as she intoned, "Nothaar, you and your health have to come first. What is the point of achieving our goals if it destroys you in the process? From our prior discussions, I would say you have, with good reason, a fear of becoming something like Lauzo's pet, just like you were with Goqanx. I don't know what Lauzo's sexual preferences are, but it's quite clear that you are ill at ease with too much of his attention focused on you, which you fear could lead to a situation even remotely like what happened with her."

"Then you think I should..." Nothaar attempted.

"You should be truthful with him," Mouza suggested. "You should tell him these exact things, how it makes you feel, and why you react that way. How he responds to this information is not your concern; he's going to believe and do whatever he thinks is appropriate. At the very least, he will know where you're coming from. When we first brought him here, you demanded he respect you as a unique, sapient being. I was so proud of you and how much progress you'd made. However, you seem to have re-gressed since then. If you really want what you said, if you really believe you deserve to be treated that way, then an important part of that is fully standing up for yourself.

"Nothaar, I won't lie to you. Being a non-*Common*, you are going to have a lot harder time than the rest of us, no matter what happens when this is all over. That said, I want to give you the tools to succeed and thrive on your own. Please, Nothaar, think of yourself and your own needs foremost."

"My own needs?" Nothaar questioned aloud. "I wonder what they even are anymore? It has been so long since I fought for myself, I am not sure I know what I want or require. For decades, I have been in the service of others. Even now…"

As Nothaar trailed off and did not complete his thought, Mouza pressed, "Even now, what?"

Locking up his own sentiments, Nothaar dismissed the line of inquiry with, "Nothing, nothing, forget it."

Just as with her earlier concern, Mouza could not hide her disappointment in Nothaar. Nevertheless, she did not push him any further, most likely because she had grown quite aware of the way he operated. Nothaar was relieved not to have to think about what the answer to her inquest actually was, and tried to suppress what it could be even from himself.

Despite his misgivings, Nothaar did end up telling Lauzo about his internal deliberation. It was not right away and took several attempts, but to Nothaar's astonishment, Lauzo was rather understanding and considerate. Lauzo tried to assuage Nothaar's unease by contending that making Nothaar uncomfortable was far from his intentions. "That said," Lauzo had submitted, "I can appreciate where you're coming from and will endeavor to be more aware of your perspective in the future. Does that work for you?"

Although Nothaar expected things to become awkward between them after this conversation, that did not happen. Lauzo instead attempted to step up and be supportive in the same way Mouza did, although Nothaar found his approach to be in an almost fatherly way. As the days and months went on, Nothaar began to think of Lauzo more as a new Baubu Yoordi, as someone who was trying to encourage him to become his best self. This was in stark contrast to Lauzo potentially becoming another Goqanx Guzyc—a person who would just use Nothaar for their own selfish purposes.

Finally, the day came when Lauzo announced that he had determined what was to come and what would be done with all the stowaways. He asked everyone to gather to hear his statement and be a part of the process. Once everyone was assembled, he pronounced, "After much deep meditation and reflection, I have decided that it would be worthwhile to help you bring your various cases to the legislative body of the government."

There was a lot of whooping, hollering, clapping, and cheering. Lauzo struggled to get the crowd to quiet down, but was unable to cut through the joyous expressions of excitement mixed with the sudden release of trepidation. It took louder voices like Ifu in combination with several others to forcefully hush the animated throng in order to allow Lauzo to continue. Once the room was mostly settled down, Lauzo reattempted his pronouncements.

"Ahem," Lauzo began. "As I was saying, I will help you bring your concerns before my administration, but it won't be happening aboard this vessel. It would be horribly suspicious if I suddenly revealed a crew of interlopers. Your presence here, no matter how honorable you believe your aims to be, complicates things far too much. Instead, here's what will happen:

"When we reach our destination, I will work with your partners in crime that got you on board to get you back down to the surface unnoticed by anyone here who would find your presence disconcerting. Needless to say, the laborers that allowed you to infiltrate this far into our sanctum can no longer be permitted to stay aboard, nor ever be employed by the government again. In other words, they will need to disembark with all of you... permanently. While you may not be dangerous, per se, they didn't know your intentions and could have exposed the entire government to a disaster of their own making. Since they can never be trusted with our safety and security again, they must go. I will let them know that should they depart willingly and disappear, they will avoid charges. That is the best offer I can make for them. From the perspective of the law, they have committed treason. If no one else ever finds out about that, then, well, it'll be best for all of us.

"Now, once we're all on the ground, the government will go about its normal activities and set up a home base in some large sports arena that can hold all of us. Given my senior position, I will be able to add a special agenda item that will allow you to come in and present your ideas. I cannot promise any results; I will not even guarantee there will be a debate and vote about it of any kind afterwards. However, I will allow an unfiltered and unedited speech to take place. After that, well, then you, too, will be free to pursue whatever comes next.

"That all said, there is no way we can allow scores of

people to speak. The legislature is not your *Conclave of Dreamers*, and we have neither the time nor the tolerance to listen to such long-winded dissertations. If there is an interest afterwards, then please, have at it. Again, I make no assurances that any opportunity will present itself. Instead, I have adopted a much simpler—though perhaps more complicated in its own way—plan for how this will all unfurl. One person will be speaking for all of you, presenting everything in a singular voice in a way that will be sure to make all the elected officials take notice."

"And we get to decide who our so-called 'singular voice' gets to be?" Ifu interrupted.

"Absolutely not!" Lauzo disputed. "There is only one among your motley assortment who can accomplish this task, and his name is Nothaar Akii."

CHAPTER 45

Underneath his mask and coveralls that hid even the smallest modicum of his skin, Nothaar's entire body was quaking. More troubling to him, though, was the fact that he was producing profuse amounts of nervous sweat—something he knew emitted an aroma that *Commons* typically found offensive. This was happening despite the fact that he was standing inside a climate-controlled environment that prevented the warmth of the outside spring day from impacting the interior temperature. A few steps away, Lauzo did not appear to be exhibiting any of these disconcerting signs, or at least the *Common*'s equivalent of them. Instead, the older man was perfectly erect and looked comfortable as he confidently spoke through a reverberating audio amplification system to the massive crowd gathered in the stands. Wherever the microphones were buried, they were completely hidden from view. Nothaar assumed they must have been embedded in the stage he and Lauzo stood upon since all sounds from their vicinity seemed to be replicated throughout the large structure they all found themselves inside of.

Although Nothaar had never physically seen or been inside a sports arena in person before, he had looked at pictures, videos, and virtual tours of some examples from the *Archive*. Still, even when experiencing these views through his ocular implants, the reality of appearing on a stage in the middle of such a place with the energy of hundreds of thousands of eyeballs staring down at him was indescribable. While Nothaar was well aware of the actual number of representatives, the population of planets, and other such significant quantities, he was ill prepared for the ordeal of seeing so many *Commons* at once. Further, he wasn't ready for them to see him, but it was far too late to back out now. After everything that had gone into preparing for this occasion, Nothaar had no intention of reversing course, no matter how uncomfortable and panicky he felt.

Before his turn to address the various onlookers came, Nothaar took one last opportunity to peer around at the setting of what was to be his ultimate triumph or greatest failure. Below the raised dais that he and Lauzo were situated upon, many members of the *Conclave of Dreamers* sat in chairs at the ground level, both patiently and anxiously awaiting the moment when Nothaar would start speaking. Due to the length of time it took for the government's Torch Ship to arrive at the planet and set up shop, Captain Bipauc and everyone else who had remained aboard the *Reimagine* were able to arrive and rejoin the former stowaways. Once Lauzo had made his pronouncement and plan clear, Ifu and the rest of their compatriots used their encrypted quantum communication methodology to alert them as to what had been decided. As such, Bipauc—whose craft had maintained a close pursuit anyway—was then able to be seated in the audience, right next to Mouza, both trying to maintain a stoic look and not betray their true feelings.

Of course, not everyone had been granted access to be spectators at Nothaar's address. There were simply too many people in their alliance to find space for all of them, so a selection process had to be undertaken. Bipauc had immediately been granted special consideration in recognition of all they had done for their various causes, so no one seemed to be put out by their presence. Among the others, Nothaar quickly spotted Ifu and Syraaq, the latter of whom appeared even more elderly and diminished, like a wisp of the person he had met for the first time so long ago. Nevertheless, her mind remained as sharp as ever, including at that instant as she seemed to intuit that Nothaar was scrutinizing her from afar despite his eyes being hidden behind his face covering. She signaled a greeting and then made the *Common*'s gesture that Nothaar understood to mean, "You've got this!"

Removing his gaze from Syraaq, Nothaar beheld the upper levels of the stadium itself. Large screens were attached to the side of the building with massive blown-up live images of the stage and its occupants being projected upon them. Ifu had told Nothaar that most *Commons* did not have ocular implants despite the widespread availability of the machinery and the ease of installation. As such, physical screens were often necessary for information and entertainment purposes. Nothaar was certainly used to the idea from the years he spent using his tablet before his own technological modifications, but was not prepared for seeing a version of himself that was several stories tall.

Watching one of the displays for a bit, Nothaar could make out other objects behind himself and Lauzo, the latter of whom continued his oration, ostensibly preparing the legislators for what was to come. Behind them, a large statue of a young woman and a much older man had been placed. The artist had posed them so that, depending upon one's viewpoint, their positions could be interpreted in multiple ways. From one perspective, it looked like each was attempting to hold the other back; while from another angle, it looked like they were coming together and about to embrace. There was something peculiar about the two figures and Nothaar came to realize what it was. At first, Nothaar thought that whoever sculpted this work of art had been using a technique that made the figures more "suggestive" of actual persons, but that was not the case. In reality, they were exceptionally detailed, which made their appearance even odder.

Assuring himself that he understood what he was observing, Nothaar determined that the depicted subjects were not *Commons* at all. The pair shared a lot of the *Common's* bodily features, but were not a complete match, although the arrangements were far closer to them than to him. At that moment, Nothaar recalled that the scouts had reported on the existence of similar effigies in various forms aboard the government's Torch Ship. Whether as sculptures, paintings, or other creative expressions, these icons appeared to be quite customary in government circles. Nothaar made a mental note to ask Lauzo about it later, assuming there was going to be a later for him.

Snapping him back to reality, the chance to calm himself via distraction ended as he heard Lauzo announce, "And here with me is a remarkable young man, someone who has seen, perceived, and been though a lot in his short life. What you are about to hear and consider will be surprising, at a minimum, and potentially disturbing to many of you. But please, listen carefully to my guest, Nothaar Akii, and all he has to tell... and show you."

With these words, Lauzo signaled for Nothaar to take center stage and stepped aside himself. Suddenly, Nothaar felt more alone than ever, with nothing to protect him from all the witnesses around him. Taking a deep breath, he prepared to speak. Just then, he apprehended that he could not get his mouth to move and felt even hotter inside his outfit. Throwing away all his prepared remarks, Nothaar ripped off his disguise and put a quick end to the masquerade before it ever really began.

The impact was immediate, first with a mumbling, then a downright rumbling. It was quite clear that the representatives were distraught by what was happening, and one managed to tap into the speaker system and yell, "Delegate Wevvok, what is the meaning of this? What is this farce you have put before our sacred body? Why have you abducted this poor, unwitting creature and brought it here? This is vile, and a violation of our laws and oaths."

Lauzo attempted to speak up, but Nothaar motioned for him to remain still and soundless. Nothaar wanted to handle this unwarranted scrutiny in his own way. Acquiescing to Nothaar's non-verbal request, Lauzo's lips remained sealed. With the older representative silent, Nothaar then forcefully rebuked, "Sir, I am no unthinking creature you can brush aside. What I am is a sapient being, the same as you and any *Common*! Lauzo Wevvok did not violate any of your decrees, regulations, directives, or principles. No, it was not he who found me, but the other way around. I sought out Delegate Wevvok and asked him for his help. It was me, in a carefully considered decision, who reasoned that he would be the person who would most likely facilitate my efforts to appear before you today. And, thus, I have been proven correct, as here we are, all together, as promised.

"As you can plainly see, although I am not a *Common* with your particular phenotypes, I am no less a person. I think for myself, I make my own choices, I question my own existence, and I have traversed the stars to see you. My name is Nothaar Akii, a designation that was given to me by my parents upon my birth on my homeworld, a place none of you have ever been. It comes from a language—now dead—that you do not understand, but one I feel the absence of every day in my heart, and miss dearly. Yet even before meeting a single *Common*, I began to teach myself the *Lingua*. This is no trick, and I am no one's plaything to put on display for your amusement. I am here for a serious reason: to talk about the future of our shared universe."

When Nothaar paused, at first there was a completely

muted stillness, an amazing accomplishment considering the number of people around him. Then, absolute pandemonium broke out. It took almost another hour for Lauzo and other representatives who were superficially running the session to get everyone to calm down enough to start asking questions. As expected, they wanted to know and understand Nothaar's origins. At first, he tried to keep it brief since Lauzo had told him that they would have limited time to make his case, but it appeared that he had the undivided attention of every single person there. As the interrogation continued unabated for such an excessively long amount of time, they had to take several breaks to relieve themselves and have meals. Eventually, they elected to adjourn for the day, choosing to extend the session into the next morning.

However, that was not nearly enough time, and further allowances were granted. For several more days, Nothaar freely shared with them every detail he could remember, aside from Lauzo's involvement and how he and his compatriots got aboard the government's ship. He decided to keep those specific details private lest it reflect poorly on their patron. At some point, though, it was made clear that everyone else who had been involved in Nothaar's escapades would be arrested since he had basically confessed to innumerable crimes. His very presence in their midst was underlined as one of them, though no one, save a few extremist members, seemed inclined to blame Nothaar for his current circumstances.

After this, Nothaar was then granted time to explain

why he was there in the first place. Given the extra intervals to say his piece, Nothaar eloquently explained all the various perspectives and recommendations from his comrades. It was quite clear that most people in the audience were far less interested in this portion and Nothaar sometimes found himself addressing a mostly empty arena. The shock and novelty of his existence was wearing off, so Lauzo diligently worked to create one last summary session with every member of the government present. This would be Nothaar's final chance.

On that day, Nothaar gave as impassioned a speech as he could muster, but he was unable to tell if he was making any headway. Then, to his surprise, Lauzo spoke up and asked, "Nothaar, we have heard all of these details and understand the various options put before us. However, what I have not heard is what you believe is best. What do you want to happen? What do you think should transpire with the Starbuilders, our entire culture, and the future of our shared cosmos? After all, you are one of the people who will be most impacted by these decisions."

For a while, Nothaar was quiet. Lauzo made a low noise with his throat, indicating to Nothaar that he needed to say something. Stalling for a few more moments to think of an appropriate response, Nothaar declared, "In all this time, no one has ever asked me that. They all told me what was best for the universe, what was best for my progenitor planet and ones like it. They told me what I needed to do for them, yet none of them asked me what I thought about any of it. I have spent so much time memorizing everyone else's opinions and plans that I never took the necessary time to think about them and what each would mean for me and my people and others similar to us on planets that are yet to be discovered."

With a gentle expression upon his face, Lauzo said, "Then I apologize on behalf of them, and also for myself for putting you on the spot like this. However, I and everyone here want to know one thing: what's it going to be, Nothaar Akii? What would you have us do?"

CHAPTER 46

Against Mouza's imperative medical advice, Nothaar decelerated his perception of time. He didn't have a program at the ready, so he was just looking out at a slow-motion version of the strange world he somehow found himself on. Although he knew that he was probably undoing years of rehabilitation and causing more damage to the receptors in his brain, he needed a bit of a stretch to organize his thoughts and reach a point where he could make a decision. There was but one question he had to answer: what did he want?

When the solution came to him, when Nothaar finally admitted the simple truth to himself, something akin to relief flooded his psyche. Despite the consequences, Nothaar recognized exactly what needed to be said, and took one last moment to gird himself for the inevitable backlash. Returning to real time, he took a final drag of recycled air before explaining his position. "Delegate Wevvok, all the representatives here today," Nothaar began, "I am on the side of the government and the Starbuilders."

"What the hell are you saying, Nothaar?!" Bipauc could be clearly heard screaming out.

Lauzo gestured for Bipauc and everyone else to stay silent as he entreated, "Nothaar, it would not be unreasonable to assume that after all of these days of testimony, your response is not the answer most people would be expecting. Please, for the benefit of all the attendees, take some time, all the time you need, to clarify what your intentions are. Specifically, what does being 'on the side of the government and Starbuilders' mean to you?"

Gratefully, Nothaar expounded, "From what I have seen and in comparison to each of the other options I have presented, I believe the government's current modus operandi is the best option for the survival of sapient beings, as well as life in general, throughout the universe. Despite the obvious drawbacks and temporary pain and suffering it causes, harvesting lonely planets bearing life from elsewhere and bringing them together into a singular system is the most logical and reasonable way to ensure our collective survival. More so, genetically modifying people like me into becoming *Commons* is a sensible practice on the whole, although much can be done to improve the execution. If the representatives would hear it, I have some ideas to better the whole process and ease the transition."

"How could you?!" a familiar voice boomed from the crowd. When Nothaar turned towards the side where he had heard this denouncement originating from, he discovered that Ifu was attempting to climb onto the stage, seemingly in an attempt to confront Nothaar. Despite Ifu's incredulousness, security guards were easily able to keep him down at the ground level as he screamed curses and made other unintelligible, belligerent sounds.

"No," Nothaar implored, "let him go. He can come up

here and we can discuss this, as logical peers."

At first, the security guards were unsure, but Lauzo made the same request and they let Ifu continue clambering up onto the stage and reach Nothaar's location. Once they were face-to-face, Ifu challenged, "How could you say such a thing like that, after everything we've been through? I thought that we were friends?!"

"What would make you think that?" Nothaar wondered aloud.

"Huh?" was all that Ifu could manage in retort.

Expanding upon his perspective, Nothaar stated, "When we first met, you and Syraaq held me at gunpoint and then shot me. After that, you basically abducted me and forced me to abandon my planet and my people, everyone and everything I had ever known. You paraded me around the universe without the least bit of my consent, using nanobots to control the very words that came out of my mouth. Then, through your own negligence, you not only allowed an outlaw to capture and abuse me, but you intentionally left me under her hegemony for an extended period of time because rescuing me sooner did not align to your schedule, plans, and ultimate use for me.

"Let us be very open: from the very beginning and as verified on several occasions since then, you have made it quite clear that you are exploiting me for your own ends. I have no specific qualms with that, but you seem to have confused the nature of our relationship and mistaken your thoughts for my own. You just presumed that I would agree with your perspective because I was an alien who was directly impacted by the actions of the Starbuilders. However, you discounted the basic fact that I am a distinct and unique individual who can make up my own mind. You dismissed the idea that I could see the cosmos and come to any conclusion other than yours. You may have convinced yourself that you were fighting for the betterment of people like me who did not have a say in the matter, but you neglected to actually ask me.

"In the short time I have known Lauzo, he has done more to learn about me and my thoughts than you ever did. Sir, you and I, we are not friends; I am just a tool for your own purposes. Again, there is nothing wrong with that. Plenty of people have relationships that are based totally on utility, too. In my nearly endless downtime between worlds, I have had the opportunity to read many of your conjectural books in the *Archive* and this is not an unusual conclusion among philosophers of various ilk. It is not that different from some of the things I remember being in the *Knowledge* from when I was a *Keeper*, so long ago. Similarly, have I not used you, as well, to assure my own survival? Nevertheless, that does not make our affiliation anything more than a loose partnership... at most."

Eyes brimmed with tears, Ifu appeared to swallow the sorrow he was showing on his face and instead spat out with the righteous—and obstinate—fury Nothaar had become accustomed to, "Everything I did, I did for you and people like you. I sacrificed everything in my life so that non-*Commons* like you could have a chance!"

"Ah, I see," Nothaar dismissively retorted, "all of my

actions were supposed to be transactional in relation to you and your cause. From your perspective, I am in eternal debt to you because you were purportedly 'fighting' for me and others who lacked any power. You see yourself as a savior figure, and I am at fault for not recognizing your divinity. Unfortunately for you, Ifuwukoogeeq, that is not how things work. Just because you, in your own head, felt that you were championing me, I am not required to do the same for you in return. My support does not come unconditionally just because of our personal connection and history together; nor do I need to adopt your viewpoint on what is best for me and my people. I can look at every specific situation and make a decision based on my own self-interests. Your sponsorship, however, seems to come with stipulations. It makes me wonder if you really do care about non-*Commons* and our worlds."

"You know I do!" Ifu retorted.

"Then, for once in your life," Nothaar responded, "just keep your mouth shut and listen. Do not tell me what I require. Hear my words and what I have to say about what I need; what I deem is necessary. I have a plan to present to the government, one that I believe is better than anything you or anyone else among our *Conclave of Dreamers* has proposed. Whether I am correct or not is up for debate, but is that not the whole reason we are here? Will you please allow me, for the first time ever, to speak up for myself, unabated?"

The fire raged in Ifu's eyes as Nothaar watched him internally deliberate what he was about to argue. Instead,

Ifu said nothing and just turned away, stepped off the stage, and returned to his seat with his arms crossed. Although Nothaar could not hear the words, he could see Syraaq trying to assuage Ifu, and the sulking Ifu attempting to push her off. Ifu was clearly upset, but Nothaar hoped he would come to see the veracity of what he had to say. Despite everything Nothaar had just professed to a massive audience, he did not hate Ifu, nor dislike him that much. Although he hoped that there would be a way for them to continue being around one another after this confrontation, Nothaar had to put it all aside to make his greater contention.

After glancing at Lauzo—who gave him an encouraging gesticulation—Nothaar illuminated, "Everyone, although I have told you much of what factually happened to me from the moment of the *Sky Shift* onward, I have not really told you that much about myself, who I am on a personal level. I have always stood out, even among my own people, due to how different I was from the average person. My approach to life, how I diligently watched and catalogued all the small details of my world, how I desired to never stop learning, it set me far apart and made me a bit of an outcast. Whereas *Commons* have the opportunity to be anything they want, my people were far less developed and were basically just trying to survive another winter without starving to death. To have the luxury to be educated and put that scholarship to use, it was a rarity to begin with. In many ways, I was lucky to find a *Keeper* to take me on and oversee the development of my talents so that they would not go to waste. Plenty of other people were not so fortunate.

"The essence of what I am trying to say is that, after all these years, it is just now that I have come to accept this basic revelation about myself. I want to become similar to the rest of you and be able to take for granted all the amazing opportunities you have at your fingertips. I aspire to be like a *Common*, to have everything you do, to know what you do. Still, I understand that I cannot really be like you no matter how hard I try. Regrettably, I will never apprehend what it means to be born as you are, to experience life as you do, and be able to choose to do something or nothing with those capabilities. I am truly envious.

"Although I have been augmented with your technologies and medicines, I will forever remain apart for the rest of my life, and not just because of my appearance. You *Commons* have an interstellar link and empathetic connection to each other and the universe that folks like me lack. No matter how much I try to absorb from the *Archive*, it will always just be words on a page and not written into my very soul as it is with all of you. No matter how you and your society really came into existence in the ancient past, it is clear as an outsider that there was a plan to turn you into masters of not only your own destiny, but of everyone's and everything's. Frankly, the design is a good one and, most importantly, is working as intended. I believe that with a few minor retrofits, this civilization can become an even better one. And considering activities like the genetic seeding updates that the Starbuilders undertake on a regular basis, you *Commons* should have no problem accepting and implementing something that would be beneficial for all of us.

"More so, though, I want to be a part of that endeavor.

"The people I came with today, it is clear what they are thinking. They hear these words and they believe that I have betrayed them. To them, I ask, 'How?' Are you, like Ifu, perturbed that I did not do what you wanted? Or are you more concerned that I have dismissed all of your ideas and proposals and schemes as just plain awful, if not repugnant? Listen, I am forever grateful for what you did for me. You liberated me from a horrible situation at the cost of several people's lives. I did not ask you to trade their existences for mine, but I am glad you have done so. For the first time since I left my homeworld, I am actually happy to be alive. You have helped me reach this point—especially you, Mouza Ori. You, above all others, have opened my eyes to the infinite possibilities, and what is important to accomplish in this vast cosmos of ours.

"That all said, after an independent analysis of all the available options, I find that what the government is already doing is the best solution for the cosmos at large. There is a reason why this culture has survived for trillions of years when all others have fallen by the wayside. No, as I said, it is not without faults, but there is an opportunity to make small corrections, to get things back on course towards brilliance. From my research, at no point has this government ever promised perfect results and justice; only the continual pursuit of both."

CHAPTER 47

"Well, Nothaar," Lauzo intoned, "I believe you have kept us waiting long enough. What is it that we—the representatives of the entire *Common's* society, the delegates of tens of the thousands of worlds—should do in pursuit of a more just and lasting system?"

Without pausing, Nothaar launched into his idea. "As Ifu and Syraaq would tell you, I have been far too contaminated to ever go back to the planet where I was born. The Starbuilders are correct in their attempts not to interfere with the development of a newly discovered species. Letting me go back there would be a mistake. Nevertheless, one of the core tenets of my profession as a *Keeper*, what my purpose in life really is, is to oversee the betterment of my people through the acquisition and distribution of useful *Knowledge*. I need a reason to continue being alive, something important to do that fulfils that goal.

"At the same time, this government has a problem. Ifu, Syraaq, Bipauc, Mouza, and all the rest are right about one thing: this administration and the Starbuilders do things to people like me against our will. Should we not have a say in the matter of what happens to our species? Most significantly, why is it that we non-*Commons* cannot determine when and how our transformation should happen? At a high level, what I am proposing is that newly discovered sapient beings need a seat at the table; we ought to be allowed to have representatives that are a part of this very council. It is inherently unfair and against the ideological aspirations of this institution to rule over anyone without their consent. The only logical solution is that we be granted the same rights as any planet that *Commons* dwell upon. Although we are not genetically alike, we share the same limitless potential as any thinking organism.

"I understand, it will not be easy to figure out a way to make this happen, but that is why I offer myself up as that first delegate. What I am saying is that I would like to stay aboard the government's Torch Ship and serve as an agent for my people. And the first thing I would advise is that we return to my former world and begin a process of recruiting a couple more individuals like myself to also take on this role and give our planet the same amount of say as any other one that is orbiting around this supermassive black hole. The reason I told you what I was like as a young person was because those are the qualities to look for in potential recruits. This is what we must investigate and discover in all other species that have not yet fully converted into being a *Common* nor reached the stars.

"And this is just the beginning. Ultimately, I would want to develop a standardized procedure and algorithm to help the government identify similarly minded individuals and personalities from future worlds teeming with sapient life. These planets may be few and far between nowadays, but they are still out there. The Starbuilders will find more, and those people deserve to have their voices heard in this chamber before anything happens to them. Instead of forcing the change upon them, they can be a part of the process from the beginning. We need to hear from the individuals who live upon the surfaces of those spheres, who understand the cultures and attitudes, and can provide critical insight into how to make the metamorphosis from their old outer shells into a new way of being as painless as possible.

"To be perfectly clear, I am not suggesting that some planets should have a right to refuse to join the union of *Commons*. The end goal will always be to make every world align to all the standards that you already expect. Once that is accomplished—and they have made the necessary technological advances at their own natural pace—they could then become a part of the larger shared community right here in this star system. Nevertheless, this approach does not need to be so distressing and abrupt. We can identify the right inhabitants, bring them up to a Quantum Ship, teach them the *Lingua* and the history of the *Commons*, and turn them into functioning members of society, just as I became. While my route was tumultuous, theirs can be smooth and full of support and understanding. And when they complete their initial training, they can then help decide the least problematic pathway towards the transition, telling us what would work best for their own unique planet and situation instead of this council and the Starbuilders forcing it upon them.

"These recruits would be the key to everything I see

as the plan forward for the betterment of all *Common*-kind. They, like me, would sit as permanent representatives until such a point that they either die from old age or their people develop enough technologically and culturally to join the community proper. Yes, I am asking for a special allowance for non-*Commons* or those in the process of becoming *Commons*, but it is what is necessary to reach a lasting and fair solution for all sapient life. As I believe I have demonstrated, your own prejudices against alien life have blinded you to the simple fact that non-*Commons* are just as proficient as you are; we just lack all your genetically encoded knowledge and general societal advantages. Given an education, we are no different. Perhaps one of them will even provide that one-of-a-kind spark that will save us all from the upcoming *Degenerate Age* and the heat death of the universe.

"I do not mean to lambast you, but it is obvious as an outside observer that your genetic programming makes you, in a way, bigoted and xenophobic. Due to being surrounded only by people who are like you, you rarely get to test these preconceived notions. That said, I am sure there is a good reason for these thoughts to be a part of you, something important in relation to the survival of the *Commons* as a whole. That said, it does not mean these feelings are best to hold onto long-term, not anymore. Genetic updates are conventional enough, so perhaps it is time to evaluate many components like these that are laced into your chromosomes. The dangers inherent with many of your base-pairs are things you cannot see for yourselves from the inside. They require exterior perspective to point out their failings.

"That is what I, and people like me, can offer. What I am saying is that it is not just a one-way relationship where non-*Commons* will expect some outsized influence combined with a never-ending social welfare support system. On the contrary, I am saying that aliens like me can give you something, something you have probably not had since you became *Commons* in the first place, whenever in antiquity that was.

"But I would be lying if I did not admit I have a personal interest, maybe even what could be described as a selfish incentive, in seeing this come to pass, too. Nothing would make me happier than getting to fly to all the wandering stars out there with you and learn about the various cultures on each planet. I am very interested in studying how a civilization perseveres and maintains their distinctiveness after becoming a *Common*. The prospect fascinates me, as does discerning even more ways to live one's life. Despite my travels, I know that I have seen but a small fraction of the worlds and peoples available right here. The *Archive* is one thing, but experiencing things with my own senses would be a dream come true, something I could enjoy for the remainder of my existence.

"Do I believe I am owed this? Perhaps, perhaps. So much was taken from me against my will. As I have told you, I lived through several virtual lifetimes and experienced many of those forfeitures firsthand. I have had more opportunities than I care to recount to mull over all that was lost to me. At the same time, I must acknowledge all that has been gained and what can still be discovered. More than anything, I understand now that I do not want to stop.

"This chapter of my life may be over, but I feel like there is a whole new universe of possibilities out there for me, right here, with the rest of you by my side."

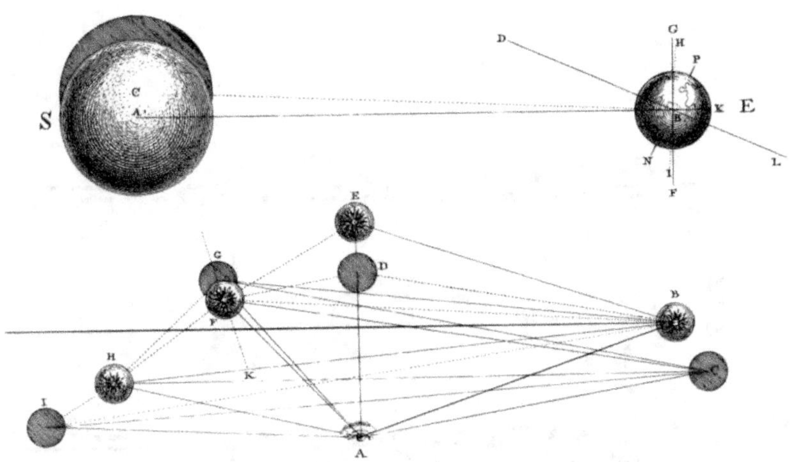

Heat Death

Epilogue I

As he was lying in bed, Nothaar Akii heard a ringing tone which indicated that someone was at the threshold to his hotel room. Plugging his perspective into the exterior camera, he was gladdened to discover that Delegate Lauzo Wevvok was standing just outside his entryway. Getting up from his prone position, Nothaar walked over to the door and commanded it to slide open. With the egress free, Nothaar stepped aside and invited Lauzo to join him inside his suite that the government was now paying for.

"Actually," Lauzo countered, "I was wondering if you'd like to go for a walk with me. There's a park not too far from here, and it's such a rare opportunity for me to be able to take a stroll out in nature."

Nothaar quickly agreed and went to grab his mask and coveralls to hide his alien features, ones that differed greatly from those of the *Commons*. "There's no need for that," Lauzo intoned as he pointed towards the various disguise-pieces still in Nothaar's hands. "The secret is out and just about everyone on the planet knows about you and that you're here. Luckily for you, we've stationed security officers all around this place so that no one can get up here and... well, no matter their intent, good or bad, you wouldn't want them around."

"Will I not draw a crowd, then, if I go out like this?" Nothaar queried as he indicated toward his distinct features. After so many years around *Commons*, he even found his own reflection to be striking and peculiar.

"It's the middle of the day," Lauzo explained, "and the majority of people are at work. Most likely, there are very few people out-and-about, especially in the park. Maybe a few people taking their pets for a bit of a meandering journey, but probably not much more than that. We can sneak out the staff exit of this building and take a circuitous route around to avoid the rest."

Once Nothaar agreed to Lauzo's suggestion, they executed it flawlessly, barely talking until they were far away from prying eyes and ears. It was a late spring day, but still rather cool despite the sun being high overhead. Upon entering the boundaries of the preserve, Nothaar had to remark, "I know you call this 'nature', but it really is just a facsimile of wilderness to me. On my homeworld, most of the land was undeveloped and plants grew uninhibitedly— not in planned patterns like these that allow wide, flat paths to pass through them. If I had groomed, even walkways like these ones when I first set out on my expedition, I could have trekked the length of the entire landmass in just a year or less!"

"Incidentally," Lauzo expounded, "my understanding is that this planet is very much like the one you came from, at least topographically. It has one major supercontinent that contains almost all of the earth above the water line with just a scattering of islands spread out over the rest of the globe. One of the reasons I wanted you to see this park in particular is because it reaches the southern-most tip of the habitable terrain. When I heard about this, it reminded me of that story you told me with... uh... um... what was that gentleman's name?"

"Baubu Yoordi," Nothaar answered. "At the time, he was the oldest person I had ever met by a significant margin. I am sure he is just a baby compared to people like you or Syraaq or others. The idea of living that long seemed completely inconceivable to me, but now..."

"Now you have probably already lived more years than he ever did, and then some," Lauzo finished. "I mean, it's really impossible to say and depends on whose perspective we're talking about, but I'd wager that you have many additional decades—if not centuries—ahead of you to make sure you blow past all prior records set by anyone from your species."

"That is, so long as I keep up with the proper preventative maintenance," Nothaar added.

For a moment, Lauzo was quiet as he seemed to be contemplating something. They walked along in a comfortable silence for a stretch until Lauzo spoke softly, "A living being like you and me is much like an entire planet. We do require the occasional 'tune-up', if you will. For instance, I talked about this world having one giant landmass, but could you imagine what would happen if we let plate tectonics happen innately and the land contracted or broke apart? Spheres like these, when they form, are meant to last a mere ten billion years, at most. If their suns did not wink out and take their life-bearing attendants with them, their own interior heat would eventually give out.

"Part of what allows a planet to have life on its surface is containing an oversized molten core that helps grant the world a relatively uniform and dependable warmth, along with some other important protections. Yet, given enough time, almost all that energy will dissipate out into the cosmos. Consequently, it most likely means it will end up with the core seizing up, or something close enough that convection stops, causing the disintegration of the protective magnetic shield. No matter which happens first, the ecosystem would simply collapse. Accordingly, on a regular basis, we have to go in and ensure that these interiors have the energetic state we desire, but not so much that continents will shift position. It's a constant balancing act of trying to let nature take the best course while controlling almost everything else in order to ensure the collective survival of our people."

"Thus is the burden of the Starbuilders," Nothaar lamented. "That name really is misleading considering all they have to do."

"But it has a really nice sound to it, you have to admit," Lauzo contended with self-amusement spreading across his face. "Propaganda and marketing are always important, even if they obfuscate the truth a little bit in order to accomplish their important overall goals."

"Fair enough," Nothaar conceded. "I am rather 'late to the party', as I have heard the saying go. As such, I will not be advocating for a name change anytime soon."

His own annoyance clearly displayed upon his face, Lauzo clarified, "Much to my chagrin, you have yet to be made an official representative of your people and world, either. Without that, I'm afraid you won't be able to promote and sponsor any potential revisions."

"And how goes the proceedings?" Nothaar probed.

Sighing, Lauzo explicated, "The government does not move swiftly. Since we *Commons* have existed as a people and a society for such an unfathomable amount of time, basically any potential law or rule has already been created. On the rare occasions when something new comes along, it takes a while to work through all the smaller committees and their like and make their way up to the greater chamber, if they ever do. Rest assured, I am doing everything I can to hasten the process, but even I am powerless against the superior strength of inertia."

"I understand," Nothaar allowed. "It is not like I am in any rush, either. Apparently, I have not even bothered to explore outside my own temporary living quarters. Perhaps I, too, should make an effort to take advantage of the area, especially now that my identity has been exposed."

"That would be a wonderful idea," Lauzo agreed. "I'll let the security guards know and they can accompany you. I'm sorry that none of your erstwhile companions will be able to join you since they are all still in detention and being questioned by the constabulary."

Turning away, Nothaar remarked, "I doubt that would be a problem. I cannot imagine that anyone from the *Conclave of Dreamers* would willingly choose to be around me, not after what I did to them."

"Pshaw!" Lauzo disputed. "People are far more capable of forgiveness and understanding than you give them credit for. They'll come around; you'll see. Perhaps there is even something you could do for them?"

"Hmmm," Nothaar thought aloud, "do you have some specific action in mind?"

"In order for it to have any meaning," Lauzo refuted, "it must be a personal gesture. As such, you must undertake this deliberation on your own. Nonetheless, don't feel pressured to give me an answer right now. Sleep on it, come up with some ideas, and let me know later."

"Okay," Nothaar acquiesced, "I will do that. Given a moment to meditate on it, I am sure I can settle on some possibility or another."

"Good, good," Lauzo said as he seemingly brushed Nothaar's concerns aside. "Ah, here we are, and just in time. These old legs of mine are about to give out on me. I could use a rest."

Following Lauzo's gaze, Nothaar observed a bench situated near a cliffside that overlooked the ocean. The two walked over and sat down, not saying anything for a while as they partook in the stunning vista. Finally, Nothaar inquired, "Is there a land of ice somewhere out there? I tried to use my telescoping vision, but could only get as far as the horizon and no further."

"No," Lauzo replied, "I said this place was similar to your world, but not an exact replica. This planet actually has no standing ice at all upon its surface, except locally in certain areas when it's winter. Otherwise, nothing permanent like that exists here."

"A shame," Nothaar pronounced. "I never got the chance to explore the one on my own homeworld, not even in my imaginary virtual scenario. I guess because I lacked the proper frame of reference, my mind and the *Eh-aye* refused to allow me to attempt the voyage."

With a laugh, Lauzo assuredly decreed, "Don't worry; when we get past this hump in the bureaucratic process, you'll have the opportunity to visit a real realm of ice on one of the many worlds in our confederation. And after you have the opportunity to spend some time on one with the frozen wind whipping across your face, I'm quite confident that you'll never want to do such a thing again!"

Returning a warm appearance of his own, Nothaar expressed, "I look forward to achieving one of my life's goals and then being happy to never repeat it. It is difficult to think about how little I have actually been able to do, see, and accomplish in all this time."

"I don't need to be a doctor or psychiatrist like Mouza Ori," Lauzo expressed, "or a therapist of any kind, really, to know that you can't blame yourself for the things that you had and still have no control over."

"In my head, I am well aware," Nothaar granted. "Nevertheless, my heart has not fully healed. I do not know if it ever will. Perhaps I am forever broken?"

Placing a hand on Nothaar's shoulder, Lauzo assuaged, "I don't think you're broken at all, Nothaar. Yes, you certainly have gone through a lot of terrible and painful things, far more than most people. Further, you've undoubtedly been robbed of a large portion of your life. And, unfortunately, you will surely continue mourning for what might have been, always second-guessing the course your existence has taken. But don't we all, in our own way?

"Yet despite everything that's happened to you, I don't see a broken man. Before me sits an amazingly put together and well-adjusted person... one who I am proud to call a dear friend. There's no limit to what's possible for you, Nothaar, and I will repeat it every day until you believe it yourself."

Giving him a silent gesture of appreciation, Nothaar turned away from Lauzo and stared out over the endless sea at the end of this world. Casting his mind outward, he envisioned what some of those potentialities might be.

EPILOGUE II

After talking for a while longer, Lauzo began to complain about his stiffening legs from sitting too long. Therefore, he and Nothaar began hiking around the rest of the park and making their way back to Nothaar's hotel. Along the way, Nothaar suddenly recalled a strange detail he had put aside for later.

"I have been meaning to ask you about something," Nothaar abruptly threw in as a non sequitur. "When we were on stage at the arena, behind us there was a statue of a young woman and an older man. It is my understanding that several similar homages are situated all over the government's Torch Ship. What are these all about?"

"Oh," Lauzo spoke, "you mean *The Sage and Her Father*. Yes, comparable effigies to it do appear quite often in government circles. You could think of them as a symbol-of-sorts related to how our régime functions."

"*The Sage and Her Father*?" Nothaar questioned aloud. "That sounds vaguely familiar. Where have I heard that before? Wait a moment, I think that was something that Goqanx Guzyc or someone aboard her vessel brought up to me at some point. If I recall, it was some type of scheduling programing? No, it was an *Eh-aye* that had rare decision-making capabilities and free-rein to select destinations for the government's Torch Ship. Knowing how uncomfortable *Commons* are with handing over any authority to computers, it was quite a surprising thing to ascertain, even back then. Now that I understand how your genetic programming actually precludes you from being able to do such a thing..."

There was a strange expression on Lauzo's face that gave Nothaar pause, something he had never seen on it before: suspicion. Lauzo quickly cleared it from his countenance and said, "Well, I suppose if anyone would have acquired the tiniest morsel of information about *The Sage and Her Father*, it would have been a successful outlaw and privateer like your Goqanx Guzyc. I guess I should've expected that someone like her would have also traded in intelligence, among her other spurious activities. Anyhow, since you already have a small piece of the puzzle and you will hopefully be a full delegate in short order, I reckon it wouldn't hurt to tell you a bit more. That is, as long as you promise not to let anyone else know about this conversation and what you are about to hear, even after you've been officially sworn in?"

His curiosity peaked, Nothaar quickly agreed to Lauzo's terms before asking, "One of the first things I noticed is that the figures do not look exactly like *Commons*. They share many similar phenotypes and are certainly closer to you than me, but they are nowhere near a full match. Are they some type of predecessor, a 'pre-*Common*' test species, if you will?"

"Honestly," Lauzo began, "I'm not really sure if they

are related to us *Commons* in any way. As far as I know, there are no pictures or videos of anyone who looks exactly like them in the *Archive*."

"Hold on," Nothaar bade. "How can that be? I understand the *Archive* is massive and there simply is not enough storage space to have an entire copy on ships and planets with limited physical storage space. However, I was under the impression that there was a central source somewhere that contained the entire *Archive*, and it was a complete record of everything ever known and recorded throughout the universe."

Lauzo had a good laugh at this before continuing, "I'm sorry, I don't mean to sound so dismissive and amused. And it's not like you'd have any reason to believe otherwise. I'm quite sure most people imagine exactly as you do. Heck, I'm pretty sure it's what I thought before I joined the government oh-so-long ago. No, I'm sorry to report the *Archive* is anything but infinite and far more limited than the citizenry would be comfortable with realizing. Think about this example:

"Your former companions Syraaq and Ifu, they both had ocular implants added early in life. You were probably not aware of this, but those two used those technological enhancements to record every moment of their lives."

"Ah," Nothaar interrupted, "so that is why, back on my homeworld, they were so insistent on building a storage medium for their personal *Archives* and then dragging it everywhere we went! Even afterwards, I could not figure out what data was so important and taking up so much space that it necessitated us hauling that thing halfway across the universe. All that audio and video must have taken up massive amounts of memory."

"That it did," Lauzo confirmed. "And now it's being used against them as evidence. I don't want to call them stupid criminals, but they basically chronicled all their felonies and didn't even protect the records with a strong encryption. It was far too easy for the investigators to gain access to their files."

"That does not surprise me in the least," Nothaar deadpanned while thinking about Ifu's hubris and Syraaq's unassailable trust in her coconspirator.

"Anyway," Lauzo segued back to the topic at hand, "That is just the recordings of two individuals. Now multiply that times trillions upon trillions of people who have done exactly the same thing over almost the entire lifetime of the universe. From a practical perspective, we just can't store it all indefinitely. Honestly, most of it is completely worthless, especially as time goes by. Who cares about a musical show that some unimportant person went to once? Most people never even look back at their own filmed memories, so why would anyone else care?"

Breaking in, Nothaar inquired, "So, is there some type of process to decide what to keep and what to trash?"

"You could say that," Lauzo cryptically concurred. "But then you might follow up that question with: how do we decide what is worthwhile and what is a waste of space? Beyond that, how could we possibly ever dedicate enough people and resources to parse through it all? The hard truth is: we don't and we can't. This is where *The Sage and Her Father* comes into play. What you heard before is partially true. It is a very advanced *Eh-aye* that has been granted special privileges, ones we would normally never cede to a machine or a piece of software. Yet, even though we do not fully understand or control *The Sage and Her Father*, we do allow it to make important assessments for us. Chief among them is judging what to prune and what to store forever in the *Archive*."

"I am still confused," Nothaar interjected. "How does it make the determination of what is worthy of being maintained? What criteria is it using?"

Giving him the *Common*'s gesture for expressing uncertainty, Lauzo further explained, "Again, we simply don't know. It's possible that *The Sage and Her Father* actually predates our society, and it may have even had a hand in its creation, if the rumors are to be accepted as fact. There are certainly reasons to think so, though. Take for instance that ancient book, the... umm... Compendium of something or other... Do you know what I'm talking about? It's that one that inspired how we use Quantum Shift technology to move whole planets into our system."

"Yes, I have heard of it," Nothaar agreed, "but I have yet to find the complete text in any local copy of the *Archive* I have been attached to. It seems that many people have heard about this tome from their grade school studies, but very few have actually read it."

"Interesting," Lauzo trailed off before picking up the thread. "Well, what I do remember is the Compendium describes scenes that were recorded on video, yet no anthropologist has ever been able to find those source materials. There does not appear to be any documentation related to the named species the Compendium is about that actually shows what they looked like. For all we know, they may appear exactly like you, or they may be the forerunners to *Commons*. Or, just as probable, they're completely fabricated and no such group of people historically existed. Yet, if they did, perhaps the statues and other works of art that represent *The Sage and Her Father* are of the same populaces. Then again, it could all be completely unconnected, and the species in the Compendium might be something else entirely. There's just no way to know because the original chronicles about them and what went into the Compendium are long gone.

"What's more, though, is there is evidence that shows *The Sage and Her Father* basically commissioned the book. So, on the one hand, it determined that the story would have value for future generations; yet, on the other, it concluded that the primary sources and everything else about the people the Compendium discusses had no value and purged them from the *Archive*. Both actions were undertaken by *The Sage and Her Father*, despite the fact that on the surface they are totally contradictory."

"I am afraid I still do not understand," Nothaar interrogated. "Is there a reason for these proceedings? What does all of this accomplish?"

"Well, I might have an answer, or at least a theory," Lauzo replied. "The example I gave is indicative of how

The Sage and Her Father operates. It will never directly ask for or demand anything. As far as we know, it has no capabilities to even speak or send messages or anything like that. How it seemingly functions, though, is to parse through the *Archive* and use it to create inspiration for *Commons* to follow—or not. At the end of the day, it's still always our choice whether to partake in any acts. However, one could look at the situation as saying the *Archive* only exists for the benefit of *The Sage and Her Father*, and for it—in turn—to use that data to influence the direction of the *Commons* on a societal level."

"This is a lot to take in," Nothaar concernedly confessed. "More so, I am surprised you are so calm about this considering how *Commons* are—as I highlighted before—genetically programmed to despise this exact situation. Even as an outsider without those directives built into my being, I am a bit disturbed by the idea of some rogue, mostly unknowable program with the free will to make such critical decisions, nonetheless manipulating trillions of people on a regular basis."

"I would be lying if I said I didn't still harbor any number of reservations," Lauzo allowed, "but they are tempered both by experience and coding. It appears that there is some type of exception built into our genetics specifically to overlook *The Sage and Her Father*."

"When you put it that way," Nothaar pressed, "it sounds like every living *Common* has been infected by *The Sage and Her Father* and carries it within their being. It makes me anxious just thinking about how far a reach this artificial program may actually have, and how much it is controlling your everyday actions."

"Then I don't think you're going to like the next part I have to tell you," Lauzo warned.

"What more could there be?" Nothaar rhetorically asked, already feeling the unease rising in his stomach.

"Try not to let this go to your head," Lauzo requested, "but I believe *The Sage and Her Father* took an interest, specifically, in you."

"How could that be?" Nothaar challenged. "I am not a *Common* and have not interacted with the master *Archive* at any point."

"That is another misconception I need to clear up for you," Lauzo clarified. "A little bit of this *Eh-aye* exists in every single copy of the *Archive*, no matter how big or small or incomplete it is. It's simply not possible to copy any part of the *Archive* without also bringing along a portion of *The Sage and Her Father* with it. Therefore, it probably became aware of you the first time you accessed your local edition of the *Archive* while using your tablet. I would wager it's even possible that it happened before then just from Syraaq and Ifu's accounts alone. Either way, I have every reason to believe it perceived you as a potential agent of change. Given what I know, I would not be surprised if it was gently nudging things along the entire time. Of course, we can never be sure. That said, after spending time with you aboard the government's Torch Ship, I saw the signs that made me consider the possibility and accept it at face value."

"That sounds akin to faith," Nothaar summarized, "almost like a religious reverence and submission. By that token, *The Sage and Her Father* would be your god, the ruler of all *Common*-kind."

Gesticulating his disagreement, Lauzo said as much to Nothaar before pronouncing, "It isn't like that. As I said before, we *Commons*—from the lowliest street urchin to the heads of our government—still make all our own decisions as living people. From my perspective, *The Sage and Her Father* is just a tool, a helping hand that can point out the possibilities. If I'd chosen to turn you and your compatriots in to the authorities, none of this would be happening now. That was always in my hands. But because I understand a bit of how this *Eh-aye* functions, I chose to listen and see where it'd bring us. Thus far, I'm happy with the results. We'll see if my fellow representatives agree with me. Even if they don't, if all that comes out of it is the pleasure of having met you, then it will have been well worth it... at least to me."

"I hope it ends up leading to much more than that," Nothaar entreated to no one in particular.

"Me, too," Lauzo agreed. "As always, though, it's in the hands of a wide array of people with various viewpoints. You mentioned in your speech about how it's amazing our society has survived and outlasted all others. I find that's because there's a system of checks and balances in place. None of the worlds can dominate the others, no faction can grow so big as to dwarf the rest, no elected official can guarantee how long they will serve, everything is about ebbs and flows. While you may see *The Sage and Her Father* as a potentially dangerous technological force, the *Commons* as the envoys of life always hold it at bay. It cannot control us; we cannot constrain it. We have reached equilibrium.

"Even *The Sage and Her Father* contains a bit of a balancing act. Forensic computer scientists—who are smarter and much more in tune with this sort of thing than I am—have found that *The Sage* is actually a distinct and separate routine from *Her Father*. However, despite this, they always move as one, no matter what, like they are handcuffed together. If you try to make a duplicate of one, you'll get a copy of both of them, no matter what you try to do in order to block it from happening. It seems like each is the counterpoint to something internal, preventing any decision or action it takes from being too extreme."

"Ah, when you put it that way," Nothaar added, "the structure of that statue makes more sense. It appeared to me like they were trying to either restrain or embrace each other. Perhaps, then, they were doing both? A parent and their child, in an eternal war, trying to decide whether they love or hate each other."

EPILOGUE III

Alone in an underground location he was told was called a "locker room", Nothaar anxiously waited for the fateful, decisive government edict that would determine the course of the rest of his life. To him, the agonizingly slow passing of the months it had taken to reach this point had seemed completely unnecessary. While Nothaar felt he was being unfairly forced to endure this uncertainty without an adequate resolution, Lauzo continually attempted to assure him the process had actually gone amazingly rapidly. "It would usually take years, probably decades, for a bill to work its way up for a full vote," Lauzo had once claimed. "Your particular circumstances have obliged the bureaucracy to move at, what is to them, an uncomfortably fast pace."

Since it was his life they were debating, Nothaar's distress was not allayed by these platitudes. Even then, he was perturbed at not being allowed to stand in the chamber while they decided what to do with him. "It's impossible," Lauzo had alleged. "There are strict rules and regulations around who is permitted in the balloting area while a formal vote is underway. The best I can do is get you into another part of the arena that is completely separated from the rest of the representatives and their staff."

True to this declaration, Nothaar found himself in just such an empty, cavernous place. It was hard for him to believe that a huge mass of people sat somewhere above him. Of course, he had been in that exact locale before and seen it with his own eyes. Thinking back to his speech before the government, it irked him to no end that he had not been invited back since. Lauzo advised him to forget about his grudges because—if all went well—those same people he was upset with would become his co-workers and co-habitants for the foreseeable future.

Just as Nothaar was about to arise from the bench he was sitting upon and begin to pace again, the door suddenly whooshed open and a stoic-looking Lauzo sauntered in. Nothaar's heart immediately sank. "Oh no," he said aloud, "how bad was it?"

Pausing for a moment, Lauzo's face started twitching. This was quickly followed by hysterical laughter and a broad happiness overtaking his visage. Gathering himself, Lauzo teased, "Oh, Nothaar, I got you, I got you good! You should have seen your face!"

"You jerk!" Nothaar yelled back. "Do you not know how scared and upset I am? Why would you do that to me?"

"Because," an abruptly serious Lauzo clarified, "I care about you, and saw that you needed to release all that tension that has been building up inside you."

For a moment, Nothaar wanted to continue arguing, but then he realized Lauzo was correct. The psychiatrist Nothaar had been meeting with as a replacement for Mouza—who remained incarcerated—had identified this exact personality trait in him. To help Nothaar work through and process his feelings so they would no longer rule him nor be such a destructive force in his life, his therapist had assigned him a number of exercises to practice between their meetings. Yet most revealing for Nothaar from this work and the in-person treatment sessions was realizing this was an issue that predated his entire experience and exposure to the *Commons*, something he had apparently been carrying around his entire life. Longingly, Nothaar wished everyone on his homeworld could benefit from the advanced medical knowledge available to him, but knew they still had a very long journey in front of them until that would be possible. It pained Nothaar to think about the struggles that were still to come for them, but fervently yearned to be able to finally provide some semblance of relief.

Retracting his initial response, Nothaar expressed his regret to Lauzo and noted, "I have erroneously taken my agitation out on you, and you do not deserve it. May I please ask for your forgiveness?"

Chortling again, Lauzo declared, "You don't need to apologize or ask for absolution; you already have my unconditional support, and my friendship. More so, for what it's worth, I'm sorry, too. I thought it would be funny to josh around with you, but I wasn't really thinking straight. I could claim that I was delirious from dealing with so many entitled blowhards out there for however long we've been going on-and-on, but that would be a poor excuse."

"No matter then," Nothaar swept aside their short

fight. "However, I must know; I cannot wait any longer. Please tell me the news is good!"

Nothaar observed a confusing mix of sentiments on Lauzo's face as the older man expounded, "Listen, it's not everything you and I wanted. Stuff changed, clauses were moved around. Promises were made, unrelated decrees were added. It's not a total win, but a compromise somehow bubbled up to the surface and solidified into an actual piece of legislation, one that sixty-one percent of the delegates could get behind and voted for. That is the bare minimum necessary for a measure to become law, which means, Nothaar, that congratulations are in order! Aside from a few technical details and a swearing in ceremony, you are hereby the first official non-*Common* representative, and absolutely not the last."

For a moment, Nothaar was unable to process Lauzo's words. It was what he had longed for, the entirety of what he had strived to make real. More importantly, it was an acknowledgement of his equality, and it came from people he admired. The relief rapidly overwhelmed him and he felt dizzy. Compelled to sit back down, Nothaar buried his face in his hands as the tears started flowing. Lauzo slowly made his way over and sat down next to Nothaar, wrapping him in awkward sideways hug, hushing him.

After a while, Nothaar was able to regain control of his emotions and wiped away the salty stream from under his eyes and upon his cheeks. "Thank you, Lauzo," Nothaar began. "This is, perhaps, the happiest day of my complicated life. It would not have been possible without you."

"You're damn right about that!" Lauzo joked.

At last allowing himself to feel satisfaction, Nothaar let the laughter escape from his insides. It was something he had not done in a long time, especially not since...

Interrupting his train of thought, Lauzo announced, "I'm glad you're enjoying this victory, but I have more good news for you."

"What could be better than this?" Nothaar queried.

"Well," Lauzo enlightened, "if we're going to have a bunch of non-*Commons* aboard our Torch Ship, we can't just serve them a bunch of slimy, bland, unappetizing 'Nothaar Chow', or something similar. I've been talking with our chefs, geneticists, chemists, engineers, and others in related fields, and they've been working on a way to adapt our meals to meet your—or anyone else's that we pick up along the way—physiology and dietary requirements. Do you understand what I'm saying?"

"That... I will be able to... eat real food again..." Nothaar, in awe of the possibilities, whispered in response as his mouth instantly began to water in anticipation.

"Yes," Lauzo agreed. "Food is one of the great pleasures in life, and you deserve to have some. By the time we are shipbound, you'll be able to partake in communal fares just like the rest of us."

"Lauzo," Nothaar uttered, "this is the greatest gift you could ever give me. I think I would rather be able to chew solids and taste flavors again even more than be a delegate to this magnificent body!"

"No need to choose," Lauzo exuberantly celebrated,

"you get to have both! However, I do have some information that I don't think you'll particularly enjoy. The council decided that your homeworld needed a name—at least a temporary one until the inhabitants come up with their own designation—in order to know which place we're talking about. Not only that, but they arrived at a conclusion on what it should be."

"How could that happen?" Nothaar challenged. "As far as I know, they do not have any familiarity with the native languages and cultures from my sphere."

"Oh, ho, ho," Lauzo giggled. "There is one word they know, even if they can't pronounce it very well."

"Please do not tell me..." Nothaar started before Lauzo quickly cut him off with giddy delight rapidly spreading across his face.

"It's 'Planet Nothaar'!" Lauzo cheered.

Groaning, Nothaar recalled, "I remember reading some piece of fiction where the names of the planet, people, and the rulers were all identical. It was terrible and I could not take it seriously! Why would they do that to me?"

"Consider it an honor," Lauzo offered. "At least sixty-one percent of them think so highly of you that they feel an entire globe should share your handle."

"Fine, fine," Nothaar dismissed. "Nevertheless, I still think it is a stupid name for an entire life-bearing world!"

"You may not have a say on that," Lauzo segued, "but there is one issue that the rest of the council is requesting your input on—the sooner, the better."

"What is that?" Nothaar probed.

Without skipping a beat, Lauzo solicited, "What are we going to do with all of those extremist malcontents, also known as your former comrades? They have all been tried and found guilty of a plethora of crimes, but since none of those activities happened on this planet, the local government doesn't want them imprisoned here, either. As part of the balancing act of competing powers that I discussed with you before, we must respect their wishes and autonomy in a situation like this."

After considering for a brief interval, Nothaar proposed, "They should serve out their sentences aboard the government's Torch Ship, with us. Then, once their debt to society is paid, we should also invite them to stay with us, if they would accept such an invitation. Not with full autonomy or free rein of movement or anything like that, but having them restricted to a small, controllable area.

"What this government needs more than anything, what you have highlighted is a major concern, is something to challenge it on a regular basis. What would be a better counterpoint to complacency than having these people be advisors to the most intractable organization in existence? Give them a committee to run and keep them busy working with each other and deciding what they want to present to the administration. If they feel involved—if they become part of the establishment—they will no longer rebel against us. Not that they could really do too much damage in any type of future uprising, but why risk it?

"Besides, it would also make the government look more open to ideas, more progressive, which would curtail other potential movements looking to create a greater and far more perilous radical change. Were you not the one who lectured to me on the importance of propaganda and appearances? What did you say; that it served the purpose of hiding the complete truth in order to accomplish what is genuinely important?"

"I can see what you're getting at..." Lauzo attempted, but Nothaar was on a roll and could not stop his mouth from expelling all his thoughts.

"Believe me, I recognize how difficult this idea is for *Commons* because of your genetic programming. You are designed to be more conservative in order to stay safe and protect and preserve life. Still, I believe we can sell this plan on the same lines, especially in regard to how it can bring about even more security to all us living beings."

"That's all fine and dandy," Lauzo interjected, attempting to get a few words in edgewise. "If that's what you believe is best, I'll start pumping the crowds and get other representatives signed up for this scheme. It'll certainly take some time, but I believe I can make it happen before we have to leave this planet for our next destination, wherever that may be. That said, I have to wonder if this is going to be a problem for you? You've been very clear with me that you're concerned about their reactions to you and thinking of you as some type of betrayer."

"As you said," Nothaar summarized, "in time, they will come to understand my actions. At least, that is now a hope I carry, too. Either way, despite our differences of opinion—and in spite of everything they did to me and how they used me—I did find them interesting to work with and would enjoy continuing to do so again. In many ways, I am grateful for the opportunity they provided me, even if they did not realize that was what they were doing."

"Are you sure this is not about Syraaq, and what happened to her?" Lauzo challenged.

With a sinking feeling in the pit of his stomach, Nothaar admitted, "I would be lying if I claimed that Syraaq's death while in detention awaiting trial did not affect my opinion on the matter. Whether it was from the stress of the situation or just her very advanced age, her passing has had an impact on my worldview. Most of all, though, I worry about Ifu. Among everyone who was part of the *Conclave of Dreamers*—and, really, throughout the entire cosmos—Syraaq was his only real companion, his only family. After we recycled her remains, it truly hit me how alone Ifu is now. I was honestly surprised to discover the empathy I experienced for him."

"Maybe that means that Ifu does, indeed, have at least one other friend," Lauzo considered. "Perhaps you've even been fooling yourself into believing that he doesn't fit into your life that way, as you told the entire legislative body. The easier thing would be to abandon him, Mouza, Bipauc, and the rest and make a clean break. After all, why drag the garbage of your past along when you are about to embark on the next chapter of your story? It takes a lot to be willing to open yourself up to the pain and consequences of your actions, to sacrifice extant comfort because you think it's the right thing to do."

"I... do not know..." Nothaar admitted. "I hear your words, I do, and I understand your point. However, I am rather unsure how I really feel in my heart. Although I suppose it would be a lot less messy if I choose the definitive ending you have outlined, that seems disingenuous and unrealistic to me. Even here and now, at the edge of the *Degenerate Age*, life must go on, and we need to find a way to coexist for our collective long-term survival."

"True enough," Lauzo agreed. "Our work goes on-and-on, and neither of us will be around to find out what truly happens. Can life actually survive the heat death of the universe? Or is the entire *Common's* society just a pipedream, a farce attempting to stave off the inevitable? The cosmos doesn't care about us and will get along just fine whether or not there are people to populate it."

"No," Nothaar contended, "I disagree. This universe, it has no meaning, no purpose, without us living beings, especially us sapient ones, to enjoy it. Though we are rare and the conditions for us to arise are difficult, it still happens, even in this unlikely era. I am proof enough of that. All of us are constructed from components formed and discharged from the deep recesses of exploding suns. The fact that there seems to be a set of rules, some type of grand astral order, directive, and intention—it cannot be equated to pure chance and randomness. Quantum particles yield subatomic specks, which in turn join forces to eventually become elements. Afterwards, those basic building blocks merge together into compounds that evolve and ultimately yield us. All of that tells me one thing: the universe wants us to be here."

"So, you're saying..." Lauzo pushed.

Nothaar made sure the *Common's* expression for contentment was clear upon his face as he concluded, "That the universe, on the whole, is the only real Starbuilder, and it uses those cosmic engines to make us."

Notes and Scribbles

Thoughts, History, and Dedications

Reading through my old notes, it seems that almost all that remains of the original concept for **Starbuilders** is the name. Once upon a time, this was a story about various sapient species who, trillions of years into the future, were barely holding on by traipsing about a massively expanded universe, finding free-floating veins of hydrogen, and then harvesting it to feed suns in their artificial solar systems. Increasingly desperate measures would have been undertaken by various factions, each completely oblivious of the others and their actions. Due to their lack of coordination, they also would have often unintentionally thwarted the plans of their unknown rivals as the resources available to all of them dwindled down to almost nothing.

Obviously, along the way, there was a fairly significant redirection which is reflected in the novel you have just read. However, not everything was cast aside as little nuggets remain here and there. Mostly, though, it lived on through the *Conclave of Dreamers*. These so-called radical extremists presented a number of these possibilities, with the *Heliocentralists* being closest to my initial notion. Nonetheless, Syraaq correctly lambasted them by highlighting that there was no net gain to be had and that the **Starbuilders** had already unsuccessful partaken in such endeavors in the past. Still, that makes me believe parts of the earliest ideas expressed in my prototype design did actually happen in this universe—or at least some version of it.

In a later pass, as I was massaging the kernel of this story, I laid out the three main characters. One was a rookie who had recently joined the **Starbuilders** and had much to learn. Another was a "gritty veteran" who ended up teaming up with our naïve newbie. Finally, there was the "primitive" who noticed a "sky shift" on their planet and was attempting to figure out what had happened. At first, their paths and journeys would have been completely separate with parallel tales that eventually converged. They would have gotten more swept up in events, rather than truly having any agency, perspective, and intentions of their own. Thankfully, I came to see how unsatisfying that would be.

Further, while writing **Aestas ¤ The Yellow Balloon**, I had decided that locking into one character's perspective worked best for the type of narratives I am trying to tell. From there, I began to nurture and water the seed of everything being from a native alien's viewpoint so the audience could learn what was happening at the same pace as that individual did. Thus, Nothaar Akii was born, although he certainly did not yet have a name at that point. Let's just say that during this process I've gained a new respect for people who develop whole fictional languages and naming conventions.

On the topic of tongues, let me be very clear about one thing: the *Lingua* that the *Commons* speak is not English—or whatever language you happen to be reading this in. The text upon the page is merely an "interpretation" of the actual words that were spoken or thought. As the author, I have given these monologues and conversations a certain parlance so they're understandable to contemporary people like yourself. Nevertheless, I see myself more akin to a translator than an exact chronicler. I'm not saying the *Lingua* did not originate from or shares anything in common with Earth-based dialects, nor am I confirming or denying that it does, either.

No matter the truth around what the *Lingua* is or isn't, I would be remiss if I did not credit Lawrence M. Schoen's ***Barsk: The Elephants' Graveyard*** and its sequel and spinoffs as the inspiration for language being encoded into DNA and/or RNA. While books about taking drugs to talk to ghosts is not in my usual repertoire, Schoen does a masterful job of weaving together exactly that with hard science fiction elements, allegories for our own world—especially those dealing with racism, refugees, and forced resettlement—and a wonderfully crafted story that deserves more attention than it has received. Of course, there are many other well-known epics about galactic empires out there, but I especially appreciated how Schoen was able to use them as a backdrop to tell a narrative about just a few characters, with the consequences being small and personal. Did you perhaps notice the influence of this style and approach in the work you have just read, too?

Despite the many real and theoretical technological solutions and cosmological conditions discussed throughout the plot, there was plenty that was left on the cutting room floor. One thing I would have liked to have delved into deeper—but there really was no good opportunity to do so—would have been a section dealing with dark energy. For those unaware, dark energy is a hypothetical solution to a difficult situation we have in our universe. As briefly touched upon at various junctures by Syraaq, Ifu, and the *Collapsers*, the universe is expanding. More so, the rate at which it's expanding is actually getting faster as time goes by. At the moment I am writing this, scientists have not nailed down what that speed exactly is, but research and efforts continue.

To answer the questions of "why" and "how", though, more investigation and experimentation is needed. Something is missing from our understanding of the equations that govern the physics of the observable universe, at least as far as we know it. To account for this, experts have filled in the gap with what they termed dark energy, an unknown force that apparently makes up approximately sixty-eight percent of the cosmos. To put that in perspective, the next largest component, at twenty-seven percent, is dark matter—which is, for lack of a better descriptor, an invisible substance that does not interact directly with regular matter but does have a gravitational impact. If you've done the math, that only leaves just five percent of the remainder of our reality to be what we think of as "normal" matter and energy, everything we are made out of and use.

When I've spent time contemplating these cosmological conundrums, I often wondered if dark energy is really an internal force. What if what we think of as an outward pushing motion from within is actually an external pulling influence? That would mean there is something "outside" our universe, perhaps another one or many universes, and as these universes expand, they get "closer" to each other and end up actually exacerbating the pulling sensation on all the other ones in some type of attraction mechanism akin to gravity. Yes, this would mean there is a multiverse, but it does not corroborate the oft-cited concept that there are parallel worlds. Marco Chung lambasted that particular potentiality in ***Compendium of Humanity's End***, so I won't rehash those arguments here. Still, there is something in this thought experiment that is worth exploring further.

I hope from all that I have revealed that you have gained a sense of how a story like this, and those still to come, are birthed into existence. Nowadays, I think it's important to highlight that everything about this specific book, all my prior works, and those yet to be written was and will be developed completely by human minds and hands with A.I. only being used in a limited research, background extrapolation, and image testing role—and, even then, solely in a partial informative position, not as an end-result decision maker. Among the other real-life individuals who made this manuscript possible are my editor

Jessica Schmidt and cover artist Xee Shan. Not only are they living beings, but they are also fellow independent contractors who do not have any protections from inferior technologies attempting to supplant their jobs. Please remember that if you want to get things done well, you are going to need a person, and these are two of the best.

That said, I'm sorry to report they are not the bestedest. That title goes to my wonderful, amazing partner Caroline. I love you[3] and thank you for being with me throughout all our crazy journeys together, and all the ones we plan to make happen in the future!

With that said, there's only one more person left to acknowledge, and that's you! Right off the top, I'm so humbled that you would spend your precious time and/or hard-earned money on this little creation of mine. Even so, I must ask a bit more of you. You see, as an autonomous artist, word-of-mouth is my primary growth mechanism. I simply lack the resources of a large corporation to brute force my goals into being a reality. Therefore, I would greatly appreciate your help in getting the news out by leaving a review, posting messages on social media, or just telling friends and family about me and this book. If you don't, I'm afraid making it to the heat death of the universe will remain tantalizingly out of reach for me.

J.P. Prag | Last Modified: November 18, 2024

ADDITIONAL READING

Some titles shown below are directly related to what you have just finished reading; others, not quite as much. Or are they? The only way to know for sure is if you pick up your copy today! Please visit **jpprag.com** to learn more about these stories, in addition to discovering general articles, current status updates, and future plans.

AESTAS

THE YELLOW BALLOON

On the floating city of Aestas soaring above the clouds of Venus, Lilit Sarkisian defends her homeland from those determined to take it from her.

https://amazon.com/dp/B0CTJ8V6NH

COMPENDIUM OF HUMANITY'S END

Was the emergence of life simply a mistake? The oldest human in the universe Marco Chung may believe so and that it's up to him to correct the error.

https://amazon.com/dp/B0CFNWW63P

254 DAYS TO IMPEACHMENT
THE FUTURE HISTORY OF THE
FIRST INDEPENDENT PRESIDENT

Will the first independent President since George Washington be removed from office simply for refusing to be a part of the bureaucracy?

https://amazon.com/dp/B0BSMH4R94

NEW & IMPROVED - BOOK 3

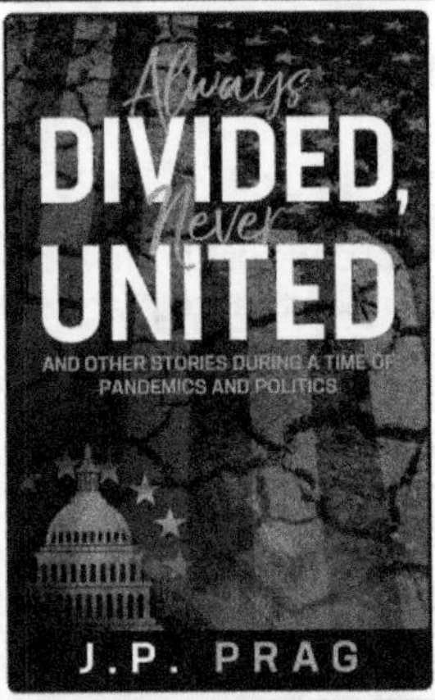

ALWAYS DIVIDED, NEVER UNITED
AND OTHER STORIES DURING
A TIME OF PANDEMICS & POLITICS

Have the troubles of our age ripped us apart more than any point in history? Or has it forever been this way?

https://amazon.com/dp/B09YDM25MB

NEW & IMPROVED - BOOK 2

NEW & IMPROVED
THE UNITED STATES OF AMERICA

Is there a way to save America and ensure justice and freedom for all? There is...if you are willing to rethink and rebuild the entire Constitution!

https://amazon.com/dp/B08FCPB5JN

NEW & IMPROVED - BOOK 1

IN DEFENSE OF...
EXONERATING PROFESSIONAL
WRESTLING'S MOST HATED

Parts of wrestling history have been
presented with overtly critical
comments and outright lies. It is past
time to bring truth to the wrestling fan!

---

https://amazon.com/dp/B08F3Y7L6K

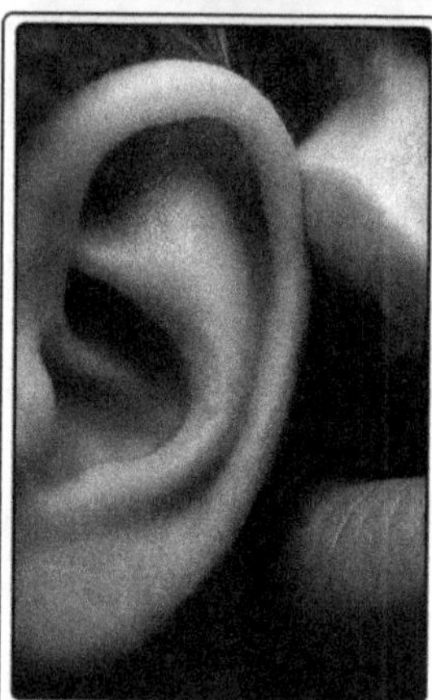

LOST RUMORS

Discovering several days of his life are
missing, Riley Furman tries to piece
together what has transpired, shattering
who and what he believes he is.

COMING SOON...

GENERATION
- WORKING TITLE -

On an interstellar generational ship,
the all-women population is tightly
controlled. That is, until a baby boy
is somehow born.

COMING SOON...

DEGENERATE ELECTRONS

- WORKING TITLE -

How does this strange boy who says they should not have even met yet know these things about her, things she has never uttered aloud?

COMING SOON...

DICTATOR AND DAUGHTER, DECONSTRUCTED

Sage Katz just got the shock of her life: the surprise return of her former dictator father! Worst of all, he now wants to repair their relationship.

COMING SOON...

HERRENVOLK

Following generations of being cut off from the world after establishing their secret society, Hitler's "perfect people" are rediscovered.

COMING SOON...

For the record, J.P. Prag is a Pisces.

Even though it doesn't mean anything, what is notable is that ten of the eighteen stars in Pisces (that are nowhere near each other) are known to host planets. One of the planets called "GU Pisces b" takes around 80,000 Earth years to circle its sun. It is also worth highlighting that some of the stars in the constellation are not singular balls of plasma at all, but are entire galaxies! Further scientific examination has revealed many other faint galaxies, nebulae, and other stellar objects within the Pisces general area. A couple of those galaxies are on a collision course, so look out for that over the next several hundred million years or so.

When not observing stellar objects at the Ladd Observatory, J.P. Prag can be found several blocks away at his home and office in Providence, Rhode Island, U.S.A. with his partner Caroline and their many tall ferns and philodendrons, lazy lying down cacti, outdoor pet squirrels (including Squirrel the Raccoon), and a stuffed sloth named Peeve and his new buddy Skvishy. That's where he wrote this and his other published works that you should add to your reading list right now!

For more irreverent details (and perhaps some pertinent ones, too?) and contact information, please visit **WWW.JPPRAG.COM**.

Version History

Number	Date	Note
0.00	2023-07-03	Draft Started
0.10	2023-07-27	Shell Outline Transfer Complete
1.00	2023-12-08	Alpha Draft
1.50	2024-02-09	Alpha Draft – Edited
2.00	2024-03-28	Beta Draft
2.50	2024-11-18	Beta Draft – Edited
3.00	2025-03-28	Final Release Form

Copyrights and Disclaimers

First Edition April 2025

Printed everywhere in the world on an on-demand basis from the nearest regional production and distribution center.

Edited by Jessica Schmidt
HTTPS://WWW.FIVERR.COM/CURIOUSWOMAN271

Cover art by Xee Shan
HTTPS://WWW.FIVERR.COM/XEE_DESIGNS1

ISBN 979-8-9874980-8-8 // eBook
ISBN 979-8-9874980-9-5 // Hardcover
ISBN 979-8-9920619-0-1 // Paperback

Basil Junction Publishing
7 Knowles Street
Providence, RI 02906

WWW.JPPRAG.COM

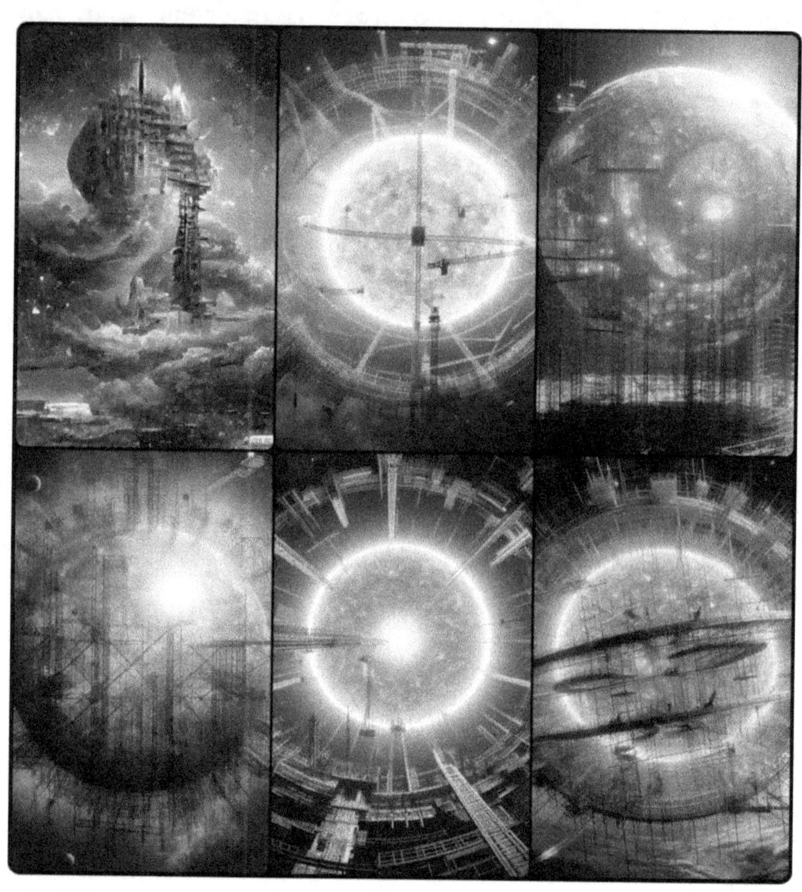

*A collage of early concept inspirational cover art developed by artificial intelligence engines **Dream.AI** and **DALL-E 3**.*